A FRENCH KING FATHERED HER,
AN ENGLISH KING MARRIED HER.
BUT KATHERINE OF VALOIS
OWED HER DEEPEST ALLEGIANCE
TO LOVE.

King Charles VI of France. Katherine's gentle, mad father. He surrendered his kingdom and his daughter to the English.

King Henry V of England. Britain's warrior King. He gave her a new life but could not protect her from tragedy.

King Charles VII of France. Her youngest brother— England's and Katherine's reluctant enemy.

Humphrey, Duke of Gloucester. Katherine's unscrupulous brother-in-law, whose ruthless ambition smashes her happiness.

Owen Tudor. The brave Welsh knight whose passionate devotion brings Katherine great happiness and great suffering.

King Henry VI. Katherine's first-born. In his young hands rests his mother's destiny.

Also by Jean Plaidy
Published by Fawcett Books:

THE PRINCE OF DARKNESS

The Queens of England Series:
QUEEN OF THIS REALM
VICTORIA VICTORIOUS
THE LADY IN THE TOWER
THE COURTS OF LOVE
IN THE SHADOW OF THE CROWN

The Georgian Saga:
THE PRINCESS OF CELLE
QUEEN IN WAITING
CAROLINE, THE QUEEN
THE PRINCE AND THE QUAKERESS
THE THIRD GEORGE
PERDITA'S PRINCE
SWEET LASS OF RICHMOND HILL
INDISCRETIONS OF THE QUEEN
THE REGENT'S DAUGHTER
GODDESS OF THE GREEN ROOM

THE
QUEEN'S
SECRET

Jean Plaidy

FAWCETT CREST · NEW YORK

A Fawcett Crest Book
Published by Ballantine Books
Copyright © 1989 by Jean Plaidy

Library of Congress Catalog Card Number: 89-29292

ISBN 0-449-22008-7

This edition published by arrangement with G. P. Putnam's Sons

Manufactured in the United States of America

First Ballantine Books Edition: June 1992

For
Mary Barron
my dear and loyal friend
of many years

Contents

Bermondsey Abbey

They have brought me to Bermondsey Abbey—a prisoner. They have discovered our secret. They have destroyed our happiness. It was what we always feared, but that does not make it any easier to bear.

They have taken Owen. I do not know what they have done to him. They have separated me from my little ones. Edmund, Jasper and Owen . . . my beautiful sons and sweet Jacina, my little daughter. Where are they and what are they thinking? They are too young to be taken from their mother.

What harm have they done?

I used to say to Owen: "When I was young, I did as they wished. I had always known that royal princesses must accept, with bland acquiescence, the fate chosen for them. This I did. I played my part in uniting my poor tortured country with England. I did all that. Now, why should I not choose my own way of life? Why? What harm am I doing?"

Owen used to soothe me, but he was at times a very worried man. How brave he was, how noble! His anxiety was all for me.

I remember so vividly those first moments of ecstasy when we knew we must be together and, constantly, we were afraid that we would be discovered, and that someone would betray us. Most of my household were my friends but there could be spies among them. How could one be sure?

I used to try to reassure myself and Owen. "I am of no importance now," I would say. "Nobody is interested in me. They have taken young Henry away from me. That is all they care about. I have lost him, Owen. I have lost my baby. Oh, I know he is the King of England . . . the boy King. It is the way with all royal children. They are always taken from the mothers who love them. But now I have a new life with you, and I will live it . . . *I will.*''

And so it was and the years passed. We were lulled into a certain blind security. We convinced ourselves that we were safe . . . most of the time.

Perhaps we were careless.

It is too late to think of that now. Here I am alone, a prisoner—though they pretend that is not so.

''Queen Katherine is resting at Bermondsey Abbey as she is in poor health.'' That is what they say.

And why is she in poor health? Because they have taken from her her husband . . . and he is my husband, for all they may say. They have already taken from her her first-born, Henry, the King of England. They have taken all her beloved children. Poor health indeed! She would be in rude health if they would restore her to her family.

None would guess that I was under restraint. When I arrived, the bells of the Abbey rang a welcome. The Abbess was waiting to greet me. She gave me her blessing and sprinkled me with holy water. I was taken to the church and stood before the crucifix, and I prayed fervently that Owen might be free and my children restored to me.

Afterwards the Abbess told me how honoured she was to have the Queen of England in the Abbey and the best accommodation which could be provided was found for me.

But I was a prisoner. She knew I had been parted from all those I loved. But pretence must be kept up. I, Queen of England, had come to honour the Abbey of Bermondsey with my presence.

There is not exactly a lack of comfort here, though it is simple, after the manner of abbeys. But I would have been happy to endure any physical discomfort if I could be with my family.

My longing for them increases every day.

I am not old. Some would say I am in the prime of life. Thirty-five might be called that. Yet I begin to feel that my life is over. There are times when I awake in the night and put out a hand to touch Owen. Then a terrible desolation sweeps over me. ''Where are you, Owen?'' I cry. ''What will become of us all?''

The peace of the Abbey is all round me, but there is no peace for me. I am envious of those black-clad figures who go hither and thither, their lives governed by the bells. It is the bells which tell me what they will be doing at various times of the day. Sometimes I hear their chanting voices. I see them working in the gardens. I envy them.

I long for news. But there is none. And I feel shut away in my own despair.

How long the days seem! I start to think of my life and what has led me to this. And then, when I think of the old days, I find myself reliving them. The hours seem to slip by and the bells tell me that another day is coming to its close.

I will go right back to the beginning. I will follow my life step by step. I will write it down, slowly savouring each scene. And I will ask myself how I came to end thus—a prisoner in Bermondsey Abbey.

The Hôtel de St. Paul

My earliest recollections are of that draughty and comfortless mansion, the Hôtel de St. Paul, in which, at that time, was incarcerated the man who was known throughout France as Charles the Mad.

There were six of us children living there: Louis, Jean, Marie, Michelle, myself and baby Charles. We had been put there because our mother did not know what to do with us, and as she had no great interest in our existence, the best thing seemed to her to be to shut us away.

Charles was just over a year younger than I. We all felt tender towards him because he was the baby and used to toddle after us with a rather bewildered look on his little face which was appealing. In truth, we were all rather bewildered.

Moreover, we were often hungry because there never seemed enough food to go round. The soup grew thinner every day until it was more like water. Louis used to ask for more. He was more important than the rest of us because he was the Dauphin—and he felt that entitled him to privileges.

He was promptly told that there was no more, so that was the end of the matter.

We had a governess who was always whispering to the nurse. "It's a shame and a scandal," she used to say. "Poor little things . . . and her going on as she does."

We listened avidly. We knew there was something odd about the place and we—at least the little ones—were quite unaware of what it was. Louis might have known something and he might have whispered it to Jean, but they were the eldest and boys. We

4

were the young ones . . . and girls at that—with the exception of Charles, who was only a baby.

Marie was different from the rest of us. When we complained about being cold and hungry she would say: "It is God's will. We must accept what He gives us and be grateful to Him."

"How can you be grateful for what you do not have?" asked Michelle.

"If you do not have it, it is God's will that you should not," insisted Marie, "and we must all be grateful to Him."

I wished I could have been like Marie. It must be wonderful to feel there was something virtuous about being cold and hungry.

While the rest of us shivered in bed at night, even after having covered ourselves with everything we could find to keep ourselves warm, Marie would be kneeling by the bed, her hands and feet blue with the cold, thanking God.

Marie was different from the rest of us, and it was Michelle and I who were the closer friends.

One day stands out more clearly in my memory of those early days than any other.

It was winter—always to be dreaded for there was never enough wood to keep the fires going, and to be cold *and* hungry is so much worse than merely being hungry.

I did not realize it at the time but it must have seemed very strange to our nurse and governess and the few attendants who were in the Hôtel that, although we lived in such misery, the days were conducted as though our upbringing was the normal one for children of our rank.

We had our lessons every day; and on this occasion we were all seated at the table in the schoolroom and our governess was attempting to teach us, when suddenly the door opened and a strange creature stood there.

We children all stared at him in wonder.

He was very pale and his hair was in wild disorder. He wore an elaborately embroidered jacket, the splendour of which was impaired by a tear in the sleeve and stains down the front.

Our governess gave a little start and for a few seconds seemed uncertain what to do. Then she rose to her feet and bowed with great respect.

We children all sat staring at the intruder.

I caught my breath in terror when he approached the table for he was truly an alarming sight.

"My children," he began, and I noticed at once that he had one of the most musical voices I had ever heard.

Louis surprised me. He must have suddenly realized who the man was, for he rose from his chair and knelt before him.

The man stared down at him. He put out a hand and touched Louis's head; and I saw the tears running down his sunken cheeks.

"You are Charles," he said, in his beautiful voice. "Charles the Dauphin."

"No, Sire," replied Louis. "I am Louis the Dauphin."

"But Charles . . ."

"Charles is our younger brother now, Sire."

"And what of Charles . . . Dauphin Charles . . . ?"

"He is dead, Sire. He was ill . . . and he died."

The man stared ahead of him and his lips trembled. He smiled suddenly and said: "And you . . . Louis . . . you are now the Dauphin."

"Yes, Sire."

"Louis . . . when did you last see your mother?"

"I do not remember. It was a long time ago."

"My child, I have been ill . . . but I am better now. Yes. I shall be better now." He looked at us children sitting there at the table watching this scene in bewilderment. He held out a hand to us.

We looked questioningly at our governess, who nodded to us, implying that we should rise and go to him.

He looked at us all in turn.

At length his eyes rested on me. "And you, little one?" I was surprised that I was no longer afraid of him.

"I am Katherine," I said.

"Katherine, my dear child . . . God bless you."

He turned to the governess. "How long have the children been living here . . . like this?"

She told him when we had come.

"These are the Children of France," he said. "It is unbelievable that they should live so."

"We were sent here, Sire. We have done our best."

"I know that well," he replied. "Now . . . it will be different. Everything that is needed will be sent. I shall command it to be done and there will be no delay.''

I remember no more of that scene, but I had learned something. The mad man of the Hôtel de St. Paul was our father and the King of France.

For several weeks after that we were warm and no longer hungry. New clothing came for us and there were fires in all the grates. There was plenty to eat. Life took on a different style.

Marie said: ''Our prayers have been answered. God is good to us.''

I heard the governess say to the nurse: ''I pray God the King stays sane.''

Her prayers were not answered for after a few months of good living, a carriage arrived at the door of the Hôtel. It brought our father. He had become the wild man again, and several strong men were needed to guard him as they brought him in.

We heard his shouting. He cried out that he was made of glass and that he was going to shatter into a thousand pieces.

I tried to visualize a glass man. I could not believe our father could be that.

I heard him call out: ''I am unworthy. I do not deserve to live. Shoot me, I beg of you.''

I was deeply puzzled and after a while the old bad times returned. It became a way of life and we accepted it as normal, as children do.

That was how it was in those days for us royal children in the Hôtel de St. Paul.

When I was a little older, I realized that I had been unfortunate to be born at a time when my country was in a more desperate decline than it had ever been—and I hope will ever be again.

I ask myself where it began, and I think, if I am completely frank, I must say that it started with my father's marriage. But perhaps it was even before that, for, as I learned so much later, my father's mother, Joan of Bourbon, who had been a good wife and mother and cared greatly for her children, suffered from periodic bouts of madness; and it seemed that she had passed this malady on to my father.

Still, I am sure his marriage did nothing to help him, and at least that was responsible for much of the trouble which arose in our country. Perhaps it is ungrateful to blame the mother who brought one into the world, but many people did blame her. So why should not I? The Bible says: "Honour thy father and thy mother," but how could I honour Isabeau of Bavaria, when I think I came near to hating her?

I saw very little of her during my childhood. There were so many of us that I believe she found it difficult to remember who we all were. It was only when we could be of use to her that she showed an interest in us. For the rest . . . we could be shut away in the Hôtel de St. Paul, to be joined by our father during his bouts of insanity. I think there were fourteen of us, but I am not sure, because many of us did not survive birth.

My two eldest sisters, Isabelle and Jeanne, had pleased her because they had made advantageous marriages—and that was, of course, the fate intended for us all. Jeanne had married the powerful Duke of Brittany when she was about six, and had been sent to him to be brought up away from the licentious Court of France as a worthy little Breton. Isabelle had made an even more brilliant match; she had been sent to England to marry King Richard, and although only eight years old had become Queen of England.

So it was only when we were needed to forge some alliance that we were important to our mother. For the most part we could be left in obscurity, looked after by servants who were fond enough of us to stay and care for us, even though they were not always paid for their services.

She was very beautiful, our mother. And she had more than beauty. Her skin was very white, her large dark eyes luminous, her dark hair abundant and curly; and she had perpetual vitality. Much as I hated and feared her, I was aware of her allure which, as I grew older, I realized lay in an insatiable sensuality. It drew men to her even though they knew it could destroy them. She was like a siren singing on the rocks calling sailors to their destruction. They knew it and yet they could not resist, for she was irresistible, even to the most austere.

As soon as my father had seen her he had become desperately enamoured of her and determined to marry her, which was just what those about him wanted, for she had been brought from Bavaria for that purpose. She had been fourteen years old at the time. He was about seventeen.

My poor father! My heart still overflows with pity for him. When we grew to know him, during his lucid periods, we all loved him. We used to be very distressed when we heard him, shouting that he was made of glass and would break into a thousand pieces.

Writing of it now, it seems incredible that members of the Royal House of Valois, the family of the reigning King, the Dauphin of France and his sisters and brothers could be living in conditions such as those prevailing in garrets in the back streets of Paris. But it was true—the only difference being that we were living in apartments which had been grand once if they were now shabby . . . and were probably more draughty than any attic in the slums.

My father had been at a disadvantage from the beginning, for he had been only twelve years old when he came to the throne. His father, known as Charles the Wise for obvious reasons, had always feared that his son might inherit the crown before he was of an age to govern.

Regencies brought trouble, said Charles the Wise. It meant that two or three ambitious men would be jostling for power—more concerned with doing good to themselves than to the country. He lowered the age of majority to fourteen, thinking he might live long enough to see his son reach that age.

My grandfather, though a wise man, was not a healthy one. When he was a very young man, his cousin, known as Charles the Bad, had attempted to poison him, and although the attempt had failed, the King had never fully regained his health, though with Joan of Bourbon he did have nine children, only three of whom survived infancy. Joan was the one who suffered from insanity.

Alas, Charles the Wise, as he had feared, died before his son, my father, reached his majority; and of course he was right when he said that regencies caused trouble.

My father was immediately taken in hand by his three uncles, the Dukes of Anjou, Berry and Burgundy. There was one other uncle who joined with them—his mother's brother, the Duke of Bourbon. They were all ambitious men and for a short time they governed in a manner calculated to bring most profit to themselves.

Those counsellors whom Charles the Wise had gathered together to assist him in the government of the country were immediately dismissed. That was the beginning of the trouble, because the uncles—always short of money—revived old taxes like the *fouage* and the *gabelle*—the hearth and salt taxes—which had always been unpopular; and the inevitable riots followed.

My father had greatly admired his father and had wanted to be like him. He loved his country, but by this time he was married to Isabeau and was coming more and more under her spell. She laughed at his seriousness, teased him and told him he should be more like his brother, Louis of Orléans. She wanted gaiety, extravagant parties, balls and masques at which she could appear in elaborate and sensational gowns. In this she was aided and urged to great extravagance by my father's brother, Louis of Orléans, who was very handsome, dashing, witty, fascinating . . . and ambitious. He must have summed up the situation. My father wanted to be a good king, to follow his father's methods . . . but alas, even more he wanted to please his wife.

Knowing my father and mother, I could well imagine the scenes between them: how she cajoled him; how he tried to resist; how she, with Louis of Orléans at her elbow, laughed at the serious young king; how she tempted him and how he succumbed.

There was constant trouble: perpetual strife with England, that old enemy; rivalry between the ducal uncles and Isabeau, with Louis of Orléans urging him to greater extravagant folly.

But my father earnestly wanted to do what was right and he knew that he was not acting as he should. There were riots throughout the country over the high taxation; affairs were going badly. He knew he must take drastic action, so he dismissed his uncles and recalled those counsellors whom his father had chosen to help him govern the country.

The most important of these was Oliver de Clisson, whom he made his Constable.

Alas, Isabeau continued to charm him to such an extent that he still allowed lavish entertainments, in which he joined, to take place.

I do believe that he could have been a great king if my mother had not been there to lure him away from his duty.

It was not to be expected that the uncles would allow themselves to be lightly pushed aside. There was constant intriguing, and one night, when Oliver de Clisson was returning home from a banquet given by the King at the Hôtel de St. Paul, he was set upon and badly wounded.

When news of this was brought to my father, he was just

about to retire to bed. He was very disturbed and wanted to know where de Clisson was, and when he was told that he had been carried to a baker's shop close to the spot where he had been struck down, the King immediately dressed and demanded to be taken to him.

De Clisson had revived a little when he reached him.

All this happened before I was born, of course, but I heard several accounts of it afterwards.

"My dear Constable," he was reputed to have said. "This is monstrous. How do you feel?"

"In a sorry state, Sire," replied de Clisson.

"Did you see your would-be assassins?"

"Yes, my lord. I saw them clearly. It was Pierre de Craon and his men."

Pierre de Craon was the cousin of Jean, Duke of Brittany. This was treachery and my father was very angry.

"He shall not go unpunished," he promised.

He was fiercely determined that Pierre de Craon should be brought to justice; and it was really this incident which triggered off his first descent into insanity, for it was during his campaign against Brittany that he had his first attack.

I heard several versions of what followed for the incident was referred to again and again, particularly when my father's condition was discussed, as it was continually through the years that followed.

My father summoned his uncles to join him in the task of bringing Pierre de Craon to justice. The would-be assassin had taken refuge with his uncle of Brittany, who would not give him up. There was some belief that the uncles may have been involved in the attempt to kill de Clisson but this was never proved. However, they did try to dissuade my father from setting out to attack Brittany and capture de Craon, but my father would not be deterred.

The weather was particularly hot even for August when the King with his army set out for Brittany.

I could picture it clearly, for the scene had been described to me so many times. My father wore a costume of black velvet; on his head was a cap of the same material, but of scarlet, ornamented with a chaplet of pearls which my mother had given him before his departure, that he might keep her in his thoughts. He rode apart from the rest because the ground was so sandy and the hoofs of the horses sent up clouds of dust. Ahead of him rode Burgundy, with Berry, Orléans and Bourbon.

As they came to the forest of Le Mans, a strange figure dashed out from among the trees. He was tall though bent and his head and feet were bare. He was in a smock which had once been white and was then stained and ragged. He caught the bridle of my father's horse and clung to it.

"Go no farther!" he shouted. "You are betrayed."

Burgundy, Berry and Orléans rushed back to the King. They seized the man, who rolled his eyes wildly and kept shouting: "The King must turn back! Danger! Danger! He is betrayed!"

Burgundy said: "The fellow's mad."

"What shall we do with him?" asked Berry.

"Let him go. He's clearly crazy and harmless. Be off, fellow, and keep out of our path."

The man stood still staring at them for some seconds. Then he went off muttering.

My father was clearly very shaken by the encounter. I sometimes wonder whether he was reminded of his own mother. It might well be that he had seen her in her moods of madness.

The madman would not leave them entirely; he moved among the trees, following the cavalcade and every now and then they would hear his shouting: "Let the King beware! He is betrayed! Go back, King, before it is too late!"

They had emerged from the forest and were on a sandy plain where there was no shelter. The sun beat down on them and the heat was intense. One of the pages, drowsy in the sun doubtless, dropped his lance, and as it clattered to the ground, the King's horse started forward.

The King shouted: "Ride on! Destruction to the traitors!" And brandishing his sword he began to attack those about him. Two of the men fell wounded to the ground.

The Duke of Burgundy immediately gave orders to seize the King, who was in a state of great excitement, galloping backwards and forwards and slashing out on both sides with his sword. Finally his chamberlain managed to restrain him. Others helped and he was laid gently on the ground. He recognized no one when they spoke to him.

They bound him up, lest the frenzy overtake him again; and so they took him back to the town of Le Mans.

The incident put an end to the proposed war on Brittany; and it was the beginning of my father's attacks of madness.

No one thought of it as such at the time. The heat had been intense and it was believed that he had been overcome by a fever which had made him delirious. Most people had seen men and women in such a state before. Moreover, he quickly recovered and was normal for about a year. The uncles at any rate were pleased to see the termination of a campaign for which they had had no enthusiasm.

A year passed. My father was still besottedly in love with my mother and she was leading him farther into the wildest extravagances. He spent a great deal of time thinking how to please her, and this resulted in balls, masques and lavish entertainments, all of which were not good for the treasury.

Then came that fatal occasion which was to show that the King's behavior in the forest of Le Mans was no isolated incident.

To surprise and amuse my mother, he secretly planned, with five of his most frivolous courtiers, to arrive at the ball disguised as savages who had come from some distant land. Isabeau was always amused when he appeared in some strange disguise and the company pretended not to recognize him—although of course they all did. He would declare himself overwhelmed by Isabeau's beauty, flirt with her outrageously . . . and the finale was that he was the King after all. It was an old trick of which everyone was aware, but it was always greeted with rapturous applause.

They went to a great deal of trouble to make their costumes. They were sewn up in linen to which tow was stuck with a sort of resin glue so that the effect was that of hairy apes. Apparently they looked quite realistic, and when they entered the ballroom there were shrieks of mock terror as they pranced round and round, in and out of the company.

Unfortunately one of the courtiers picked up a torch and came too close to the masquerading group. In a few seconds, several of them were alight. The resinous substance which had been used to stick on the tow burst into a great blaze, and the hairy savages were, in a matter of seconds, engulfed in flames. Frantically they tried to tear off their inflammable costumes, but in vain.

Someone shouted: "The King! Save the King!"

For he was there . . . my father . . . in the midst of that writhing mass of flame. It would have been the end of him if the Duchess of Berry, recognizing him, had not pulled off a heavy cloak from a man standing nearby and wrapped it round the King.

"Do not move!" she cried. "Keep still!" She pressed the cloak round him and, by a miracle it seemed, saved his life.

However, several of his friends perished and the incident brought on the second bout of madness.

He did not know where he was. He wanted to attack those around him. He kept shouting that he was made of glass and the glass was melting. He was not their King. He was an evil sinner, responsible for the deaths of those who had served him well. They should kill him.

That was a tragic night.

For some months he remained in a clouded world apart from reality . . . and then, suddenly, he regained his senses. He was able to take over his duties again. But he was a sad man. The knowledge was there. It was the second time he had gone into a frenzy—the first started by the man in the forest of Le Mans and the second by the terrible accident resulting from a foolish masquerade for which he held himself to blame. Those who had shared that folly with him had died. He had killed a man at Le Mans. He was now sure that he was subject to fits of insanity. The people had called his father Charles the Wise, and they were now calling him Charles the Mad.

A wonderful doctor was found for him. He came from Laon and his name was William Harsley. He looked after my father and he understood his madness; he even saw signs when one of his attacks was coming on, which was very helpful.

With Dr. Harsley's help, my father came to accept his madness, for when he emerged into sanity, he was well enough to take up the reins where he had dropped them and conduct the business of state. But always he must be watchful and the knowledge that there was madness in his blood put a perpetual shadow over his life.

During the years that followed, between his bouts of madness, he continued to be the uxorious husband, and he and my mother had many children; in fact, a birth was almost a yearly event. Many of them died but some survived.

The uncles, Burgundy being the leader, came back into power after pushing out the ministers my father had restored. During his sane periods my father attempted to govern but he—and those about him—were ever watchful for the first signs of insanity.

There was the usual trouble with England but the prospects in this direction were brighter when my sister Isabelle married Richard II, and there was a truce between the two countries which was to last for twenty-eight years.

Alas for treaties! It was the year 1396 when my sister went to England.

And that was the state of affairs in France when five years later, on a dark October day, the fourteenth, in the year 1401, I was born.

I was no longer a baby. I was beginning to take notice of what was going on around me. At six years old, when one lives in very unusual circumstances, one is perhaps more aware than a child living normally would be; one is watchful for happenings which could change one's life.

Perhaps the fact that my father was under the same roof when he was mad and departed when he was sane, and we were never sure when the change would take place, made me more perceptive than most children would have been.

All of us, except Marie, developed a talent for gleaning gossip, mostly by keeping our ears open when we moved among those around us. We did not have many servants, and those who were there were devoted to us, for they were not always paid as they should have been; they had to wait for my father's sane periods. But sometimes their resentment would overcome their discretion and they would speak their minds.

I discovered that the name of my uncle, Louis of Orléans, was constantly being mentioned . . . and my mother's with his.

"It's a scandal . . . a disgrace. I cannot understand why the poor King endures it. Cannot he see what she is . . . or does he try to pretend she is not?"

I asked Michelle what they were talking about, and being slightly older than I, she assumed a patronizing air.

"Oh, you're too young to understand."

"I can understand if you can."

"Well," she said, "our Uncle Orléans is very friendly with

our mother . . . too friendly, they are saying . . . and when our
father is shut away, the Duke of Orléans is . . . well . . . he is
king.''

She looked at me triumphantly, so I pretended to look knowl-
edgeable, though I was not sure of the significance of her remarks.

I soon learned though that throughout the Court it was a well-
known fact that the Duke and my mother were lovers and that
my mother preferred the Duke to the King because he was more
handsome, more light-hearted and more merry than my poor
father could ever be . . . even when he was not mad.

There were two people at that time who brought comfort into
my life. One was Guillemote, who suddenly came to my notice.
I was not sure how long she had been in the Hôtel. I think she
may have come to look after young Charles but she extended
her care to all of us. She was a jolly, rosy-cheeked young woman.
She seemed mature to me but I have learned since that she was
about sixteen years old when I first noticed her. She was rather
buxom, different from the people around us. I think it was because she came from the country.

I grew to love her. She had a way of rubbing my hands when
they were cold and if I fell and hurt myself she would kiss the
wound and make it better—which seemed a wonderful remedy.

I did not realize it at the time but I think she supplied a certain
motherliness which I missed without knowing it.

People always seemed to know when my father was coming
out of his bouts of madness. He would be much quieter and Dr.
Harsley would send a message to my mother telling her that the
King appeared to be moving towards normality.

On this particular day there was a great deal of excitement at
the Hôtel because we were going to have important visitors. Our
governess gathered us children together and we were taken into
the hall to await their arrival.

Our mother was coming.

I could not remember what she looked like, so long was it
since I had seen her. We were all a little nervous. Louis looked
sullen. He did not like our mother. He blamed her because we
were all banished to the Hôtel de St. Paul. He would have liked
to be at the Louvre, or Vincennes or wherever the Court was.

Her image remains with me to this day.

There was a flurry of excitement as she came into the hall.

She looked wonderful . . . just as a queen should. She was magnificently dressed in a velvet cape with a gown which sparkled with jewels. Her thick, dark, curly hair was shown off by a slender crown of diamonds. She had the most magnificent pink-and-white complexion I had ever seen. There was a little white dog with her. She was carrying him and scolding him, now and then, in a tender, petting sort of way. A few paces behind her was a beautiful man whom I knew because Michelle had told me he would probably be there. It was our Uncle Orléans. He was almost as splendid as she was. He wore rose-coloured velvet, and his jewels glittered only slightly more discreetly than hers.

There were several other ladies and gentlemen with them . . . all very beautiful and grand to behold. I noticed among them one young woman because she had one of the sweetest faces I had ever seen.

We children stared in awe, and when my mother turned to us and cried out loudly that we were her dear little ones and how happy she was to see us and how sad it was that we could not always be together, I thought Louis was going to ask why we could not be. But he was, I believed, as over-awed as the rest of us.

We bowed as we had been taught. My mother patted Charles's head while he looked up at her with those bewildered eyes, and then Louis did what was expected of him and ceased to look sullen.

I noticed the lady with the pleasant face smiling at us. I returned her smile and she seemed pleased.

The Duke of Orléans—our splendid uncle—gave us an amused smile and they all swept past.

I believe they went up to my father's apartments, and we were taken to the schoolroom by our governess. The adventure was over.

There was tension throughout the Hôtel until the party left; and when they had gone, I discovered that the lady whom I had particularly liked remained behind.

In due course I discovered why and who she was and her coming made life considerably more comfortable for all of us children.

She was Odette de Champdivers and she came from Burgundy. Hers was a beauty different from that of my mother. It was by no means flamboyant. I thought of her as cosy. I learned that she had been chosen by my mother to look after my father.

I heard some gossip about her.

"They say Madam has had enough. Well, who wouldn't? How many is it? Thirteen, or is it fourteen? That's enough for any woman. Every time the King comes out of his madness there's another little one to mark the occasion. So . . . she sent Odette along to make him happy. And who's to say they're all his anyway?"

"Be careful now . . ."

"Oh, I'm not the first to raise that point, I can tell you."

So Odette was with us, and she kept him happy. He was much quieter now. He did not have to be chained to his bed. Odette was there. She made sure that his clothes were clean; she cooked his food; she was gentle and loving, and my father was not the only one who grew fond of her.

Sometimes she came to see us children; and when she did she was shocked by the way we lived and set about changing it. Our food was not adequate, she said. We were growing children and we needed new clothes from time to time.

Odette began to give orders and they were obeyed.

So, with Guillemote and Odette de Champdivers, life at the Hôtel de St. Paul became more tolerable.

Because I was so young, there were great gaps in my knowledge which made it difficult for me to grasp all that was going on around me. I pieced together what I heard and a great deal of conjecture was necessary; but I really was beginning to understand a little, and it is so much easier to bear adversity if one knows the reason for it.

I remember very clearly the day my sister Isabelle came to the Hôtel to see us.

She was twelve years older than I and had been sent to England at the age of eight. I was not born at that time. I was overawed to meet her . . . the Queen of England—for I supposed she was still that even though the King was dead, and she a widow had returned to France.

She was very beautiful, I thought, and I was surprised and flattered when one of our attendants pointed out that there was a striking resemblance between us. But there was a sadness in her beauty, and the reason for this soon became clear to me, for she still mourned her late husband, although it was some years since he had died.

She and I were specially drawn to each other from the beginning and she talked to me frankly.

I learned something of the terrible trepidation a young girl can feel when she is sent to a new country to be the wife of a man whom she has never seen before.

Isabelle told me about her experiences.

"But as soon as I saw Richard," she said, "I was afraid no longer. I went to a new life . . . I left all this." She smiled and looked thoughtful. "It was not so happy here. There were troubles, even then. We travelled to Calais. Our father was with us. His illness had only just started then. He was very handsome in those days. He met the King of England who was to be my husband and they embraced. He liked Richard. Who could help that? Everybody loved him . . . except those wicked, cruel men who wanted to take his crown."

She was overcome with emotion and I tried to soothe her.

I wanted to hear how happy she had been in England, how she had loved her wonderful husband who was so good and kind to her. How she had never known such kindness until she met Richard.

She wept a great deal and I would sit silently beside her, holding her hand, not knowing how else to comfort her. But I believed I did . . . just by sitting there and listening to her.

"I had been frightened, of course, but as soon as I saw him I knew it would be all right. I was glad, Katherine. Glad that I had come. Was that not wonderful?"

I agreed that it was. "Was he so handsome?"

"He was the most wonderful man I had ever seen . . . or ever shall."

She was crying again for him.

"Why should *that* have happened to him?" she demanded. "What had he ever done to deserve that? I wish you could have known him, Katherine. He said he was surprised when he first met me. He had expected me to be pining for my home and that he would have to comfort me. I told him I liked being his wife and Queen of England better than being a Princess of France. He was very touched and we loved each other from that moment. I had to do my lessons when I reached England for I was only a little girl. Not much older than you are now, Katherine.

But he used to come and sit with me and listen to me. He laughed a lot. He was never stern. And he bought me fine clothes and we used to ride together . . . and the people cheered us. I was so happy, Katherine.''

"Yes," I said. "Yes."

"And then they killed him. They were not content with taking his crown.''

"Who?" I whispered.

"Henry Bolingbroke . . . he who calls himself Henry IV of England. He sits there on Richard's throne . . . and the only way he could keep it was by murdering Richard. And they wanted me to marry . . . *his* son. It was to keep my dowry, of course. Oh, they are wicked.''

"His son?" I asked.

She nodded. "Henry of Monmouth." Her lips curled in contempt.

It was the first time I had heard the name of the man who was to play such an important part in my own life. Afterwards, looking back, I felt how strange it was that I did not have some premonition at the time. But I did not, and Henry was then just a name to me. He was the son of that wicked predator who had stolen the noble Richard's throne and murdered him.

"Henry of Monmouth?" I repeated.

"He is still called that by some, because it was in Monmouth that he was born. He is odious. I hate him. How could they think I would marry him!''

"Never mind, sister," I said. "You are home now. He cannot harm you here.''

"But they would marry me . . . to my cousin of Orléans.''

"But he is our mother's . . . ''

"No . . . no . . . not the Duke. Charles, his son. Oh, Katherine, I do not want to marry. I want Richard to be alive. I want to go back. I want to be Queen of England.''

"If you married . . . this Henry of Monmouth . . . he will be King one day.''

She shuddered. "Perhaps. Most of all . . . I want to be left alone. I want to spend the rest of my days thinking of Richard.''

"Poor, poor Isabelle.''

"If only those traitors had not succeeded. It is so unfair . . . so cruel. Richard was a good king. He thought he had got the better of his enemy, Bolingbroke, because he had sent him into exile. How pleased he was about that! He ought to have had his head . . . when he could have. But he did not, you see. He was too kind and Bolingbroke was his cousin . . . the son of John of Gaunt. He might have known that Henry would have his eyes on the throne. John of Gaunt would have liked to be King . . . and he passed on that ambition to his son.''

''But Richard came first.''

''Oh yes. Richard. Richard was the son of the greatest of King Edward's sons—the Black Prince. He used to talk of his father. He had been a great hero to him. When he died, Richard had been about nine years old. Richard was wonderful. Oh, Katherine, it is a tragedy to be a king . . . and so young . . . with scheming men around one.''

''Like our father,'' I said.

''Yes, our poor sad, sick father. But Richard was wise and clever. He quelled the peasants' revolt when he was only fourteen. He had the makings of a great king. I cannot describe him to you, Katherine. He was so handsome. His wonderful golden hair . . . his nobility of countenance . . . and he was my husband. He was never impatient with my youth and innocence. He was always tender, calling me his Little Queen. People called me the Little Queen. It was because I was small and young. I thought it was going to be so wonderful . . . and it would have been, but for those wicked men.''

She was silent for a few moments and I prompted: ''That Bolingbroke . . .''

''We thought all would go well when he was sent into exile. He was the one who made the trouble. We all knew that. Richard used to talk to me sometimes . . . very seriously. He used to tell me how troubled he was. Then he would laugh and say: 'What of it, eh, Little Queen? I want you to try this sweetmeat I have had them make for you. And look at this brocade. How would you like a dress made of that?' I cannot explain to you, little sister.'' And again she broke down in tears.

It grieved her to recall that happy past but her only comfort was in talking of it.

''It was while he was in Ireland,'' she said, ''that Bolingbroke returned to England. Richard had taken a loving farewell of me. I had wept at his departure and he had said he would be back soon. He said: 'And see how you are growing.' He reminded me that soon I should be done with the schoolroom. I should be

at his side . . . his true Queen. We would have children . . .
heirs to the throne. It was a wonderful prospect before us. We
only had to be patient for a little while.''

''And it did not come to pass,'' I said sadly.

She shook her head. ''The traitors. Richard had been so good
to Bolingbroke's children.''

''That was Henry of Monmouth. He was one of them.''

''Yes . . . he and his brothers. When their father was sent
into exile he took charge of them. They never suffered for their
father's sins. And when Richard returned from Ireland . . . the
country was in the hands of Bolingbroke who called himself
Henry IV, and Richard the King was their prisoner.''

''How can we know what will happen to any of us?'' I said,
speaking from experience.

''It was so sad . . . so heartbreaking, Katherine. They came
to me at Windsor and said I was to leave at once. They took me
to Wallingford, which was like a fortress. I stayed there . . .
while Richard was their prisoner. His one thought was of me.
Later . . . after he was dead . . . I was told that he found comfort in writing to me. He called me his mistress and his consort.
He cursed the men who had separated us. He was filled with
grief because of it. He knew that he was hourly in danger of
death and he wrote that he had lost his joy and solace . . . and
by that he meant me. How I wished that letter could have reached
me.''

''It would only have made you more sad,'' I told her.

She shook her head. ''If only they had let me be with him. I
would have died with him most willingly.''

''Do not talk of death, sweet sister. You are young yet and
there is much to live for.''

''With Orléans?''

''Will you marry him then?''

''Do you think I shall be allowed not to? Our mother and our
Uncle Orléans wish it . . . and that is enough. It will come to
pass.''

''But you refused Henry of Monmouth.''

''That was different. I think that our mother and the Duke,
who are the rulers of France when our poor father is in his sorry
state, did not wish it. If they had . . .'' she shrugged her shoulders ''. . . it could well be that by now I should be the wife of
that monster.''

I shivered with her.

She went on: "He lives riotously. He is the friend of the lowest and frequents the taverns of London, mixing with rogues and vagabonds . . . and lewd women. I could tell you tales of what I have heard. But I forget, sister, you are only a child. You would not understand."

"I do understand," I insisted. "I listen to them talking. That tells me much."

She laughed at me and kissed me. "It does me good to talk to you. You may be a child but you have the sympathetic ear. You seem to care."

"I do care," I assured her. "Tell me more. Tell me about Richard and the wicked Bolingbroke and Henry of Monmouth."

"They were all against Richard. They welcomed Henry. They kept me a prisoner and they took me to Sunninghill."

"I have heard of that," I said. "Our father was so worried about you that it made his illness worse."

"They told me lies. They said that Richard was well and free. Oh, why did the people turn against him? All he wanted was to live in peace. Why do people want kings who lead their countries into war? Why do the people have the power to depose a good, kind king? They cheated me. It was the Earls of Kent and Salisbury. They told me that they had driven the usurper from the throne and I was to place myself at the head of the men they had brought with them and march to join Richard, who was waiting for me. How can I tell you of the joy I felt then! I was dizzy with happiness. I was in a delirium of joy. I was advised to send out a proclamation that Henry was no King. There was only one King . . . Richard. We marched to Cirencester . . . and into the trap. Richard was not free . . . not waiting for me. They had found someone who looked like him and dressed him up as the King. I knew at once that he was not my Richard. They did not deceive me. And then I understood that I had been betrayed. Bolingbroke's plan had been to capture me, and to show the people that I was the leader of a revolt. He could not execute me. He dared not because I was the daughter of the King of France. Besides, he wanted me for his son Henry. I did not see Richard. I never saw Richard again. They murdered him in Pontefract Castle."

"Are you sure?" I asked.

She nodded. "It was like something which had happened before, some said. There was a king once who asked his knights why they did not rid him of a turbulent priest; and the result was the murder of Thomas à Becket. They told me that Bolingbroke, one day, said to his knights: 'Have I no faithful friend who will deliver me from one whose life will be my death, and whose death my life?' I do not know if this be true or if it be rumour . . . but Richard died soon after. Some said it was Sir Piers of Exton who took a company of some eight persons and went to his prison and there slew him. I do not know if this be true. Others said Richard starved himself to death. He would not eat. His grief was too great because he had lost the crown, but I like to think that his greatest grief was for me. And he died and I was the widowed Queen."

"My poor, poor sister."

"I was thirteen years old. It did seem a great deal to have happened in a not very long life. They kept me at Havering Bower. Our father was too ill to demand my return and Henry said I should be treated with great honour. It was unfortunate, he said, that I had been given to Richard who was too old for me, but now there was another, younger prince eager for my hand. Again and again I refused young Henry and it was good luck for me that our mother and Uncle Orléans did not want the match. We have no say in our destiny, Katherine. It happens to us all. When we have once done what they call our duty to the state, we should have the freedom to please ourselves."

"Yes, we should," I agreed.

"But I was a child still. There was a lot of haggling over my jewels. Henry would not give them up. Then there was this matter of the dowry. This went on for a long time while I was kept in semi-captivity. Two years passed and at length I was allowed to return home to France without any of the valuables about which they had been quarrelling. I was fifteen years old. You were only a baby at that time."

I nodded.

"I am surprised," she went on, "that they have left me so long. They might have forced me into marriage by now. I know why though. It is because they are unsure which marriage would be profitable to them. I live in fear that they may decide after all to send me to England."

"As the wife of that . . . Henry?"

"Yes. I believe they would have done it if our Uncle Orléans had not wanted me for his son Charles."

"Our mother will surely say that you must do as our uncle wants."

"But there are times when our father is aware of what is going on. There are others, too. I know they hesitate. I was terrified when Henry Bolingbroke said that if I were given as wife to his son, he would give up his crown, and his son should be King of England and I the Queen."

"Second time Queen of England!" I cried.

"There is more to life than crowns, sister. I would forgo the greatest crown on Earth if it meant I had to take that man with it."

"Poor Isabelle! How frightened you must have been."

"I was glad then that our mother is so enamoured of our uncle. Of course, she was very much against the match with England because he was. I am sure that was the reason why, after a good deal of deliberation, it was refused. We even had an embassy from England to settle the matter. It was a time of great anxiety for me. Just imagine going to England a second time . . . with all the memories of the first. I don't think I could have borne that."

"But it did happen," I soothed.

"No. But did you hear what Orléans did? He sent a message to the King of England, saying it was the duty of noble knights to protect the rights of widows and virgins of virtuous life. He referred to Henry as the plunderer of my goods and the murderer of my husband; and he challenged him to a duel to settle the quarrel between them and decide the matter of the return of the dowry."

"And what did Henry say to that?"

"It was an absurd challenge in the first place, and Orléans must have known that it would never have been accepted. Henry's reply was cold and dignified. There was no example in history, he said, of a crowned king's fighting a duel with a subject, however high that subject's rank might be. As for the implication that he had been responsible for Richard's death, God knew how or by whom his death was brought about, and if the Duke of Orléans implied that it had been brought about by his, Henry's, order, the answer was that he had lied. I knew that was the end of my fears and that I should not be sent to England. It was a great relief, sister, I can assure you.''

''And Charles of Orléans?''

''I fear it may come to marriage with him. You see, I am of an age to be married . . . and that is the fate of all princesses.''

She was right. I did not see her for some time, but Odette, who came to see us frequently while our father was sleeping, told me that our sister Isabelle was now betrothed to her cousin, Charles of Orléans.

''He is a gentle boy,'' said Odette. ''Quite a poet. I pray they will be happy together.''

I prayed too. So did Marie and Michelle; and we listened eagerly to the stories we heard of the fêtes and banquets which took place at Compiègne where Isabelle, in the company of our mother, joined up with the Duke of Orléans and his son.

Isabelle was nearly twenty years old and Charles was younger.

It was five years since she had left England, but I knew, for she had made it very clear to me, that she still mourned Richard.

It was about this time that an event took place which shocked the entire country and changed the course of our lives.

It was a dull November evening. The Duke of Orléans had been with my mother, as he often was. It was eight o'clock and he was returning to his hôtel in a very merry mood, probably thinking that all was going well for him. His brother, the King, was never going to return to complete sanity and his relationship with Queen Isabeau gave him the position for which his ambitious heart had always craved; he was, in all but name, ruler of France.

It was not the sort of night when many people would be out unless it was necessary, and the streets were deserted. He had two squires with him, and one or two servants on foot, carrying torches. Suddenly some twenty armed men sprang upon him. The squires' horses took fright and bolted, and, brandishing their swords, the armed men fell upon the Duke.

''Do you know that I am the Duke of Orléans?'' he is reputed to have demanded.

''Yes,'' was the reply. ''You are the one we want.''

One of his men attempted to defend him but was immediately struck down. Another was badly wounded and crawled into a nearby shop.

Everyone was talking about the murder of the Duke of Orléans. We had heard so much of our Uncle Orléans. He was the most discussed man in the country. His liaison with my mother, his usurping of his brother's rights . . . it had all been common knowledge and everyday gossip; so even the children could not be prevented from hearing of it.

Odette told us a little of what had happened. She was wise and I believe she thought it would be better for us to know something near the truth rather than form our opinions from the random gossip which would undoubtedly be circulating.

"Who killed him?" I asked.

"That is something which has to be discovered," replied Odette.

"Why did they kill him?" Michelle wanted to know.

Odette surveyed us for a moment and then she said: "A man in the Duke's position would have many enemies. They will discover why in time."

"Why was he out in the streets at night?"

"He had been dining with the Queen, they say."

"He always dines with our mother," said Michelle.

"Did no one see who did it?" asked Marie. "They must have heard the noise."

"There were one or two people who peeped out. We heard through them that a cobbler's wife opened her window and shouted that murder was being committed. She was told sharply to be silent, and shots were fired at windows where lights appeared. A woman said that there were men with masks over their faces and they shouted to all in the houses to keep away from the windows and put out the lights."

"And did they?" Louis wanted to know.

"They dared do no other . . . and when the men had gone away and there was silence in the streets, some of them crept out and saw the Duke lying dead on the cobbles. They carried him into the church of Blancs-Manteaux. Now the question is, who did it?"

There was great consternation when the instigator of the crime was discovered. He confessed to it himself. We could not believe it and what seemed so strange was that he should have confessed.

The murderer of our Uncle Orléans was our father's cousin, the Duke of Burgundy, known as Jean the Fearless.

He said: "I confess, so that none may be accused of putting the Duke of Orléans to death. It was I and none other who caused the doing of what has been done."

There was upheaval everywhere.

"This was no ordinary murder," Odette told us. "The effect of this will be felt throughout the entire country."

And she was right.

Burgundy, after making his confession, returned to his mansion, the Hôtel d'Artois, and then, taking six of his most trusted men with him, made for the Flanders frontier. The Duke of Bourbon was angry, because, so stunned had everyone been, no one had attempted to arrest him.

The shock had brought my father temporarily out of his madness. It surprised everyone that the moment this had happened he seemed to pick up the threads and behave as though he had not been away from his state duties.

He was deeply disturbed by the death of his brother—though many of the servants wondered why, since Orléans had taken over not only his authority but his wife, and had hardly shown himself to be his friend.

We were avid for news. Surely Burgundy would be captured and brought back for trial? He had committed murder and, although he himself had not actually carried it out, it had been done at his command.

The Duke's widow came to Paris to demand justice. She was very sad, which was surprising, for he had been a neglectful and faithless husband to her.

It was December and bitterly cold, I remember, and one of our main concerns at that moment was keeping warm. The Duke's widow was the daughter of the Duke of Milan; she was a quiet, peace-loving woman and had been completely subservient to her husband; but when such people's determination is aroused, it can be surprisingly firm. Thus it was with Valentine Visconti, Duchess of Orléans.

She came to the King, begging him on her knees to avenge her husband's murderer. He must be brought to trial, she said.

My father assured her that this should be done and said that he regarded what had been done to his brother as though it had been done to himself.

Soon after, however, my father lapsed into insanity again. There was a half-hearted attempt to raise a cry against Burgundy; but people were now remembering the overbearing attitude of the Duke of Orléans, and his extravagances, and he was fast ceasing to be one of those heroes whom the dead become—particularly when they are cut off in the prime of their manhood.

Christmas came and, although people were still talking about the murder, nothing was done to bring Burgundy to justice.

And then . . . I remember the day well—a cold February day with clouds scudding across the sky and that dreaded wind seeping into all the rooms. There was excitement in the streets. Jean the Fearless, Duke of Burgundy, came marching into Paris, with a thousand men at arms. The people came rushing into the streets in spite of the cold. They were shouting. I heard them clearly: "Long live the Duke of Burgundy!"

Crowds followed him to the Hôtel d'Artois, which was strongly fortified. It was soon clear that no attempt would be made to arrest him. The people, for one thing, would not allow it. Moreover, Burgundy had his fighting force with him. The people did not want battle in the streets of Paris.

There was consternation in the Hôtel de St. Paul when Burgundy did not so much ask as demand an audience with the King.

How could our poor father confront his warlike cousin? He was deep in the delusion that he was made of glass and it was time someone shattered him, which was what he wanted more than anything.

My little brother Louis was frightened. He was twelve years old and he was the Dauphin, so, since the King was not fit to see Burgundy, the duty fell to him.

Odette tried to comfort him. "You will not be alone with him, my love," she soothed. "The princes and the lords and the counsellors . . . they'll all be there. They'll tell you what to say."

Louis was trembling when he went to face Burgundy.

Of course, there was none of them who could stand up against Jean the Fearless. I had heard it said that everything would be different in France if Burgundy had been King. And that was what he wanted, of course . . . and Orléans had wanted the same for himself.

Burgundy's case was stated with eloquent fervour by a monk whom the Duke had chosen to speak for his defence.

Yes, he had had Orléans killed. Orléans had been a criminal and a tyrant whose aim had been to take the throne from the King and his children and keep it for himself and his own. In this the Queen had aided him. The killing of Orléans had been a justifiable act, and it had been undertaken in the interests of the welfare of France.

As soon as Burgundy had entered Paris it had been seen that the people were with him; and when Valentine Visconti had come to Paris to avenge her husband, they had not shown any great sympathy for her; and when the scandals about Orléans and his incestuous relationship with the Queen were remembered . . . it seemed inevitable that Burgundy, instead of being condemned for what he had done, would be hailed as the country's saviour and a hero.

Burgundy had prepared a paper for my father to sign. In this he had laid down that he, Burgundy, and his heirs should live at peace in the realm in respect of the death of the Duke of Orléans and all that followed concerning it; and that from the King's successors and all people, no hindrance to the affairs of Burgundy should be offered at this time or that to come.

My father—lucid again—was prevailed upon to sign the document. He did say that, although he himself cancelled the penalty, he could not answer for the resentment of others, but it would be for him, Burgundy, to defend himself against revenge from some quarters which might be inevitable.

To this Burgundy graciously replied that all he cared for was the King's good graces. As far as other men were concerned, he feared nothing.

Nor did he. He was, after all, Jean the Fearless. He had cleverly rid himself of the man most dangerous to his own interests and managed to make of the deed a virtuous act performed for the good of the country.

My mother might have been deeply saddened by the loss of her lover but she had greater concerns, for if he were regarded as a menace to the country, what of herself, who had worked and lived side by side with him?

When my father signed the letters exonerating Burgundy from blame, it was tantamount to admitting that the murder of Orléans had been a just act committed against a man who was a danger to the state.

The day after the signing, in the late evening, six men and women arrived at the Hôtel de St. Paul.

My father was in his room, sunk in melancholy, calling out for someone to kill him, so it was no use appealing to him.

We were all in the schoolroom with our governess when Odette came hurrying to us. Guillemote was just behind her. I knew something dramatic was going to happen because Odette was distraught and Guillemote looked frightened.

"The Queen's men are here," said Odette. "We must obey . . . but it will be all right. You must not be afraid. The boys are to be taken to her."

"Not to our mother!" cried Louis.

"You see . . . there is unrest in Paris . . . she wants to take care of you."

"I won't go," said Louis.

"My dear," said Odette quietly, "you are frightening the little ones. No harm will come to you. Your mother wants to look after you. It's natural."

"It is not," insisted Louis.

"You will be all right. Please . . . Louis . . . remember little Charles. Look after him. You must take care of your little brothers."

"I will," said Louis. "I will look after them, but I don't want to go. I want to stay with you, Odette."

"I know. You'll be back soon. I'm sure of it. Come . . . go graciously . . . remember you are the Dauphin . . . and if you do not go willingly . . ."

Louis said no more.

And the boys were taken away.

I heard later that that night they left Paris with my mother for Melun.

Michelle had come close to me and taken my hand. Marie was praying and an expression of acceptance was creeping over her face.

The boys had gone. Now it was the turn of the girls. We were not as important as the boys but still we were royal princesses, and had our uses, so we must not be taken over by Burgundy.

Odette said: "You are to go into a convent. That will be pleasant for you. You will learn much. You will all be very happy and clever."

"Are you coming with us?" I asked.

She shook her head.

"My place is here. But you three will all be together."

"Is Guillemote coming?"

"No. But there will be the three of you . . . sisters to look after each other. You will be very happy there. It will be so much more comfortable than St. Paul. I can promise you that."

We flung our arms round her and told her that we did not want to leave her. Then we turned to Guillemote who was trying hard to smile and told us we should be very happy in our convent where we would learn to behave like princesses.

The days in the Hôtel de St. Paul were over. Soon after that we left for the convent of Poissy.

Poissy

Life was different at Poissy—more quiet and orderly. The nuns were severe, but kind; we were fed and clothed adequately and our education, which had hitherto been somewhat neglected, received immediate and assiduous attention.

Marie was very happy. She was in her natural element. She was one to whom life would bring exactly what she wanted, and she knew then that she wanted to become a nun. It was different for Michelle and me. Michelle was already betrothed to the eldest son of the Duke of Burgundy; for me, nothing had so far been arranged.

We rose early—about five in the morning—and the rules of the convent were that every one of the hours between that time and darkness, when we retired, must be spent in some useful occupation. For Michelle, Marie and myself it was mostly lessons. We learned Latin, and English and music lessons were given every day. We had to learn to converse intelligently, and great stress was laid on good manners at table . . . and elsewhere, of course. The Mother Superior was a deified figure. She was benign yet aloof and we all were in great awe of her. We would walk in the gardens where we learned the names of flowers and herbs and their uses, and were allowed to grow some of our own, and when we wandered through the sequestered paths of the gardens we could chatter a little.

It was a very different life from that which we had lived in the Hôtel de St. Paul. Here we were shut away. In the Hôtel there had been a smattering of gossip to give us ideas—if vague ones—of what was happening. To the uncertainty of life there had been added a whiff of excitement. We had never known when our father was going to recover and our life-style change for a while. Then his lapses into madness had been equally unpredictable. Now life in the convent fell into an ordered routine. One knew what one would be doing at any moment of the day.

Occasionally visitors were allowed, and Isabelle came to see us.

She had now been married to our young cousin Charles who, on the death of his father, had become the Duke of Orléans. He was younger than she, and I could see, merely by looking at her, that she was not exactly unhappy in the marriage, so that that which she had so much dreaded had turned out to be tolerable after all.

"Charles is very gentle and sweet-natured," she told me. "Of course he is very young, but he loves me. Isn't that wonderful, Katherine . . . for he was forced into this marriage . . . even as I was. He writes poetry. It's really very good. It is not only I who says so. I think I have been fortunate in having two good, kind husbands."

I knew all would be well with her now because, although she referred to Richard, she did not look downcast as she had before.

I said to Michelle later: "I believe she is quite happy. She seems different." And Michelle agreed.

It was from Isabelle that I learned something of what was happening outside the convent walls.

She told me that Burgundy had remained in Paris, imposing his rule on the city. He had been there for four months and would still be there but for a revolt in Liège.

"He sent troops to suppress it, but they could not do so, and he had to go himself. When he was gone, our mother came back to Paris. Louis was with her. Poor Louis. It is all rather bewildering for him. I think he rather wishes he was not the Dauphin. He's such a boy really and always so nervous because he is afraid he will do—or even say—the wrong thing. Who would be born royal? I often think, Katherine, how much happier we might be if we were just simple people. We should perhaps be able to lead our own lives. Well, our mother came back with Louis, and Berry and Bourbon are with her. They are against Burgundy. And what do you think our father has done? He recovered a little but he is always afraid that his madness is going to break out. He has said that he cannot go on like this and he thinks it would be wise to pass on the government of the country to the Queen, our mother! You can imagine what consternation that caused.''

''Our poor father, he must be completely mad.''

''Louis is quite alarmed, wondering what this is going to mean to him. And Valentine Visconti upset him terribly by coming to him, kneeling at his feet and asking for justice for her murdered husband.''

''What did Louis do?''

''He said he would give her a speedy reply. Poor little Louis, it will not be for him to decide what shall be done. And in the midst of all this came the news that Burgundy had completely subdued the people of Liège and was preparing, with a victorious army, to return to Paris.''

''Were they all alarmed?''

''I am sure they were. In any case, they all left without delay. They have gone to Tours. Our mother has taken the King and the Dauphin with her. What will happen next I do not know, but I can see that it will take a long time to heal this rift between the houses of Burgundy and Orléans. It worries me, Katherine. I wonder how my Charles will react. He is not a fighter. He is not like his father either. He will never be an unfaithful husband. I know it.''

I smiled at her and held her hand tightly. I was so pleased that she had ceased to mourn for the long-since-dead Richard of England, and life had turned out well for her after all. She had been given a chance of happiness and I was sure that, with her sweet and gentle disposition, she would attain it.

I began to notice a serenity about her. It was some weeks before she told me.

''Katherine, what I have always wanted is to come to pass. I am going to have a child.''

I embraced her and we both shed a few tears. They were tears of happiness. I was thinking how wonderful it was that in the midst of all this turmoil there could be this joy. And who deserved it better than my sweet sister Isabelle?

One of the saddest events of my childhood happened during my Poissy days.

I remember it well. A nun came into the room where we were doing our lessons with other daughters of the nobility. She went straight to the one who was teaching us, and a whispered conversation ensued. I was glad of a little respite from the tedious task of translating a passage in Latin, when the nun who was taking the class said: "Will the Princesses Marie, Michelle and Katherine please step up here to me."

We obeyed at once.

"The Mother Superior wishes to see you," we were told. "You may go to her now."

Michelle and I exchanged glances, wondering what sin we had committed, for it was not often that the Mother Superior wanted to see pupils, and when she did, it usually meant they were in deep disgrace.

But it was not for that purpose that we had been summoned. How I wished it had been!

The Mother Superior smiled at us in a kindly fashion when we entered her sanctum. She said: "You may sit." And we did.

"I have some bad news for you," she went on. "It will be a shock, I fear. It concerns your sister, the Duchess of Orléans."

"Isabelle . . ." We murmured her name.

"It is God's will," said the Mother Superior. "We must always remember that. And she has gone to a happier place."

I sat there, numb, realizing the significance of what she was saying. I thought: the baby. It is the baby.

None of us could speak. We were too shocked.

"Your sister is now with God and His angels," said the Mother Superior. "We must not grieve. We must rejoice in her happiness. She is beyond all earthly pain."

I sat there thinking of her . . . all her unhappiness since the loss of Richard . . . the hopelessness she had experienced, and then had come her marriage to Charles and she had shown signs of being happy again. And the baby . . . how she had wanted the baby!

Life was cruel. To have dealt such blows and then to give a glimpse of happiness before snatching it away.

The Mother Superior came to us and laid a hand on each of our heads.

"Bless you, my children," she said. "I think you may want to be alone."

So we went out, Michelle and I not looking at each other,

Marie accepting the blow with quiet resignation as the will of God.

I ran to our dormitory and flung myself on my bed. My throat was dry. I was still numb with shock and misery. It was not until I was in bed that night that I began to weep. And then I could not stop.

How we missed her! We had so looked forward to her visits. For so many years we had not known our beautiful sister. Then she had come into our lives, only to be snatched away. If they had not forced her to marry; if she had not become pregnant, she would still be with us!

I was angry with Fate and filled with apprehension as well as sorrow. We were moved around as the men of power wished to move us, and if we died, that was an end of our usefulness and they ceased to think of us, for we were then no longer a means of patching up a quarrel, no longer a bargaining counter in a treaty.

Isabelle herself had said how lucky were those who were not born royal and could lead lives which they themselves had some power to arrange.

Moreover, I knew little of what was going on outside the convent walls, for we had depended on Isabelle to inform us. Nuns do not gossip; and in any case they are shut away from the world even more securely than their pupils. I did not know that the quarrels between the houses of Orléans and Burgundy were growing to menacing proportions which were to have a dire effect on the state of our country. There could be few situations fraught with more danger: a mad king who longed to be good and wise as his father had been and whose periodic lapses into madness had loosened his grip on the helm of state; a powerful, sex-crazed wife who was ready to plot treacherously against anyone who stood in her way; rival princes—ambitious men all of them—seeking to grasp the power which seemed there for the taking when the King was mad; and the Dauphin was only a boy.

The strongest man in the country was the Duke of Burgundy. I believe many were of the opinion that, if the King could not govern them, Burgundy should take his place. Burgundy certainly thought it, and there was open hostility between the houses of Burgundy and Orléans.

I did not know this at the time, but my mother, realizing that Burgundy was the stronger man, was attempting to throw in her lot with him . . . against my father and her own son.

The Treaty of Chartres had been devised and everyone was delighted because it was meant to establish peace between the princes. But at the very time the treaty was signed, a man of great ambition and energy stepped into the forefront of events. It could not have happened if Isabelle had lived.

This man was Count Bernard of Armagnac. He had a daughter, Bonne, and he saw a way to power through a marriage between her and Charles of Orléans, the widower of my sister Isabelle.

I cannot guess what Charles felt about this. I was sure, from what Isabelle had told us, that he had been devoted to her. To marry so quickly after her death must seem like faithlessness. But he, no less than Isabelle, must do what he was told to do, and because it was believed by his ambitious uncles that the Count of Armagnac could be a useful ally the marriage took place.

No sooner was he connected with the royal family than Armagnac made his presence felt. With Berry and Brittany he placed himself at the head of the anti-Burgundy faction, and so powerful did he almost immediately become that from then on, instead of being called the Orléanist party, it was known as the Armagnacs.

What was tantamount to civil war was raging throughout France.

I was oblivious to this strife and my convent life went on in its peaceful way. It was sad when Michelle went away to marry the son of the Duke of Burgundy, and for a long time I felt very lonely. There was only Marie now at Poissy with me, and she was so immersed in preparing herself for her vocation that I saw very little of her.

There were no ways of learning what was happening outside. Each day was ordered by the bells. Lessons . . . reading . . . walking . . . prayers at regular intervals. I had my friends . . . girls like myself, highborn and therefore knowing that one day they would be presented with a fate which they would be forced to accept.

It was a strange life—so different from what it had been in the Hôtel de St. Paul.

I often thought about my father. I guess, of course, that little had changed. There would be the periods of madness, the interludes of lucidity. And my mother, what was she doing now?

But for so long I had lived in the sheltered atmosphere of Poissy that I had been lulled into acceptance of the life around me. I knew that change must come sometime, but when it did, it found me unprepared.

I was at this time twelve years old, what I suppose would be called well-educated, but unaware of much which it would have been good for me to know. My early years in the Hôtel de St. Paul had taught me something about the unpleasant side of life, but perhaps then I had been too young to absorb it. The Hôtel where I had lived with my brothers and sisters and my mad father seemed unreal in the saintly atmosphere and rigorous routine of Poissy.

The quiet life came to an end as suddenly as it had begun.

I was coming close to an age when a princess becomes useful to those around her.

The Mother Superior sent for me, and once more, thinking that I was to be mildly reprimanded or reminded of some duty, I blithely went to her.

With her was a ruddy-faced man. I knew he was a foreigner before he spoke, but in those first moments I was too amazed at the presence of a man in the sanctum of the Mother Superior to think of anything else.

Then I heard her telling me that he had come to paint my portrait, and I was uneasy.

He was Flemish, said the Mother Superior, and a great artist.

He said in his atrocious French: "I come from Her Highness the Queen herself. She bids me paint a picture of Your Highness. Ah, but you are beautiful. That is good . . . It is always good to have the beautiful subject. I will make a fine portrait of you, my lady."

"The picture is to be painted at once," said the Mother Superior. "Those are the Queen's orders." She turned to the painter. "Where should the sitting take place? What about this room?"

He looked round and nodded his head. "It is good," he said.

"Who is it wants this picture?" I asked.

"But it is the Queen, your mother, my lady."

"But . . . for whom . . . does she want it?"

He raised his eyes to the ceiling and lifted his shoulders.

The Mother Superior said: "I will have a room made ready for you. How long do you think it will take you to paint this picture?"

Again that lifting of the shoulders and the upward glance. Then he said: "That I will tell you . . . soon. Once I have made my start. The Princess is very like her sister, I am told."

"You mean the late Duchess of Orléans?"

"And Queen of England, eh?"

"There is a resemblance," said the Mother Superior.

He nodded, smiling.

My alarm increased as the sittings progressed. There was something decidedly ominous in this need for a picture. Why had my mother, after years of neglect, suddenly remembered me and wanted a picture of me? There was one answer. It was for a suitor. That was why royal princesses had their portraits painted.

I remembered Isabelle's telling me that she had been painted and the portrait was sent to England; as soon as Richard had seen it he had fallen in love with it.

And now it was my turn, because I was a child no longer.

There was spasmodic conversation during the sittings which took place each day—one hour in the morning and one in the afternoon.

"It is not good to sit too long," the artist told me. "Sitters become tired . . . and that is not what we want to show in the painting, you understand?"

"Should you not paint people as they are . . . tired or not?"

He looked at me reprovingly. "No . . . no. I want to paint one beautiful picture. A lady at her best. That is what we want."

"But if there are defects . . . ?"

"It is my task to find the perfections, eh? You understand? Let us say she has beautiful eyes, so we make the observer see those eyes. She has a nose that is a little . . . how shall we say? . . . not little. Sometimes we do not see this . . . so I will paint the picture at a time when it is not seen."

I laughed. It was true that my eyes were my best feature and I had always been aware that I had inherited the Valois nose. Fortunately, in my case, this was not so very noticeable . . . but it was there.

I discovered that he had brought with him a picture of my

sister Isabelle. He set it up so that he could glance at it while he painted.

I said to him: "Why do you have my sister's portrait there?"

He smiled secretly: "There is a likeness, you see."

"But you are not painting her portrait."

He shrugged his shoulders and looked at the ceiling.

I thought it was rather mysterious.

I said to him: "Do you know why my mother wants this portrait?"

"Oh . . . but you are her dear little daughter."

"Is that what she told you? 'Go and paint a picture of my dear little daughter' ?"

He nodded.

"She wants it for someone."

He smiled secretively.

"Do you know for whom?"

"Madame Princess, I am only the painter. Kings and queens do not share their secrets with me."

"Is there a secret then?"

"How should I know of secrets, my Princess?"

"So you really do not know for whom this portrait is being painted?"

"Ah, Princess, I am only the painter."

He did know, I was sure. I wondered if my mother had cautioned him against telling.

At last the picture was ready. It flattered me, I thought. He said: No. It was myself . . . at my best, which was what he had aimed for.

"It is more like my sister Isabelle than it is like me," I said.

That seemed to please him.

In due course he went away, taking the picture with him.

A few days after he left, messengers from Court arrived.

I was to prepare to leave Poissy for Paris.

A Marriage Is Arranged

My mother sent for me and, filled with apprehension, I went to her apartments. One of her women was waiting for me.

"Madame la Reine," she announced, "the Princess is here."

I went into the room.

It was so long since I had seen her that I had only vague memories of her.

She was stretched out on a couch, dressed in a gown of pale lavender colour. There were pearls and diamonds at her throat, on her arms and in her ears. She glittered. She had grown very fat; and now that I was older I suspected that her dazzling complexion owed something to art. Two little white dogs were on the sofa with her.

She looked as voluptuous as ever. Her hair was a little darker than I remembered it, and the luxuriant curls were arranged in careless elegance. She was startlingly attractive still.

Her eyes sparkled as she saw me.

"My dearest, dearest child! Come to me." She held out her hands. I went to her and kissed one of them; then she drew me to her. "Let me look at you. There." She kissed my cheek. There was an alertness in her eyes which belied her languor. "But it is true," she went on. "You are beautiful. Alas, you remind me of my dear Isabelle." She picked up a lace handkerchief and held it to her eyes. "My dear, dear child. It broke my heart. So young . . . and poor Orléans. He's consoled himself now . . . and lost little time in doing it. But he had no say in the matter, of course . . . with Armagnac in control. But let me look at *you*. Bring a stool and sit beside me. Stop that silly barking, Bijou. He is jealous, you know. He cannot bear me to look at anyone but him. Naughty, silly little dog."

I sat beside her, fascinated by the folds of white flesh . . . the brilliant eyes, the delicately tinted cheeks.

I did not know what to say but I realized, with relief, that I was not expected to speak very much. All I had to do was agree with what she suggested.

"My dear child," she said, "It has been a great grief to me that I have been so often separated from my dear children. You do not understand what a mother's feelings are." Her expression changed from second to second. Now she was the bereaved mother, her beautiful features set in lines of melancholy. She quickly brightened and her smile was dazzling. "But that is the way of life for us. I have had so many trials. Your dear, dear father."

"And there was the death of the Duke of Orléans," I said.

She looked at me sharply. I could see angry lights appearing in her eyes. But that quickly passed. I knew what she was thinking: The child is innocent of everything. What could she know, shut away in Poissy?

"There have been many tragedies for France," she said. "And for the Queen. Well, they must be her tragedies, too. We have lived through some stirring times . . . but I have always put my personal griefs behind me and thought only of my country. But why are we gloomy? I have the most wonderful news. My pleasure now is planning for my family. My thoughts are all for them . . . my dear, dear children, whose company was often denied to me . . . but now they are growing up and I can plan for them as I am doing now for you, my child. You will see what your mother has in store for you. I have a grand match for you."

"A marriage . . ." I said fearfully.

"A marriage, of course. What else?" She was slightly irritable. She wanted me to be young and innocent but not stupid. "You will bless your mother when you hear."

"Please, Madame . . . may I hear who this is?"

She leaned towards me. "You will never guess. You would never have dreamed. The King of England has a son . . . his eldest son . . . heir to the throne. Who else would I think good enough for my dearest daughter, Katherine?"

"That is Henry," I said. "Henry of Monmouth."

"But of course. He is a handsome young man . . . full of vitality . . . charming, amusing, witty, good-natured . . . kind. Everything that a young woman could wish for in a husband."

"Isabelle did not think so."

She frowned. "How do you know?" she demanded.

"She told me. She would not have him . . . and she knew him. She had seen him . . ."

"Your sister . . . your dear, dear sister . . . was not always wise. In any case she was only a child. She could not know what was good for her any more than you can. Never mind. You have a mother to plan for you." She was smiling at me benignly, forgetting, no doubt, those years of neglect. I had an impulse to ask her where the loving mother had been then.

"Your sister was so young," she went on. "She was so enamoured of Richard, which was good and right that she should be, but like all children she was without judgement. Of course, she had a wonderful life in England . . . as you will see, my dear. Who would not wish to be Queen of England? And you will be that . . . in time. I have heard that the King suffers from some illness; he cannot last long. And then Henry, your husband . . . will be King of England. And you will be beside him, his Queen. Is that not a wonderful prospect? And should you not be grateful to your mother for making all this possible for you?"

"Isabelle could have remained Queen of England if she had married him."

"Oh, an end to this harking on Isabelle! Isabelle . . . God rest her soul, has been taken from us. We loved her dearly but at times she could be a little foolish . . . as most young people are. They do well to listen to their elders . . . those who make the young people's future their greatest concern. Then all will be well. Well, let us now say that Isabelle's loss will be her little sister's gain. Now listen to me. You are very like your sister. This comes out in your portrait."

I said: "It was painted with that purpose . . . to show the similarities between us."

My mother smiled slyly. "I am sure it will please the Prince."

"But . . . I do not want . . ."

She waved a hand and there was a warning in her eyes. I could see how fierce she would be in anger. She did not want to know what I thought unless it was in favour of the match. If

I was proposing to object I had better be silent. In any case my views in the matter were immaterial.

"Now," she went on, "an embassy will be here shortly. The Duke of York is on the Continent. He will come to Paris to discuss certain matters. Naturally he and his embassy will wish to see you." She looked at me archly. "And take back a report. We must see that it is a good one."

I was silent.

"You must learn to be more animated. We do not want the English to say you are dull. Isabelle was full of life. You must try to be like her. They will speak to you in English and you must reply to them in their language . . . show them that you are not stupid. I have dressmakers coming tomorrow. There are many preparations to be made. You must make a good impression on the King of England's ambassadors."

I knew that there was no escape and I was filled with foreboding.

I longed for the peace of Poissy.

The period of preparation had begun. I was with my mother often. She, who had spent a lifetime adorning herself, knew exactly how to accentuate the good points in others. Colours were chosen with the utmost care; the cut of a sleeve, the fall of a skirt . . . they were matters of great moment. She applauded or abused the dressmakers in accordance with what she considered their deserts. One would have thought we were going into war, or that some matter of great importance to the country's welfare was being decided.

Jewels were chosen for me. I had to practise my English; I had to learn to dance—a matter which, to my mother's chagrin, had been somewhat neglected at Poissy. I was kept so busy that I had little time to brood on my situation—which was a good thing.

My dead sister was constantly referred to—"Isabelle did this . . . she had a habit of . . ."—until I felt I was impersonating her. And how I longed for her to be with me, to advise me . . . to help me . . . to explain what I had to do. The odious Henry of Monmouth had sought her at one time . . . and ardently, it seemed. She had turned from him in horror. He had never seen me . . . but his father was seeking me on his behalf. He might not want me any more that I wanted him.

Oh, Isabelle, I thought, if you were here, you would tell me what to do. You would help me to evade this fate which they are determined to press upon me. You did it. How can I?

But Isabelle was gone and I was alone; and I was completely at the command of my indomitable mother.

At length the ambassadors came. I had conversed with them in their own tongue and they had graciously applauded me on my command of their language, which I believe was due to politeness rather than truth, for I had stumbled a little. But it seemed my looks and my demeanour were acceptable; and there was reference to my likeness to my sister Isabelle.

My mother was not displeased.

"You did well," she told me, and she patted my head. "I could have thought it was Isabelle all over again." She perfunctorily dabbed at her eyes for a few moments.

The English emissaries were still in Paris, and negotiations went on. I heard that the demands of the King of England were too great; on the other hand they were not refused.

Every day I dreaded to hear the outcome, for I knew that once they reached an agreement—and it was certain that both sides wanted the match to take place—my fate would be settled.

But something happened which was to give me a respite—if only temporarily.

My mother sent for me and I knew at once that she was excited but a little uncertain.

"There is news from England," she said. "This will undoubtedly delay our plans. I hope not for long. The King of England has died. Prince Henry has become King Henry . . . King Henry V."

She was smiling at me coyly.

"Well, what do you say?"

"I . . . I was wondering what difference that would make."

"Delay undoubtedly. Perhaps he will want to strike a harder bargain. It was hard enough, God knows, before. But now he is the King . . . we shall see. Do not fret, child, I am sure your father and I will manage to get this wonderful match for you . . . however much we have to pay for it."

I shivered and was silent, and she pretended to construe my attitude as one of delight.

"I know how you feel," she went on. "It is a dazzling prospect. A Queen . . . you, my little Katherine. You will learn what that means. I am a proud woman. Two daughters of mine Queens of England. Is that not a wonderful triumph?'' She was smiling, gazing ahead. ''Of course . . . he will be busy for a while . . . getting himself crowned and dealing with matters of state. We know that full well. So it may be that we have to wait for a few weeks or so . . . months mayhap . . . before he can give himself up to the delights of marriage.''

I escaped to my own apartments, and there I shut myself in with my thoughts.

A few months. At least it was a respite.

The embassy sent to assess my worthiness to become the bride of the King of England had departed. I wondered what sort of report would be given of me.

I gathered that I looked sufficiently like my sister to please them; and I fervently hoped that it would be a long time before Henry wanted to think of marriage. He was fourteen years older than I and from what I had heard had been on particularly friendly terms with a great many women: but of course that was different. He would have to marry, and the sooner kings married the better, for one of their first duties was to get heirs.

The thought made me shudder. How grateful I was to Henry IV for dying when he did. It ensured me a few weeks—perhaps months—of peace.

There was a great deal of speculation about Henry. He had been such a wild and reckless youth that people were asking what sort of king he would make. Many people said England would be ill-governed. Perhaps that was wishful thinking, for an ill-governed England would suit France very well. Heaven knew France was in a sorry state. There was what was tantamount to war between the Burgundians and the Armagnacs; the King's periods of lucidity were growing more and more infrequent; the Dauphin was young and inclined to flaunt his authority, and there were sycophants all round him; he was not on good terms with his mother, who objected to his attempts to interfere with her plans. She, I believed, was intriguing first with the Armagnacs and then with the Burgundians. This internal strife had weakened the country to a considerable extent, and across the Channel was a new king who had not been tested yet but had made it clear that he was casting covetous eyes on France.

All were watching events on the other side of the Channel.

There were rumours that the new king had changed his character overnight. There was no more roistering with rowdy companions, no more frequenting of low taverns. He threw these habits off as though they were a cloak and revealed his true nature—a young man with a mission to rule his country well and make it great.

"It cannot last," said some. "It is just a phase. He is a wild young man. He goes from one mood to another. No one changes like that overnight as it were."

Others said he had long wanted the crown and that he had been impatiently waiting for his father's death to take it. There was a story in circulation that when his father lay sick he had taken the crown and tried it on and had very much liked the feel of it upon his head.

This man they had chosen for me seemed to have many facets and moods. He was a rake; he was a dedicated king; he cared only for the life of pleasure, yet he had waited with the utmost impatience to shoulder the burdens of state.

It was difficult to know what to believe. I wanted to find out all I could about him, while I prayed that I might never have an opportunity of discovering whether it were true.

I was often in my mother's company, and sometimes I felt that the more I saw her, the less I knew her. I had very soon learned that it would be unwise to show any defiance of her wishes. I had a habit of lowering my head in case she should read rebellion in my expression. I was always wishing that I might be sent away from Court. I longed for Poissy. But even if the negotiations did hang fire, I was still an important pawn in my mother's game; and she wanted to keep me under close surveillance.

I was afraid of her. Large, voluptuous, perfumed, there was something snake-like about her. I saw it in the sudden venom in her eyes when she considered her enemy; and if I refused to fall in with her wishes, I could qualify for that description.

She must be at the centre of some plot. I knew that she swayed between Burgundy and Armagnac, feigning friendship with each in turn and being the friend of neither. Yet, in spite of her love of intrigue, she wallowed in voluptuous indolence. Her sensuality was her most outstanding characteristic; and it must be satisfied at all cost. When I think of her now, it is to see her reclining on a couch in her splendour, lapsing into voluptuous ease, nibbling sweetmeats, calling to her little dogs, petting them, scolding them, popping sweetmeats into their mouths, stroking them while they watched her with attentive adoring eyes. I think she cared more for her pets than for any people. I supposed it was because they were completely hers to command. They obeyed without question. She did not have to manipulate them. But then I believed she enjoyed manipulating people; of course, she could fly into wild rages if those about her did not dance to her tune.

She had her lovers—several of them. I remember especially Louis de Bosredon, whom I particularly disliked. He was a nobleman who came from the Auvergne and she had made him her steward so that she could keep him close to her.

He was good-looking and very conceited. He gave himself airs, and I had heard it was said that, because the Queen liked to have him in her bed, he thought he was all but the King of France.

He clearly did not realize how short-lived the Queen's favour could be and that she never seemed to show any regret for her lost lovers. Even in the case of the Duke of Orléans, whom many believed had had a special place in her affections, she had shown no great sorrow when he was murdered.

My mother was anxious to keep my brother Louis close to her and to guide him in every way. He was a child no longer and many believed that before long he would be King of France. My father was growing less and less capable of understanding state affairs and there was a good deal of speculation about his abdicating in favour of the Dauphin. Courtiers were aware of this; and with every day Louis growing more important in the eyes of those about him—and in his own.

No one was quite sure which side the royal family supported . . . Burgundy or Armagnac. The Queen was so devious; she swayed between them. But Louis suddenly developed a very close friendship with the young Duke of Orléans and they were constantly together. They even dressed alike; and therefore Louis became a friend of the Armagnacs. The people followed the Court, and the Burgundians who had been in high favour in Paris were no longer so. It was fashionable now to stand with the Armagnacs. It was amazing how quickly people took up causes, and they were completely fickle. There was fighting in the streets and, I am grieved to say, often murders. Anyone who dared say a good word for Burgundy was set upon.

I felt a great sorrow for my country. People did not see that the continual bickering between two great houses could do nothing but harm to everyone.

It was not to be expected that the Duke of Burgundy would allow himself to be ousted from his position of power; and when his secret negotiations with the King of England were disclosed, there was a great outcry against him.

My mother was enraged.

"The perfidious scoundrel!" she cried. "He thinks he is the King of France . . . no less. How dare he! I'd have his head for this. Jean the Fearless! I'd give him something to fear!"

I do not know why she talked to me about it. I supposed it was because at that time she talked to anyone, so furious was she.

"Do you know what he has done? He has sent men to London, trying to persuade the King there to consider *his* daughter."

My heart leaped with hope. Could it be that I was to be supplanted? I was sorry for the girl, but what an escape for me!

"He is offering his daughter as wife to Henry. Does he think he can achieve that? The upstart!"

Burgundy was no upstart, I wanted to say. He was more royal than she was. But of course I lowered my eyes and kept quiet.

"I never heard of such arrogance. Her name is Katherine," she added wryly, as though that made the offence even more treacherous. "Yes . . . he hoped to get ahead of *me* . . . ahead of your father, by bringing about a marriage between that wretched daughter of his and the King of England."

"And . . . what did the King of England say to that?"

"What do you think? He is making high enough demands for you. Do you think he would think twice of Burgundy's daughter?"

"She is royal."

"She is not the daughter of a king. He is a king, is he not? He will take you in time . . . never fear. But he strikes a hard bargain. Burgundy is mad."

That was not true, but perhaps he had been a little unwise.

My hopes that there would be a substitute were dashed. My

father was brought out of retirement and set up in the council chamber.

He must sign certain documents which would be delivered to the Duke of Burgundy without delay, informing him that on pain of forfeiture and treason, he must not enter into any treaty with the King of England either for his daughter's marriage or for any other reason.

My mother laughed in derision.

"The man is undoubtedly mad. Does he think Henry would take such a match? No . . . no . . . he'll look higher. He is the King of England, is he not?"

I could see that my hope of escape had been too optimistic.

We heard that the new King was displaying great energy. He was extremely popular in a way his father had never been. He was young and virile; Henry IV had been old and ailing. In fact, his last years had been plagued by a terrible illness. Now there was a great driving force in the nation. The shipyards were busy; there were preparations for war which was always a matter for concern; and already the young King had distinguished himself on the battlefield.

There was a rumour that he was thinking of claiming France. His great-grandfather, Edward III, had had an obsession that France, in truth, belonged to England, which was due to the marriage of Edward II to Isabelle of France. Edward had waged war in France. Poitiers and Crécy were still remembered.

Henry sent messengers to France. He was ready now to open negotiations for the marriage.

"He liked the portrait of you," my mother told me. "No doubt it reminded him of Isabelle. He was most upset that he did not get her."

But when she saw the demands Henry made, my mother was less euphoric.

"Really!" she cried. "He asks too much. He is too sure of himself. He is young . . . and feeling his way, no doubt." She smiled indulgently. She had a weakness for young and virile men.

I was glad of his demands, for it seemed they were too great to be met. Postponement at least was something.

I heard that he was demanding Normandy, Anjou and Maine and that I was to bring a dowry of two million crowns.

"It is outrageous," said my mother. "Even if we were inclined to concede the territory . . . where could we find two million crowns?"

Negotiations flagged once more and the trouble which had begun by Burgundy's perfidious act in trying to arrange a marriage for his daughter behind the King's back caused further outbreaks of fighting. It was almost as though we were at war.

In the midst of all this the bargaining was renewed.

The Dauphin Louis could talk of little but Henry of England. He jeered at him. How dared he make such demands? The English had no right to be in France. They had gained much through Henry II's marriage to Eleanor of Aquitaine, and their son King John had obligingly—as far as the French were concerned—lost it all. Now those lands were back where they belonged, and that was where they should stay.

I had opportunities of talking to Louis now and then. How different he was from the younger brother I had known in the Hôtel de St. Paul! He was now longing to be King. He thought my father should give up the crown and pass it to him without delay.

"He is sick of mind," he said. "He will never be able to govern. If I were King, I would subdue Burgundy for a start. I would stop this fellow of England daring to make such demands. If I were King, I should tell him to marry you, sister, and think himself honoured."

"Why should he?" I asked. "He is a King."

"And are you not the daughter of a King? When you are Queen of England, you must always think of your native land. You must work for France . . . when you are Queen of England."

"It may turn out that I never shall be. The matter has been discussed many times and there is always some hitch."

"It will not always be so. Oh, if I were but King, how different everything would be!"

I could see why my mother kept a close watch on Louis. I wondered what would happen when he became King. He had no love for her and he would certainly not brook her control. What would she do then?

I asked him to tell me what he knew of Henry. "For, if I am to be his wife, it will be good for me to know," I said.

"Oh, you will deal with him, sister. Any woman could. He is but a boy."

"He is fourteen years older than I am."

"He has spent his life roistering in taverns in low company."

"I have heard that he has spent some time on the battlefield."

"Just a soldier. He will never be able to govern England. I have no fear of him."

"Some people seem to."

"They would be frightened by their own shadow. I shall be King one day . . . then you will see."

"Louis," I said earnestly, "how necessary is this marriage to France? Must it be?"

He looked at me shrewdly. "It is of importance," he said. "We have had trouble with the English. There is always trouble with the English. Such a marriage might put an end to it. They have this notion that they own our land. It was due to all those marriages . . . years ago. Well, France is mine and I intend to hold it."

"And I must marry Henry of England?"

He nodded his head. "It seems to me that most people in France think it would be an excellent conclusion . . . and I am of the opinion that the English are of like mind."

"Then . . . providing he does not ask too much . . . it will take place?"

"Yes, sister. It must. For France."

I could see that unless Henry made outrageous demands— which he was capable of doing—my fate was certain.

Disquieting news was coming from across the Channel. Henry was demanding subsidies from his Parliament. "For the defence of England and the safety of the seas." What did it mean? There was a great deal of shaking of heads and uneasy speculation.

Henry's demands, which included me, could not be met. And it seemed he was preparing to make even greater demands.

Alarming statements were coming from England. The crown of France, in fact, belonged to him, declared Henry. The English did not recognize the French law precluding women from ascending the throne, which law was the reason why the throne had not come to Isabelle, wife of Henry's ancestor Edward II. These claims had been raised before and had caused strife between our countries; and now here they were again.

The King was more or less offering an ultimatum. Unless I was given to him in marriage with a dowry of 840,000 golden crowns, fifteen towns in Aquitaine and the seneschalty of Limoges, he would have no recourse but to come over and take the crown which, after all, was his by right.

My brother Louis laughed aloud.

"The arrogant young pup!" he said. "To whom does he think he is talking? Does he realize that he is challenging the mighty land of France?"

But was France mighty? For years it had been ruled by a mad king and his rapacious wife; there was fighting between the two greatest houses in the land. Was France in a position to defend itself?

There was a hasty meeting of the Council; and the Archbishop of Bourges sent to the King of England a reply which was both moderate and adequate.

Did the King of England really think that he could turn the King of France from his throne? he asked. He must be thinking that out of fear he had entered into negotiations for his daughter's marriage. This was not so. It was done out of the love of peace. The French did not want war. They did not wish innocent blood to be shed. In the event of war, the French would have right on their side. They would confidently call upon God Almighty and the Blessed Virgin to aid the King's arms and loyal subjects, and the English armies would be driven out of France and their King would meet death or capture.

Such bold words might have deterred some but not King Henry.

He now made it clear that negotiations were at an end. If the French would not give him what he wanted, he had no alternative but to come and take it by force.

It was said that he was determined on war.

My father was in one of his lucid periods. He was horrified at the prospect of war. He wrote to the King of England saying that if he came to France he would receive him and they might enter into discussion. He added that it was a strange way of wooing his daughter—covered with the blood of her countrymen.

Louis was boasting about what he could do to the English if they dared set foot on French soil. With a few of his friends he contrived what he thought was a joke. He had a cask of tennis balls sent from Paris to London, with a message to Henry that the balls were more fitting playthings for him than the weapons of war he was proposing to use against France.

Knowing Henry, as I did later, I could well imagine the mood in which he received the tennis balls.

His reply was typical of him. "These balls," he said, "shall be struck back with such a racket as shall force open the gates of Paris."

It was tantamount to a declaration of war.

On 7 August in that year 1415, Henry set sail for France.

At that time I was nearly fourteen years of age.

It was just a month after he had landed when Henry took Harfleur. It had cost him a great deal and there were rumours that his army was plagued by sickness.

He marched on, however.

The terrible events of the previous month had aroused my father from his madness. He listened to the accounts of the capture of Harfleur and declared he would place himself at the head of his army and go with it to meet the English King.

It was his Uncle Berry, I think, who begged him to consider what he was proposing to do.

"Remember Poitiers?" he said. "Remember Crécy? It is better that you should not be there. It we lose the battle, we cannot lose the King or the Dauphin as well."

My father hesitated. He must have known that his presence would be a cause for alarm rather than an inspiration. What if madness should seize him on the battlefield—which was not unlikely? What harm would that do? It was agreed that he should not go . . . nor the Dauphin and his brothers Jean and Charles. It was also decided that it would be unwise for Berry, Brittany and Burgundy to risk themselves either.

When I heard this, I felt that they were preparing for defeat before the battle had begun. But although it was more than fifty years since the Battle of Poitiers had been lost, Frenchmen had never forgotten it.

The Battle of Agincourt would be another of those which would be remembered for a long time. It was 25 October and I had now reached my fourteenth birthday. There was tension throughout the Queen's apartments.

All the flower of the nobility—with the exception of the very highest in the land, whom it had been decided could not risk their lives—was there.

In trepidation we waited for the result.

I heard more of that battle later on. Henry himself described it to me. He glowed with pride and enthusiasm when he did so, and I could not help catching it, even though it had meant such a bitter defeat for my own countrymen.

"The French were doomed from the start," Henry told me, "in spite of the fact that there were so many of them. We had come from Harfleur . . . there was sickness in our ranks, and a soldier will often fight better when he is defending his homeland. France was mine by right but these men of mine . . . well, they wanted victory . . . they wanted the spoils of victory . . . but home for them was England. The French were confident . . . too confident. Fifty thousand of them at least . . . all drawn up in their heavy armour. Compared with them, we were very few. Some Englishmen quailed when they compared the numbers of French with ours, and I had to remind them that one Englishmen was worth ten Frenchmen." He laughed that rather raucous laugh of his to which I had become accustomed by that time. But I never forgot his description of the battle.

"They were so confident, your poor deluded Frenchmen. They had the numbers. There they were in their shining armour . . . elegant to look at but oh so heavy to wear. They spent the night before drinking, dicing, betting on how long we should last against them. A soldier should have confidence . . . but the right sort of confidence . . . which is not the foolhardy sort. There must be no vanity in that confidence. The French did not have the right kind. We spent the night in preparation. I had my scouts all over the ground. I knew where it was marshy due to the excessive rains. I knew where I wanted my men and I knew where I wanted theirs. I made sure the French were huddled together without enough space to move freely. I had them on the sodden ground. I knew that, however pretty their ornate armour was, it was too heavy for easy manoeuvre. And there we were, with the whole width of the field to move in, with the archers on our wings and the woods to protect our flanks. I wore a crown in my helmet that all should know I was there among them. And at the end of the day the French had lost 10,000 men and the English . . . some say fourteen, but I'll confess it might have been a little more . . . perhaps a hundred or two. Small though against 10,000. I did not know the name of the place and asked it of a peasant who said: "It is Agincourt, my lord." And I replied, "Henceforth this shall be known as the Battle of Agincourt."

That was Henry's version, and I think it must have been an accurate one for he was not a man to hide the truth.

In any case, no one could fail to admit that that was a sad day in France's history.

There was despondency throughout the Court. There was scarcely a family in the land which was not plunged into mourning. The Duke of Burgundy had lost his two brothers—the Duke of Brabant and the Count of Nevers. I heard he cursed himself because he had not been present. He had given orders that his son—who was the husband of my sister Michelle—should not be allowed to go, and although the young man had attempted to disobey his father's orders, he had been restrained by the Duke's men.

It was a day of shame for France, and that meant England's glory.

The Duke of Burgundy, in a moment of despair, sent a message to Henry with his gauntlet challenging him to single combat. He wanted to avenge his brothers, he said.

By this time I was beginning to realize that Henry was not the man I had first thought him to be. Isabelle's account had been of that rash youth, that frequenter of taverns. This was a different man, a man of great wisdom . . . a king and a conqueror.

He at once saw the folly of fighting a duel with the Duke of Burgundy. Weighty matters such as he was engaged in were not solved by such methods. He was the victor of Agincourt, but he was fully aware that this was by no means the end of the struggle. Victory could easily turn sour, and he had no intention of allowing his to do so. Moreover he knew of the strife in France; and he believed that, with a little diplomacy, because of Burgundy's intense hatred of the Armagnacs, he might consider them a greater enemy than the English. Henry was more than a great soldier; he was a diplomatic king, always looking far ahead beyond the triumphs of the moment.

His reply to the Duke was almost sycophantic, which amazed all, for it seemed incredible that the victor of Agincourt could write in such a humble manner. I was as surprised as any, for, of course, I did not know Henry at that time.

He wrote back: "I will not accept the gauntlet of so powerful a prince as the Duke of Burgundy. I am of no account compared with him. If I have had a great victory at the expense of France, it is through the grace of God. The death of the Duke's brothers has afflicted me sorely, but neither I nor my soldiers caused their deaths. Take back this gauntlet. I will prove to the Duke by the testimony of my prisoners that it was the French who accomplished his brothers' destruction."

I wondered what Burgundy's feelings were when he received that reply. He must have realized the cleverness which lay behind it. It could have been the beginning of that rapport between Burgundy and the English. The latter were not so much the Duke's personal enemies as the hated Armagnacs.

I remembered my brother Louis's rage when he realized the extent of the defeat at Agincourt. All his arrogance had disappeared; he was a different man from that one who had laughingly sent the tennis balls across the Channel. He looked more like the bewildered boy I had known in the Hôtel de St. Paul.

He trembled with rage. "What will happen now?" he shrieked. "What will happen to us all now?" He went into a sort of frenzy. I think those about him must have feared he was going to have an attack similar to those suffered by my father. Blood frothed at his lips. He was a terrifying sight and had to be hurried to bed.

He was very ill for some days. I went to see him.

"I shall soon be well," he said. "It is just a fever."

"You must rest," I told him.

"So says the physician. Then I shall be well. It is the war. I should have been there, Katherine. I should not have allowed them to be so . . . ignobly beaten by those barbarians."

I looked at him sadly. Did he really believe that he could have turned the defeat at Agincourt into a victory? He seemed very like my little brother then . . . vulnerable . . . like the rest of us . . . constantly having to remind himself that he was the Dauphin when he was really a frightened boy.

I was present when my mother came to him.

"My dear, dear son," she cried. "You are sick. Oh . . . but *I* am going to look after you."

"I am well looked after," protested Louis.

"But at such a time, my love, you need your mother. You have had a shock. Have not all of us? This terrible tragedy which has befallen our country . . . I know exactly what is good for you. I am going to nurse you back to health.''

The idea of our mother in a sickroom was rather startling. Louis stared at her disbelievingly; then suddenly I saw a look of horror creep over his face. He turned to me and there was a tragic appeal in his eyes. "Katherine," he said, "don't go . . . you will stay.''

"There is no need for Katherine to be here," said our mother firmly. "She knows nothing of nursing.''

Did she? I wondered.

I said boldly: "I will stay with you, Louis, if you wish.''

"Katherine . . .'' He reached for my hand, and I was again reminded vividly of that little boy.

"Now, now,'' said my mother. "My poor boy. Katherine should go now. We do not want too many people in the sick-room. Poor, poor Louis. You have suffered a great shock. It is best for you to be with your mother.''

I stood still looking at Louis.

"Go now," she said to me with a show of irritation. She turned to look at Louis. "We shall soon have you well. You shall have the very best attention. I shall send for my physician. He is the cleverest doctor in France.''

She gave me a little push away from the bed. I wanted to refuse to go because I thought Louis was trying to say something to me, but we had been in awe of her too long, and I knew those purring kittenish moods could suddenly break into violent rage.

I bowed my head and turned away. I could not bear to look at Louis.

I heard that his health did not improve even though she had sent for her physician.

I cannot say whether the rumours were true but inevitably there *were* rumours, for everyone knew there was conflict between the Dauphin and his mother.

When the physician came, he gave Louis what he said he thought would be an immediate cure. Louis was very ill and by the following day he was dead.

Rumour persisted. Some said Louis had been in moderately good health. Why should he die so suddenly? Was it the shame of Agincourt which had hastened his death? He had been certain that the French could not fail to win. He had boasted of inevitable victory; and the shock of defeat had killed him.

Others said he had been spitting blood for some months. Innumerable royal children had died from that complaint.

But the whispers were there. It was poison. Everyone knew that the Dauphin hated and feared his mother; and everyone knew that that was something she would not endure.

Whatever the truth was, the Dauphin Louis was dead, and my brother Jean had now stepped into his shoes.

Jean had never been like Louis. He had always comfortably assured himself that he would never have to face that great responsibility. Now he had been proved wrong.

Our mother lavished care on Jean, which he had never known before. He was timid; he was no braggart like his brother; all he wanted was a peaceful life.

Like all of us children, he was afraid of our mother and now that her attention was turned on him, he was terrified.

The Armagnacs were always at his side. He could not escape to the peace he so desired.

He was only just eighteen years old. I remember well the last conversation I had with him.

"I'd rather be anywhere than here, Katherine," he said. "I'd rather be cold and hungry at the Hôtel de St. Paul."

I tried to comfort him. "Most people in your position would feel like that at first," I said. "This has been thrust upon you. You weren't expecting it."

He nodded. "And our mother . . . she is always there now."

"You must remember that you are the Dauphin," I said. "It is you who will be the King."

"I know. That is what terrifies me."

It was April of that year 1417 . . . a momentous one. Jean was coughing blood. He was almost pleased when the doctors said he must rest. Gratefully he kept to his bed, and a few days later he quietly died. Poor Jean. I think he was rather relieved to leave a life which had become so frightening to him.

My younger brother, Charles, now fourteen years old, had become the Dauphin of France.

Poor Charles, I do not think he wanted the honour any more than Jean had. He was of a melancholy nature and wept when he heard the news. His two brothers—whom he had believed would protect him from high rank—had gone . . . and now there he was, the new Dauphin of France.

"I shouldn't have the title, Katherine," he told me. "It is not mine by right."

"What do you mean, Charles?" I said. "You are the next in line."

"Ah, but I do not believe I am the King's son."

"What?"

"When I was born, our mother was having numerous lovers. One of them could be my father."

"You must not think like that, Charles. After all, it could apply to us all."

"Our mother is a wicked woman, Katherine."

I was silent.

"Do you think she poisoned Louis?" he asked.

"No . . . no . . ." I cried, although it was not strictly true.

"And what if she decided to poison me?"

"She will not. She would not dare."

"But if I am a bastard I have no right to the throne."

"Charles, do not think of such things. You will be all right. You must be. You are the last son. You are safe."

He hugged me suddenly. I was very sorry for my little brother who was so afraid of being Dauphin, and even more so when he looked to the future and saw himself King of France.

Henry did not stay in France after Agincourt. Some less clever, less astute victors might have attempted to continue with the campaign. But his army needed rest and replenishment. Several of his men were sick, so he fortified his gains and with his sick and wounded and much depleted army he returned to England. But we all knew full well that that was not the end. He would return.

The strife between Armagnac and Burgundy continued while each blamed the other for the defeat at Agincourt. If only my countrymen had stood together, everything might have turned out differently.

We were in Vincennes. My mother kept me with her. She was certain that soon Henry would be demanding our union, so I was an important bargaining counter.

"A daughter's place is with her mother," she said, glibly ignoring any reference to the years of my infancy when I might have needed a mother and had been neglected with my brothers and sisters. But that was her way. Truth was bent to suit her purposes of the moment.

I think she was more indiscreet than ever in Vincennes. There were numerous lovers and she made little secret of her tendency to select presentable young men and invite them to her apartments for a cosy session.

The favourite was still Louis de Bosredon, and he was becoming more and more insufferable.

He had several clashes with one or two highly placed officials in the household, but when complaints were made to my mother, she shrugged her shoulders and laughed. She treated Louis de Bosredon like one of her little dogs . . . to be petted and scolded light-heartedly and pampered. Louis de Bosredon was clearly delighted with his success.

I do not know how long he would have continued to please her—he had had a long run—but it was inevitable that one day he would go too far.

· It so happened that my father had been getting a little better since the battle of Agincourt. It was possible that such a devastating event may have done a little to arouse him to his responsibilities and had given him a little impetus towards sanity.

However, he was better and he decided to come to Vincennes to see the Queen.

On the road he met Louis de Bosredon.

I cannot imagine how Bosredon could have been so foolish. He must have been intoxicated by his success. He had spent the night with the Queen, and I imagined it had been such a satisfactory encounter that it had robbed him temporarily of any common sense he might have had.

It is only by heresay that I know what happened at that meeting on the road, but, of course, everyone who had witnessed it could talk of nothing else. Bosredon behaved as though he were the King and my father some vassal.

My father was at first amazed that a subject could show such a lack of courtesy and offer none of that homage which was due to the Crown. It was more than an insult to him; it was an insult to France.

He ordered that Bosredon should be arrested without delay.

And then he rode on to Vincennes.

From a window I saw his arrival. He went straight to my

mother's apartments, and there such a scene ensued, the like of which had never taken place between them before.

He must have known she had many lovers. He was a tolerant man. He knew of her ardent nature. Perhaps he thought it was natural that she should be unfaithful to him during his absences. He himself had Odette de Champdivers to comfort him in his seclusion. He had even had a child by her. However, he had not reproved my mother before. But the insolence of Louis de Bosredon must have ignited years of resentment. He had indulged her; he had been besotted by her; but he would not have her lovers insulting the Crown.

We were all amazed. We all cowered in our rooms, waiting to know what would happen next.

He was accusing her not only of infidelity towards him but of treachery to France. She had her spies everywhere. She was with the Armagnacs. She was with the Burgundians. Anything that suited her purpose at a certain time. He was tired of being treated as though he were of no account.

He sent for the guards. She was under arrest.

He shouted his orders. The Queen should be taken to Tours. There she should be guarded night and day. Every letter she wrote must be examined. All her actions must be reported.

My mother was astounded. What had happened to the poor mad husband who had always been her slave? She tried to protest. She exerted all those wiles which had never failed before. But the King had had enough. He was no longer to be duped.

His country was in dire straits; the enemy was waiting to deliver the final blow; and one of France's bitterest enemies was its Queen.

And now she was his prisoner.

So my mother was taken to Tours, and I was united with my father.

I travelled back to Paris with him, and there I was with him often. Now and then he talked to me sadly of the past.

He said: "It is my tragedy, daughter, that I have my periods of insanity. I am sane now, but for how long? How do I know? Perhaps it would have been better for me if I had been completely mad. These trips back and forth are sometimes more than I can endure. I trust young Charles will have a happier reign than I. Alas, poor child . . . he is little more . . . this has overwhelmed him. I trust he will not suffer as I have done. But sometimes I fancy he has no stomach for the task.''

He liked to have me with him, and I was glad of that time we spent together. I wished it could have been longer. He was so different from my mother, gentle, innately good and kind.

He talked of my mother a little and with much sadness.

''In the beginning it was perfect,'' he said. ''Too perfect, I suppose. My child, I am afraid of perfection. There is often a canker somewhere. If you could have seen her when she first came to France. She was enchanting . . . a child . . . younger than you are now . . . but she never seemed like a child. She was so eager and loving. I never saw anyone like your mother. There are few of her sort in the world.''

I thought that was not such a bad thing.

He said to me one day: ''And you, daughter, you have a happy life ahead of you. You will leave this tortured land. You will be the wife of a great king.''

''Do you think, Sire, that Henry is a great king?''

''He has all but conquered us, has he not? Oh, he had a wild youth, but they tell me that, as soon as the crown was placed on his head, he changed. It was like a miracle, they say. He put aside his frivolities. He gave himself up entirely to his country. It is a rare man who can do that, Katherine. Perhaps that is greatness. I think you will be fortunate to marry such a man.''

''Shall I ever, do you think? For so long there has been talk of it.''

''Much has to be settled. He wants this marriage, depend upon it. We both want it. It is just a matter of settling terms. The King of England asks too much of us, but after Agincourt . . . it seems inevitable. My reign has been disastrous. We have gone from bad to worse.''

''It was not your fault, dear Father.''

''Perhaps if I had not been plagued . . . perhaps if I could have kept a firm hand on the reins . . . perhaps, daughter . . . it may be then that this strife within our country might not have happened. There is nothing which destroys a country more than civil war and when you have two great houses within their country fighting each other . . . then that country will fall into despair . . . as ours has. But we shall emerge. It may be, Katherine, that you will play your part in rebuilding our great nation.''

''How, dearest Father?''

"You will know when the time comes. Perhaps it will be through this much-talked-of union. Your husband will be our conqueror . . . but he will always remember that it is your country which he has conquered."

"And what of my mother?"

His face hardened. "I want to trust her," he said almost piteously, "but I cannot. I would if I could. If only I could."

His lips trembled and his eyes were melancholy. I was afraid—as we often were—that the madness might be coming upon him once more.

There are many who said Louis de Bosredon met his just deserts.

When he was arrested and imprisoned he was 'put to the question.' I do not know what form of torture was applied but he did not endure it for long. He could not, I was sure, have borne the thought of his beautiful body being mutilated in any way. He quickly confessed to anything they wanted him to. His punishment was that he should be sewn into a sack and thrown into the Seine. A fitting end for an arrogant coxcomb, many said. So this was done and the sack, on which was written 'Let the King's justice run its course,' was thrown into the river.

The Armagnacs rubbed their hands with glee. This was a direct attack against the Queen who had been in secret communication with Burgundy.

My mother was not the woman to accept captivity with quiet resignation. Intrigue had always been one of her most exciting pastimes; and consequently she excelled at it.

She had not been at Tours for more than a month before she conceived the idea of getting in touch with the Duke of Burgundy. It was the King and the Armagnacs who had imprisoned her; therefore she knew that Burgundy would be prepared to defy their authority. I do not know how she managed to smuggle a note out of her prison but I guessed she had contrived to cajole one or more of her guards by that time.

Burgundy was only too eager to aid her in her escape, and from then on they were allies—at least on the surface.

Isabeau was allowed to leave her prison only to go to Mass at the convent of Marmoutier, which was just outside the city's walls, and on the occasions when she went there, her guards went with her.

While she was in the convent's church, a company of sixty men, led by their captain, entered. Seeing that these were Burgundians, her three guards urged her to act with caution while they tried to decide how they could smuggle her out of the church.

It was she who surprised them when she addressed the captain.

"Where is the Duke?" she asked.

"On his way, Madame."

"Then arrest these three men."

When the astonished guards found they were prisoners they realized that the Queen had led them into a trap.

In due course the Duke of Burgundy arrived.

He kissed the Queen's hand.

"My dearest cousin," she said. "I should love you beyond any man in the realm. You have rescued me from my enemies. You have set me free. I will never fail you, my dearest friend. I know your aim has always been one of devotion to the King and your country. May God bless you."

The Duke knelt at her feet, and in due course they set out, followed by his men, for Chartres.

My mother was free. It was fortunate for her that my father, overcome by all the distress brought on by the situation between them, had had to retire once more to the Hôtel de St. Paul and the ministrations of the tender Odette.

My mother sent a declaration to all the important towns, in which she stated that, owing to the King's unfortunate seclusion, the government of the country was, for the time being, at Chartres, and with her was her good cousin, the Duke of Burgundy, to help and advise her when necessary, until the recovery of her good lord, the King.

So my mother was free and, with Burgundy beside her, had regained her power.

The Armagnacs kept control of the King and the Dauphin; and the conflict in my country was stronger than ever.

In the meantime Henry had returned to France and was laying siege to Rouen.

A few men from the besieged city escaped and came to Paris. They had a terrible story to tell. The people had been determined to hold out until help came to them. Poor deluded men and women! What help could they expect? Nevertheless, they had fortified their ramparts; they had forced all those who could not bear arms or were too feeble to withstand the siege to leave the city; they had hoarded food and had prepared themselves in every way.

Twelve hundred helpless men and women were sent out of the town; and the miseries they endured are too distressing to brood on. I was especially sorry for the pregnant women who had nowhere to go. They gave birth unattended outside the walls of the city. Death stared them in the face, and their greatest fear was that their newly born infants would go unbaptized. Friends from within sent down baskets that the new-born children should be brought up to be baptized, and when this was done, they were lowered down to their helpless mothers and left to die.

How cruel was war! I should hate those men who came over to our country and caused so much misery—and all for a crown!

The people inside the city's walls suffered too. They were forced to eat cats, dogs, rats, anything that came to hand. And the winter was approaching.

They were very brave, those people of Rouen. If those in high places had shown the same dedication to their country, we should not have been in the sorry plight we were.

When the fall of the city was imminent, the men of Rouen decided to fight to the end rather than give in. They planned to stand together and fight outside the city walls after having set fire to it. They were courageous and Henry admired courage. He declared he would spare the lives of all citizens—with one or two exceptions—if they would surrender peacefully; and so a compromise was reached.

Henry said later that one of the proudest moments of his life was when he entered Rouen—that city beloved of his ancestor Richard Cœur de Lion and which King John had lost with the English possessions in France.

Our resistance was coming to an end. These disasters could not continue. The English were marching through Normandy, and everywhere cities and castles were falling into their hands.

We were ready to make terms.

My mother returned to Paris. She behaved as though there had never been a rift between her and my father, who had now lapsed into a state of melancholy. Everyone around him was watchful lest he should slip into violent madness.

Dr. Harsley had left Court, deciding that his own health demanded that he should live a quiet life in the country. So my father was taken back to the Hôtel de St. Paul, to Odette, whose company, I was sure, was more beneficial to him than any doctors would have been.

My mother had commanded that, as I was now of some importance and had my part to play in bringing peace terms to a satisfactory conclusion, I should be under her care.

I was given an apartment and several attendants. What a delight it was to find my old friend Guillemote among them.

We greeted each other rapturously. She had changed a little. She was slightly more plump but there was still the same rosy face—the face, I always thought, of a good woman and one on whom I could always rely.

"I have thought of you often, my lady," she said, "and wondered how you were getting on."

"The convent was more comfortable than . . ."

She nodded.

"But I missed you. So did Michelle and Marie."

"Michelle is a grand lady now. I wonder if it has changed her."

"I suppose we all change. I must have changed a good deal."

"You've grown up . . . which was to be expected. And the boys . . ." She turned away to hide her emotion.

"I know. Both Jean and Louis . . ."

"And little Charles?" she went on quickly. "Such an important man now. The Dauphin, no less. I trust all will be well with him."

"Guillemote," I said, "we are together again. Let us stay so."

She lifted her shoulders. "If it is in our power, my lady."

"I shall do my best. I shall not let you go away."

"They say you are going to make a grand marriage . . . across the sea."

"I shall be important then, Guillemote. I shall be the one who says whom I shall have about me."

She smiled rather sadly. "I shall never forget the day they took you away. There was such sadness. Nothing was the same.

I wept until I had no tears left. All my little ones gone, especially you, Madame Katherine.''

''Well, Guillemote, don't be sad now. We are together again.''

''Mademoiselle de Champdivers was good to me. She is a good woman. I think she arranged that I should come here to be with you.''

''Yes,'' I said. ''I know she is good. I am thankful that my father has her to look after him.''

I felt considerably comforted to have Guillemote so near.

The King of England was now ready to talk peace; and my mother was making arrangements into which she entered with the utmost enthusiasm. She was sure that I would be instrumental in softening the peace terms.

''This betrothed of yours strikes a hard bargain,'' she said with a coy laugh. ''Now, child, we must make you so desirable that he will decide . . . for your sake . . . to modify the terms. You are handsome enough. Yes . . . just a little like me. And amazingly like your sister Isabelle for whom he once had a great desire. He will see her again in you . . . and therein lies our hope.''

My emotions were in a turmoil. I was about to take the most important step in my life and it might well be that soon I should be married to a man whom so far I had never seen. But I had a vivid picture of him in my mind. I saw him as Isabelle had seen him; and again as quite a different person: the wise, shrewd conqueror. Was it possible for a man to change as drastically as he was said to have done? It seemed hardly likely. But surely this rash and frivolous youth of Isabelle's version could never have conquered France.

Earlier I had been terrified of union with him; now I had to admit to a certain excitement. I wanted desperately to see him, and my fear of what might follow was swallowed up in my excitement.

''Your complexion is good,'' my mother said. ''You have a lovely soft skin and your eyes are very fine. They are like mine. Your mouth and teeth are good. But your nose, my dear. That comes from your father. The Valois nose. A pity! But it is not too marked in you. You must smile. You look so solemn. You must look *interested*. I shall expect you to charm him. He is a soldier . . . no doubt a little rough . . . and English manners have never had the grace of the French. Never mind, you will act with grace and charm . . . and if you do that, he will be enchanted. Now, try this.''

It was a gown shaped to my figure, coming up high to the throat. It was discreetly adorned with jewels and there was a strip of ermine down the front. On my head was an arched crown, from which a veil flowed down to my shoulders.

My mother clapped her hands. "That is good," she said. "Oh, daughter, I have hopes of you."

I felt a little thrill of pleasure and for once did not recoil when she kissed me.

The meeting was to take place in Pontoise, and a splendidly decorated barge was made ready to take us there.

My father, who, under Odette's ministrations, had recovered a little, was to accompany us.

"It is necessary that he is there," said my mother. "As long as he remains quiet, all will be well."

Close to the river, pavilions had been set up and there were elegant tents made of green velvet decorated with cloth of gold.

As we sailed down the river, I could not stop myself from watching my poor father. I thought, he should not be with us. How did he feel . . . he who had lived so much of his life in a clouded world . . . to be sailing down the river to meet the conqueror of his country? His father, the Wise Charles, had left him a prosperous land, a proud kingdom . . . and under him, it had come to this. He had to look to his daughter to charm the King of England sufficiently for him to accept her as part of the peace terms. It was humiliating . . . distressing beyond words— and I suffered with him.

My mother looked beautiful in spite of a certain obesity which only seemed to add to her voluptuousness. She was animated and I understood that what she craved most in life was excitement, and the significance of this occasion could not stop her enjoying it.

As for myself, I felt I had left my childhood behind me for ever.

We disembarked and, as we approached the royal tent, I saw Henry.

He was very tall and slender; and what struck me most about him was his immense vitality. He was comely enough, with a pleasant oval face. I noticed his long, straight nose. I usually

looked at people's noses, as people do look at the features of
others when they are particularly aware of their own. His complexion was fresh and he looked as though he lived much of his
life in the open air. He had brown hair and eyes of the same
colour, very bright and, I noticed with relief, quite gentle, though
afterwards I learned they could flare into sudden wrath. I was
agreeably surprised and I felt great pleasure as his eyes eagerly
turned on me and I knew that he was not displeased.

He bowed to my parents and then took my hand and
kissed it.

He sat opposite me and, while he talked with my parents and
members of the Council, his eyes strayed again and again to me.
I lowered mine and he smiled. I was feeling more and more
reassured with every moment.

I was disappointed to learn that, in spite of his openly expressed admiration for me, he did not lower his demands.

My mother said: "Let him wait awhile. I know he is enamoured of the Princess. He will agree to modify his terms. Give
him time."

He was disappointed, I believe, because my father and his
advisers would not capitulate—but he would not give way; and
the meeting over, he continued with his campaign throughout
Normandy, with alarming results for the French.

I liked to think that he did intend to lower his demands, because he asked for another meeting, but by the time he arrived
at Pontoise it was to find the tents had been removed. Only the
Duke of Burgundy remained with a few of his men.

Henry said with some rancour: "Cousin, understand that we
will have the daughter of your king or we will drive him out of
his kingdom."

The Duke replied: "Sire, you may do so, but before you have
succeeded in driving the King and me out of this kingdom, I
doubt not you will be heartily tired."

So in spite of the meeting, it seemed that we had advanced
very little.

But my mother did not accept this. She knew men, she said,
and a spark had been struck between myself and the King of
England, and he was the sort of man who would not rest until
he had what he wanted.

* * *

I thought a great deal about Henry. At last he was a living person to me. I had seen him, though briefly, but it was enough to show me that he was not the man Isabelle had known.

My life since I had left Poissy had not been a happy one. I lived in fear of my mother. There was a suspicion in my mind, which I could not dispel, that she had poisoned my brother Louis. Of Jean, I was not sure. I knew that she despised my brother Charles. I thought he was safe, though, for there was no son to follow him; so it was to her advantage to keep him alive. I was fond of my father but I was in a state of perpetual anxiety about his health. I thought of a new life . . . away from it all, away from the conflicts which had surrounded me since the day of my birth. I thought of Henry as my husband, of myself as Queen of England. I thought of children of my own. Yes, I longed for children.

I had come to the conclusion that I wanted a better life than that which I had hitherto known and that I might find it with Henry. I prayed that these negotiations would not fail. I was no longer a child. The years were slipping by. I was now eighteen years old. For so long I had been told I was to marry Henry. Should I ever do that?

During this uncertain period, there took place one of those events which was to shake the whole of France so violently that, temporarily, even the state of our country was forgotten. My brother Charles, the Dauphin, was under the control of the Armagnacs, and I believed he had now come to terms with his fate and, attempting to prepare himself for the role to come, was eager to make peace with Burgundy.

My father was becoming so feeble that even in his most lucid moments he was unfit to govern; and this must have made Charles feel that he must learn quickly and do his best to bring a stable government to the country.

He had now established himself at Bourges, where a small court had gathered about him. He was very serious, which might have been good had he not been of such a melancholy nature. I knew that he was haunted by the fear that he was illegitimate and therefore had no true claim to the throne. In view of the life our mother had led, it was a doubt which might come to us all. I felt fairly sure of my own parentage. I had my nose to thank for that.

Charles clearly saw that the reason we had fallen so low was the strife between our two great houses and, as he was involved with the Armagnac faction, he renewed his efforts to make peace with Burgundy.

I like to think that my brother was led astray by evil counsellors. I cannot believe to this day that he planned what happened. Or if he did, it was because he was convinced that it was for the good of France.

What he did was to arrange a meeting between himself and the Duke of Burgundy when they would discuss how to bring about peace between the two rival houses. The meeting was to take place at Montereau. They would both come in peace and unarmed in order to show their confidence in each other.

I think the Duke must have been a little suspicious, for, although he might trust the Dauphin, the young man was in the hands of the treacherous Armagnacs. However, the meeting was arranged.

I heard that several men close to the Duke thought he was taking a great risk by going unarmed among his enemies and warned him not to agree to the meeting; but after a good deal of consideration the Duke decided that he must go.

"It is my duty," he said. "If we can make peace, the Dauphin and I can stand together against the English."

It was a never-to-be-forgotten day in September when he set out for the rendezvous.

The Duke arrived as arranged and was met by one of Charles's men, a certain Duchâtel, who greeted him with great respect and told him how delighted the Dauphin was that he had agreed to come. It was time they settled their differences and stood together against the English, who were the real enemy of France, instead of fighting each other.

This seemed a satisfactory beginning but, as the Duke was preparing to go with Duchâtel to the Dauphin, one of his own men came running to him and, throwing himself on his knees, begged the Duke not to go. "You will be betrayed, my lord," he said. "I am sure they mean to kill you."

The Duke turned to Duchâtel and said: "You heard that, my lord. It is what the people round me have in mind."

"They are wrong," Duchâtel assured him. "I swear they are wrong. The Dauphin loves you. You are his close kinsman. All he wants is to end this strife, and that all Frenchmen stand together for France."

The Duke bowed his head and said: "I trust your word. In God's holy name, do you swear you have not murder in mind?"

"My good and most noble lord," replied Duchâtel, "I would rather die than commit treason to you or my lord. I give you my word that the Dauphin wishes nothing but reconciliation."

"Then let us proceed," said the Duke.

When he came to the Dauphin, the Duke took off his cap and knelt before him. The Dauphin appeared to be seized with emotion and made him rise and cover his head.

Then, changing his mood abruptly, my brother began upbraiding the Duke. He had not cared for the good of France, he said. He had followed his own inclination. He was wanting in his duty.

The Duke must have been surprised at this sudden change. He had come to talk peace, not to listen to a harangue against his actions.

He said haughtily that he had done what he had thought was right and would do it again.

My brother, alas, was no diplomat. I think that secretly he must have been afraid of Burgundy, who had a very powerful and overbearing personality and considered himself equal to—perhaps greater than—the highest in the land.

Duchâtel ran up and shouted: "The time has come!" He lifted his battle-axe and struck the defenceless Duke.

I wondered if Burgundy had time to realize that he had stepped into a trap. Had he forgotten that he himself had brought the Duke of Orléans to an untimely end? That had happened twelve years earlier but such things are never forgotten.

Vengeance had been brewing for years. It had been decided that the murder of Orléans should not go unpunished.

As the Duke fell to the ground, others came forward, their swords unsheathed.

There were several who were eager for revenge; and there on the ground lay the once-mighty Duke. They fell upon him with their swords.

The murder of Orléans was avenged.

The Duke's followers waited at some distance, as had been arranged. They did not know what had happened until they were set upon and, weaponless as they were before armed men, they were forced to fly.

There were some among the assassins who wanted to strip

the Duke's body and throw it into the river. But my brother, already regretting the part he had played in the murder of his kinsman, would not allow that. The Duke's body was prepared for burial, albeit in a pauper's shell, and taken to the Church of Notre Dame in Montereau to be interred.

And so died Jean the Fearless, the Great Duke of Burgundy. The new Duke Philip was the husband of my sister Michelle.

I wondered what Michelle was feeling now, for she was happy with the heir of Burgundy, and I wondered how this would affect their relationship, for her brother would be held responsible for the murder of her husband's father.

It was small wonder that I felt a desire to escape from the scene of this strife.

It was not to be supposed that the murder of such an important personage as the Duke of Burgundy would not arouse a storm of condemnation.

The next day, when the news was spreading throughout the country, the Parliament and all the leading dignitaries met. They were determined to bring the criminal to justice. People were crowding into the streets, demanding that the murderer be delivered up to them.

My poor brother was thrown into a state of deep depression. All he had wanted to do was to stop the quarrelling between Burgundy and the Armagnacs. He had been led into this. Only the death of Jean the Fearless could bring peace, he had been assured, and, young and inexperienced as he was, he had believed them. And now this terrible deed was on his conscience. Never would he be able to forget the look of horrified reproach in the eyes of the Duke as he fell, when, in those fleeting seconds, he realized he had been betrayed. Charles would be haunted by the murder all his life.

There was an attempt to justify the deed.

The conspirators said that the Duke had been greeted in a friendly fashion but he had suddenly started to abuse the Dauphin. He had been ready to draw his sword.

As the Duke's supporters had made it clear that he had come to the meeting unarmed, this carried little weight. But, said the conspirators, the Duke had attempted to attack the Dauphin, and it was then that they had found it necessary to despatch him with speed. It was through his own madness that he had died.

This story was quickly proved to be untrue when two of the knights who had accompanied the Dauphin declared that they had known the Duke to be unarmed; they had seen him walk into the trap; they had wanted no part in such treachery; they cursed those men who had planned the murder and so betrayed the honour of their master, the Dauphin. They would rather have died before they had been present on such an occasion, and they had played no part in it.

There was condemnation throughout the country.

As for Henry, he was determined to turn the murder to his advantage.

It was a great loss to France, he said. The Duke of Burgundy was a true and honourable knight. Through his death he, Henry, had reached the summit of his wishes, for one of the greatest Frenchmen was no longer there to oppose him.

The murdered man's son, now Philip, Duke of Burgundy, was deeply grieved by his father's death. He was filled with hatred for the Dauphin and the Armagnacs. He was determined to bring them to disaster, and to this end he threw in his lot with the English that he might stand up in arms against the true enemies of France, the Armagnacs.

I could imagine Henry's glee. At least he had profited from the terrible deed.

The Dauphin and his Armagnacs were doomed. My brother was overcome by remorse and despair. This wicked deed which was to have silenced the Burgundians had succeeded in making them stronger and—an unforeseen development—who would have believed they would have ranged themselves beside the English!

The result of this alliance did not take long to show itself.

There was no alternative for the Dauphin but to make peace with the conqueror of his country.

Henry was triumphant.

I accompanied my mother to Troyes, where I was to be formally betrothed to Henry. I felt a sense of relief that it was to happen at last. My longing to be free from conflict was now intense. I had seen Henry only briefly, but I felt I knew a great deal about him and I was ready to trust myself to him.

I went with my mother to the church of Notre Dame in Troyes. Henry was already there. He had arrived on 20 May with his brothers, the Dukes of Clarence and Gloucester, and 1,600 men, chiefly archers, to remind all that they must accept him as the conqueror or take the consequences.

Lodgings had been prepared for him at the Hôtel de Ville.

I remember now the moment he came into the church. He looked godlike in shining armour, and in his helmet was a fox's tail decorated with gems.

As he approached me, he gave me a most warm and loving smile. Then he took my hand and that of my mother and led us both to the altar.

My mother explained to him that her husband, the King, was too indisposed to be present.

Henry graciously inclined his head. He would know that my father was suffering from another of his mad spells—which was not surprising considering that this ceremony was tantamount to the surrender of France to the conqueror.

The terms of the peace were read aloud so that all might hear.

It was as though my father were speaking and, when I thought of him alone in his room at the Hôtel de St. Paul, I was glad that he would be unaware of what was happening about him. He would be happier that way. At least he did not know that he had lost a kingdom.

"I, Charles VI, King of France, give my daughter Katherine in marriage to King Henry V of England.

"King Henry shall place no hindrance in the way of our retaining the crown for as long as we shall live.

"It is agreed that immediately on our death the crown and kingdom of France shall belong perpetually to King Henry and his heirs.

"During those times when we are prevented from taking part in the affairs of the kingdom, the power of government shall belong to King Henry, with the counsel of the nobles and sages of our kingdom.

"King Henry shall strive with all his might to bring conflict in this kingdom to an end and bring back peace to those cities, castles, places and districts that belong to the party commonly known as that of the Dauphin or Armagnacs."

As I looked round among those assembled in the church to listen to the terms of surrender, I wondered what their feelings were to hear this solemn renunciation of their country to an invader.

Philip, Duke of Burgundy, was present. Now the ally of the conqueror, he was in deep mourning for his father.

Henry was beside me. He had taken my hand, and on my finger he placed a ring encrusted with jewels. It was one worn by English queens at their coronations, he told me afterwards.

I felt a certain contentment. It seemed now, that my marriage with Henry was certain.

It was a little more than two weeks after that ceremony, on 3 June, that I was married to Henry and became Queen of England.

The ceremony took place in the parish church of Troyes, and I doubt the people of that town had ever seen such a magnificent spectacle before.

My husband wanted everyone to realize that he was, in all but name, the King of France; and all the pomp and glory were an indication of his power.

It touched me deeply that this mighty warrior could be tender towards me. I felt happy and secure and I thanked God that, out of the terrible tragedy which had befallen France, at least this had come about.

The truth was that I was proud of him. He was triumphant and I wanted him to be, even though his triumph was the defeat of my country.

My mother was pleased with me. She cared nothing for France, only for herself, and I believed she craved excitement so much that she would have welcomed it whatever it cost.

She was ingratiating towards my husband, exerting all her wiles. Not that he appeared to be aware of the feminine allure which had led men like Louis de Bosredon to destruction. At the same time I had a feeling that he was assessing her in his shrewd manner and wondering how she could be of use to him.

After the ceremony, Henry and I sat side by side, and he spoke to me in his rather anglicized French and I responded in my quaint English which amused him.

I told him I should improve my English. I had learned to speak it, but the manner in which he spoke was somewhat different from that of my teachers.

"You must not change it too much," he said. "It is charming as it is, Kate." He went on, "I shall call you Kate. It sounds more English. Kate, I would not have you change one little bit."

I blushed and hung my head for there, before them all, he kissed my lips.

He prided himself on being a soldier. He told me he lacked the fancy manners of prancing courtiers.

"So much of my life has been spent on the battlefield," he said. "It makes a man rough and ready perhaps . . . but honest, Kate . . . an honest man who says what is in his mind. If you want me otherwise . . ." He lifted his hands in mock despair.

I said: "I would not want you other than you are," at which he laughed and kissed my hands and said I delighted him and that I was all he wanted in his bride, which was how he had known it would be from the first moment he saw me.

And I refused to remember that he might have married me long ago if he had accepted the terms offered. I understood why he had refused. He was a man of great ambition. He wanted France . . . as well as me.

But why should I think these thoughts? I was newly married. I was excited. I believed I had left the melancholy days behind me. I was starting a new life.

Queen of England

The Archbishop of Sens had blessed the bed and prayed God to make it fertile. We had been ceremoniously put to bed. This was the moment about which I had thought a great deal. No one had talked to me of what was expected of me. Isabelle's marriage with her King of England had never been consummated; and afterwards, when she had married the Duke of Orléans, she did not speak of such matters. My mother had told me nothing. She was the sort of woman who would have been born with the knowledge of everything that would be required of her.

I felt inadequate. I need not have done. Henry was a gentle and tender lover, and I was greatly relieved to discover that, instead of irritating, my innocence enchanted him.

During the night a grand procession came to our bedside with wine and soup as though to fortify us against the night's activities.

When they had gone, Henry took me into his arms and laughed.

"The interruption was untimely," he said. "Forgive me, Kate. I had to agree to it. Here am I, in a new country which has suddenly become mine. There will be enemies all around me. Of course, they are very agreeable now. They have to be." He laughed again and I laughed with him. "But how do I know who is plotting against me? How do I know when someone is going to creep up to me and thrust a dagger in my back?"

I shivered and clung to him, which pleased him.

"Fret not, sweet Kate," he said, "and know this: I am a man who is able to take care of himself as well as those about him.

You will be taken care of from now on. So have no fear. But I think it as well to follow the customs of the country." He laughed heartily. "Who wants soup and wine? There are other matters with which to concern ourselves than drinking soup and wine."

And I laughed with him and was happy. I thought I was the luckiest princess in the world, for although my country had been defeated, my happiness had come out of it. And I was no longer merely the Princess of France. I was Queen of England.

The morning had come. We broke our fast together side by side . . . he now and then leaning over to kiss me.

"So," he said, "how goes it with you, Kate? How feels it to be my wife?"

"My lord," I replied, "it makes me wondrous happy."

"That is what I wanted to hear . . . and truth it is . . . is it not?"

"It is the truth, my lord."

"Then I am the happiest man . . . not only in France but in the whole world. There will be a feast today. It must be so. In truth, Kate, I think these feasts a waste of time."

I nodded, smiling.

How wonderful it was to be together. There was an intimacy between us but I felt there was much of him which I had yet to know.

I was able to meet his two brothers during that morning. I warmed towards them because it was clear that they both admired him.

There was Thomas, Duke of Clarence, and the younger Humphrey, Duke of Gloucester. I should not have wanted to marry either of them. Thomas looked rather delicate and Henry told me afterwards that he had sent him home after the fall of Harfleur because he was anxious about his health. Humphrey was different. I could see he had great vitality. He was very handsome and—said Henry—aware of it.

After the meeting Henry talked a little of them.

He said: "You will get to know my brothers very well in time. They are my good friends all of them."

I said that I had seen by their expressions that they honoured him and were very proud of him.

He smiled at that, well pleased that I had noticed or that they had betrayed their feelings.

"Then there is John," he went on, "the Duke of Bedford. He is younger than Thomas. Humphrey is, of course, the youngest."

I had guessed that that was a sore point with Humphrey. I felt he must be rather vain—although he had been very gracious and charming . . . perhaps a little too charming? The idea occurred to me that I might have to be a little wary of Humphrey.

But this was no time for misgivings. I had been married but one day and I had every hope that a happy future lay before me. I thought there would be weeks ahead when Henry and I would get to know each other really well; I was sure that the more I knew of him, the more attractive I would find him.

I had a rather rude awakening at the banquet that afternoon. We were side by side on the royal dais, contentedly listening to the musicians. It was a great delight to find that Henry was fond of music. He played the harp, as I did. He would play to me, he said. I should play to him; and we should play together.

One of the courtiers was talking to Henry, saying what a happy occasion this was, with which Henry agreed.

"We must celebrate it, Sire, so that the French do not forget."

"I promise you this is something which will never be forgotten," replied Henry.

"But there must be celebrations, my lord."

"What do you suggest?" asked Henry.

"Well, in the first place, we should stage a tournament. We should show the French our skill."

Henry was silent for a few seconds. Then he said coolly: "Tomorrow we lay siege to Sens."

"My lord! So soon!"

"It is not soon. It is late. And there you may tourney to your heart's content . . . not in play, sir, but in very truth. I do not anticipate great resistance. But we do not dally here celebrating my wedding . . . while there is work to be done."

The man looked crestfallen and moved away.

I said: "Is this true? Are you going to fight tomorrow?"

"Yes," he said. "I shall begin to take Sens tomorrow."

"But," I began, "it is so soon after . . ."

"War waits for no man, Kate. I have you. You are mine now. We shall be near. I shall keep you with me. Have no fear. You

will be safe . . . and when there is time, I shall come to you
that you may console and comfort me.''

He smiled at me tenderly. I wanted to protest but I knew him
well enough to understand that nothing would deter him.

So . . . two days after our wedding, he was planning to continue to beat down any resistance in the country he had already
won.

Well, I had married a soldier . . . a conqueror. I should have
to remember what was important to him. He loved me . . . in
his way, but nothing could prevent his going to war when he
thought it necessary. Conquest . . . marriage . . . they came in
that order.

I did wonder then if it was plain Kate of whom he was enamoured or was it the Princess of France?

We had been married such a short time and already he was
planning to go to war.

So two days after my wedding day I was alone. He had girded
on his armour and gone, though not far.

He had said: ''This will take but a short time. Soon I shall
be back with you.''

''And then?'' I asked.

He stood looking at me, raising his eyebrows questioningly.

''And then,'' I went on, ''there will still be war.''

He came towards me and took me roughly into his arms. He
planted a rather noisy kiss on my lips.

''You're a soldier's wife, Kate. And a soldier follows the for-
tunes of war.''

I was lodged with my mother, close to the town of Sens.

Henry's brother, the Duke of Bedford, had joined him. Each
day I wondered whether he would come.

I did not enjoy my mother's company, although she treated
me with some respect nowadays. The Queen of England was of
more importance to her than the Princess of France had been. I
was gratified when I remembered that I was of higher rank than
she was; she the wife of the deposed monarch, while I was that
of the conqueror.

She was very fat now. She would lie about, nibbling her
sweetmeats, and would not be parted from her dogs. I wondered
how many lovers there were nowadays. Was she still as eager
for them? One thing she had not lost was her love of intrigue.

It seemed a long time before Sens surrendered, but it was only six days. Then Henry came to me. I thought he would be exhausted, but quite the contrary; he was elated.

There was a passionate reunion, but a short one, and I sensed that most of the time his main preoccupation was with his captains. He told me his next objective would be Montereau, which was in the hands of the Armagnacs.

He said: "Young Burgundy is eager for the fight. There he is in his elaborate mourning, vowing vengeance of his father's murderers. I'll swear he cares more for his father in death than he ever did in life. He cannot wait to get to Montereau. Now I have a plan. I want you to be near . . . but not too near. I want to be able to come and see you when there is a chance. So I am moving you to Bray-sur-Seine . . . you and your household . . . with your mother, of course."

"I hope that you can come often," I said.

"I hope so, too. Now prepare for the move. But first there will be our triumphant entry into Sens."

"Shall I be there?"

"But of course. Are you not the Queen of England?"

So I prepared myself for the entry into the city. I often thought of it afterwards and how incongruous it was that I, who belonged to the defeated House of Valois, should enter into the fallen city in the role of conqueror. But such was Henry's personality that I felt I belonged with him and not with my family.

The Archbishop of Sens, who had performed the ceremony at our wedding, led us into the city. He was overjoyed because, after having been expelled by the Armagnacs, he was now reinstated by Henry.

We entered the great cathedral to the sound of a glorious anthem, and Henry turned to the Archbishop and said: "Recently you gave me my wife. Now, my lord Archbishop, I restore yours to you this day." Which was a way of telling him that the archbishopric was given back to him.

What a happy day that was! But it was disappointing that war must go on. Henry was busy preparing, and when a battle was imminent I could see that he had no thought for anything else; and as soon as one town had fallen to him, he was preparing to take the next.

We moved to Bray-sur-Seine and settled in to await the fall of

Montereau. My father, who had recovered a little, joined us there.

I was glad to see him but at the same time sad, for there he was, robbed of his royalty in a way, although he still held the title of King which Henry had graciously allowed him to keep. But he had no power; every decision must be made by Henry; and as soon as my father was dead, Henry would be King. I often thought of my brother, the Dauphin. This affected him more than anyone, for he had expected to take the crown; I knew that he had not wanted it and it had suddenly been thrust upon him, but having tasted power he did not want to lose it . . . particularly in such a humiliating way.

But he was our enemy now. The ill-advised murder of the Duke of Burgundy had put him firmly in that unfortunate position—a Dauphin without hope of fulfilling his destiny.

My father might be sunk in melancholy, but my mother was as eager for intrigue as ever. She was constantly in my company, telling me what I should do. I did not consider that she had made such a success of her life that I needed to emulate her. I would listen to her and shrug my shoulders. I should do what Henry wished.

How long the days seemed without him! They were enlivened by visitors from England who had come to pay homage to me as the new Queen. My mother was delighted to receive them. She still behaved as though she were the Queen, and her manner had not changed since the days when she held great power.

She received the visitors graciously, with me standing beside her. I accepted this. In spite of everything, I could not help feeling sorry for her. I could not believe that she was still attractive to her lovers; moreover, I myself was happy and when one is happy one is inclined to be sorry for anyone who cannot possibly enjoy the same bliss—and therefore one is lenient towards them.

The Duchess of Clarence—my sister-in-law Margaret, who had arrived with the English party—was very agreeable to me.

She told me a great deal about life at the English Court and how it changed with each king. With Richard it had been elegant and gracious; it had been less so with his successor.

"The King's father was not a happy man," she said. "I think he had Richard's death on his conscience. He was always afraid that ill luck would come to him through it. Henry IV was a haunted man.''

"My sister Isabelle has told me something of what happened."

"Ah, our Little Queen. I heard she was most enchanting."

"She loved Richard."

"She was only a child."

"I suppose children can love."

"That is so, of course."

"Will the English like me?"

"They will love you."

"But I am French. Do they not see the French as the enemy?"

"They will see you as the King's wife, and he is their idol. And when he returns as the conqueror, you will see how dearly they love him. They will applaud everything he has done . . . including his marriage."

"I do understand."

She looked at me quizzically. She said: "You will make many friends in your new country, but I will be the first."

I held her hand and pressed it.

Another time she talked of her childhood. There had been great tragedies in her family and we could sympathize with each other. Three years after her father's death, when her eldest brother was only twenty-five years of age, he had been beheaded for treason, and his head had been set up on London Bridge.

"Why?" I asked. "Why did they do such a thing?"

"Well, it was all due to the new King . . . the father of the present Henry. Richard was King and Henry's father, who became King Henry IV, thought he would be a better king than Richard. My brother was loyal to Richard. If Richard had been victorious then, it would have been Henry IV who lost his head. My brother rose against Henry. He set himself at the head of a company of men and went to the Little Queen."

I cried out: "My sister told me of this. They deceived her. They said that Richard was alive and free."

"My brother believed it. That was why he was so confident. He had seen a man who was exactly like the King. It was a trick. However, my brother was captured and that is how his head came to be on London Bridge."

Our conversation brought back to me those days when Isabelle had been with me and told me of her love for Richard.

I talked to her then of my childhood, of my sisters—Michelle who was now the Duchess of Burgundy, and Marie in her convent.

It was a great pleasure for me to have such a companion. It passed the days while I was waiting for the siege of Montereau to end. So the Duchess of Clarence, my new sister-in-law, became my friend.

The people of Montereau put up a strong resistance. They knew that outside their walls, fighting with the English, were the Burgundians led by Duke Philip. Montereau had been the scene of the murder of the late Duke Jean the Fearless and they guessed Burgundians would want their revenge. This knowledge doubtless strengthened their resistance.

It was inevitable, though, that in due course the town should fall to Henry.

Soldier that he was, he was not a violent man. He wanted victory not revenge. He killed only when it was necessary to do so, and if those who were conquered fell in with his wishes, he would be lenient with them. He made no effort to avoid the hardships his men endured and shared them with them. That was one of the qualities which made him the greatest soldier of his age and was the reason why his men were prepared to follow him anywhere.

Therefore there was no undue slaughter at Montereau.

He told me that Philip of Burgundy made a drama of the occasion. He called attention to his bereavement. With dramatic ardour he visited the place where his father had been buried in a pauper's shell. He ordered that a pall should cover it and lighted candles be placed around it. He then took a solemn vow that he would dedicate his life to bringing his father's murderers to justice. He would make it his unswerving duty to do so. And to this cause he would place his body, his soul and all he possessed.

"It was effective," commented Henry. "But I believe his devotion to his father was slightly less intense during the latter's lifetime. I believe he went so far as to curse his father for not allowing him to be present at Agincourt. Jean gave orders that his son was to be guarded and not allowed out. Philip made an attempt to escape and was restrained. I believe he thinks that, if he had not been prevented from being there, the result of the battle would have been different.''

I told him how pleased I was to have his brother's wife, Margaret, with me and how we had become good friends.

''She is a good woman, and Clarence is a good man. I'll confess that of all my brothers I love him best—though I suppose many would point out that Bedford is the more worthy. But one does not always love people for their worthiness. And Clarence . . . Thomas . . . has always been my special friend. I suppose it was partly because he was the nearest to me in age.''

''I think she is sad because she sees so little of him.''

''He is a soldier . . . like the rest of us.''

''Would it not be wonderful if these wars could be over!''

He laughed at me. I was not sure whether he agreed. I had seen the excitement in his eyes at the prospect of battle; and I knew that, tender and loving as he was to me, the real excitement in life for him was in conquest. I wondered what he would have been like if there had been no war to occupy him.

I had no opportunity of finding out.

No sooner was Montereau in his hands than we must move on to Melun.

I with my family and our attendants were housed not far from the camp.

Henry was thoughtful and kind to my parents; none would have believed that my father was the conquered king and Henry the conqueror. He was most anxious for my father's comfort.

He said to me: ''The house is far enough for your father not to hear the cannon. I am sure that would disturb him. And yet it is near enough for me to be able to ride to you now and then should the siege take longer than I expect. That was why I chose it.''

I was amazed at his concern. He had had musicians brought to the house in Melun, because he had heard that when my father became uneasy and showed signs of another lapse, he could be soothed by music.

When Melun fell, the next objective was Paris.

I wondered how I should feel, riding into our capital side by side with its conqueror. Henry was uneasy too; he thought there might be certain hostility, and for that reason he chose to go on in advance. He said he did not want to put me in any danger;

and before I entered the city he must make sure that all would be well.

So it was with my mother beside me that I rode into Paris. I was amazed at our reception. Banners hung from the windows, wine was running from the conduits in the streets and the cheers were deafening.

I was relieved. They bore me no resentment for having joined the conqueror, and I knew that their greeting was not given out of fear but love for me.

So we spent Christmas in Paris and we were happy. Surely, I thought, this must be an end of hostilities. What more did he want? I was bold enough to ask him.

"France is mine," he said, "and what pleases me most is that I have made my French Princess Queen of England. But you will learn, little one, that there is often as much strife in holding what one has gained as in taking possession of it. To have is important, but it must not be forgotten that one must hold."

However, for that Christmas we gave ourselves up to pleasure. He could be as merry as any. We danced and sang; we played the harp together.

It was a wonderfully happy Christmas.

I might have known it could not last.

My friend Margaret, Duchess of Clarence, told me that the English were getting restive. They were not pleased that their King should desert them and spend so much of his time away from his own land. Conquests were all very well and when the conquering heroes returned they could be certain of a rapturous welcome, but Henry was first and foremost King of England, and that should not be forgotten.

Margaret said: "I heard news from England. Humphrey of Gloucester is Regent while the Duke of Bedford is in France and . . . well, it is not that the people do not like Humphrey . . . but he is not like Clarence or Bedford. He likes a little riotous living. He frequents the taverns. He is overfond of women. Mind you, he is full of energy and has great charm. He is something of a scholar, too. He is an odd mixture of a man. But . . . he is very ambitious. I have always fancied that he is a little envious of Henry . . . oh, full of admiration, of course, but in my opinion he is deeply discontented because he was born his father's youngest son instead of his eldest."

"He sounds a little . . . dangerous."

Margaret lifted her shoulders. "One to be watched," she suggested.

Margaret was right. Messengers came from England. There were letters for Henry, and he shut himself in with them for some little time.

It was not long after that that he talked to me. It was night, and we were alone. He put his arms round me and said: "How do you fancy a sea voyage?"

I looked at him in astonishment and he went on: "The Channel is not at its most inviting in the winter, but crossing it is a necessity, I fear."

"You mean . . . England?"

He nodded. "And soon."

Everything was "soon" in Henry's mind. He could never brook delay. Once he had made up his mind, the deed was as good as done.

"I must return," he said. "I have been away too long. When all is said and done, England is my first responsibility."

"And France?"

"I am going to appoint your mother Regent."

"My mother!"

"I think she is devoted to your interests."

I looked at him in astonishment and he went on: "Because they are hers. Moreover it will be in name only. My brother John will remain in France. He will be in charge of everything."

"But my mother . . ."

"Kate," he said solemnly, "conquerors are never popular with the conquered. They are treated with honour only because the alternative would be too painful. A conquered people should be treated with care. They have been deeply humiliated by the conquest. The wise conqueror lessens the humiliation wherever possible. So I shall call your mother Regent and my brother John will, of course, make sure all goes well for us."

"You trust John?"

"Absolutely. I am fortunate in my brothers. Thomas . . . dear Thomas . . . and John . . . good John and . . . er . . . Humphrey . . ."

"Humphrey is now looking after affairs in England for you."

"Humphrey is the youngest." He smiled affectionately. "He can be a little wild. I understand that."

"As you were once," I said.

"As I was once. It helps me understand Humphrey. He is a little like me. He will grow out of it."

"You grew out of it when you became King. Humphrey will not have a crown to change him."

"I should have grown out of it in any case . . . as he will. But . . . at the moment I must go back. I know all will be well here in John's hands and very soon we shall return to France."

I was excited at the prospect of going to England. For one thing I should escape from my mother. I should indeed feel a few regrets to part from my father; but I was young and wanted new experiences. I was fast falling in love with my husband and the new life he offered; and to be with my father was a continual sadness, for one could not help sharing something of his sorrows and therefore one's happy exhilarating existence must be tinged with the sadness of his.

As I said, Henry could not endure delay. We were going to England; therefore we should set out at once. It was winter, but, to Henry, that was of little consequence. He would have preferred spring, of course; but this happened to be winter and that was when we should go.

The Duke of Bedford had arrived with 6,000 men to escort us to Calais.

I liked my brother-in-law, John, as soon as we met. He was more like Henry than any of the others, not so much in appearance as—I was to discover—in character. He was a clever man, but slightly less clever than Henry; he was shrewd, brave, clearsighted and resourceful. But it seemed to me that with all these qualities he just slightly failed to equal Henry. I think, too, that he was clever enough to know this, and I liked him for that. Henry was his hero and he was content to serve under him.

Humphrey was clever but the difference between him and John was that John realized his limitations in regard to Henry; Humphrey did not, and all through his life he would tell himself, I would have equalled my brother Henry. The only reason I did not is because I had the misfortune not to be born my father's eldest son.

I felt I was beginning to know my new family, and the experience was agreeable. My friendship with the Duchess of Clarence was now to be repeated with the Duke of Bedford.

We reached Amiens, where I was lodged with the bailiff.

Several of my countrymen and -women came to see me there. They brought me presents and wished me well. It was comforting to know that they still held me in high regard. In fact, I think many of them were delighted to be at peace and were grateful to me for helping bring that about. There is no greater destroyer of happiness than war, when lands are devastated by ruthless soldiery and cities destroyed. Oh yes, it was a great relief to these people that the war was largely at an end, and their Princess was happily married to Henry of England.

We embarked at Calais. I do not want to dwell on the discomforts . . . I might even say torments . . . of that strip of water which had to be crossed. It is best forgotten. Henry, of course, was unaffected; but that did not mean he had no sympathy for those who were not. My relief at sighting the white cliffs of my new country was intense.

As soon as we alighted we were greeted by crowds of cheering people, and this continued throughout the journey to London.

"One of the first things we must do," said Henry, "is to have you crowned. It will then be seen that you are the Queen in very truth."

It was shortly after my landing on English soil that I was crowned in Westminster Abbey. There was not much time to prepare, but by now I had learned that, with Henry, everything had to be done with the utmost speed. I often thought of how my mother would have revelled in preparing me for that great event. Instead of which I had only three busy weeks in which to make myself ready.

I went from the Palace of Westminster to the Abbey, where I was crowned by the Archbishop. It was a solemn and impressive ceremony, as coronations must be. I was too moved and overwhelmed to remember all the people around me.

The banquet which followed remains more memorable to me. I think that was because of the people I met there.

There was the Duke of Gloucester, that Humphrey whom I had already met briefly, and of whom I had heard so much. He had arranged the feast and he stood bareheaded before me. We surveyed each other with the utmost interest. He was good-looking—rather like Henry; he had great charm; and I could see, by the way his eyes appeared to take in every detail of my appearance, that he was attempting to assess me in many ways. I supposed he was thinking that as the King's wife I would have some influence with him; he was wondering, I guessed, to what use I would put it. He studied me with other objects in mind and I thought I detected faintly lecherous lights in his eyes. My opinion that I would have to be watchful of Humphrey was confirmed.

Another who interested me was Henry Beaufort, Bishop of Winchester. Margaret had mentioned him to me in my conversations with her, and I knew of this connection with the royal family. He was a brilliant man, a son of John of Gaunt, himself a son of Edward III, and Katherine Swynford, whom John of Gaunt had eventually married, after she had been his mistress for several years. The children had all been legitimized when the marriage took place. They were clever and ambitious and, Margaret said, the rest of the family was inclined to look down on them as, although made legitimate, they had been born out of wedlock. There had been trouble between Henry Beaufort and Gloucester and I was sure resentment lingered.

Another whom I met on that occasion was James I of Scotland, who was Henry's prisoner and had been in a kind of captivity for the last seventeen years. He was treated with the respect due to a king, but he was a prisoner nonetheless. He was handsome and charming and he did not seem as though he were a captive. I wanted to know more about him and I decided I would ask Henry at an appropriate moment.

The banquet was sumptuous but as we were in Lent it consisted mainly of fish; the only diversion from the Lenten abstention was brawn served with mustard.

As I looked at the table weighed down with fish of all kinds—soles, crayfish, lobster, roach, lampreys, congers and other varieties—my thoughts temporarily flashed back to those days in the Hôtel de St. Paul, where there was only a crust or two to be shared by six hungry children.

The table had been decorated with tableaux, all bearing some significance to the occasion. There was one of St. Katherine, my patron saint, discoursing with doctors, and in the right hand of the statue of the saint was a scroll on which was written in gold letters ''Madame le Reine.'' There were others depicting Henry as the conqueror of France.

I was exhilarated and happier than I had ever been before. I believed that I had escaped from my troubled country for ever and that my marriage was one of those romances which began in strife and ended in happiness ever after.

It was wonderful to be given such homage; I, the daughter of the defeated King, to be showered with blessings by my wise and all-conquering husband!

It was even more wonderful to be alone with Henry afterwards. He was pleased with the day's proceedings and, I think, delighted to see me overwhelmed by the welcome and honours I had received.

I wanted to talk to him. I wanted to tell him of what I had endured in the Hôtel de St. Paul, to make him see those cold and hungry children, wondering about that wild man, our father, who was confined close to us.

I could not believe all this had happened to that frightened little girl. But here I was . . . Queen of England . . . beloved by her husband and his people. It seemed too wonderful to be true.

He embraced me with passion, and it was not the time for talking of such things.

I was too excited to sleep; and I think he was too. We lay side by side in the stillness. I reached for his hand.

I felt a great desire then to learn something of the people whom I had met at the banquet. There were so few occasions when it was possible to talk to Henry of such things.

"Are you happy, Kate?" he asked.

"Beyond all my dreams," I answered.

"Then so am I."

"It is wonderful that you came into my life. You have carried me away from all the strife . . . all the fears . . . everything that made life so . . . uneasy."

"That is what I intended to do. Shall you be happy in England, Kate?"

"If you are with me."

He pressed my hand and there was silence.

After a while, I said: "Tell me about the King of Scotland."

"James? A pleasant enough fellow."

"He seemed . . . quite charming . . . and not like a prisoner."

"He has been with us for many years. It must be seventeen years since he was captured."

"Seventeen years a prisoner?"

"He's better off here than in his own land. When we took him, his life would not have been worth much if we had sent him back. Warring uncles, you know."

"I do know . . . indeed."

"A child king . . . that is one of the worst ills which can befall a country. Let us thank God that you and I are young. We'll have sons . . . many of them . . . as my father did. See how useful my brothers are to me. But to be a child and a king . . . that means trouble. There are too many seeking to rule . . . fighting each other. You know that, with your Armagnacs and Burgundians. There's nothing unusual in it, Kate. It was the natural course of affairs . . . So we must get to it. Let us get sons . . . we must waste no time."

I was happy that night but the next day Henry said: "I must get up to the north. There is a little trouble there. I have been away too long."

"When do we leave?"

"I shall go today and you will stay here for a while. You will be more comfortable here."

"Without you?"

"It is not for long. Just a short trip up to the north. I shall have to go to France soon and I shall have to replenish the army. Money, Kate. That is what I need and it has to come from the people. So to the north first to settle them down . . . and then to the countryside to show myself as the conqueror, the King of France to be. I want to show them how their money is spent. They love victories. Well, praise God! I have had some of those."

"So you will go as a soldier . . . not as a husband."

He slapped his thigh and laughed. "There you have it, Kate. That's the answer."

I was bitterly disappointed. All the euphoria of last night had gone. I knew I had hoped for too much. He would constantly be going off and I should have to face long periods without him. It was my fate and I should have to accept it.

Before he went, he said: "I'll be with you by Easter, Kate. We'll celebrate the feast together."

I felt lonely without him and with only Guillemote—how thankful I was that I had been able to bring her with me!—and the few friends I had been able to make since my arrival to keep me company. It was so different from what I had hoped.

Easter seemed long in coming. I was excited when on Palm Sunday I left Westminster Palace for Windsor.

I loved Windsor on sight and have done so ever since. I was thrilled as we came through the park and forest and up the long walk on either side of which grew stately elms. I was thinking of Henry and wondering how long we should stay in this beautiful spot.

I hoped the people of the north had settled down and that his subjects were prepared to give him what he wanted. Then I thought that, if they did, soon his army would be off to make fresh conquests. What conquests? Had he not subdued France? Bedford would act as his deputy there. I wondered if I could persuade him that it was his duty to remain in England. The idea was ludicrous. It would amuse him though. I could imagine his laughing at me.

There was so much to occupy me at Windsor. I loved to roam through those stately rooms; I loved to walk outside, to stroll round the castle, to touch those grey stone walls. When I heard that Edward III had started to rebuild certain parts of the castle and Richard had finished it, that seemed to bring Isabelle close to me. I was sure she had stood where I was standing, for Richard would have brought her here; he would have shown her the mews which he had built for his falcons.

Each day I looked for Henry. Good Friday came . . . a day spent in prayer and meditation; then Easter Day and he still did not come.

"The King must be here soon," I said to Margaret, Duchess of Clarence.

"Yes, in time," she answered. "It is always so with kings. One can never be sure. Something may have happened . . . something which needs his attention."

"Something more pressing than his desire to be with me," I said a trifle bitterly.

"You married a soldier, my lady," she replied.

It was during the period while I was waiting for Henry to come to Windsor that I met Margaret's daughter, Jane. I had noticed this lovely young girl about the Court and had wondered who she was; and I was particularly pleased when Margaret presented her to me.

I congratulated her on having such a beautiful daughter. She saw that I was puzzled because I knew she had not been married long enough to Clarence to have a daughter of such an age.

She explained to me: ''Her father was John Beaufort, Earl of Somerset. He was my first husband.''

She talked to me then about her sons Henry, John and Edmund; but it was Jane on whom she doted. I supposed that a mother in her position saw little of her sons, who were always taken away from their own home to be brought up in the household of some nobleman where they would learn the chivalric arts. I had always thought that was sad and that my brothers, sisters and I could have had a far happier childhood if we had not been born royal; but the same applied to all noble houses.

I discovered that Margaret's first husband had been the eldest son of John of Gaunt by Katherine Swynford; so there was royal blood in the veins of her children.

I wondered a great deal about Margaret. Was she happy with the Duke of Clarence? He had seemed to me a charming man when I had met him—but very briefly, of course.

It was pleasant to get to know Margaret. It helped to pass the time while I was waiting for Henry to come as he had promised.

Easter had passed when a message came from him.

He could not come to Windsor but I was to leave at once and go to Leicester, where he would join me.

Overjoyed, I prepared to leave.

It was wonderful to be with him again. I forgot all my resentment that he had not kept his promise to come to Windsor.

I was happy, but when he explained to me that I was to take part in his journey through the country, I understood why I had been summoned.

''You see, Kate,'' he said frankly, ''you are important in this. I am asking them for money. I need money. I have to keep an army in France. I have to prepare to take the crown when the time comes.''

He paused and looked at me uncertainly, realizing I knew that he was talking to me about the death of my father, which must take place before the crown was his.

''Forgive me, Kate. I have the manners of a rough soldier. I should know better.''

There was something endearing about him in such a mood.

It was characteristic that he could see faults in himself and did not hesitate to admit them. If he were wrong, he never pretended to be right. He was like that with his men. It was one of the reasons why he had their complete loyalty.

He put his hand over mine and I clung to his.

"You understand me, Kate. I know your fondness for your father. Poor man. His is a sad fate. He will never be wholly sane, I fear; and I do not think he values his life greatly."

"That is true," I said. "In his frenzies he called for those about him to kill him."

"On his passing I shall be crowned King of France and that has to come, Kate. Well, I want the people to realize the achievement of our armies. I want them to understand that we have become mighty and will be mightier still. I want them to see you beside me."

"As part of the spoils you have brought home from France," I murmured.

He laughed and swung me up in his arms. "There is no booty which has delighted me more."

So there I was beside him, through those triumphant rides, listening to him as he talked to the people, eloquently rousing them to patriotism . . . making them see that it was imperative that they pay for the glory which was theirs.

It was wonderful to see the effect he had on them.

We visited every church on the route where he thanked God for His help in the past and reminded Him that it must not be withheld in the future.

Henry was deeply religious. He was indefatigable in his condemnation of the religious sect who called themselves the Lollards.

"Lollards?" I said. "What a strange name."

"It comes from the German *Lollen*, I once heard," he told me, "which means, 'to sing.' I suppose they earned their name because they are always singing hymns. John Wycliffe started it off. Writing . . . preaching heresies. There could have been a serious rising against us. Fortunately we discovered this in time." He was silent, his brow furrowed. "A man I knew well at one time," he went on after a pause, "it was in the days of my youth. John Oldcastle . . . he was the head of it. He was the last man I would have believed would have turned to religion. He changed. Men change. A crown changed me and these her-

esies changed him. And what we were, we are not today. But
. . . it is in the past. But I am moved when I think of John
Oldcastle. He was hung up and burned alive."

I caught my breath in horror.

Henry nodded slowly and sat very quietly, staring into nothing.

Then he roused himself and said: "A man one has once been
merry with . . . we drank together, laughed together . . . sported
together . . . but we could not see into the future then. No . . .
I cannot believe this of old John Oldcastle." He stood up
abruptly. "Life goes on," he said. "I'll pray for the old fellow
tomorrow. Pray with me, Kate."

I would indeed, I said: and I fancied all that evening he went
on thinking of his one-time friend who had turned traitor through
religion.

I could not forget the man. He had once been Henry's friend
and yet he had come to a terrible end. Henry had been fond of
him once. How could he have allowed that to happen?

He might have been a traitor, yes, but surely he could have
had a less horrific death? Henry could have stopped it—and he
had not done so. He was ruthless. I had known that. He pursued
his ends with unswerving determination. How else could he
have achieved so much?

Into my love for him there crept that night a little fear. Our
courtship had been brief. I had been enchanted by the genial
conqueror. But how much did I know of Henry? He was a man
who could allow an old close friend to die in such a terrible
manner.

I knew that we must soon be parted. I had learned that would
be the pattern of our lives. I must therefore give myself up to
the pleasure of his company while it was there for me to enjoy,
for how could I know, from day to day, from hour to hour, when
it would be snatched away from me?

It was about this time that I made a wonderful discovery. I
believed that I was with child, and that drove all other specula-
tions, doubts and fears from my mind.

I had meant to wait until I was certain before I told Henry,
but I could not keep the news to myself.

I had never seen him so delighted. I laughed and exulted to
see his joy.

"I believe," I said, "that something can be more important to you than a victorious battle."

"Battles are won . . . or lost, but this is our child. Yours and mine, Kate . . . and England's. Our little king. We shall call him Henry. Yes, he must be Henry after his father and grandfather. King Henry VI of England."

"Henry, please do not be so sure that it will be a boy."

"But of course it will be a boy. You do not think my firstborn could be anything else!"

"He's mine too."

He laughed out loud. "You were meant to be a mother of sons. And suppose . . . just suppose that this one is not a boy. The next will be . . . and the next . . . and the next . . ."

"Please, let there be one at a time. I am not even absolutely sure. I did not mean to tell you until I was . . ."

He lifted me up and danced round the apartment with me. Then suddenly he stopped, remembering the precious burden I carried within me. He put me down rather gingerly. "We must take care of our son, Kate," he said gravely, "the utmost care."

I often saw him watching me with a tender smile on his face. He was even more pleased with our marriage. I knew he was thinking what a big part it had played in his plans for France, and now it was successful in that all-important way. We had been married quite a short time and had not been together a great deal, but there were already signs of fruitfulness.

He was a very happy man.

We were in Yorkshire and Henry planned to go farther north. The going had been rough and I had seen him on one or two occasions cast anxious looks in my direction.

When we retired for the night, he was very serious. "You are tired, Kate," he said.

"Not more than usual after a long day's journey."

"We must think of the child. I have to go on to the north but you shall not come with me. We will find a suitable spot and there you will stay and rest for a while."

"But, Henry, I want to be with you."

"God bless you, Kate, and do you think I do not wish that too? But you are going to await my return. The way may be rough and I'll not have you taking risks with the child. You will stay comfortable while I continue the journey. It will only be for a week or so. Then I shall return and find you refreshed and ready for the journey south.''

I felt a little melancholy. It was only for a week or so, he said, but I knew Henry. Something could happen which needed his presence . . . and it could be a long time before I saw him again.

I tried to protest but he was adamant. In fact, he was so accustomed to having his orders obeyed without question that it did not occur to him to take my objections seriously. I knew it was no use protesting; and I was not yet entirely certain that I was going to have a child.

The next morning we set out.

''We are not far from my castle of Pontefract,'' said Henry. ''You shall stay there and wait for me.''

Pontefract! It was a castle I had heard spoken of with dread by my sister Isabelle.

When I saw it, I thought it was as I had imagined it when I had heard of Richard's last days there.

As we rode towards it, I thought it was like a prison; but perhaps that was because I was thinking of Richard's meeting his miserable and mysterious death within its walls.

It looked formidable—a fortress built on a rock. The walls were high and flanked by seven towers. There was a moat with a drawbridge which was lowered as we approached.

The castellan was waiting to pay homage to the King.

Food was prepared for us and while we feasted in the great hall Henry explained to the castellan and his wife that I should be staying there for a short while and the utmost care must be taken of me. I was in a delicate state and in need of rest. It was for this reason that I was not continuing with the King on his journey.

The place filled me with revulsion. I kept seeing Isabelle's sad face when she had told me of the last days of her husband. And here I was . . . within those very walls. I wanted to get away.

I knew it was no use talking to Henry. His mind was made up, and in his thoughts he was already on his way, calling people to his side, assuring them how necessary it was, for the honour of England, to meet the heavy taxes that were essential to the success of his operations.

When I lay in my room, I fancied I could hear the cries of

those who had suffered in this grim place. It was more than twenty years ago that Richard had died . . . and Isabelle herself was dead now.

I must not be fanciful. I must, as Henry said, try to rest here. There was the child to think of.

I was glad to have Guillemote with me, and Margaret and her daughter Jane were among my attendants. I found their presence particularly comforting; but I could not shake off this heavy pall of melancholy which seemed to be a part of this dismal castle.

I longed to be away. I was sure it would be far better for me to be riding through the countryside, perhaps a little exhausted at the end of the day, than here where sad memories were coming to me.

Yet the place had a fascination for me. Isabelle seemed to be with me; and when, on my first day, I learned that her second husband, the Duke of Orléans, was actually in Pontefract, she seemed nearer to me than ever. I knew that Orléans had been captured at Agincourt but Henry had not mentioned, when he had told me I was to go to Pontefract, that Orléans was a prisoner there. Perhaps he had forgotten.

However, it was a shock for me to discover that we were under the same roof, and I felt that fate was playing some sinister trick, to bring Isabelle's second husband to the very place where the first had died.

I used to wake in the night and put out a hand to touch Henry. Then I would remember that he had gone and where I was . . . in Pontefract Castle . . . and a certain terror would creep over me. I remember sitting up in bed and looking round the strange apartment for a few seconds before remembering. Then it came to me that somewhere not far away Richard had been incarcerated . . . a prisoner . . . and waking as I had, listening for a step close by, wondering if an assassin was lurking in a dark corner . . . And what had happened? Had his end been like that?

There were ghosts in this place. I knew it. I could sense that terrible things had happened here.

I could hear Isabelle's voice. "I do not know what happened at Pontefract. Some say he was murdered . . . slashed to death by Bolingbroke's men; some say they starved him to death; others that he starved himself. How can I know, Katherine? Perhaps one day I will."

And somewhere here in this castle was Orléans, the husband who had made Isabelle happy as she had thought she would never be after the tragedy of her first marriage.

It was small wonder that I could not rest happily in Pontefract. I should have told Henry that I would be unhappy here. Would he have understood? No. He was too practical perhaps. And in any case he would be thinking ahead to his next project: money to get to France. Rebels to subdue. There would always be rebels in a conquered country. I kept thinking of his old friend John Oldcastle . . . hanging over the fire. And he had been an old friend. Henry could have stopped it. But the man was a heretic; he had planned rebellion. Did Henry never think of those old days? This John Oldcastle must have been one of those who had accompanied him on his tavern adventures. I wondered what those adventures had involved. I believed that on one occasion Henry had become caught up with the law.

I began to ask myself, what did I know of Henry? He loved me, I was sure. I was good-looking . . . for a princess. I was attracted by him. I was about to bear his child. I had been all that a conqueror could have asked for.

I knew the King, but what did I know of the man?

Those were uncomfortable days at Pontefract for within those evil walls I was prone to introspection. Henry should never have left me there.

I had a compulsion to wander around the castle. I liked to talk to the men-at-arms. I found them courteous and respectful. Surely they would not dare be otherwise to Henry's Queen; but I found them friendly, too.

I thought I detected in one of them a certain sadness. He was older than the others. I approached him once when he was alone and I boldly asked him how long he had been in the castle.

"All my life, my lady. I was born here. My father was a guard before me. It's a tradition in the family, you might say."

"Were you here when . . . King Richard . . . ?"

He looked wary, but he nodded.

"That was a long time ago, my lady. I was a young man then."

"Could you show me where he was lodged?"

He hesitated for a moment. I said: "I should like to see it. My sister was his wife."

"Yes, my lady, the Little Queen. I hear she was a very beautiful young lady."

"She was. She is dead now."

He crossed himself and murmured something like "God rest her soul."

"Could you then . . . ?"

"People don't go there much now."

"I should like to."

He hesitated for one more moment. I wondered whether it was against orders. But I was the Queen. I could not be refused.

I stepped into the small room. It looked dark and eerie.

"So this is where he lived . . . and died. Did you see him?"

"I was young then. It wasn't talked of in the castle. You see this pillar here . . . from the floor to the roof? You see these notches in it? I heard it said that these were made by the axes of his murderers as he fled around it. But who's to say whether that be true?"

"Did you believe it?"

He was cautious. He was doubtless remembering that I was the King's wife and that the King was the son of that man who had taken the crown from Richard.

"There's some said that he starved himself to death," he said. "Who's to know? Others said he was starved by them. Some say he escaped from Pomfret."

Pomfret? I was puzzled for the moment; then I remembered that Pomfret was another name for Pontefract. I had heard that the man who had built it had named it after Pomfret, a town in Normandy which the place resembled.

"Escaped?" I said.

"Some said he reached Scotland and was befriended by the Scots King and lived in Scotland for many years."

"Do you believe that?" I asked.

"No, my lady. He died in this room."

"Murdered?"

"Hacked or starved to death. 'Tis murder, every way you look at it."

"You feel it here . . . do you?" I asked, and then wished that I had not expressed such a fanciful thought.

But the man nodded.

I had another experience while I was at Pontefract. I talked with the Duke of Orléans.

I said that he was my brother-in-law and I wished to see him. Our hosts were unsure whether my wish should be granted. But they remembered that I was Queen of England, and if Henry had not wished me to see Orléans, either he would not have brought me to Pontefract or he would have given orders that I was not to see him.

So here was another sad reminder of Isabelle.

Charles of Orléans looked older than when I had last seen him. Captivity was not as irksome to him as it might have been to some people. He was a poet rather than a warrior and I had always fancied that he would rather have lived in peaceful obscurity than in the blaze of one near the throne.

I was taken to his apartments in the castle. They were very comfortable, and it was obvious that he was treated in accordance with his rank. He was a prisoner only in the fact that he was not able to leave the castle without guards.

He embraced me warmly.

"I hear what goes on now and then," he said. "Our poor country is in a sorry state. We have been ignobly defeated, and because of that . . . I am here, and you also."

"Yes. The war has had a great effect on our lives. Tell me, Charles, are you treated well?"

"I do not complain."

"What do you do here?"

"I am allowed to walk. Sometimes I ride, if there are enough guards available to accompany me. I write . . ."

"Your poetry, of course."

"It satisfies me. You understand, Katherine?"

"Yes, I do."

"I brood a great deal. I pray for forgiveness."

"For the death of Burgundy?"

"I never wanted that, Katherine."

"I know."

"All this strife within. It was certain to lead to ruin. I remember those days with Isabelle. They were the happiest of my life."

"She was happy with you, Charles."

"I know. That makes it all the more sad. If only she had lived . . ."

"Then you would not have married again."

"I did not want to. Armagnac decided . . . and it had to be. My life ever after has been like something out of a nightmare . . .

until I was captured at Agincourt. Sometimes I wished I had gone the way of so many others.''

"No, Charles, you must not say that."

"And then . . . Isabelle is dead . . . if only she had lived!''

"She would be mourning now . . . separated from you as she would be. At least she did not have to suffer that.''

We talked of Isabelle. He read some of his poetry to me and when he did so his face was transfigured with a certain contentment; and I believed that he was happier in his prison than he had been as the tool of the ambitious Armagnacs.

It was long since Isabelle had died but I felt her close to me during those days in tragic Pontefract.

I was relieved and delighted when Henry came riding into the castle.

He kissed me fondly. I was now sure that I was pregnant and I told him this, to his great delight.

"Did the people respond as you wished to your plans for taxes?" I asked.

"To a man . . . and woman,'' he replied jubilantly.

"Does that mean you will soon be leaving England again?"

"Nay,'' he cried. "I would not want you to travel. I shall stay in England until my son is born."

I was happy. I was going to forget all my misgivings. Henry loved me and I loved him. I would not ask myself so many questions. I would stop wondering how deep his affection for me went. I must learn one of the great lessons of life which was that people were as they were, and to attempt to change them could prove fatal to any relationship.

So a few weeks passed. We were in June, and June is a beautiful month. My baby was due in December. It was a long time to wait, but I looked forward to the waiting months because Henry would be with me.

He was looking forward with great excitement to the birth. What if the child should prove to be a girl? But even if it were, we should love it, and the fact that I had become pregnant so quickly augured well. I knew that Henry was looking to a happy future when his family would be as numerous as that in which he had grown up . . . or perhaps he visualized more children, as everything Henry did must be better than others.

I might have known that such happiness could not last.

I remember the day well—a hot June day. I had awakened to a feeling of intense happiness. I was feeling very well, no longer experiencing those early inconveniences which sometimes are the lot of pregnant women. The days were full of contentment. I was growing fonder of Henry, and our love for each other was a great joy; we played our harps together as we lived, in harmony.

Thoughts of the coming child absorbed us both. We talked of the event continuously.

It was in the early afternoon when messengers came riding to Westminster. I knew from their demeanour that something terrible had happened. I was with Henry when he received them. There were two of them and they both knelt before the King; I could see that they were desperately afraid to give him the news.

"It was at Beaugé," they said.

"Yes, yes," cried Henry impatiently. "Tell me the worst. Our forces have been defeated?"

The men were silent for a few seconds. Henry roared out: "Speak! For the love of God, tell me!"

"It is the Duke, my lord . . . the Duke of Clarence."

"They have taken him . . ."

That terrible silence again and then: "He was slain, Sire."

I watched the emotion in Henry's face. This was his brother . . . his best-loved brother. Slain! I thought of Margaret . . . a widow once more. Oh, the tragedy of war! Why did men have to make it? How much happier we should all be without it!

Henry began questioning the men. They stammered out what had happened.

I could not bear to see the misery on Henry's face. He loved all his brothers but Clarence was the one closest to him. It was more than that. I knew that he was thinking that the line of victories had been broken. This was defeat. The French had beaten the English. And the reason? Because he was not there.

I knew him well enough to read his thoughts. He had indulged himself; he had given way to a desire for family life. He had been spending time with his wife, contemplating the birth of his child, and consequently the French had beaten the English, and his beloved brother had been killed.

The messengers feared the wrath which was sometimes the reward of bringing bad news; but Henry was too sensible for that. His grief was intense but it was under control.

He fired questions at them. He wanted to know all that had happened.

It was something like this: when we had come to England, Bedford accompanying us, Henry had left Clarence behind as Captain of Normandy and Lieutenant of France. Clarence had carried on with Henry's advance and had reached Beaufort-en-Vallée. My brother Charles, the Dauphin, had signed no contracts with Henry. I could imagine his wrath when he heard that our mother and father had given away his birthright and I had become Henry's queen. Naturally there would be many who would deplore the surrender of France and would rally around him. Moreover, the Scots were the perennial enemies of the English, and there were many in France who had gone there to support the French.

I understood the attitude of Henry's brothers towards him. They recognized his brilliance and all regarded him with a certain awe and sought to emulate him. Bedford was the only one who realized that, efficient as he might be, he did not, nor ever could, compare his skills with the military genius of Henry. Clarence believed that he could equal it; Gloucester, I was to discover, was deluded enough to think he could excel it.

I guessed that what Clarence wanted was to present Henry with as great a victory as Agincourt—with himself, Clarence, as the hero of the day.

When he heard that the Dauphin was marching on Beaugé with a strong force, he was impatient to go into battle. His main army was not at hand and could not join up with him for a day or so; but he was eager for glory, and with a very small force he rode in to the attack. It was brave but it was folly.

I watched Henry half close his eyes and grind his teeth as he listened.

Clarence's little band of knights were quickly overcome and in the fighting which ensued Clarence was slain.

Henry stood numb. I guessed what emotion he was suffering. Grief at the loss of a beloved brother and there would be the realization that the aura of invincibility, which he had built up and which he believed was one of the elements of victory, had been tarnished.

Oh, foolish Clarence! Henry would never have acted so. He would have waited. He would have taken no risks. Great planners only took risks when it was necessary to do so. Henry would never have been so foolish as to attack without the means to win. But others were not Henry.

"My lord," went on the messengers. "The Earl of Salisbury recovered the bodies of those who were slain. They are sending the Duke's body back to England."

Henry nodded. He stood silent for a few moments; then he dismissed the men. They needed refreshment and rest; they had ridden far and fast.

They were relieved to go.

I looked at Henry and I knew that the peaceful days were over. He was shedding the role of lover, husband and prospective father. These were forgotten in that of the conquering king.

"I must leave for France," he said, "as quickly as possible."

I had known it would happen. The next days were spent in feverish preparation. I scarcely saw him and wondered when I should again.

The day came for his departure. He expressed regret at leaving me but I knew that his heart was in France.

On the last night we spent together he spoke about the child.

"Perhaps you will be back by December," I said. "You should be here when he is born."

"I shall do my utmost to be here, but who can say? I did not plan to leave England until after he was born." Then he became very solemn. "The boy must not be born at Windsor," he said.

Not at Windsor! Indeed, I had thought that my confinement should take place there. It was the place I loved best of all the castles and palaces of England. I had promised myself that I would go there and await the birth of my child. And now he was saying it must not be Windsor.

"No," he repeated, "I do not want him to be born in Windsor."

"I cannot think why you should say that. It is the most beautiful place I know. I felt happy there . . . at peace with myself and the world."

"Windsor is a fine castle . . . yes. The park and the forest are indeed majestic. But there are other places. And remember this, Kate: I do not wish my son to be born at Windsor. Do you understand?"

"I understand."

"Then, sweetheart, that is settled."

That night, as I lay beside him, I was thinking, when shall I see him again? By that time I shall surely have my son . . . or perhaps a daughter. That was the one thing of which I felt certain.

And the next day he was gone.

After he left I went to Windsor. A mood of serenity had settled upon me. There was a certain relief in not having to ask myself when the summons would come to take him away. He was gone and there was no point in thinking about it any more. I knew some months would pass before he returned. Moreover, there was the baby to think of.

In six months' time the child would be born, and as the days passed I could forget everything but that wondrous fact.

Guillemote was in her element. She loved babies and was looking forward to mine with as much excitement as I was myself.

Since I had come to England I had grown very fond of four of my English attendants. They were Agnes and the three Joannas. We often laughed about their having the same name. They were Joanna Courcy, Joanna Belknap and Joanna Troutbeck. With these friends around me, I could not feel that I was in an alien land.

I knew we should all be happy at Windsor. Each day when I awoke I would remind myself that I was a day nearer to the great occasion which was to take place in December. My own child! That was what I wanted more than anything on earth.

We talked about the child continually. Guillemote was making tiny garments. She remembered me, she said, when I was little more than a baby.

"I watched you grow," she said, shaking her head and thinking back, I knew, to those days in the Hôtel de St. Paul. We should never cast off the memory of those days—any of us who had lived through them. Guillemote could only have been a young girl when she came, but they would live in her memory for ever.

It was about three weeks after Henry had left that Jacqueline of Bavaria arrived and the peace of Windsor was broken; one cannot say that it was shattered exactly, but it was ruffled.

Jacqueline was a disturbing person; moreover, she was filled with resentment against life.

I remembered her slightly from the old days when I had seen her once or twice, for she had been my sister-in-law, having been married briefly to my brother Jean.

She had gone back to her birthplace, Bavaria, when Jean had died, for she was the daughter of the Count of Hainault, Holland and Zealand and Margaret of Burgundy, sister of Jean the Fearless, the murdered Duke.

When her father died, she had inherited all his lands and had married the Duke of Brabant, who was her cousin and also a cousin of Philip, Duke of Burgundy. However, her uncle, at one time Bishop of Liège and known as John the Pitiless, had usurped her possessions, having tricked her second husband, the weak Duke of Brabant, into signing them away.

As a result she was in exile and had been given refuge in England, where she was treated with great respect. This might have been partly due to her connection with me, for I suppose the Queen's former sister-in-law could not have been denied a haven.

I said to Guillemote: "We must be patient with her. We must let her talk of her wrongs. It helps her. She has suffered so much. Imagine being an exile . . . and robbed of one's inheritance. She is just about three months older than I."

"She looks years older," said Guillemote.

"She certainly looks experienced," added Joanna Courcy.

"One would expect her to be after having had two husbands," said Agnes.

"I remember her . . . just a little," I told them. "She came to France when she was married to my brother Jean. He was Dauphin for a while."

"She reckoned she would be Queen of France," said Guillemote.

"Well, she might have been . . . had he lived. But he died, as my brother Louis had before him."

"Two Dauphins . . . to die," said Joanna Belknap. "How very sad . . . and strange."

There was silence. I knew what they were thinking. I had thought it myself many times. It was suspicious . . . and my mother had liked neither of them. But did she like my brother Charles any more? For a few moments I was back in that unhappy past; my mother exerting her power over us all; my father shut away in darkness. Michelle was happy, I believed, with

Burgundy, but how did it feel to live with the fact that her brother had been in the plot which had resulted in the death of her husband's father? Marie was the only one who had found peace, in her convent. Charles . . . poor little baby brother . . . had lost his throne and was now trying to regain it. The Duke of Clarence had died because of that.

But I had escaped. I was the fortunate one. Here I was, happy at Windsor . . . awaiting the greatest event of my life. I must forget the past. I was beginning to. It was only now and then, on occasions like this, that it was brought back vividly to me.

Jacqueline was often in my company. I supposed she thought that, in view of the family connection between us, I should have her with me. She talked on and on about her grievances and I would feign to listen sympathetically while my thoughts were elsewhere. Would the child be a girl after all? I wondered. A little girl would be delightful, but of course it must be a boy. Henry wanted a boy. The country wanted a boy. The bells would peal out and everything that had gone before would be worthwhile because of this child.

Jacqueline was saying: "Of course, what they all wanted was Hainault, Holland, Zealand and Friesland. They were mine. That is why they were so eager to have me."

I looked at her. She was quite comely; but there was something mildly repellant about her. It is due to what she has suffered, I told myself.

"They were ambitious for me," she went on. "Both my mother and my father. It was a great blow to my father that I was not a boy. How highly men rate their own sex."

I agreed. "It is because men lead other men into battle," I said. "People always want war . . . or conquests. I do not think they like it overmuch when it goes against them. But for war, Henry would be here now. We had to marry to make a harmonious union between our two countries. But for war my father could have remained King and Charles would have followed him peacefully. But they had to make war, and what men would want a woman to lead them? When you come to think of it, what woman would want to lead them? That is why they always want boys."

"If Jean had lived . . ."

"What if Jean had lived? Do you think Jean would have been able to stand out against Henry? Jean, less than any, wanted the crown."

"They would not let me remain a widow for long," she was saying.

"And you were not happy with your second marriage?" I asked perfunctorily, because I knew the answer already.

"How dared they marry me to such a weakling!"

"Well, he is your own cousin and therefore cousin to Philip of Burgundy."

"He is a fool. He allowed my wicked uncle to rob us of our estates."

"Money! Power! It seems there is always conflict where they exist. Oh, Jacqueline, do you not wish sometimes that we had not been born into families such as ours?"

She looked at me in astonishment. "No! No!" she cried. "I would not have it otherwise. We are the ruling class. We have the power."

"Until we lose it. Look what has happened to you! What has happened to my family!"

"That was war. And all is well with you now. You have made your way to the winning side. All would have been well with me if they had not forced me into marriage with Brabant . . . and if my wicked uncle had not seen how he could cheat the fool and rob me of my rights."

I knew so well by now the story of Jacqueline's second marriage to the Duke of Brabant who had foolishly allowed himself to be tricked by her scheming uncle, who had made a treaty with the Duke that all the property left by his late brother to his daughter should pass to him.

"Brabant should have fought for my rights," she cried in anguish. "Our marriage will be annulled. Yes, I shall be free of the fool. But look at me! What have I now? I . . . who was once the greatest heiress in Europe?"

I sympathized. We did what we could to help her, but her continual ranting about her wrongs wearied us.

"One day," she said, "there will be someone who will help me regain what was stolen from me."

"I hope so, Jacqueline," I replied.

I did indeed. Then she would go back to her own country and leave us in peace.

Meanwhile I continued to plan for the baby.

* * *

The time was passing . . . July, August, September.

I watched the leaves turning to bronze. Time was passing and Henry showed no sign of coming home.

I thought, a little resentfully, that he should have been here for the birth of our child.

I left Windsor and went to Westminster. October came.

I said to Guillemote: "I long to be at Windsor."

She replied: "Well, you could go there and return to Westminster for the birth. There is time."

So we went to Windsor.

Jacqueline stayed at Westminster. She had been given a comfortable pension by the state which had mollified her a little. I was glad of that.

I wanted to spend my time peacefully waiting . . . in the company of my dear Guillemote and my faithful ladies.

November had come.

Guillemote said: "If the child is not to be born at Windsor, we should begin to think of leaving. You will not want to travel in a week or so."

"Guillemote," I replied, "I do not want to travel now."

"I thought the King expressly said that the child must not be born at Windsor."

"How could he get such a fancy, Guillemote? Henry . . . the practical soldier . . . to have such a whim. I love this place. I don't feel so happy anywhere else. It is pleasant not to have Jacqueline always with me. It is so delightful here. I feel safe and secure. Just a few more days, Guillemote."

"A few more days," echoed Guillemote. "But no more."

But when those days had passed I still felt reluctant to leave.

"They say a pregnant woman's whims should be satisfied," I reminded Guillemote.

"How shall we move later on? You will not be fit for it."

"No, Guillemote. I shall not be."

I do not know why I did what I did. It was like some compulsion. Each day I put off the departure. I thought he could not really have meant it. It was such a fanciful notion and Henry was not a man of fancies. It was just said on the spur of the moment. And I did not want to leave Windsor where I was so happy.

I was still at Windsor when December came. The weather had turned cold. Bleak winds swept through the park and the forest and there were flurries of snow in the air.

"You could not leave in this," said Guillemote. "The King would not wish it and I would not allow it."

"No," I said. "It is too late now, Guillemote."

Then came that wonderful day when my child was born.

I lay on my bed and they brought him to me and put him in my arms. Happiness surged over me. My child had been safely born and he was perfect in every way.

"A beautiful boy," they said.

I thought of Henry's joy when the news reached him. But I had disobeyed him and my son had been born at Windsor.

What did that matter? It was a slight matter when he was here, alive . . . healthy.

I looked at his little red face, the tiny nose, the little hands, perfectly fitted with miniature nails . . . and on his head I pictured a crown.

Henry VI was born, and I was happy as I had never been before.

Each morning I awoke to a sense of excitement. I would go to the cradle and gloat over my son. Because Henry was absent there had as yet been no arrangements as to the setting up of a royal nursery. I could keep him with me as any low-born mother might. That was wonderful.

Guillemote and I would talk of him endlessly. When he whimpered, there was a race between us to reach him first.

Those wonderful days were only overshadowed by the thought that they could not last.

Immediately after little Henry had been born, news had been sent across the Channel to his father. I was very proud because I had given him not only a child but a son.

When the messengers returned, I sent for them and I asked what the King had said when the news was imparted to him. I wanted to know each detail.

"His joy was great, my lady. He first asked news of the boy. He was a little sad because he had been out of England at the time of his birth. Then he asked where he had been born."

I felt a twinge of alarm. He had been so insistent. I could hear his voice echoing in my mind: "The child must not be born at Windsor."

"And," I prompted, "you told him . . . ?"

''We told him that the Prince had been born at Windsor.''

''And what said he then?''

The messengers looked at each other and were silent for a moment.

''Yes,'' I repeated. ''And what said he?''

''He said nothing for a moment, but he seemed uneasy. Then he said slowly: 'Are you sure that the Prince was born at Windsor?' 'Without a doubt,' we told him.''

''And then?'' I asked.

''It seemed, my lady, that a cloud came over his joy. He murmured something. Then he turned to us and said: 'I, Henry born at Monmouth, shall small time reign and much get; but Henry of Windsor shall long reign and lose all.' It was strange, my lady, and as though someone spoke through him. It was so clear . . . we remembered the exact words he spoke. Then he closed his eyes and murmured: 'But if it is God's will, so be it.' ''

I was overcome with awe, and my conscience was greatly troubled. After the messengers had gone, I kept asking myself what he could have meant.

Then I demanded of myself why I had allowed it to happen?

It was the weather, I assured myself. But I could have got away earlier. Why had I so blatantly flouted Henry's wishes? I had never done so before.

It was nothing, I assured myself. It was just a fancy of Henry's.

It was no use. I could not console myself, and the terrible feeling of guilt remained. I was not able to dismiss the matter from my mind, and it cast a slight gloom over the happiness of those days.

Live in the moment, I admonished myself. Little Henry is yours now. For how long? I wondered. They would give him the grand household which they would say was the right of a prince, especially one who was heir to the throne. They would give him all that when what he wanted most was a mother's love and care. It was foolish to let this fleeting happiness be marred by a sense of guilt over a very trivial matter.

One of my dearest friends was Johan Boyers. He was a doctor of philosophy who had been assigned to me as my confessor. I was attracted to him because he was a man to whom I could talk freely and he had helped me over one or two trifling matters.

At our next meeting I said to him: "There is something on my mind. It is of small account really, but it is worrying me."

"Then let me hear it," he said.

"Before he went to France, the King talked to me earnestly about the child we were to have."

Johan nodded. "It was his great concern. He spoke to me of it. Above all things he wanted a son. I rejoice that God has seen fit to grant his wish."

"Before the King went he asked me not to allow the child to be born at Windsor."

"And you disobeyed his wishes?"

"I cannot understand it. I did not want to. But I love Windsor. It is the place where I am most content. I went there when the King left. I missed him very much but my ladies are my good friends and I became deeply content thinking of little else but the child."

"It is natural, my lady."

"But . . . I did not leave Windsor. I meant to . . . but something held me there."

"Because you wanted so much to stay?"

"Yes. Yes, I did. But I did not forget that Henry did not want the child to be born there. I kept telling myself that I would go . . . in time."

"Did you have a compulsion to stay?"

"Yes," I said eagerly, "I think I did."

"And the King knows?"

"One of the first things he asked was where was the baby born."

"And when he was told?"

"He made a strange remark. He said that Henry of Monmouth would gain a good deal and not reign long and Henry of Windsor would reign for a long time and lose a great deal. It seemed such an odd thing to say."

"He may have been quoting some old prophecy. He must have had a premonition before he left, as he said he did not want the child to be born at Windsor."

"It is baffling."

"And what did he mean about reigning a short time? He is a great king. The people love him. He must reign for many years . . . and then . . . in due course . . . there will be another Henry to follow him."

"But why did I stay? If I had known of this prophecy . . . or whatever it is . . . before, I should have done everything possible to get away from Windsor. And yet I had this compulsion to stay."

Johan was thoughtful for a while, then he said: "If we are going to take any account of this prophecy, we must say that it is God's will that it should have happened as it did. There was nothing you could have done to change it."

"I could have left Windsor. I could have made sure that my child was not born there, then he would not have been Henry of Windsor."

"What is to be will be. If you had known of this you could have acted differently, it is true. But it was clearly not meant that you should know. You will forget this matter. It is a fancy which came into the mind of the King."

"He is not given to fancies."

"Perhaps we all are at times."

"I wish that I knew what it meant."

"God's ways are mysterious. People have strange fancies . . . all of us do at times. Let us pray that all will be well with the King and his son."

I was ready to do that with fervour.

And after a while I ceased to worry. It had just been a fancy on Henry's part. Such prophecies were meaningless. I had a strong and virile husband and a healthy baby.

I must rejoice.

The baptism of my son was carried out with the ceremony due to the heir to the throne. I said to Guillemote that it was difficult to imagine our little one with such a grand title.

Henry had chosen his godparents: his brother John, Duke of Bedford, and Henry Beaufort, Bishop of Winchester, Henry's father's half-brother. They were both men who were held in high esteem. His godmother was Jacqueline of Bavaria, who was immensely delighted to be given this honour. She was sure that it meant Henry had her good at heart and in time might even help her to regain her lost provinces.

Little Henry, I am proud to say, behaved with impeccable decorum at his baptism and he was the object of much admiration.

The time was passing and I knew that change must come.

The inevitable happened. It was a summons from Henry for me to join him in France.

At first I made wild plans for taking the baby with me. Then I thought of the unpredictable stretch of water between me and Henry. It would be May, I reminded myself; and that would be very different from February when I had crossed before. Then I remembered the rough going across country and I knew I was deluding myself. Of course the baby would have to stay in England.

The Council had decided these matters for me. I was a fool to have thought it possible. I should never have been allowed to take little Henry with me.

It was arranged that he should be left in the care of his uncle Humphrey, the Duke of Gloucester, while the King and I were in France, so I had to prepare myself to say farewell to my baby.

"Well," said Joanna Troutbeck, "you won't see the baby, but the King will make up for that."

I wanted to say that nothing would make up for parting with my baby, but of course there would be some consolation in Henry's company, though experience had taught me not to expect too much of that. There would be the usual battles, the partings, the reunions, and never knowing from one hour to the next when he would be gone.

Duke Humphrey came to see me and the child.

He was very charming and told me I need have no anxieties about my son. Everything could be safely left to him.

He did not appear to be the sort of man who would interest himself in nurseries. But he would not have to do so, of course—just make sure that the right people were about the child and did their work efficiently. I should insist on Guillemote's staying with him.

Jacqueline was with me at this time. She showed an interest in her young godson, but I was never sure how deeply her feelings went. I imagined she gave more thought to her lost possessions than to her godmother's vows.

She met Humphrey. After all, the boy was under his care and she was his godmother. It should make a common interest.

I could see that they were rather attracted to each other, and it was not long—as I had guessed would be the case—before Jacqueline was telling him of her wrongs.

He knew what had happened, of course, and why she was in England, but he listened with the utmost sympathy.

"My dear lady," he soothed, "how you have suffered! That uncle of yours is indeed a wicked man. And your husband . . . he allowed it to happen!"

"My husband no more!" she cried. "We are divorced. The Pope has annulled our marriage."

"The Pope has agreed to this?"

"The Spanish Benedict."

"He whom some call the anti-Pope?"

"Anti-Pope or not, he has been a good friend to me."

"Then I will say he is a good pope."

They laughed together. I had never seen Jacqueline so merry before.

She talked to him about the importance of what she had lost. Hainault, Holland, Zealand and Friesland . . . all gone to the wicked uncle through treachery.

"But I do not despair," she said. "One day some gallant and noble knight will come to my aid."

Duke Humphrey was smiling at her.

"There can be no doubt of that," he said. "God speed the day."

At length he left, reluctantly, and I remarked to my ladies that he had talked more to Jacqueline than to me.

"He seemed taken with her," said Agnes.

"In my opinion," said Joanna Courcy, "he is taken with Hainault, Holland, Zealand and Friesland."

We all laughed, and I set about getting on with my preparations to leave.

John, Duke of Bedford, was to escort me to France. I had said my farewells to my baby and left him in Guillemote's careful hands. She had assured me that I had nothing to worry about. The Duke of Gloucester had given me his word that when the baby's household was arranged Guillemote should remain with him.

The crossing was fairly calm, and on landing I was accompanied by Bedford and 20,000 men to Vincennes.

Henry was in the wood there with my parents, waiting to greet me.

What an emotional reunion that was! Henry embraced me

with fervour. I had been a little worried as to what his reaction would be after I had disobeyed him regarding little Henry's birthplace; but he did not seem to remember that in his joy at seeing me.

My father embraced me with tears on his cheeks. I was fearful that the deep emotion might bring on one of his periods of madness.

"My daughter . . . my Katherine . . ." he murmured. "I am so proud of you."

My mother, plumper than ever, gloriously apparelled, perfumed and sparkling, kissed me with an outward display of affection.

"My dear, dear daughter," she cried. "How wonderful for us to be together again. It has been so long. And now there is the little one. How I wish I could see him! Later on he must come here to be with me."

Never, I thought; but I smiled pleasantly.

I rode side by side with Henry to our lodging, and at last we were alone.

I thought he looked a little strained and when the first passionate reunion was over I asked tentatively about his health.

"I'm well enough, Kate," he said. "A soldier's life is not an easy one. We go from place to place, and Meaux was an obstinate city. I did not think they could hold out so long."

"I was hoping this fighting would be over."

"I doubt we shall ever be completely at peace here. These people . . . they have too much resistance."

"They resent the conqueror. That is natural."

"I know. I'd have a poor opinion of them if they were otherwise. But it makes the going hard."

"They will go on resisting for ever," I said.

He nodded grimly. "That may be so, but when they rise against me, they will be put down. Never fear. Now . . . tell me of our son."

"He is wonderful and beginning to know us. Everyone dotes on him."

"And strong . . . and healthy?"

"He is the son of his father!"

It was the wrong thing to have said, I knew, because I saw a shadow pass across his face. Is he as well as he pretends to be? I wondered.

I knew that sooner or later he would broach the subject of Henry's birthplace and I decided to mention it first.

"I am sorry," I said, "that I did not get away from Windsor in time for the birth."

"What kept you?"

"It was the weather," I said quickly, suppressing the impulse to tell the truth and say, my own inclination.

"You left it until it was too late to venture out?"

I nodded. Then I was contrite. I put my arms about him and wept. "I am sorry, Henry. I am sorry. It was my fault. I should have gone before . . . I wanted to . . . I really did. But it was some compulsion."

He stroked my hair and kissed me tenderly on the brow.

"Fret not, Kate," he said. "You cannot go against what is to be."

"I should have, Henry. I could have . . ."

"Let us forget it."

"But you were so determined. It has spoilt your joy in our son."

"It does not do to be fanciful. All will be well with our son . . . and with me."

"You will make it so," I said. "You are brave and strong; and nothing can ever succeed against you."

"Except God's will," he reminded me. And then he added: "We can do no good by speaking of it. So forget it. It has to be. And we have been apart so long. I have thought of you constantly, and now you are here . . ."

I felt an immense relief sweep over me. I was forgiven. Indeed it seemed as though there was no question or need of forgiveness. If he believed the prophecy and that fate had decided it should come to pass, there was nothing anyone could have done to change it. On the other hand . . . if it were fanciful nonsense, why bother with it?

So . . . we would forget it. No harm could come to any of us while we had Henry to guard us.

I gave myself up to the pleasure of being with him again after our long separation.

It was Whitsun Eve when, beside Henry, I rode into Paris. How moving it was to ride through my native city. My mind slipped back, as it must do once again, to those days of poverty in the

Hôtel de St. Paul, and I marvelled afresh at the strangeness of fate which had brought me back to ride side by side with the conqueror.

I did wonder what the people thought as they watched me—their own princess—now the wife of the victor.

They lined the streets all the way to the Louvre, shouting their loyal greetings.

My parents were not riding with us. That would have been too humiliating for my father, so he and my mother had gone by a different route to the Hôtel de St. Paul.

I was richly clad with a crown on my head, to remind these people that I was their future Queen as well as the Queen of England.

It seemed disloyal when their real queen was with my father on the way to the dreary Hôtel de St. Paul.

We rested that night at the Louvre.

Henry was very understanding and had noticed how quiet I had become.

When we were alone in our apartment, he took my chin in his hand and looked earnestly into my face. "This is a strange day for you, Kate," he said.

"It is certain to make me feel a little bewildered to be back here in the city of my childhood."

"All that is behind you," he insisted. "We are here and this is how it should be. Think of this, Kate. I can do more for France than your father could."

"If he had never lost his senses . . ."

"Enough of these ifs. Life is made up of them. Come. We are together. The people of Paris are glad to see peace. You are their Queen . . . you who were their Princess. They will accept me, Kate, because I am *your* husband."

"Let there be peace and I shall be happy," I said fervently. "Then we can go home to . . ."

"To our child," he finished. "How is England for you, Kate, then?"

"Home is where my son is . . . where you are."

"Then it is in two places at this time."

"I would it were in one."

"It will be so ere long, Kate. I promise you."

The next day was Whit Sunday, and a great feast was held in the Palace of the Louvre.

"It is an important occasion," said Henry. "The people will want to see us."

"They were always allowed into the palace on Whit Sundays . . . to watch the King at table."

"Then they shall do so on this day."

I was carefully dressed and a crown was placed on my head. Henry looked equally splendid. We sat on the dais and about us were all the highest nobles of France and England.

The banquet was served and the people crowded into the palace to watch, just as they had when my parents occupied the places where Henry and I now sat.

I noticed that many eyes were fixed on me.

I wanted to say to them: I do not forget you. I am still French. I married the King of England who is soon to be King of France, but it was all done in the name of peace.

I knew that at the Hôtel de St. Paul my parents would be sitting in lonely state this Whitsun. How did it feel, I wondered, to know that people had flocked to the Louvre to pay their homage to those who, on the death of my father, would be King and Queen of France? I felt ashamed that I might be seen as a daughter waiting to take the crown from her mother when my husband took that of my father.

I longed for the peace of the nursery, where all such matters seemed of little importance because little Henry had begun to crow with pleasure.

Henry sat beside me, quiet and dignified. Glancing sideways at him, I thought he seemed tired and I knew that, but for his sun-tanned skin, he would be looking a little pale.

I was longing for the feast to be over. I, too, was tired. I thought, soon we shall depart and the remains of the food will be distributed among the poor who have crowded in here to watch us.

After what seemed a very long period, that time came.

We left and I heard later that the people were sent away without the food which it had been the custom to distribute, that there had been a great deal of complaint and the crowd had at one time threatened to become quite ugly.

"Where is the food?" they had demanded. "Are we to be robbed of our rights as well as our true King and Queen . . . ?"

Joanna Courcy, who had accompanied me to France, said:

"I cannot imagine why it was done. I hear it has always been the custom. I heard it was on the King's orders."

I spoke to Henry about it later.

"It has always been the custom," I said. "The people have always had the food that was left over from the banquet. That is why they come."

"It is not my custom," replied Henry.

"But . . . they expect it."

He shrugged his shoulders. "I did not promise to follow their customs."

"But the people . . . seeing us eat all that food when some of them must be in need . . ."

I should have seen that he was exhausted. But I did wonder why he had given such an order. Surely it could not have mattered to him? Was it just to be different; to show them that in all but name he was their King and the old customs of French kings should be dispensed with?

He did not answer. He sat on the bed, looking more tired than I had ever seen him.

I should have dropped the subject, but something prompted me to say: "It is simple matters such as that which cause revolts."

"Have done!" he said sharply. "The people will have to grow accustomed to my rule. When I say something is to be . . . it will be and that is an end of the matter."

I looked at him in astonishment. It was the first time he had spoken harshly to me.

I was worried about him, and I longed more than ever to be back at Windsor with my beloved child.

Henry slept heavily that night. He had not risen when I awoke. I was accustomed to finding him gone and I sat up in bed and looked down at him anxiously. He looked ill and I was overcome with tenderness, for in his sleep he reminded me of my son. There was a vulnerability about him which I had never noticed before.

"Oh, Henry," I murmured, "what are you doing? How can you endure these perpetual battles . . . ?"

He opened his eyes and saw me studying him.

"Well," he said, attempting to smile. "Do you like what you see?"

"No" I said boldly. "I think you are unwell."

"Enough," he said, and I was aware of the look of irritability in his face. "I am as well as ever. It is late, is it not?"

"You have slept longer than usual."

He leaped out of bed. "Why did you not wake me?"

"I have only just awakened myself."

"And wasting time contemplating me and coming to the conclusion that my looks do not please you."

"You need rest," I said.

"I need rest as much as I need an assassin's knife. For me, Kate, there is no rest until there is peace throughout this land."

"And then I doubt not you will have other plans for conquest."

"No. I plan to go on a crusade."

I stared at him.

"I'd take you with me," he added.

I did not answer. I knew that would never come to pass.

That very day there was news. My brother Charles, the Dauphin, was on the march. He was going to attack the enemy, the Duke of Burgundy.

Burgundy was now Henry's ally, and when he heard the news he said: "I must go to the aid of Burgundy. It would be a disaster if he were defeated by the Dauphin."

"Need you be involved?" I asked.

He looked at me as though I were foolish.

"But of course I'm involved. The Dauphin had a victory when my brother Clarence was killed at Beaugé. That gave the enemy hope, and hope is something we must not let them regain. You do not understand these matters. I shall have to leave at once."

"Could you not send your army and remain for a while?"

"Remain here . . . when my army is on the march! What are you thinking?"

"Just that at this time you seem to be in need of rest."

"I? In need of rest! When there is an army to lead?"

"So . . . you will go?"

"Kate, sometimes you ask the most foolish questions."

"I would you could stay behind."

He turned from me impatiently. But a few seconds later he turned back and took me into his arms.

"Fret not," he said. "I will be back with you ere long."

"I pray that you will," I said.

* * *

I went with him as far as Senlis.

There he decided I might be too close to the fighting. "Better," he said, "that you go to Vincennes."

I said: "I shall be close to you here."

I saw the impatience in his face. "You will go to Vincennes immediately."

So I left for the castle in the woods of Vincennes and he went on to Senlis.

It was only a few days later when I heard the sounds of shouting below my apartments in the castle. I looked down from my window and I could scarcely believe what I saw. Some men were carrying a litter and in it lay Henry.

I hurried down. He was very pale and half-conscious. It would be useless for him to attempt to hide his condition now.

One of the bearers spoke to me. He was tall and very good-looking and spoke English with an accent I did not recognize.

He said: "The King has been forced to leave the army. He could go no farther."

"I see. Can he be brought up to the bedchamber?"

"At once, my lady."

They carried him up. He lay on the bed . . . breathing deeply.

The tall bearer said to me: "My lady, you should send for a priest."

I knew then how ill he was.

He was in fact dying. It seemed incredible that one so strong, so seemingly invincible, could be so suddenly struck down.

I said to the bearer: "We will nurse him back to health."

He looked at me rather sadly and with such pity that I was deeply touched.

It was some hours before I could convince myself that this really was the end.

Henry had suffered from dysentery for some time. It was the soldier's disease and taken for granted, so was lightly brushed aside. Now he seemed to have some disorder of the chest, for he coughed a great deal and his breathing was difficult.

The physicians shook their heads gravely, implying there was little they could do.

The Duke of Bedford left the army and came to his bedside. I was glad of his presence. He was the one of Henry's brothers whom I had always trusted most.

"Be of good cheer," he said to me. "He will recover. He always achieved what to others would seem impossible."

I tried to smile but it occurred to me that this time he was fighting a more formidable enemy than the French.

The confessor was with him. Henry managed, between gasps, to ask forgiveness for his sins. What were his sins? Those peccadilloes of his youth? Or the blood which had been shed on the battlefields of France? He did not mention that.

His confessor was reading the seven psalms. He came to the phrase "Build thou the walls of Jerusalem" when Henry feebly lifted a hand as a sign for him to pause.

He said between gasps: "When I had completed my conquests in Europe . . . it was always my intention . . . to make a crusade to the Holy Land."

I wished that these thoughts would not enter my head at inopportune moments, but I could not help wondering whether he thought a crusade to the Holy Land would compensate for the misery and bloodshed he had brought to my country.

The harrowing bedside scene continued and I felt I could endure it no longer.

I whispered to the physician: "He will recover, will he not?"

The man did not speak; he just looked at me as though begging me not to demand a direct answer.

"I would like the truth," I insisted.

"My lady . . . it will be a miracle if he lasts for another two hours."

Henry asked for his brother Bedford, and the Duke, who was already at his bedside, came forward and took Henry's hand.

"I am here, brother," he said.

"John . . . you have been a good brother to me."

"My lord King, brother . . . I have always sought to serve you."

"I know. You were the one . . . I always trusted. John . . . now it will be for you. You must hold what I have gained. There is my son . . . a baby. There is Kate . . . my wife. Comfort Kate, John. She will be the most afflicted creature living . . . so young . . . and the child, John . . ."

"I will do all you wish. I will do as you would."

Henry nodded and closed his eyes. He looked as though he were at peace.

We stood at his bedside in silence, and into my mind came

the strange prophecy I had heard. "Henry of Monmouth would reign a short time and gain much." The first part had come true.

I was filled with a sense of awe and deep loss. I had one thought: I must get back to my son. He had lost his father. He was not yet a year old and he was King of England.

I tried to look ahead but the future seemed dark, mysterious and foreboding.

Looking back now on those days at Vincennes, I realize that for most of the time I thought I was living through some evil dream. It was hard to accept the fact that Henry was dead. He had been so vital. If he had been killed in battle, it would not have been so unexpected. But to die like this . . . in such a short time . . . seemed impossible.

There was a great deal to be done. He must be given a worthy funeral. The people of France must be made to understand that the death of the great conqueror did not mean that the English grip on the country would be lessened. He had brothers to carry on with his great schemes of conquest.

I wondered what effect this was having on my parents at the Hôtel de St. Paul. I could imagine that my mother was busily scheming. As for my poor father, he had long given up hope of regaining the crown and I was not sure that he would want it if he could. His only pleasure nowadays was keeping away from conflict.

John of Bedford was a great help. Deeply grieving as he was, he took over the arrangements for the funeral and, oddly enough, it was the tall squire who had helped bear the litter to Vincennes who gave me the greatest comfort.

I singled him out among the others. It might have been because he had a kindly face which showed at the same time a strength of character. I liked the lilting way he spoke English. My own was less than perfect and I had often found it difficult to follow those who did not speak the language in the way Henry and the people around me did. He was from Wales, and the Welsh accent was musical and pleasant to listen to. I was glad of Bedford's efficiency but he was not a man to whom one could talk easily, and this man had a soothing manner which might have been due to his voice.

I was able to ask him how the King had been at Senlis before he had allowed them to remove him from the army.

"It must have been a difficult decision for him to make," I said. "I am sure he did it with the utmost reluctance."

"With the utmost, my lady," replied the Welshman. "He had been fighting against the disease for some time."

"You were close to him, I believe."

"Yes, my lady. I was with him at Agincourt and ever since he has kept me near him."

"He thought highly of you, I expect."

"I was honoured to serve him."

"Tell me about him. He was much loved by his men, was he not?"

"It is my belief, my lady, that he was loved more than any king before him, and I doubt that any who follows him will be loved more."

"You cared for him very much."

"All his men cared for him. There was no one like him. He was the greatest soldier who ever lived, in my opinion, my lady. All who have been privileged to know him should be proud."

"He was friendly with his men, was he not?"

"He was always kind and generous. His men knew what was expected of them—which was absolute devotion to duty . . . as he always gave himself. His decisions were quick. He always knew what should be done. 'It is impossible,' he would say. Or 'It shall be done!' We all knew exactly what to expect, and it never varied."

"You make him sound almost impossibly perfect."

"He was as near perfection as a man can be. He was just. Some would say he was stern. He was, it was true. He made his laws and expected absolute obedience to them. That is the way of great rulers."

"Sometimes I wonder . . ." I began. "Sometimes I think . . . of the cries of women and children who have lost their men and their homes in battle. Such cries haunt me."

"I know," he said. "I understand."

"And I cannot help thinking . . . why should there have to be war?"

"The King believed firmly that France belonged to him. He planned to bring better rule to that land." He paused, remembering, I supposed, that he was speaking against my family.

I smiled at him and then began to ask myself why I was talking thus to this man. I could not understand myself. I was, of course, in a highly emotional state, and he had such a kind face, such a sympathetic manner.

I wanted to hear a vindication of Henry. I wanted to forget those terrible doubts which had come to me. I thought of him on his deathbed, when it had not occurred to him to ask forgiveness for the sufferings he had caused to so many innocent people.

"My lady, the King considered the men as he did himself. He was never vengeful to an enemy, never vindictive. He was always merciful. He forbade pilfering and disrespect to women. He shared the hardships of his soldiers, he gave them example after example of his own bravery."

"You make a hero of him."

"He was a hero, Madam."

I smiled, I had been greatly comforted by my conversation with this man.

I said to him: "I do not know your name."

And he answered: "It is Owen Tudor."

They made an effigy of Henry. It was life-size, constructed from boiled leather and painted to make it resemble his living self. On the head was set a crown, in the right hand a sceptre and in the left an orb. The effigy was put upon a carriage and we set out.

It was an impressive cavalcade, with noblemen such as the Duke of Exeter and the Earl of March carrying the banners of the saints, and 400 men-at-arms in black armour riding with the bier. I followed at some distance.

Our first stop was St. Ivian in Abbeville, where we rested for a day and night, and all through that day Masses were sung for the saving of his soul.

At length we came to Calais.

It seemed long since his death, for it was at this time 12 October and he had died on the last day of August.

There followed the journey across the Channel, and how relieved I was when I saw the white cliffs looming ahead. I thought of my child. It was nearly five months since I had seen him. Would he know me? I wondered. How foolish! Of course he would not. He had been too young to know me when I had left.

But he would have been safe in Guillemote's care. But what would happen now that he was King?

Never had I wished so much that I had been born in humbler circumstances. If I were but a humble noblewoman coming home to her child, I could find some contentment. Why did people crave for crowns? As far as I could see, they brought nothing but unhappiness.

As soon as I stepped on English soil, the ceremonies began again.

Waiting on the shore were fifteen bishops and numerous abbots in their mitres and vestments; and the solemn procession set out for Blackheath.

The funeral took place on a dark November day when Henry was buried in the Chapel of the Confessor in Westminster Abbey. It was more than three months since his death and I still could not get accustomed to the fact that I would not see him again.

I had ordered that a statue should be made in silver plate with a head of pure silver gilt and set on his tomb with an inscription to say it came from me.

And when it was over, I did what I had been longing to do for some time. I went down to Windsor to see the new King of England, who was not quite one year old.

True Love

It was more than three months since Henry had died when I arrived in Windsor. Guillemote and my ladies were overcome with emotion. We embraced each other joyfully.

Guillemote said: "He is well. He is waiting for you."

I ran up the stairs with the ladies behind me. I threw open the door and beheld my son. He was seated on the floor playing with a silver whistle, and in that moment the loss of my husband and my concern for the future were forgotten. I ran to him and knelt beside him. He regarded me solemnly, and my happiness was tinged with sadness because he did not recognize me. I was a stranger to him, and he was not sure what I was doing in his nursery.

I seized him in my arms. "Henry," I cried, "little Henry . . . this is your mother come to you."

He drew himself away, frowning; then he looked round him and, seeing Guillemote standing there, he gave a little crow of triumph and held out his arms to her.

She picked him up. "There, my precious. 'Tis your mother who loves you and is waiting to tell you so."

He turned his head slightly and regarded me with suspicion.

Guillemote sat down and beckoned me to sit beside her.

"There," she crooned and placed him on my lap. She knelt down beside us and I noticed how he clung to her hand.

"Poor little mite," she went on. "He does not know his mother. It is so long, my lady, and he is very little. It will come. He learns quickly, our little one."

Henry did learn quickly. In less than ten minutes he had accepted me. He had made up his mind that I meant no harm. I was a friend of his dear Guillemote, and if she accepted me, so would he.

I wondered if I should ever equal her in his affections, and I was filled with resentment against a fate which separated a mother from her baby.

I was greatly relieved to be at Windsor again with my ladies around me. How relaxing it was to be able to talk without considering one's words first.

"It is so good to be with you again," I told them. "I hope we shall be left in peace for a while."

"My lady," said Agnes, "you will make your own decisions. You are the Queen Mother now. It will be different from being Queen. There will not be so many duties."

Joanna Troutbeck took my hand and kissed it. "We felt for you so much," she said. "When we heard the news, we wished that we were with you."

"It was so sudden . . . such a shock," I told them. "Who would have thought that Henry could . . . just die like that?"

"He seemed different from other men . . . immortal," said Agnes.

"And now he is proved to be as all men are. They must go when they are called."

"We will do anything . . ." said Joanna Belknap.

"We want to help all we can," they told me.

"I thank God I have my baby. Do you think they will take him from me?"

"If they try to, you must protest."

"He is the King . . . and kings are the property of the State, they say. Oh, how I wish he were not a king! When I think of that little head weighed down by a crown . . ."

"Doubtless," said Agnes, "he will hold it dear. Most men do."

"It was a crown which killed his father . . . or the determination to hunt for it."

They looked at me in amazement; and I went on, "Oh yes, he was killed in war as much as any man. Had he not wasted his youth and strength on the battlefield, he would be alive today."

There was a brief silence and I thought: I must not talk thus.

I have come here to forget . . . to be with my child . . . to make a new life.

I went on: "You must tell me what has been happening while I have been away."

"The biggest news is the marriage of the Duke of Gloucester," said Joanna Troutbeck.

"Is that so?"

"To the Lady Jacqueline of Bavaria."

"But I thought she was married to the Duke of Brabant. How can she therefore marry the Duke of Gloucester?"

"The marriage was annulled. Or so she claims. The anti-Pope obliged and she was free. So she has married Duke Humphrey."

"There will be trouble surely?"

"It would seem that neither of them cares very much for that."

"But Brabant is the cousin of the Duke of Burgundy. They are connections of mine. As for Jacqueline, she was once my sister-in-law."

"They are snapping their fingers at all those who object," said Agnes. "The Duke of Bedford, we have heard, is furiously angry. Burgundy is not the man to brook interference and he naturally had his eyes on Jacqueline's possessions. The Duke of Bedford fears he may lose Burgundy as an ally through this. There is a great deal of gossip about it at Court."

"They have been very rash," I said. "Are they very much in love?"

"As was said before, I think the Duke is very much in love with Hainault, Zealand, Holland and Friesland," said Joanna Troutbeck.

"And Jacqueline?" I asked.

"She is in love with the belief that he, as her husband, will fight with her to get her possessions back."

"So it is a love match between them both and these possessions rather than that of Jacqueline and Humphrey for each other?"

"Well," said the cynical Joanna Troutbeck. "Is it not for such reasons that marriages are often made?"

I nodded sadly. "As mine was. Was I not fortunate to marry a man like Henry?"

"And he to marry you, my lady."

"Yes, it was a good marriage. We were happy together . . . when we were together."

They began to talk of other matters. I could imagine their whispering to each other when I was not there as to how they could turn my mind from those happy days I had spent with Henry and stop my repining.

I had not been in England more than a week or so when messengers arrived from France. I knew they brought news of some calamity, and waited with trepidation for what they had to tell me.

They hesitated for a little while until I begged them to speak. Then one of them said: "It is the king, your father, my lady."

"My father? What of my father?" He had been a source of anxiety for so long. What more could there be to fear?

"He is dead, my lady."

I was silent, thinking of my first glimpse of him when I was a child. Vividly I remembered the wild-eyed man who thought he was made of glass. I could remember the bleak despair in his eyes.

"The people of Paris mourn him deeply."

I nodded, not trusting myself to speak.

"And now he has gone to his rest, my lady, the rest for which he had so much longed."

"So . . . he was in Paris?"

"Yes, my lady. The people cheered him when he came to the city. It warmed his heart to hear the shouts of 'Noël.' The people always loved him . . . even when he could not come among them . . . even when he was shut away from them."

Love and pity were very close, I thought.

"He lay in state, my lady, for three days . . . his face uncovered that all might take a last look at him. He was in the Hôtel de St. Paul, and crowds went in most devotedly to pay their last respects to him."

"Yes," I murmured. "He was well loved."

"You should have heard the prayers, my lady. The people knew him for a good man. He was sadly afflicted. They said how different the fate of France might have been if he had been well enough to lead the country. They prayed to God for the soul of their dear prince. They said they would never again see one as good as he was. 'Now it is all wars and trouble,' they said. 'Prince, go to your rest. We must remain to our tribulations and sorrows.' They likened their plight to that of the children of Israel in captivity in Babylon.''

I listened impassively; and suddenly they were covered with embarrassment. They had been thinking of me solely as my father's daughter and then had realized that I was the conqueror's widow. I had left my own country and adopted his. It was an awkward situation in which they found themselves. They would have liked to say more, I knew, but they had said as much as they dared.

''How did he die?'' I asked. ''Was he at peace at the end?''

''They say so, my lady. They say he welcomed death with open arms. He was tired of life. Fate had ill-used him.''

I thought: Yes, he had always wanted to go. There was nothing for him here but those long periods of darkness followed by brief lucid periods when he would know that it was during his reign that France had been lost, and his own son, the Dauphin, had been deprived of his inheritance. He had had to stand aside and see another proclaimed King of France. What did they think of me? Where was my place in all this? My little son was usurping the rights of the Dauphin.

''They took him to St. Denis, my lady. The Duke of Berry made a speech over his open tomb. He said: 'Lord have mercy on the soul of the most high and excellent Charles, King of France, sixth of the name.' ''

I nodded . . . he *was* King until the end. Henry had agreed that he should retain the title until his death. I was glad that Henry had not robbed him of that, empty as it was.

''Immediately after the Duke of Berry had spoken, there followed a cry of 'Long live King Henry, by the grace of God, King of France and of England!' ''

I felt I could bear no more, so I thanked them for coming and dismissed them. I wanted to be alone.

There were so many memories . . . and all sad ones. I wondered about my mother. What was she doing now? She was no longer Queen of France. That was no loss to France. I was filled with a deep resentment towards her. Much of the tragedy which had befallen my father and his country was due to her. And now where was she? I doubted not that she would be looking after herself. She would have her luxuries . . . her pets . . . her lovers. And she would not shed a tear for that poor tragic man whose life and whose country she had helped to bring to disaster.

But what was the use of recriminations, of brooding on the past? I had to go on with my life. I was in a new land. I had become a widow. Perhaps they would send me back to France. But I was the mother of their King, so they could hardly do that. I must think of my son. Therein lay my future. I must forget my tragic past. My allegiance was to my new country.

I went to the nursery and gazed down on my sleeping child— King Henry of France and England.

The Duke of Gloucester called at Windsor.

What a handsome man he was! Far more attractive in a way than his brother of Bedford. He wore his hair closely cropped, as Henry had worn his. It was the best style for a soldier; and because it had been favoured by the King, it had become fashionable. That would change now, I supposed, with his passing. But just now Henry was very much with us. Humphrey had a love of fine clothes, which Henry, being mostly at war, had no time for. He now wore a blue houppelande caught in at the waist with a jewelled belt. The full sleeves billowed out, and his long pointed shoes were the same colour as his houppelande.

He studied me with a mixture of appreciation and speculation, as I guessed he did all women. His eyes were rather like Henry's, but Henry's had been clearer. Under Humphrey's were the beginnings of pouches, which was an indication, I believed, of his indulgence in the pleasures of the flesh. I knew that he was quite unlike Henry in character and temperament. He liked good living; and wine and women played an important part in his life. Yet there was a certain aestheticism about him which was an intriguing contrast to that side of his nature. He was a great lover of the fine arts.

Bedford was more like Henry in character than Humphrey would ever be—though a pale shadow of him.

I was beginning to think that Humphrey's life was guided by an overweening ambition.

"My lady Queen, my dear sister," he said, taking both my hands and kissing one after another. "This is a grievous time for us both. How sad my heart is for myself . . . and for you."

"You are kind, my lord."

"I would there was something I could do to alleviate the pain you are suffering. Henry was a wonderful husband . . . a wonderful brother. There has never been, nor ever will be another such as he.''

"I believe that to be true. I believe, too, that I must congratulate you on your marriage.''

"You are most kind.''

"I was surprised to hear of it. The King knew nothing of it, I believe.''

"No. It happened after his death.''

"My lord Bedford . . .''

Humphrey raised his eyebrows. "Speak not of it, sweet sister. I have had scolding enough from that quarter.''

"It was a dangerous thing to do, perhaps.''

"But love laughs at danger.''

"Yes, I suppose so. And my kinsman, the Duke of Burgundy, what thinks he of the match?''

"Ranting and raging, I doubt not. Poor little Brabant being his kinsman, Burgundy will have his eyes on Jacqueline's possessions.''

"I daresay you propose to win them back for her.''

He smiled at me and bowed his head. "We shall see what happens,'' he said. "In the meantime I am here on a mission. I looked after our little King well during your absence. Do you agree?''

"Yes, and I thank you.''

"It was a sacred duty. He is an important little boy . . . the most important in the land. He will help you overcome your sorrow, I trust.''

"I know he will, and I am grateful to you for acting as his guardian while I was out of the kingdom.''

"It was a pleasure as well as a duty. If anything had happened to that child, I should have had to answer to the people. They will adore him when they see him.''

"He is too young as yet to be exposed to the people.''

"Oh, give him a taste of it. I'll warrant he'll love to hear the people shout for him. Which brings me to the proposition which I have been commissioned to put to you. Parliament is to be meeting in a week. The Council has decided that the monarch should be present.''

"My baby!''

"Yes, madam. You will drive through the streets of London

with the child on your lap. I can promise you it will be a most affecting sight.''

''But . . . he is too young.''

Gloucester lifted his shoulders. "He is already a king. He will have to grow accustomed to seeing the people. He cannot begin too soon. You will be with him all the time. And . . . it is the wish of the Council. I think you should prepare to come to London.''

I looked at him in dismay. It was clear to me that the peaceful days were over.

So I went to London for the meeting of Parliament, and I rode through the streets seated on what looked like a throne set up on a chariot, and on my lap was my baby son.

How he delighted them! There is nothing like a baby to touch the hearts of the people. They marvelled at him; and indeed he played his part magnificently. I had feared he might scream and cry, but instead he seemed very interested in everything that was going on. Only when the shouts were particularly loud did his little fingers curl more tightly about my hand.

They had dressed him in fine robes, which pleased him. He kept stroking the cloth of gold and velvet and chuckling to himself.

He had quickly grown accustomed to me, and there were times when I thought he knew that I was his mother.

Guillemote said I had weaned his affection from her and that I was the important one with him now. That delighted her as much as it did me. Guillemote was a good woman—a mother to me in my early days and one of the best friends I ever had.

There he sat, my little one, interested in the crowds and music and appearing to listen with solemnity when the proclamations were read out in his name.

I sensed the loyalty of the crowds. Their great hero was dead but he had left them his son who one day would be a great king.

That was the mood of the people that day.

I returned to Windsor, glad to be back but still glowing from my son's triumph in winning the hearts of the people of London.

I felt I was moving away from my sorrow, and if they would allow me to keep my son, I could be happy. But I knew, of course, that that was hardly likely.

For a year I was left in peace—if peace it could be called, to be continually in fear that something could happen at any moment to disrupt it.

I think I was fortunate to be left so long undisturbed. There were reasons, of course.

It has often amazed me how significant a part Humphrey of Gloucester played in my life, for I think it was largely due to him that I was, at this time, left in peace. I do not mean that he arranged it. Humphrey was not the man to concern himself with other people's comfort. But this reckless marriage of his with Jacqueline of Bavaria had caused such anxiety to Bedford and those about him that they could give little thought to anything else.

The King was a baby. He was with his mother and her household, so there was no immediate need for him to be a concern of the State—even though he was King—until he was a little older. His affairs could be dealt with later.

The great trouble was that Jacqueline had been married—still was, some believed—to the Duke of Brabant. Burgundy had arranged that marriage and was eager for those rich provinces which Jacqueline had inherited to remain with the Burgundians. And now Gloucester was threatening to take them.

I knew there was trouble between Bedford and Gloucester and that Bedford said this could never have happened if Henry had lived. He would never have allowed Gloucester to marry Jacqueline while the help of Burgundy was necessary to England. Gloucester had placed that in jeopardy and had done a great disservice to his country.

Gloucester snapped his fingers at Bedford and was, so I heard, planning to take a force to the Continent, not to help his brother consolidate Henry's gains as he should have done but to fight his own little war for the possession of Hainault, Holland, Zealand and Friesland.

In the secrecy of our royal nursery I said to Guillemote: "Perhaps we should be grateful to Gloucester."

She looked at me with an expression in her eyes which told me she was cautioning me.

"I know, I know," I said. "He is undermining England's cause. But let us be frank with each other, dear Guillemote: but for that, they might be turning their attention to us."

She admitted that was so.

"I dread the day when they make their plans. They will take him from me, Guillemote. I could not bear that."

She put her arms about me and patted my back, as she used to in the old days when I myself was little more than a baby. "There," she said. "It has not come to that yet. Let us hope it does not . . . for a long time."

"It will though, Guillemote. Royal children are never left to be happy with their mothers."

"This will be different."

I smiled sadly at her, shaking my head.

"You are with him now. Just forget what may come. Be happy in the moment."

I realized the wisdom of her words and I determined to try to do as she said. For the time being Henry was with me, and Duke Humphrey was pursuing his wildly ambitious plans. They would all be too concerned with him to think very much about Henry.

So I wanted to make each day last as long as I could. But every morning when I awoke I could not help thinking that this might be the day. Then I would dismiss the fear. Not yet . . . not yet. Why, it might be a year before they took some action.

That was my mood during that time. Perhaps that was why I behaved in a rather reckless fashion now and then. I certainly did when I appointed Owen Tudor as Clerk of the Wardrobe, which was a post which would keep him close to me.

"He is very handsome and not much older than you are," said Guillemote, who, over the years, and because she had known me more or less as a baby, often spoke more familiarly to me than the others did.

"What of that?" I said.

She lifted her shoulders and raised her eyes to the ceiling. "You are the Queen," she said.

Was she implying that Owen Tudor was too young and attractive to live so close to the Queen who was perhaps only a little younger than he was?

I laughed at her. Yes, I was indeed reckless. I think it was because I missed Henry. Perhaps I regretted those times when we had been separated while he had pursued a war which had in the end taken him from me altogether. Perhaps it was because I lived in fear of the desolation which would come upon me when they—as they undoubtedly would—brought certain highly born ladies into the nursery to take charge of my son and decided that caring for him was not a suitable occupation for a queen.

Owen's coming into my household brightened my days. He was very sympathetic and understood my anxieties. Young Henry had grown fond of him.

He was now entirely my child. He recognized me as his mother; and I believe there is a special bond between a child and its mother, in spite of early separation. Even with my own mother, whom I hated, there was a certain link. I liked to think that I was especially loved by my son.

He was now taking notice, babbling a few words which Guillemote pretended were "*Maman*" and "*Gee Gee*"—for herself, of course—but I am not sure whether others recognized them as such.

I would walk in the gardens and wish that Henry could have been with me playing under the trees, as any normal child might have done with his mother; but although I was left in peace with him at this time, it must never be forgotten that he was the King and he could never be allowed to go out without his guards.

But at least in the nursery he was living the life of a normal child.

I found myself often looking for my Clerk of the Wardrobe and detaining him that I might chat with him. The strange manner in which he spoke attracted me. He was different from the others about me. I supposed it was because he was not English. Henry had liked him, too. He had rewarded him for his bravery at Agincourt by making him an Esquire of the Body.

I would not admit even to myself that the memory of Henry was fading a little. He had been a good husband; we had lived intimately together; I believed we had loved each other. Yet always for me there had been reservations which I had not recognized at the time, and I was beginning to be aware of them now. Henry had been unreal to me in a way . . . remote . . . a hero . . . someone not quite human, in spite of his earthy conversation and manners—the manners, as he had often said, of a soldier.

He *had* been a hero—the most loved king the English had ever known. Many had said so and many would in the years to come. He had been dedicated to his kingship, and the fact that this great king had emerged from a rather disreputable youth made him something of a mystic figure. I had idealized him with the rest. I had been proud of him. But was that love?

My thoughts were now occupied . . . not with my loss of him but with my fears that my son would be taken away from me.

I felt I did not know myself and that Owen Tudor in his way was helping me to find the person I was.

Sometimes we would sit together and talk. He had a small room in the apartments where he kept his accounts.

One day I went to this room and found him alone. He immediately rose and bowed as I entered.

I said: "Sit down, Owen Tudor." And I sat too so that we faced each other.

"Tell me truly," I said, "how does it feel for a brave warrior to be thus engaged, on boring accounts?"

"My lady, I am happy to be here," he said.

"Perhaps you are . . . as I am . . . tired of war?"

"They were great days under the King."

"They brought about the humiliation of my country."

"But the triumph of the King's armies."

"One country's victory must be another's defeat."

"That is so, my lady."

"Are you sure you do not want to return to fight?"

"I have had my fill of fighting. The King is dead. Having served with the greatest, I would not wish to do so with any less."

"So you will stay here. Perhaps one day you will guard the King and be beside him as you were beside his father."

"Who can say, my lady?"

"I think it would be what my husband, the King, would have wanted. He thought highly of you."

"He was gracious enough to do so."

"Did you not fight bravely with him at Agincourt?"

"It was a great honour to be close to him in that battle."

"He mentioned your name to me. I remember it well."

"And rewarded me, too. Being Esquire of his Body was the greatest honour I had known at that time. There were some who complained that I was too young for the post, but the King said that there were qualities which were of more importance than years. He was a great king, my lady. There was never one like him before, nor ever will be after. That I know. I shall never forget the day he saved his brother's life."

"His brother's life? I did not know of this. Which brother?"

"The Duke of Gloucester, my lady. I was nearby and saw it all. It could have been the end of the Duke. The Duke of Alençon was in command of the enemy, and I saw him strike down the Duke of Gloucester with his own hand. The Duke lay on the ground for a few seconds. He would have been killed, but the King was at hand. He dashed forward and knocked the sword out of Alençon's hands. He saved his brother's life then."

"The Duke must have been thankful to him."

Owen was silent and I went on: "Was he not?"

"It is difficult for a proud man to acknowledge a debt."

"But for a life!"

"That would make him feel even more indebted."

I wanted to pursue the point but Owen would not be drawn into it. He was wise really . . . wiser than I was. He taught me discretion.

These tête-à-têtes were becoming frequent. They were easy to arrange because of his position. I was known to set great store by clothes, and as he was my Wardrobe Clerk I would have a certain amount to say to him. I suppose one of my ladies might have conducted the necessary business but it was not unnatural that I should want to do it myself.

I liked to listen to his musical voice with the accent which was now becoming familiar to me. He was proud of his ancestors with the unpronounceable names. I used to laugh as he reeled them off and I used to make him say them again, syllable by syllable.

How he loved to talk of Wales! I said: "I think your heart is still there, Owen Tudor."

"A man's heart often stays where he first saw the light of day, my lady. And you?"

I shook my head firmly. "No, Owen Tudor. I was very unhappy there. Home! That was the Hôtel de St. Paul. You could not imagine it. Those cold and draughty rooms. Guillemote will tell you. She came to us when we were there. She looked after us . . . poor, hungry, shivering little children. We were kept there by our mother, who lived in luxury with her lover and spent so much on garments, perfumes and little pet animals that there was not enough to feed her children. And all the time there was the fear of that wild man . . . our father . . . who was often chained to his bed in a room more dismal than ours."

I was startled by this outburst. This was no way for a queen to talk to one of her subjects. I stopped abruptly: "I . . . er . . . Forget what I said. I was carried away. It was what you said about one's home. I never had a real home, Owen Tudor. This Windsor . . . with my son . . . is the best home I ever knew."

I left him then. I was too emotional to remain. I sat alone in my apartment. Why had I allowed this to happen . . . to talk so frankly, so intimately . . . to my Clerk of the Wardrobe?

I wanted to tell Guillemote about it. But no. It was something I could not say to anyone. I could not understand it myself.

I insisted that Owen tell me about his family. I loved to hear him talk; he had a love of words and could be carried away by his own rhetoric.

"My sire, my lady," he told me, "was one Meredydd. He lived in Anglesey, that island at the head of wild Wales. He was what is known in those parts as Escheater of Anglesey, and I pray you do not ask what his duties entailed for I cannot tell you. Yet I know this: later he revelled in the post of Scutifer to the Bishop of Bangor, and I can tell you that that was a grand name for butler or steward. He married my mother. She was named Margaret, her father being Dafydd Fychan ap Dafydd Llwyd, which means that he was the son of the last named."

He made me laugh and I was eager to hear more.

"My father Meredydd was a man of wild temper. If a word was uttered against him that did not please him, it would be his hand to his sword. I do not believe any were surprised when he killed a man."

"Owen Tudor!"

"Alas, 'tis true, my lady. 'Twas before I entered this world. Perforce he fled to the mountains taking Margaret with him, and there in the shadow of great Snowdon, I was born."

"And you left Wales to come and serve the King?"

"There I had good fortune. Look you, is it not so? A man knows this one . . . knows that one . . . and that can be another step up the ladder to fame. My father's mother was a connection of the great Owen Glendower who was of some use to England. His own son, in time, entered King Henry's army and so brought me to it."

"So that is how you came to be with us?"

He looked at me earnestly and murmured: " 'Twas the greatest good fortune I have ever known, my lady."

"I am pleased. I often think that a warrior such as you will want to be off again . . . fighting."

"My lady, I am more content here than I have ever been before."

It was fulsome. But he was Welsh, I reminded myself. He had a poetic soul and might sometimes choose words for their musical sound rather than because they expressed the truth.

But I continued to look forward to our meetings; and they took my mind away, now and then, from the haunting fear that I might lose my son.

Margaret, Duchess of Clarence, was with me again, and I was delighted to see her, particularly as she brought with her her charming daughter of her first marriage, Jane.

Margaret was happier than she had been at our last meeting when she was mourning her husband. Now she had settled down to a life of widowhood and I could see that the centre of that life was her daughter.

I found a great pleasure in their company. I, myself, was fast recovering from the shock of Henry's death, and my nightly prayers were that I should continue in this state.

There was another visitor to Windsor. This was James I of Scotland.

It was not quite true to call James a prisoner in the ordinary sense. He was just being held in England until such time as the Scots paid his ransom.

James was a delightful companion. I had liked him from the moment I met him. I felt I knew him fairly well for he had been with us on our triumphant entry into Paris. Henry had taken him to France in the hope that he would be able to persuade the Scots there not to fight for the French. I believe he had not been very successful in this; but James himself had fought side by side with Henry in several battles and I could not believe that for one moment he saw himself as an enemy. He had been in exile for so long. I think at this time it was nineteen years. But he had always been treated as royalty. The only difference was that his liberty was curtailed. For instance, he could not ride out and return to Scotland. I had a sneaking notion that he had no desire to. Conditions above the border were somewhat harsh compared with the south; and while he was treated in a royal manner, I supposed James felt no restraint—or very little—in not being allowed complete freedom. He was happy enough to be in England. In any case, he never showed any nostalgia for his native land to my knowledge—in fact, he could scarcely have remembered it, for he was about ten years old, I believe, when he had been captured.

He had lived hardly any of his life in Scotland, for he told me that when he was eight years old he had been put into the care of the Earl of Northumberland to learn the manly arts and for a while was educated with the Earl's grandson, who later became known as "Henry Hotspur."

It was another case of a minor being too young to take over the government of his country; and his old, sick father decided he would send his young son to France for safety. His efforts failed, for the ship in which James was being taken was intercepted by the English; and that was how James came to be a prisoner awaiting the ransom to be paid.

He was writing a long poem about his life which he called *The King's Quair*, and he used to read extracts from it to us which we found both moving and entertaining.

So I grew very fond of James and hoped we should go on enjoying the peaceful days together for a long time.

It was inevitable that, as they were both at Windsor, one day James should meet Jane.

I remember the occasion vividly. James was in my apartment and we were looking down on the gardens as we chatted. Suddenly Jane came into view.

She looked up at the window and, seeing me with the King of Scotland, she bowed her head; then she looked up again and smiled.

"What a beautiful girl!" said James.

"Yes, is she not."

"Who is she?"

"She is the daughter of the Duchess of Clarence. Her father was John Beaufort, the Earl of Somerset."

"Oh . . . a Beaufort."

"Yes. The Duchess's first husband. Poor Margaret, she has been twice widowed."

"Yes," he said. "It is sad for her."

At the earliest possible moment I presented Jane to him. James was clearly bemused. I was not sure of Jane. She was perhaps more in command of her feelings. They talked together for some time and I noticed that his eyes never left her face.

I fancied a certain radiance had touched her too. It was rather charming to see the effect those two had on each other.

I talked to Margaret about them.

"I think there is no doubt that James is falling love with Jane . . . or, more likely, has already fallen."

"I trust that is not so."

"But why, Margaret? I should like to see James happy. Poor young man! Think of his being a prisoner for nineteen years."

"It has been a very comfortable prison."

"If Jane married him, she would be Queen of Scotland."

"A queen without a crown . . . a queen without a throne."

"If the ransom were paid, he would return to Scotland."

"They say it is a barbaric land, and the ransom will never be paid."

"James does not seem barbaric, and the ransom will surely be paid one day."

"He has been brought up in England."

"Margaret, I thought you would rejoice. I think it is wonderful to see two young people so happy. If they are in love, they should be allowed to marry."

"Well," said Margaret. "It has not yet come to that."

I watched the courtship grow. This was love . . . true love. It was something I had missed. Henry had never been like that.

I could see it all clearly now. He had been kind to me . . . gentle . . . loving . . . but it was not love such as the King of Scotland had for Jane Beaufort. I felt envious. I would have given a great deal to be loved like that.

They talked to me about it.

"We are going to marry," James said firmly.

"Then I wish you all the happiness in the world," I told them.

Jane embraced me. "Nothing will change our minds," she said. "They can forbid us as much as they like . . . we will marry. We have made up our minds."

"You will," I said. "But do not do anything rash just yet. Surely the King's ransom must be paid."

"Surely soon," said James.

Margaret was less optimistic.

"Will they pay his ransom after all these years? It must be

nearly twenty now . . . just because he has fallen in love with an English girl?''

"They must want their king back."

"After all these years? You can depend on it—for every one who wants him back, there will be two against it."

"Why are you so pessimistic, Margaret? Let us hope."

And so the golden days slipped by.

Trouble with Burgundy through Humphrey's marriage continued to hold the attention of those who might otherwise turn it to the education of my son, which was a blessing to me. And here in Windsor I had Henry to love and to cherish and I could watch the growing love and courtship of Jane Beaufort and the King of Scotland. And there was Owen.

Happy days when I could forget the shadow hanging over me.

The summer was passing. I lived through the golden days treasuring each one as though it might be the last. I watched with mixed emotions the progress of my son. Each day he seemed to change; he would soon pass out of babyhood. They would be made aware of that passing and they would take him from me. He was now taking a few uncertain steps. Guillemote and I would stand him on the floor, a few paces from each of us, and he would take his tottering steps before stumbling into our arms. We clapped our hands in rapturous applause and he would clap with us, his face a picture of delight. There were happy moments like that to be treasured and I knew I should remember them for ever.

Humphrey of Gloucester remained in conflict with the Duke of Burgundy, much to the chagrin of the Duke of Bedford. But I was not thinking very much of that at this stage. I was immersed in my happy days at Windsor, watching the ever-growing love between James and Jane—and envying them.

James was becoming an impatient lover. There was nothing he wanted so much as marriage with Jane. I was deeply aware of his single-mindedness. For him there was one goal. How lucky Jane was to be loved like that!

He talked to me about it.

"I must be recalled to my kingdom," he said. "I must have a home to offer Jane."

"I am sure Jane would be happy to marry a poor prisoner," I replied.

"I know. It is so with us both. There is nothing . . . nothing but each other."

I said: "Such love is rare with kings."

"A king can love as wholeheartedly as a shepherd."

"I know, James. You have shown me that. I wish I could help you."

"I have an idea."

"Tell me."

"My countrymen have always been a thorn in the flesh of the English. Now some of them are in France . . . and of course they are fighting with the French."

"Well?"

"What if I promised to withdraw them all if they would send me back to Scotland?"

"Could you?"

"I could try."

"They would still demand the ransom."

"Perhaps my countrymen would agree to that."

"You are of an age now to govern. Do you think they will like you? You have been here so long that you are more English than Scot."

"I can play the Scot at a moment's notice."

I laughed at him. "What do you propose to do?" I asked.

"Offer to recall all Scotsmen from France, for one thing."

"Try it."

It was about a week later when he came to me in triumph.

"Thomas of Myrton has left for Scotland," he told me.

"They have sent your chaplain."

"He seemed a good man to send."

"And you think he will succeed in making terms for your release?"

"I have told him he must. I want to go back . . . with Jane as my Queen, and that is what I am going to do, Katherine."

"I shall pray for you, James."

"And your prayers will be answered, I know."

"There are some times when I am sure that if one believes fervently that something will come . . . it does."

A few months elapsed before Thomas of Myrton returned from Scotland, but when he did, it became clear that his journey had not been in vain.

James was beside himself with joy.

"It is going to be!" he shouted.

Jane was with him and they both hugged me. All my ladies gathered round, ceremony forgotten. Everyone was kissing everyone else.

"Listen to me," said James. "It is true. The treaty has been signed. It was done in York between the Scots and the English. The English drove a hard bargain but my countrymen accepted it. Sixty thousand marks paid in instalments of 10,000 over six years. Am I worth it, do you think?"

Jane smiled at him, her eyes shining with joy. "Every mark," she assured him, "and more."

"Assuredly so," he cried. "And the Scots are prepared to pay it! Oh, yes, I repeat, your country drives a hard bargain, Jane. All the Scottish troops are to be withdrawn from France. So that we must try to do. And here is the best part. It is hoped that I will marry an English lady of noble birth."

Everyone laughed and clapped their hands.

"And what did you reply to that?" I asked him.

"I replied that I would do so with the utmost pleasure. And . . . here she is. I have already found her. I am determined to take her, and no one else in the world will do for me."

It was a solemn moment as the lovers clasped hands and gazed soulfully at each other. We were all silent, watching them.

Then the laughter rang out.

"This," said James, "is the happiest moment of my life. But . . . there is better to come."

Oh, to be happy like that! To be loved for oneself . . . and not for a crown. How I envied those lovers!

I thought that everyone in the castle must.

I went into the wardrobe room. Owen was sitting at a table writing.

"Have you heard the news about the King of Scotland?" I asked.

Owen said he had not.

"You will. The whole Court will be talking about it. He is a very happy man today. Do you know, a treaty has been signed between the Scots and the English? He is going back to Scotland with the Lady Jane."

"That is wonderful news," said Owen. "Indeed, the King of Scotland must this day be a very happy man."

"Happiness shines out of them both. I am afraid I am a little envious of them."

"All the world is envious of lovers."

"You too?"

"Everyone, madam."

"I am ashamed of myself."

"Your Grace should not be."

"But I am, Owen. I say to myself, why should this happen to them when I . . . oh . . . I think Jane Beaufort is one of the truly fortunate women."

He was standing before me, and suddenly he put out his hand and touched mine.

"I understand," he said.

I said in an embarrassed voice: "You see . . . I was never loved wholeheartedly. Henry loved his battles more."

"He was a great king."

"James is a king."

"It is different."

I shook my head. "No, Owen, it is just true love and . . . half love. That is the difference. I have never been loved as Jane is. I have never been loved as my little Henry is loved. My mother gave me no love. I and my brothers and sisters were just encumbrances in her life to be sent off to live in near squalor . . . out of her life . . . out of her thoughts. We were of no importance to her. Then I was married and I was happy. I had dreams . . . but dreams are . . . only dreams. What was I to Henry? A means of bringing harmony between our two countries . . . a line in a treaty."

"It was not so," said Owen. "He cared for you deeply."

"He cared for his conquests more. James cares nothing for anything but Jane. That is how I would be loved."

Then he said a strange thing! "My lady, perhaps you are."

I looked at him in silence. Then suddenly he bowed and, turning, left me alone in that room.

After that I thought a great deal about Owen. It would be foolish of me to pretend I did not know he harboured a special feeling towards me, as I did to him. I was content with my life as it was at this time. I wanted it to go on and on. I wanted Henry to remain a baby while I went on seeing Owen frequently.

It was absurd, of course. Owen was a handsome young man

about my own age; he was brave, good, kind, understanding and clever. But what was he? A squire from some wild country beyond the borders. I did not know very much about the geography of my new country, but I had heard that there were certain remote parts which gave trouble from time to time and that they were inhabited by races not entirely English.

I wanted to learn more about the Welsh.

Guillemote, because she had actually come with me from France and was French herself, understood me well and, being inclined to speak more frankly to me than the others, plucked up courage to comment on what was becoming obvious to them all.

"Do you think you see a little too much of your Wardrobe Clerk?" she asked.

"Owen Tudor!" I cried, taken off my guard.

"That was the man I was thinking of, my lady."

"See too much of him! But there are certain matters which I have to discuss with him."

"They seem to be very long and animated conversations."

"I think, Guillemote, that you are . . ."

"Forgetting my place. Forgetting that I am speaking to the Queen. Oh, I know what you mean. But I do not forget also that I looked after you as a baby. Who was it you came to when you cut your knees . . . when you saw bogeys in the night? Tell me that. It was Guillemote. You may be a great queen but you are still my little one . . . to me. And let me tell you this, there are greater dangers when you grow up, my lady. And when I see you walking into them, I shall say so . . . and if that means stepping out of place . . . if it means talking to the Queen as though she is a child . . . then I will talk."

I smiled at her lovingly—Guillemote, my comfort in the dark days in that dismal and often frightening Hôtel, Guillemote who had come into my bed to cuddle me and keep me warm, Guillemote who, I think, would have given her life for me.

"I'm sorry, Guillemote," I said. "I know you love me. I know that everything you do is for my good. You do not have to tell me that, Guillemote."

"So now I will speak. It is true that you are shut away at Windsor. But people notice. They say how friendly you are becoming with the Clerk of the Wardrobe. Do you need to talk so much of silks and brocades? He is a very handsome young man, and his manner . . . and yours . . . is not quite that of a queen and her wardrobe clerk.''

''I like the man, Guillemote.''

''That much we know.''

''I find him interesting to talk to. He comes from a fascinating background. I did not know anything about the Welsh until I came to this country.''

''There are other ways of learning. I think of you as my little one still. You have always been precious to me. If I saw you running into danger, I would be after you. I would take you up in my arms . . .''

''I know, Guillemote, but I am not a child any more.''

''No. You are not a little princess. You are on more dangerous ground. You are a queen . . . and a queen in a strange land.''

''It is my land now, Guillemote. I became the queen of this country because my husband was king and now I am still a queen.''

''That is what I say. So take care.''

''Why should you see danger, Guillemote?''

''Because I know you well. When you talk of that man I hear in your voice and I see in your eyes . . . what he is becoming to you.''

''I admit, I enjoy talking to him.''

''That is clear to see.''

My lips quivered as she put her arms round me. She rocked me to and fro as she used to do when I was a child.

''I understand . . . I understand,'' she murmured. ''But you must take care. A queen could never mate with a wardrobe clerk, and a Welsh one at that.''

''What does his country matter?''

She shrugged her shoulders.

I went on: ''I did not know of these other races here. I thought they were all English. We did not hear of the Welsh in France.''

''There is much we did not hear of. And it is not only the Welsh in him. Think of it. He is a soldier from nowhere. What could come of this? Nothing . . . nothing . . . but misery. That is why I say, dear Princess, my dear, dear Queen, take care.''

I put my arms about her and clung to her for a few seconds. Then I withdrew myself.

''What are you thinking of, Guillemote? How could you ever think I would have such a thing in mind!''

She looked relieved. "It was silly of me. Of course you would not. It was merely that . . . oh yes, it was foolish of me."

"Guillemote," I said, "we will forget this nonsense."

I knew the peaceful days must soon come to an end.

It was a year since Henry had sat on my lap and we had ridden through the streets of London. I often smiled to remember how quiet and solemn he had been, listening with what seemed like pleasure to the shouts of the people.

There came a message from the Council. The King's presence would be needed at the opening of the Parliament.

He was now nearly two years old and had grown considerably since he had made his first public appearance. He was not the docile infant he had been.

Preparations to leave for London began.

I did not see Owen Tudor before we left. I had avoided him after my conversation with Guillemote.

Her remarks had made me assess my feelings more honestly. I saw that I had allowed myself to slip into a very pleasant relationship without realizing that it would be noticed and might be misconstrued by those about me.

It had been so comforting to be with him, to discover something of his background and to talk to him about my early life and his. He had listened with great attention and sympathy and made me see those days less grimly than I had before. I would find something to laugh at, though previously I should have thought that impossible.

We were young. Twenty-one or -two is the age for gaiety and romance. Two people as we were, put together, with similar tastes, must be attracted to each other . . . and such attraction could quickly strengthen into something deeper.

Yes. I was in love with Owen Tudor, if being in love means a lifting of the spirits when a certain person appears, of wanting to be with him above all else, of feeling completely at one with him, wanting to reach out and touch him, to be close to him and never go away.

Yes, that summed up my feelings—but I was the Queen and he was a humble soldier from the remote country of Wales.

Guillemote was right. I should be watchful of myself. More than that . . . a wise woman would send him away . . . right away . . . out of Windsor . . . out of the household.

Send him away! Give the impression that I no longer wanted him in my household, when he had made Windsor such a happy place for me!

Of one thing I was certain. Wise or not, I was not going to send Owen away.

In the meantime I had to consider the journey to London. I was afraid. They would realize that Henry was growing up and that it was time they took him out of his mother's care.

He was my child. I had borne him. Why should I allow them to wrest him from me? I wanted to keep him with me. I wanted to keep Owen with me . . . to go on as we had been.

We left on Saturday 13 November. I remember the day—dark, gloomy, typical November with a mist in the air. I always felt there was something ominous about mists. I remembered the last occasion. The weather had been similar then.

Henry was quite happy. He was with me and was interested in everything he saw.

I think he was forward for his age. He babbled a lot and could say a few words, and one of these was a decisive "no" when something was done which he did not like.

But he enjoyed the journey, sitting on my lap as we rode along.

We spent the first night at Staines, and he awoke next morning in a bad mood. Where were his familiar surroundings? Where was Guillemote?

I said: "We are going to have a great deal of fun. We are going to open Parliament."

He was dressed with difficulty, protesting all the time, and when he was taken out to the litter, in which we were to make the journey to London, he screamed and kicked out at everyone who approached him, except me. And me he regarded with reproachful eyes.

"No, no, no," he said emphatically.

He kicked and struggled when it was attempted to lift him into the litter.

We could not very well travel through the villages where the people would come out to see him and discover that their little King was a bawling and protesting child.

There was a hurried conversation. It was decided that it would be better not to leave and that we should, therefore, stay another day in Staines.

One of the guards came to me and said, ''My lady, it is the Sabbath Day. We believe it is because of this that the King refuses to travel.''

I stared at him in amazement. Could he really believe that Henry was aware of what day it was?

He said, ''They are saying, my lady, that he is going to be a great and pious king and as such he will believe in keeping the Sabbath holy.''

My scowling and red-faced infant looked anything but pious to me; but I was glad they had construed his behavior in this way and thought it better not to raise contradictions.

So that day was spent at Staines. I was dreading the next for fear of more tantrums, but Henry awoke in a sunny mood. He chuckled with glee when he was being prepared, and his mood did not change when it was time for him to get into the litter with me. He held my hand firmly and allowed himself to be placed in it, smiling the while.

His demeanour confirmed the belief that his anger had been because they were trying to make him travel on the Sabbath Day; and thus the rumour of his pious destiny was first founded.

The rest of the journey was uneventful. He was interested in everything. He laughed and I taught him to wave at the people, which naturally delighted them.

We had another stop at Kennington, and it was Wednesday when we rode to Parliament. Henry was dressed in a gown of crimson velvet and wore a cap of the same material. On the cap was set a crown—very small, to fit his little head. He was very interested in this and kept putting up a hand to touch it proudly. They had given him a tiny sceptre to hold, which drew his attention from the crown.

The occasion was a great success. He played his part well, showing an interest in the people and now and then saying a word or two in his baby language. He raised his hand in acknowledgement of the cheers and waved to the people.

They adored him.

''God bless our little King!'' they shouted; and even his father, returning as the triumphant conqueror, could scarcely have received a more enthusiastic welcome from the citizens of London.

This impeccable behaviour continued throughout the ceremony.

He appeared to listen to the speeches with great solemnity, staring at the faces of the speakers and now and then giving a little grunt or crow as though in acquiescence.

He was a great success and I was proud of him, though at the same time very uneasy. They would be more than ever reminded that he was growing up, and that was what I most dreaded.

Soon after the opening of Parliament we left Westminster. I was conducted to Waltham Palace, where I stayed for a few days and nights and from there went to Hertford. It was not Windsor but it was almost as good, for I found my household assembled there waiting to welcome me. And among them was Owen.

When they all greeted me, he looked at me with such love and longing in his eyes that I could no longer be blind to his feelings for me; and my own response would have told me—if I had not known already—that I returned his love.

We were to spend Christmas at Hertford, which was an indication of what was to come, for this had already been decided for us and was not of my choosing. I knew that those who had chosen would now determine how and where the King should be brought up and were reminding me that they had not forgotten their duty.

I felt a certain feverish excitement that Christmas, I was on the brink of change. Poor Guillemote, she would suffer with me. We had to console ourselves. I would not think beyond this Christmas.

Guillemote said: "They may take him away, yes. But we shall still see him. You are his mother. He will ask for us . . . he will cry for us. They cannot deny the King his wishes. This has happened to all queens. They are never allowed to bring up their children after the manner of humble women."

"The fact that it has happened before and to us all does not make it any easier to bear, Guillemote."

She shook her head sadly. Then she looked intently at me. She knew me so well, and knew that I could not help thinking of Owen.

It was then that the thought came into my mind: I will not lose everything.

James of Scotland joined the household with the Duchess of Clarence and her daughter Jane. We were all caught up in the excitement of the coming wedding. The lovers lived in a dream of happiness which was wonderful to share in. And I did share it. I was uplifted by the knowledge that I too was loved.

I said to James: "How well everything has turned out. It is like a miracle."

He agreed. "It was worth being a captive all those years to come to this. For think you, if it had not been so, I should never have met Jane."

"And that makes everything that has gone before worthwhile for you?"

He looked at me, astonished that I could ask such a question.

"But indeed it does. To think that, if I had not been taken a prisoner by the English all those years ago, I might well have been in Scotland now, separated from Jane by hundreds of miles . . . never knowing the one woman in the world for me existed. Can you imagine a greater tragedy?"

"Perhaps, if you had never known Jane existed, you would not have missed her."

"What a travesty of life that would have been!"

"So you would stay a prisoner if it was the only way you could be with her?"

"I would rather be in the darkest dungeon with her than on the grandest throne without her."

That is love, I thought. And when it comes it must be taken with both hands. It is only fools who turn their backs on love.

I was not entirely surprised when Richard Beauchamp, Earl of Warwick, called at Hertford to see me.

I had met him on other occasions. Henry had mentioned him to me with respect and affection; and moreover, Warwick had been in France at the time of our marriage and had taken part in my coronation.

Henry had said to me: "There is a man whom I can trust. Such men I keep close to me. I feel blessed that there are men like Warwick at my side."

And I had always thought that Warwick deserved his confidence.

He kissed my hand and thanked me for receiving him so graciously, while I tried to remain calm, though guessing what he had come for made that difficult.

My fears were soon realized.

He said, "My lady, you will know that I was honoured by

the late King's confidence, and to me he left the greatest of all tasks—the care and education of his son, our gracious King Henry VI.''

I bowed my head in acknowledgement.

''Your Grace has been in deep mourning this last year and I know that you have derived much comfort from living quietly with our dear lord, your son, who is very young yet.''

''That is so,'' I said. ''He is a baby still and needs his mother.''

''It was noticed with what regal dignity he conducted himself at Westminster.''

I thought of the screaming infant who had manifested his disapproval at Staines by noisy and scarcely regal protestations. Henry was a baby, in spite of the miniature crown they had set upon his head.

The Earl went on: ''It is time he was given his own household. He must begin to learn that he has a great position to fill.''

''I think he is hardly of an age to realize what that means.''

''It is never too early to begin to learn. The late King entrusted me with his upbringing and education and I am determined to do my duty in a manner which would have had his approval.''

''I understand this, but he is . . . as yet . . . very young.''

''Responsibility descends early on royal heads, my lady. I have engaged for him a nurse in the person of one Joan Astley. A very worthy lady, the wife of Thomas Astley. She is well experienced with children and will be a careful and a loving nurse.''

''My woman Guillemote has looked after my son with the utmost loving care and he is very fond of her.''

''I am sure of that, my lady. But the King must have a qualified nurse and one who has the approval of the Council and myself.''

I knew it was hopeless. He had had my husband's commands to form my son's household, and in the eyes of these men, the matter of great importance was not that little Henry be surrounded by those who loved him but that he learn how to be a king.

I should have been prepared. I knew it had to come. I had in fact been expecting it all through the year. Yet I felt stunned.

Whatever they said, whatever I tried to do, they were going to take him away from me.

I heard myself stammer: "This . . . Joan Astley . . . she is . . . er . . . kind . . . ?"

"She will know exactly how to treat the King."

"The King is but a child. He needs his mother."

The Earl smiled at me benignly. "The King will have great responsibility. He cannot shelter forever in the loving arms of his mother."

"In a year or so . . . perhaps."

"The King is no longer a baby."

What was the use? I felt angry. Why should some hard-headed man who knew nothing about the ties between a mother and her child decide our lives for us? My baby might be—rather sadly— a king, but he was only a child . . . my child. I wanted to rage and storm at this man who was smiling so confidently, sure that he knew what was best for my child.

"Mrs. Astley will be arriving within a few weeks," he went on. "And, of course, equally important is his governess. I have chosen Dame Alice Butler . . . a most worthy lady."

"You mean . . . she will be in charge of his household?"

He smiled and inclined his head.

I felt limp with dismay and anger. I knew that the Earl was only following custom. I knew it was the fate of all queens to lose their babies in this way . . . but that did not make it any easier to bear.

I wanted to shout: "No, I will not allow it."

Wild plans were forming in my mind. I would run away. Guillemote and I would take Henry and find some humble place in which we could live in peace.

How foolish of me! I should have known that they would choose for me. They were going to take my baby away from me. Some would say I had been fortunate to have had him to myself for so long.

The Earl may have had a glimmer of understanding, for he was not an unkindly man, merely insensitive to a mother's emotions.

"Your Grace will be highly satisfied with the ladies whom I have chosen," he said. "They will be kind yet firm . . . exactly what his Grace the King needs. The Council have decided that, in view of the very important posts they hold, they shall be highly paid. In fact I can tell you that their salaries will be £40 a year, which is equal to the salary of a Privy Councillor. So you see, my lady, what importance has been attached to this matter. We are giving Dame Alice permission to chastise the King if that should be necessary.''

I cried out in alarm: ''No!''

The Earl looked at me almost pityingly. ''It is considered necessary for most children at some time. It will just be a little light punishment to teach the difference between right and wrong.''

I felt in despair. Facing it was even worse than I had imagined.

He went on: ''The King will have his own Court and children of his own age—heirs to baronies and so on—to be brought up with him. So he will not lack company.''

No, I thought bitterly, except that of his mother!

''The King's Court will become an academy for the young nobility which seems a highly satisfactory arrangement.''

I was too emotional to trust myself to speak.

''Your Grace will find that the Council has been equally assiduous in its care for you. All the dower palaces will be at your disposal, the only exceptions being Havering and Langley, which, as your Grace knows, are in the possession of Queen Joanna, widow of the late King's father, King Henry IV.''

I was not listening. All I could think was: it is as I feared. I have lost my son.

With a heavy heart I travelled to Southwark for the marriage of James and Jane.

How I envied them! They would be setting out on a new life. My ladies had shivered at the thought of the Court of Scotland and wondered how James would be received after spending so long away from his native land.

''It will be different,'' said Joanna Courcy, ''for there is no doubt that we are different from the Scots.''

''They are his people,'' insisted Guillemote, ''and blood is strong.''

''But he has become one of us,'' said Agnes.

''Have no fear,'' I told them. ''He has Jane, and while they are together, they will be happy.''

They all sighed and I guessed they were thinking, with a little envy—as I was, of the lovers.

They were so radiantly happy, and as soon as the wedding was over they would set out for Scotland.

It was a very impressive ceremony, held in the church of St. Mary Overy, and immediately afterwards we adjourned to the adjacent palace, which belonged to Henry Beaufort, Bishop of Winchester. He was Jane's uncle and delighted, of course, that she was marrying into the royal House of Scotland. The Bishop was one of the richest men in England, for he was the second son of John of Gaunt, Duke of Lancaster, and Katherine Swynford, although the Duke had married Winchester's mother after his birth and he, with his siblings, had been legitimized by Henry IV.

I was watchful of Winchester during the banquet. I had heard a great deal about his quarrel with the Duke of Gloucester, and I knew that the two were declared enemies and that, if Henry had been living, he would have taken sides with the Bishop against his own brother.

Gloucester wanted power. His life-long regret was that he had not been born the eldest son. For a man such as he, to be the youngest was a tragedy . . . for him, but not indeed for the country.

I did not know a great deal about politics but I was aware that Gloucester's schemes were all for self-aggrandisement and that Winchester, in spite of his reputation for being haughty, arrogant and in his opinion as royal as the King, was a man of intellectual brilliance; and he did realize the importance of putting the country first.

I remembered Henry's once saying: ''A man may be what he wishes if he does but remember that he is an Englishman and owes his first allegiance to England.''

I felt sure Winchester did that.

I watched him at that time, presiding at the feast. All those things which had been said of him I felt to be true; and I firmly believed that Humphrey, with his wildly ambitious schemes, would be no match for him.

Margaret, Duchess of Clarence, was beside me. It was with great emotion that she had watched her daughter married to the King of Scotland.

I took her hand and pressed it.

I whispered to her: "I never saw two people so radiantly happy as those two."

She smiled and nodded.

I returned to Hertford. They were already preparing to move the King's household to Eltham.

I went into the nursery to look at him. He was asleep. I watched him in silence, and Guillemote came to stand beside me.

"Soon he will be gone away," I said.

"Yes," she answered.

"How can they do this to us?" I demanded.

"It is the custom and we knew it had to come."

I did not answer.

"They will be kind to him," she went on. "I have spoken to Mrs. Astley. She seems a good woman, overawed by her task. I think he will like her."

"He will cry for us, Guillemote."

"I hope not too much. He is interested in everything around him. There will be his new surroundings . . . new people."

"You do not think he will forget us, Guillemote?"

"Oh, no, no, no. But I hope he will not think of us too often . . . just at first . . ."

I stooped and kissed him. There would not be many more times when I could steal into his bedroom and see him thus informally . . . yet it was a blessing any peasant woman might have enjoyed with her son . . . day or night.

Who would be born royal?

Poor Margaret had her moods of sadness, too.

She said: "It was a beautiful ceremony; and Jane looked so happy, did she not?"

"Jane looked wonderful."

"She was always first with me. I loved her more than I ever loved anyone else . . . from the moment she was born."

"I know," I said.

"And now . . . she has gone. I may never see her again."

"You will travel to Scotland. It is not so very far. And they will visit the Court here."

She shook her head.

"You must not be sad, Margaret," I said. "Think of Jane.

She is happy. I never saw two people so happy in the whole of my life. Remember her as she was at her wedding, Margaret.''

''I do. We both know that one of the tragedies of a noble-woman's life is that she must lose her children. Why do they envy us . . . those tillers of the soil . . . those peasants? I know they must work hard for their livings but they have their families about them. Ours are taken from us to be brought up in other houses . . .''

I put my hand over my eyes and she cried: ''Oh, forgive me, Katherine. I am selfish. Jane is happy. It is what she wanted.''

''Yes, Margaret,'' I said. ''And they are going to take my baby from me. They are going to bring him up as a king . . . which they say a mother cannot do. They are setting up others to take care of him . . . those who can make of him a king.''

She put her arms about me and we wept together.

It was no use telling myself that what I suffered had been en-dured by every queen before me. I was going to lose my baby.

Guillemote had tried to comfort me. I should not lose him entirely. I could see him often. I was his mother, was I not? He would want to see me. He would demand it.

We smiled together and I was remembering the storms when he had refused to leave Staines in the litter. He would want to see his mother and he would demand to.

I thought of Dame Alice Butler, who had ''the power to chas-tise.'' Oh, no, I could not bear that.

I sent for Owen. I had to see him. I wanted to talk to him. I thought that he alone at this time could give me comfort.

He came and stood respectfully before me.

I said: ''As you know, we shall be leaving here soon. The King is going to have his own household which . . . is what I have been expecting for some time. It will be soon. They are making plans now. I shall need . . . some new gowns.''

I faltered. It was useless to pretend I had sent for him to discuss purchases of material. I was horrified to find that my eyes were filled with tears. I said: ''They are taking him away from me, Owen. My baby . . . he will be without his mother . . . without Guillemote . . .''

''They say that Mrs. Astley understands children well. The King has already seen her. He seems to like her . . .''

"He will want his mother . . . and his mother . . . she will want him."

He knelt before me and, suddenly taking my hand, kissed it.

"I should be brave," I said. "I knew it had to come. For months I have been dreading it. They left us alone together longer than I expected. But now it has come. Very soon they will take him away. He will be as a stranger to me."

"He will never be that."

"Others will be around him. They will teach him to forget his mother. There will be others to take my place."

"I think a child never forgets his mother, my lady."

"But I shall not see him, Owen. I shall be alone."

He put my hand to his lips and kept it there.

I went on: "The King of Scotland has left now . . . taking Lady Jane with him. They are so happy. They did not mind leaving us in the least, though they were kind enough to say they would miss us. But they want nothing more than each other. Oh, how I envy them! To love like that and to be loved. It seems to them that all the world is smiling at them. Her mother wept because she had lost her, but she was proud, I think. The Bishop was there . . . the Bishop of Winchester. He is very grand, handsome, dignified . . . and so royal . . ."

"Well, is he not, my lady, the son of the great John of Gaunt?"

"Legitimized by his loving half-brother . . . my husband's father."

"He was a wise king. He knew that it is better to have certain people with him than against him."

"The Bishop indeed looked worthy of his royalty. He was pleased by the marriage. Everyone was pleased. What perfection . . . to love like that and to have everyone smiling approval."

"Methinks they would have been happy without the approval."

I looked at him earnestly. I felt there was something he wished to say and dared not. I knew that I should have to be the one to put away pretence, stop hiding behind conventions and speak the truth.

"Do you really think they would have been, Owen?" I asked.

"I am sure of it. With them it was true love. Who could doubt that?"

I shook my head. "No," I said. "I do not doubt it. And they would be right."

It was enough. It was the spark which set light to the fire.

We stood close, smiling at each other. There was no need for words in that moment. His arms were about me and he held me tightly.

Then I heard him say: "For so long I have loved you, Katherine . . . Queen of England."

And I replied: "I love you too, Owen Tudor."

That night we became lovers. It was reckless. I am amazed now, looking back, at our courage. I was in a state of despair. I was going to lose my child. I was not the sort of woman who could live without a husband. Moreover, I was in love. This was different from what I had experienced with Henry. I had believed I was in love with him. I had been fond of him. I had found life with him fulfilling to a certain extent, even enjoyable. But it could not be compared with the feelings I experienced with Owen.

This was reckless love . . . love which refused to be denied, which had not been arranged for the benefits it would bring to both sides in a war. This was different. This was dangerous, unsanctified love . . . love which was so overwhelming as to be irresistible.

And having tasted it, there was no going back.

He told me how he had loved me from the beginning, how he had contemplated asking that he might be relieved of his post, and how he could not bring himself to do that.

I listened avidly, drinking in every word, revelling in this wild passion which I vowed I would never lose.

It was my due. It was the due of every woman. They had taken my child from me; they should not deny me my lover.

We were both fully aware of the dangers.

"I have good and faithful women about me," I told him. "They would never betray me."

"You are too gentle, my love, too trusting. You expect everyone to be as kind and good as you are."

"Dear Owen," I assured him, "I can trust my Joannas and Agnes, and Guillemote would die rather than betray me."

"I have noticed their devotion and have often rejoiced in it."

We talked of little that night but our love for each other . . . how it delighted and alarmed us at the same time.

"No one can love where people want them to because it is convenient," I said. "Love is not like that. It is there . . . one does not say it is suitable . . . therefore we will love."

"You have suffered so much," he said.

"My dear Owen, all our troubles will be shared from now on."

"Katherine . . . is it possible . . . do you think . . . ?"

"Have I a timid lover?"

"Not timid . . . the only anxiety I have is what trouble this may bring to you."

I put my fingers over his lips.

"I will not listen to such talk," I said. "For tonight in any case we are together. It is wonderful. At last we have broken through the barriers of convention and admitted our love. Nothing must spoil this night."

Nor did it. That was for later. On this night we had found each other.

That was enough.

Dangerous Love

I knew I had changed. I knew that Agnes and the Joannas looked at me incredulously and that there was a hint of fear in Guillemote's eyes.

But they said nothing. Nor did I.

I was happy . . . as happy as Jane on her journey to Scotland. I was happy as I had never thought to be in the whole of my life.

I could think of nothing but Owen. I wanted to hear about his life, of those early days in Wales. I wanted to hear about Cadwaladr, an ancient ancestor who had defended Wales from King Henry II. I wanted to hear more of his father, the outlaw, who had fled from the neighbourhood when he had killed a man. It all seemed so wildly romantic and I loved to hear him recount those stories in his beautiful musical voice.

I was obsessed by Owen.

"We must not show our feelings," he warned me.

"You must not look at me as you do when people are present," I admonished him.

"Do you not like it?"

"I adore it. No, no, forget what I said. I care not. Please look at me like that."

"How do I look at you?"

"As though you love me."

"Which is no more than the truth."

Lovers' talk. Lovers' ways. I could not help it. Life was wonderful suddenly.

I was losing my baby but I had my love to comfort me. Owen was making life wondrously happy for me.

I will not lose all, I reasoned with myself.

Guillemote was strangely silent. She seemed a little aloof. I had betrayed too much and she was wondering what would come out of this. She would guess the truth, I knew. I had been so desolate at losing my child; and she would know that I must have something in my life to help me replace that loss.

She said nothing, though I knew the time must come when she would.

The household had been taken over now. Dame Alice Butler and Mrs. Astley were in charge of it. There was no place for me. Henry's Court moved to Windsor, and I stayed on in Hertford.

It was easier here for Owen and me to meet, for the King must necessarily be under constant scrutiny; and it would be more so now that he had his own household. Thus I could live more or less privately, for a time at least. I should be grateful for that.

I became more and more aware of that anxiety in the looks which my dear ladies cast in my direction, and they appeared to be a little embarrassed when Owen's name was mentioned.

Guillemote could contain herself no longer.

She came to me one day and I guessed what was on her mind because for the first moments she was silent and she looked at me in a puzzled sort of way.

"My lady," she said solemnly at length, "are you aware that you have changed and that it is . . . noticeable?"

"Changed? In what way, Guillemote?"

"Something has happened. I knew it . . . and what matters is that others know it."

"We all know that the King has his own establishment now. That is certain to make change."

"After all your sorrow, you seem to have accepted that separation. Is that because . . . ?"

"Because, Guillemote?"

"Because you have found consolation?"

"Consolation," I mused. "Oh, Guillemote, it is more than that."

"It is Owen Tudor, is it not?"

I nodded. It was no use pretending with Guillemote. She was too good a friend and she knew me too well.

She said: "This is . . . reckless."

"I know."

"Have you thought what it might lead to?"

"Listen, Guillemote . . . I married once to please them. This time I suit myself."

"But it is not a question of marriage. A queen cannot mate with a . . ."

"A brave soldier," I cried. "My husband thought Owen was one of the finest men in his army."

"But you cannot . . ."

"I cannot help it, Guillemote."

"Well, it was understandable. You were overwrought. You saw Jane with the King of Scotland. Your baby has been handed over to his nurse. I knew it. It happened. But now there must be no more."

I felt suddenly confident to manage my own life. I laughed at her. I said: "Guillemote, it is for me to decide what there shall be . . . for Owen and me."

"He is the Clerk of the Wardrobe."

"He was the companion of my late husband."

"He is a penniless Welsh squire."

"And I am the Queen who loves him."

"Holy Mother of God, has it gone as far as that?"

"It has, Guillemote."

"They will discover."

"They?"

"The Duke of Bedford, the Bishop of Winchester . . . the Duke of Gloucester. Gloucester . . . now he is a mischievous one. I would not want him to know. You are placing yourself in danger, my lady."

"I care nothing for danger."

Her next words frightened me. "And there is one whom you might place in even greater danger."

"What do you mean?"

"Owen Tudor, of course."

I was terrified, for she was right.

"Yes," she went on. "He is the one they would blame. You . . . well, you might be shut away in a convent . . . away from the world. But wardrobe clerks who aspire to queens . . . well, I would not want to dwell on what might happen to him. *Mon Dieu!* They could call it treason."

That sobered me.

And Guillemote was satisfied. She had made me pause to think.

For a few days I would not see him. Then, when I came upon him, he looked so doleful that I asked myself why I was listening to Guillemote's dismal prophecies.

Owen said: "It is days since I have seen you."

"I have been afraid," I told him. "Guillemote knows."

"Does she? She would keep our secret."

"She is completely loyal . . . but she talked to me."

"You are on such familiar terms that I am not surprised."

"She is worried about what will happen if we are discovered."

"She has a point there," he agreed.

"They would separate us . . . and Owen . . . what charge would they bring against you?"

"Whatever it was, I should count everything worthwhile."

"It must never be," I said quickly.

"We must be doubly careful and make sure that we are not discovered."

"Everything she says is because of her care for me, I know."

"Perhaps I should go away."

"You could not. I should forbid it."

"How did Guillemote discover?"

"She said it was the way I looked."

"You are beautiful . . . always."

"People in love betray themselves sometimes, Owen. I listened to her. She made me fear for you."

He was silent.

"I could not bear it if anything should happen to you, Owen."

"I will take the utmost care to preserve myself for you."

I knew it was useless. We could not stay away from each other. It had begun and it must go on.

So through all the days my thoughts were of Owen; and all through the nights we were together.

We lived in a state of bliss. This was the most wonderful experience which had ever befallen me. I had not known there could be anything like it, and I marvelled to contemplate that, if Owen had never come my way, I should have lived my life without it.

I had thought I loved Henry, but now I realized that that had been a pale shadow of this exciting relationship.

Henry's kingship, his need to conquer, had been the driving force of his life. To him love was a light adventure, pleasurable and rewarding in a way but something apart from the main purpose of life. Whereas I was everything to Owen and he to me. Not only was there this all-absorbing, awe-inspiring passion but there was the need for secrecy which gave an added excitement.

There were times, of course, when I wished that we could live in peaceful harmony, openly and unafraid, but the fact that we were living dangerously, in those early days, did add a thrill of which we could not be unaware.

I was not cut off from my son. I was allowed to visit him. It was not like living under the same roof, but at least I could assure myself that he was not unhappy. Dame Alice was a good, serious-minded woman, determined to do her duty; and Henry appeared to accept her.

It was clear to me that Joan Astley was ready to devote that loving care to her charge which the best nurses give unstintingly, and I could see that he was safe in her hands. She would protect him and if—which I fervently hoped would not be the case— Dame Alice felt at times that she wished to avail herself of the permission to chastise him, Joan Astley would be there to comfort him.

Henry showed his pleasure in seeing me and was not over-distressed when I left—a fact which both saddened me and made me rejoice.

Guillemote, who had accompanied me on the visit, said: "It is not as bad as we feared. He will be happy enough and he will not forget us."

"A child should be with his mother," I insisted.

"There would be many people around to watch us . . . if he were with you," she reminded me.

She was right, of course. She was worried about me—which I realized she had good reason to be.

Owen was still a soldier at heart; his life had been governed by the war in France and he was very interested in how it was progressing. He listened avidly to the news of what was happening across the seas as well as in England.

Neither of us wanted to look too far ahead. Each of us knew that if our relationship was discovered we should be in trouble . . . deep trouble. Marriage would be out of the question, I was sure.

I should be disgraced and Owen would be accused of treason. That worried me a great deal; but in the first flush of our passion I could think of little else but the joys of the moment.

There were times when we lay in bed when Owen would whisper to me of what was going on in France.

"It is always dangerous," he said, "when a country extends its dominions. Communications have to be kept up. Armies have to be sent to guard the outposts. It is never easy. If the King had lived . . ."

"If the King had lived," I retorted, "we should not be here now . . . like this."

He was silent. He had a great reverence for Henry. I think he was deeply concerned that he had become Henry's widow's lover.

"The Duke of Bedford is very good, they say," I said.

"There was only one King Henry V, and he was the greatest soldier the world has ever known."

"What do you think will happen now, Owen?"

"I think the Duke of Gloucester will make a great deal of trouble."

I shivered. "I am afraid of Gloucester."

"He is a man to be watched. But now he is going to Hainault with a company of men to fight for his wife's rights . . . so he will be out of our way."

"I hope he will stay there. Do you think he will regain Hainault? It was what he married for. Poor Jacqueline. I wonder if she knows?"

"I feel she must. Or it may be that she prefers to delude herself. But from our point of view it is good that he has gone. As far as England is concerned, I believe what he has done may prove disastrous."

"You mean his quarrel with Burgundy?"

"The Duke of Bedford will do everything within his power to keep the alliance with Burgundy, but it seems as though his brother will do everything he can to destroy it."

"Gloucester thinks only of his own good."

"Which is what he is doing now. He will jeopardize the English and Burgundian alliance for the sake of regaining his wife's estates for himself. It is unfortunate that the Duke of Brabant is the Duke of Burgundy's kinsman. This could well cost England Burgundy's friendship, and that is something they cannot afford to lose.''

''At least he is out of the country. I have for a long time had a feeling that he is against me. I feel afraid for little Henry while he is here. He wants to be King of England, and there are others in the way. Clarence died. There is Bedford, of course . . . and now he has married and strengthened his alliance with Burgundy through his marriage to the Duke's sister. But if Bedford died without heirs . . . and if something happened to Henry . . . then Gloucester would be King of England. I cannot bear to think of that.''

''It could not get to that,'' said Owen. ''I do not know what the outcome of all this will be, but of one thing I am sure, and that is that Gloucester, by his conduct, is putting the alliance between England and Burgundy in jeopardy.''

''Let us forget all about them,'' I begged. ''Gloucester is far away. He is not concerned with us now. And we have found each other. Swear that you will never leave me.''

''Not of my own free will, my dearest.''

''Then I am happy.''

Henry, Bishop of Winchester, called to see me.

The visit of such a man must necessarily alarm me. I was constantly wondering whether my relationship with Owen had been discovered beyond my intimate circle, and what the consequences would be, so I received him with a good deal of trepidation.

He was gracious, very dignified, very much aware of his royalty and position in the country. He made me feel that it was an honour for him to visit me.

I hoped I did not show my anxiety, but if I did, I supposed he would attribute it to my realization of the honour he did me.

Henry had thought very highly of him. He had said to me once: ''My uncle has enough dignity to balance his illegitimacy, for although my father most wisely legitimized him, the fact does remain that he was born before his parents' union was sanctified by the Church. He cannot forget this, and it irks him, so we must forgive him that little extra dignity he has to exercise to remind us all that he is equal with the highest in the land.''

I thought that summed up Henry Beaufort exactly.

Henry had said he was a good man to have working for him; he was exceptionally intelligent; he knew that allegiance to the Crown would serve his best interests, and therefore he was loyal to the Crown. "But I trust Beaufort," Henry had said, "and I have always known he was a good man to have on my side."

Beaufort was a man who would stand up for what he considered best for the country, while making sure, if it were possible, that what was done was profitable for himself.

His recent quarrel with Gloucester had shown that Gloucester held great power, particularly while his brother Bedford was in France acting as Regent there for young Henry. Yet Beaufort had made no secret of his disapproval of Gloucester's marriage to Jacqueline of Hainault because he knew it would be detrimental to the alliance with Burgundy, which was all-important to England, even though this created great antagonism between the two men and could be harmful to him.

I told him that I was well and said I trusted he was in the same happy state.

He assured me that he was and then came to the point of his visit.

"Your Grace will be aware that His Highness the Duke of Gloucester is causing some dismay abroad."

"I know he has gone to Hainault to regain his wife's estates."

"His wife!" said Beaufort. "There is some doubt that she is that."

"Did not the Pope grant her a divorce?"

"The Duke of Brabant does not accept that. There are many who say she is still married to him and that the alliance with the Duke of Gloucester is no marriage at all."

"But he has gone . . ."

"I regret to say that the actions of the Duke have been . . . quite dangerous . . . to me . . . to the whole country . . . and perhaps in particular to his brother the Duke of Bedford who is striving to consolidate the great victories won for England by the late King."

"I have heard of this," I said, great relief sweeping over me, for I realized he had not come to talk of my affairs. I had been in terrible fear that he might have come because he had heard something about Owen and me.

"I have done all in my power to stop his leaving for the

Continent," went on the Bishop, "but I have not been successful in doing so."

I was wondering why he should be telling me all this, for I was sure that, like most of his kind, he would think the opinion of a woman not worth having.

He went on: "The Duke of Gloucester has taken Hainault. There was no opposition. The Duke of Brabant was unable to prevent this. Hainault has now recognized Gloucester as its ruler."

"Then there will be no fighting," I said.

He looked at me with faint contempt. "The Duke of Burgundy will certainly not allow this to pass unchallenged. He is hurrying to the assistance of his kinsman. You misunderstand the gravity of this situation. In order to go to Brabant's assistance it was necessary for Burgundy to conclude a truce with France. You can guess what that means."

"The English are losing their ally."

He was silent for a moment. Then he said: "Now I come to the point of my visit. The Duke of Burgundy has challenged the Duke of Gloucester to single combat . . . a duel between the two of them to settle the dispute."

"Surely not!"

"But indeed it is so, and the Duke of Gloucester has accepted the challenge. I know it seems incredible, but it is so. That duel must not take place. If it does, one or the other will be killed. You can guess the consequences. If Gloucester kills Burgundy, the Burgundians will be in revolt against him; and if Burgundy kills Gloucester, it will be the same from the other side. One thing is certain: it will be the end of the alliance between Burgundy and England. And that alliance is of the greatest importance to our success in France."

"I realize that."

"This duel must be stopped. And you may help in some small way . . . but we cannot afford to neglect any means . . . however small . . . to bring an end to this folly."

"What do you expect me to do?"

"Philip of Burgundy is married to your sister. He is devoted to her and she to him. If she could be persuaded to beg him not to continue with this ridiculous gesture, it could be a help."

"It is long since I saw my sister."

"Nevertheless, she is your sister. What we wish you to do is write to her . . . tell her exactly what this would mean . . . a rift between us . . . further trouble for France . . . the prolonging of the war. You could help perhaps.''

''Do you think the great Duke of Burgundy would listen to me?''

''No. But he might listen to his wife.''

''I see.''

''We are asking the Queen, your mother, to do her best in the matter,'' he went on. ''We are determined to try anything . . . just anything . . . to prevent this disaster. Write immediately. I will take your letter and see that it is delivered to your sister by special courier. You must do this for the sake of your son, the King.''

Writing to Michelle was an emotional experience. I could only see her as the poor frightened little girl in the Hôtel de St. Paul. Although she had been slightly older than I, I had always felt I had to protect her. Our sister Marie had had her unfaltering faith to sustain her. Poor little Michelle had suffered with the rest of us, but she had seemed weaker than I. She always seemed to be colder and more hungry. It was difficult to imagine that shivering little mite as the Duchess of Burgundy.

She had always seemed rather simple, less able to cope with our desperate situation than the rest of us. Yet she had married the great Duke and he cared for her. Even when her brother had been involved with the men who had murdered his father, he had not turned against her.

He must truly love her, and because of that these men, who made it their business to know what was going on, thought she could influence him.

I wrote to her, trying to eliminate from my mind the image of that shivering little girl as I did so. What could I say. ''Dear Michelle, you are the Duchess of Burgundy, I am the Queen of England . . . my little son is King and now I am the Queen Mother. I have lost my husband. Do not lose yours. Please try to stop this duel. Persuade your husband that it is not worthwhile. Beg him not to risk his life. You must not become a widow . . . as I have.''

I went on in that strain. And all the time I was thinking of those days when my father was alive and we children were living in poverty and neglect while our mother sported with her lovers.

And what of her? What would she write to Michelle? We had

all hated her. No. No, hatred was too strong a word. We had all feared her, and we had always known that no good would come to us through her.

The Bishop was pleased with my efforts; he took my letter and rode off.

Guillemote came to me one day and said: "The Duke of Gloucester is back in England."

"Oh," I replied. "What of his duel with the Duke of Burgundy?"

"People say that he has come back to prepare for it. They are also saying that he is heartily sick of the whole affair. He thought he could take Jacqueline's possessions easily . . . and it seemed that he might but for Burgundy. But Burgundy will take them from him. It looks as though the Duke of Gloucester is getting away from it all and leaving Jacqueline to face Burgundy alone."

"How can he do that? It is so dishonourable."

"I don't think the Duke would give much thought to that. The rumour is that he is tired of Jacqueline and greatly enamoured of one of the ladies who went out with Jacqueline from England . . . if lady she can be called."

"You have been listening to gossip, Guillemote."

"How can one learn what is going on if one does not listen to gossip? We learn more from that than from what they call news. From that one hears of victories which turn out to be defeats . . . winning today . . . losing tomorrow. No, it is the gossip in which the real news is wrapped up. Believe me."

"I do believe you, Guillemote, and what is this news about the Duke's new friend?"

"A voluptuous piece, by all accounts. Irresistible . . . saucy . . . luscious . . . everything that would appeal to His Grace's jaded tastes . . . which poor Jacqueline failed to do."

"Who is this charmer?"

"Lady Eleanor Cobham . . . daughter of Lord Cobham."

"I have heard of her."

"And doubtless you will hear more now. They say the Duke is so enamoured of her that he has lost his love for Hainault, Zealand and the rest."

"And poor Jacqueline I am sorry for her."

"In any case she will be rid of the Duke."

"What will happen to her?"

"Burgundy will overrun the place in a very short time, I am sure. Doubtless she will be his prisoner. He might send her back to Brabant."

"And what of this duel?"

Guillemote shrugged her shoulders. "I have heard nothing of that," she said.

"It will be rather pointless when Burgundy is in possession. Oh, how I wish that he had stayed in Hainault."

She looked at me sagely and nodded.

I had heard from Michelle. She had been pleased to get a letter from me.

It brought back so many memories, she wrote. "How different our lives are now. Who would have thought when we were living as we did in the Hôtel de St. Paul that we should come to this? I have been happy since my marriage. I believe you were happy in yours. It was so tragic when it ended. I have spoken to the Duke, my husband. I have pleaded with him. He always listens to me. He is very tender. I am hoping he will not fight this duel. I am praying for it . . ."

I could not believe that Gloucester would want to fight. Of course, he had had to accept the challenge. It would have been against his nature not to. People might have thought he was afraid. He must always present that image of the dashing, reckless, devil-may-care charmer. Strangely enough, people accepted it. They closed their eyes to his follies. They thought it was noble and chivalrous to go to fight for his wife's possessions, to win back for her all that she had lost. They did not see that he was winning back those lands—not for her—but for himself.

The people were deceived. They loved him. They would cheer him in the streets, they would welcome him back. They preferred him to the Bishop of Winchester who, in spite of his arrogance and avarice, had the good of the country at heart. No, the people liked the swashbuckling, licentious Duke far better than the serious-minded priest.

The Bishop did have the courtesy to call on me again.

"I am pleased to tell you," he said, "that our efforts were successful. I am sure that the letter you wrote to your sister helped; and your mother, too, played her part. The duel would have been a disaster. In the end, the Pope forbade it. But the

Duke of Burgundy has been moved by the entreaties of his wife. So we can be grateful for this mercy.''

I said: ''But the friendship between England and Burgundy?''

''It has been considerably impaired, but the Duke of Bedford is very clever. His wife is the Duke's sister, which makes a bond. We must hope to repair the damage.''

''And the Duke of Gloucester is now in England . . .''

''I very much doubt he will want to venture to Hainault again.''

''But his wife will need help.''

The Bishop shrugged his shoulders and smiled.

I felt very uneasy. If the Duke of Gloucester had abandoned hope of ruling Hainault, then he would seek power in England. That alarmed me not a little.

They were uneasy days. Gloucester's health had suffered. How he had thought he could stand up to a duel with the Duke of Burgundy, I cannot imagine. I think a great deal of his defiance was bluster.

I should have been grateful, I supposed, that he seemed to become immediately absorbed in his quarrel with Henry Beaufort, for it would turn his attention from my son. How he and Henry Beaufort hated each other! I suppose it was largely because their temperaments were so different, and Beaufort, with his strong sense of duty to the State, was appalled by Gloucester's self-interest.

The people of London took up the quarrel—some siding with Gloucester, others with Beaufort. There were even riots in the capital between the two factions. The feud became so fierce that widespread civil unrest was feared. This became so alarming that emissaries were sent to the Duke of Bedford, begging him to return to England, where his rule was needed as urgently as it could possibly be in France.

I daresay the Duke of Bedford was a disillusioned man. Gloucester's reckless acts were costing him the friendship of Burgundy. It could not have happened if Henry had lived. Henry would never have allowed it. Bedford would know that, but it must have been hard to realize where he had failed.

I was greatly relieved when he arrived in England; and from that time peace returned. Gloucester and Beaufort were obliged to make a public show of reconciliation, and if it might not have been entirely genuine, it calmed the general unrest which had broken out among the supporters of both sides.

Gloucester swore not to aggravate Burgundy further, but when the Duke of Bedford returned to France, where his presence was urgently needed, Gloucester sent Jacqueline the help she asked for.

Meanwhile there were many rumours about his torrid affair with Eleanor Cobham, a very flamboyant and decidedly handsome woman who attracted attention wherever she went—especially when it was whispered that she dabbled in witchcraft. The Duke was said to be completely enthralled by her.

Oddly enough, his profligate ways seemed to enhance his popularity; the more sullied his reputation became, the more the people cheered him. His once-handsome face was becoming bloated and he was beginning to look like the dissolute rake he was; but they continued to love him.

Then came the day when I heard that the Pope had—very likely at the instigation of Burgundy—annulled Gloucester's marriage to Jacqueline. I am sure that he breathed a sigh of relief. He could now forget his commitment to her—of which he had long grown weary—and devote himself entirely to the wiles of his fascinating mistress.

Unfortunately Bedford had returned to France, taking Beaufort with him, and Gloucester slipped into his old role of Protecter of the Realm, which caused me qualms of uneasiness.

While all this was happening, life had become very agreeable to me. I had my secret love which filled me with excitement and pleasure. The more I knew Owen, the more I realized how very much he meant to me. I could be deliriously happy, and the trials of England and Burgundy seemed very remote. In my happiness, I wondered how people could be so foolish as to involve themselves in making war.

Love absorbed me. I had Owen and, with the help of my faithful ladies, who were delighted to see my contentment, I managed to live my secret life.

Then there was Henry. No longer a baby, he was an adorable child—now five years old and a somewhat serious little boy. Already he was aware that he was apart from the other boys in his household. He was quite fond of Dame Alice Butler and he dearly loved Joan Astley; but he never forgot that I was his mother, and it was a great joy to me to see his pleasure when I visited him.

This I was able to do fairly frequently. I must not interfere, of course, with their methods of upbringing, but I had long realized this and made no attempt to do so. He loved me as his mother; he had Dame Alice and Joan Astley, and there was Owen to comfort me when I felt sad, as I sometimes did after visiting my son.

He was a strange child. He could change quickly. Sometimes he would seem a normal, fun-loving boy and then suddenly he would become serious, a little puzzled, perhaps faintly worried. When he rode out, I would sometimes be with him, for it was natural that as his mother I should be, and it satisfied the people to see us together. The people clearly loved him. He was very much aware of them. I had seen him touch the miniature crown on his head rather nervously now and then. I think it must have been a symbol to him. It was something of which at times he was proud and could at others fill him with apprehension.

There were times when we were together and I would hold him to me. He would cling to me. Then he was like the baby I had known. He liked to hear stories of his early days. He would sit listening intently, holding my hand or sometimes clutching at my skirts as if he feared I would leave him. Then he was indeed like my little one. But when he was quiet and seemed a little anxious, I knew he was remembering he was the King.

Dame Alice told me that he was good at his books but he did not excel as he should at outdoor games. She believed that he had little fancy for them.

"It is well," she said, "that there are boys of his age here. He can watch them. Some of them are very skilful . . . riding . . . archery and such like. But the King always prefers his books. It is a pity. He should have enthusiasm for both."

"We are all different," I said, "and it is very important that he should do well at his lessons."

"A king must excel in all ways," she said with a touch of severity.

I used to talk to him about his father—the greatest warrior the world had ever known. He listened with a kind of awed anxiety.

I said to him: "But there are better things than war, Henry. It is better for countries to live in peace with each other than go to war . . . killing . . . maiming each other. There are wonderful things in the world . . . books . . . music . . . pictures.''

He was pleased with that. I knew that those about him constantly talked to him of Agincourt and Harfleur.

He liked to hear about his ancestors, and the Earl of Warwick had given instructions to his tutors that he must be fully cognisant of the history of his country.

I thought sometimes that they were forcing him out of his childhood too soon. It was true he was the King but could they not let him forget that for a few years? Apparently not.

I wondered what effect coming face to face with the people had on him. He certainly liked their applause and responded to it in a manner which delighted them; and youth is so appealing, particularly when it wears a crown.

He said to me once: ''They like me, do they not?''

''It is clear that they do,'' I replied.

''Yes, but Dame Alice says it is the crown they are cheering, not me.''

''Dame Alice may be right.''

''Then why do they not carry the crown through the streets? Why do I have to be under it?''

''The crown needs someone to wear it and it is the possession of the King.''

''Then it must be the King they cheer as well as the crown.''

I could see that my son was developing a logical mind.

It brought home to me the fact that he was growing up, and I feared for him. I could not shut out of my mind the thought of Gloucester's ambitious face.

A message came that I might spend Christmas and the New Year with Henry at Eltham Palace. I was delighted. I would travel there with my household, and that would include Owen, so I could enjoy the festivities in the company of both my son and my lover.

Henry had, that Whitsun, been knighted by his Uncle Bedford. It had been a solemn occasion, for after the ceremony he himself had knighted a few of his young companions.

He had described the occasion to me at some length and I had been saddened a little because I felt more strongly than ever that they were forcing him to grow up before his time. How I wished that he could have enjoyed a little more of his childhood more simply with me and Guillemote . . . and Owen too.

I was very pleased to see that Henry had quite a liking for Owen, who had taken great pains not to put himself forward. In view of the nature of our relationship, Owen felt a little embarrassed. I think he felt himself to be in the position of stepfather to the little King.

It was in a state of happy expectation that we arrived at Eltham. I could not restrain my excitement as we came through the magnificent avenue of trees and saw the stone walls and lofty archways of the palace. We passed into a cobbled courtyard.

Henry was waiting to greet us.

I wanted to pick him up in my arms, but I must remember that, although he was my little son, he was also the King. He smiled at me happily, so the formal greeting was not important. We should have an opportunity to be alone, when we would cast off convention and revert to the old easy-going relationship which was more natural to us.

How happy I was to be with him! He told me what had been happening to him—how he had to ride every day and practise archery. He wished it was not quite so often but he was very fond of his horse. Best of all he loved his books. The Earl of Warwick, though, said he must not neglect sports or the study of arms for them.

"The Earl of Warwick will know best," I said.

He accepted that rather dubiously; but I think on the whole he was a docile pupil.

He was very interested in the Christmas festivities. He had been allowed to take a hand in decorating the great hall and had helped bring in the yule log.

He had a present for me, he told me. It turned out to be a pair of gloves. He watched me unwrap them and put them on, studying me to see whether I was pleased with them.

I kissed him. I told him they were perfect. How had he known that I had always wanted such a pair of gloves?

"Dame Alice helped me to choose them," he said modestly. "But I really wanted that pair for you."

"They are the best gloves in the world," I told him, "and I shall always treasure them."

I was speaking the truth. I have them to this day. I often unwrap them and think of the time he gave them to me.

He told me that Jack Travail and his band of merry men were coming to amuse us and there would be mummers. He and his little companions would play all sorts of games. It was going to be a wonderful Christmas. "And," he added, "*you* are here with me." A remark which touched me deeply.

Among his Christmas gifts were some coral beads. He was delighted with them, and he told me that Dame Alice had said that they had belonged to King Edward.

"But," he said, "there were three Edwards and she was not sure to which one they had belonged. I wish I knew. Do you know about the kings named Edward? One of them was a great warrior . . . like my father, but not so great of course. There were battles called Poitiers and Crécy—though they were not like Agincourt. He did not win the whole of France, though he did quite well. Then there was one who was always fighting in Scotland. But she didn't tell me much about the second one. When I pressed her, she said, 'You will know one day. But that time is not yet. It will depend on your tutor.' He was the second Edward, and he is the one I should like to know about."

I told him that I had learned my lessons at a place called Poissy in France. I could not enlighten him about the second Edward but I would find out if I could.

I did find out later, and when I learned of the life of King Edward II, I felt very sad, thinking of the tragic fates which could befall kings. And it occurred to me that the second Edward was probably the one to whom those coral beads had belonged; and I rather wished they had not fallen into my son's hand.

But that Christmas was a time for rejoicing.

There was great merriment when the boys played their games. I noticed they were all a little deferential to Henry, though most of them came from the noblest families in the land. They played blind man's buff and hide-and-seek, and when Jack Travail arrived with his merry men, he devised new games and did little comic sketches which amused them mightily. He had brought with him some portable organs which provided special delight. I said afterwards to Owen that it was wonderful to see my little boy enjoying fun naturally, unencumbered, however briefly, by his kingship.

I could not help thinking how wonderful it would be if we could slip away . . . taking Henry with us, and go with a few

friends to some quiet place away from the ceremony of the Court
. . . somewhere where we could live in the style of certain gen-
tlefolk away from the turmoil of state affairs.

I think I must have been lulled into an even greater sense of
security than ever, which made me careless. It was the relaxed
atmosphere, the festive celebrations, the pleasure of having my
son near me. I was bemused by my contentment.

It seemed nothing at the time. It all came about quite naturally, though it brought home to me the fact that I was being
watched and that every little action of mine was noted, considered and judgement passed upon it.

The young people had retired to their beds and there was
dancing in the great hall. Owen was present but naturally he did
not sit with me. We had to remember that in public he was the
Clerk of the Wardrobe and one of the guards, and as such naturally would not be with me.

I sat watching the dancers, not wishing to dance myself. There
was a great deal of laughter and chatter, and the musicians were
playing tunefully. Often my eyes went to Owen across the hall,
and our eyes conveyed tender messages.

Some of the courtiers had organized a competition.

"What are they doing?" I asked idly.

One of the men came up to me and said: "It is a contest, my
lady. We were discussing who of us could leap the highest in the
dance and turn the greatest number of times. Then someone
said, 'Let us put it to the test,' and that is what we are doing."

I clapped my hands and said: "Let us all see then. Let us
discover the champion."

"Perhaps Your Grace will be the judge."

"Why certainly. I will judge."

They gathered round me.

"The test is who can jump the highest and turn the most
number of times, is it not?" I said.

"Yes, my lady. They must jump while turning . . . as in the
dance."

"Well, let the trial begin. Who is to be the first?"

The contest started. The men came and danced before me,
twirling and leaping into the air. The watchers shouted the number of times they turned and gave their opinions of the height of
the leaps.

We had almost decided on a winner when someone said: "Come on, Owen Tudor, try your luck."

"I am no dancer," protested Owen.

It was true. I had watched him in the ballroom with great tenderness. I would not have him like those mincing, prancing men who prided themselves on their agility in the dance. Again I thought of Gloucester, who, of course, was the perfect dancer. It was amazing how frequently his image came into my mind. It was a man's place to excel at things other than dancing.

Owen was embarrassed and continued to protest.

"Come on, Owen Tudor," someone cried. "Are you a coward then? What will Her Grace think if you refuse to dance before her?"

Owen stood there slightly flushed. I smiled at him encouragingly.

"It is only a game," I said.

The musicians started to play. There was nothing he could do but attempt to dance, which he did clumsily, twirling round and round.

"Higher, higher," shouted one of the courtiers.

Owen leaped, lost his balance and fell straight into my lap.

I put out my hands and caught him. For a few moments I held him against me. I was not aware that I held him longer than I would normally have held anyone who had fallen upon me in such an impromptu manner until I became aware of the deep silence in the room. The musicians had stopped playing. Everyone seemed to be very still . . . listening . . . waiting for something to happen. I heard myself laugh.

"My lady . . ." stammered Owen.

"I do not think that Owen Tudor will win the prize," I said as he stood up before me.

Owen looked overcome with embarrassment. "I am sorry . . ." he began.

I waved my hand. "You did protest," I reminded him. "I shall blame all those who forced you to it. Come, let us continue with the game. I am eager now to see who will be our winner."

The music had started. There were two more competitors who wished to try their luck. But something had happened. People were watchful. Secretive glances passed between them.

* * *

It was not long before Guillemote raised the subject.

She made a habit of brushing my hair before we retired for the night. It was then that we discussed the events of the day and night.

She came to the point in her usual candid way.

"It was noticed," she said.

"What was noticed?"

"You and the Tudor."

"What was noticed?" I repeated.

"That he fell into your lap."

"How could they help noticing? They were all watching the contest. Owen did not fall purposely."

"It was the way you received him."

"Received him? He fell into my lap. How should one receive a dancer who falls into one's lap?"

I laughed at the memory. "He looked so funny," I said. "Poor Owen, he did not want to do it. They should not have insisted. He knows he cannot dance. And why should he? Dancing is no occupation for a man of intelligence."

"And wit . . . and all perfections," added Guillemote.

I was silent. She looked at me accusingly.

"Did you not realize? It was the way you held him . . . the way you looked at him . . . the way he looked at you. It was clear to everyone in the room."

"What are you saying?"

"My dear . . . my dearest mistress . . . how long do you think you are going to keep this a secret?"

"What . . . a secret?"

"What is going on between you and Owen Tudor."

I was silent. She placed the hairbrush on the table with an angry gesture. "Secret!" she cried. "After this night it will be a secret no longer."

"My dear Guillemote, how could I help it if he fell?"

"You could not help his falling. It was afterwards. They are whispering about you. Don't you see how dangerous it is? You are the Queen."

"It was nothing," I protested. "It was all over in a few seconds."

"Long enough for you to have betrayed your feelings . . . and he, too. It was the way you looked at each other . . . the way he stayed there . . ."

"For a second or two?"

"It was too long. The looks were too ardent. And there were all those watchful ones who have already been . . . speculating. My lady, my lady, I beg you to think what you are doing . . . of what would happen if it were known to some of your enemies."

"Guillemote, you are frightening me."

She suddenly took me into her arms as she used to when I was a child.

"There," she said in the old manner. "Perhaps they did not notice after all. It is just because I watch over you too much. I care too much . . ."

"Oh no, Guillemote, do not say that. Go on caring . . . caring too much."

She stroked my hair.

"You should give it up, my dearest. It is dangerous. I do not know what would happen if it were found out . . . in certain quarters. Give it up now . . . before it is too late."

"I could not, Guillemote. I have lost my child . . ."

"He is here . . . under this very roof."

"It is not the same. You know they have taken him away from me. Dame Alice and Joan Astley . . . they are closer to him than I am. They have taken him away from me . . . no matter what you say. And as he grows older he will be farther from me. I love Owen, Guillemote. I just could not face life without one of them . . ."

"I know." She sighed and kissed my cheek. "But you must be more careful. It becomes dangerous . . . and have you thought that one day they might want to make a match for you?"

"I will not allow it, Guillemote. I married for state reasons once. When I marry again, it will be for love."

"You are the Queen, remember."

"Yes, I am the Queen and I will not allow them to arrange my life. I will do as I wish."

She nodded her head gravely and her eyes were full of fear.

It was soon after that that I made a discovery which, while it filled me with the utmost alarm, both excited and delighted me.

I was pregnant.

Why I should have been so surprised, I cannot imagine. Owen and I had been passionate lovers for some months. We had been living together, oblivious of everything around us. It was only when I had had to go to Court that we had to restrain ourselves.

I felt dazed with the wonder of it. A child—mine and Owen's. How wonderful it could have been, if only . . .

As the realization of what this could mean swept over me, I began to tremble. What should I do now? How could I keep this secret? And it would have to be kept secret.

I will not part with this child, I told myself. I will do anything rather.

I had to think. I had to be clever. I was in a difficult situation and I must find a way out of it.

I did not want to say anything to anyone until I was absolutely sure. In the meantime I must begin to plan. What would be the reaction of those about me? But why should they govern my life? I was the Queen. I was the mother of the King and they had taken him away from me. Why should I not have a life of my own . . . children of my own who were of no interest to the state? It was unreasonable to deny me this. But I knew they would. I wanted to say to them: I will go right away. You can take away my title of queen. I do not want it. I only want to live in peace.

Wild plans came into my mind . . . plans which I knew it would be impossible to carry out. There was one thing only which I clung to, and that was my determination to keep this child with me . . . to bring it up as my own.

I was now sure that I was going to have a child.

When I told Owen, his reaction was the same as mine had been—that wonder and delight . . . and then fear.

"Owen," I said, "what are we going to do?"

He was silent for a moment, then he said slowly: "There will be trouble."

"I know. But . . . what can they do about us?"

"They can separate us to begin with."

"I will not have it, Owen."

"My dearest, you will have no say in the matter."

"No say in the management of my own life!"

"You are the daughter of a king, the widow of a king. It puts you in a dangerous position."

"Why . . . why . . . Henry is dead. They have taken his and my child from me. Why should they take everything else?"

He said: "We need to consider this very carefully."

"First tell me that we shall not be parted. We must marry, Owen. We owe that to the child."

He nodded slowly.

"Then," I said, "I shall care nothing for the rest. We will fight them, Owen."

"We must decide how."

For a few moments he held me tightly in his arms. I knew that he was overcome by the wonder of what had happened, as I was. He was visualizing this child we should have . . . our very own . . . belonging to us . . . no pawn of the state, this one. Our child . . . Owen's and mine. When I contemplated that, it was difficult to dwell on the problems we faced. But we had to be very careful . . . for the sake of the child.

"My dear one," said Owen. "We have to think of this very clearly. We must be very clever. We must look straight at all possibilities . . . however alarming. We shall need the utmost skill to bring ourselves through this."

I watched him intently. He was frowning. I could see he was contemplating the problem which loomed ahead of us with deep concentration, knowing full well that it could bring disaster to us both.

"How I wish," he said, "that you were not the Queen."

"It is an empty title," I replied. "It always was. It brought me no power. It only made a prisoner of me. I cannot tell you how often I have wished that I had been born in some humble cottage."

He laid his hand on my shoulder and smiled gently at me.

"We shall need all our energy . . . all our ingenuity to bring us through this, Katherine. Let us think of that . . . and that only. We are going to marry in spite of everything and everyone. We are going to have our child. No one is going to spoil our lives. We must think as best we can how we are going to bring this about."

"Why should this concern others? They have taken Henry from me. Is that not enough?"

"We must not brood on what has already gone. We have to plan, Katherine . . . plan logically. You are the Queen . . . mother of the King. Any children you may have might consider they have a claim to the throne."

"How could they? They would not be Henry's. They would be yours and mine."

"I am thinking of what would enter the minds of some people. We must consider these things, Katherine. This is what makes our position doubly dangerous. If in high places it was thought that a marriage would be right for you, it would be to a prince of their choosing."

"But I would never agree to that."

"I am trying to think of how this will seem to them. The fact is that, if you and I married, our children would be legitimate. It would doubtless be our marriage to which they would object most strongly."

"Nevertheless, we are going to marry, Owen. We must marry. There is the child. And Owen, I will *not* be separated from you and my child. It is my right to be happy with my family."

"We will marry," he said. "Oh Katherine, we have to tread with great care. We have to be very clever. You could not have the child here. It would be known throughout the Court at once."

"Then what? Let us run away. Let us go to Wales. I should love to see your country, Owen. The mountains . . ."

"We should never escape them. If we ran away they would say we were really dangerous. No, we cannot run away. We have to find a way of living our lives . . . in secret."

"Here . . . surrounded by all these people?"

"It will have to be somewhere else. One of the small, quiet manor houses. There are several you could use. But it would have to come about naturally. There are some of your household whom you could trust . . . and mind you, they must be those whom you could trust absolutely."

"Guillemote . . ."

"Guillemote, of course."

"And the Joannas . . . Agnes, and my confessor Johan Boyers . . . I could trust him."

"That is the idea. A small household . . . and everyone in it your friend."

"No one knows as yet . . . not even Guillemote."

"Tell no one. But what we must do is move as quickly as possible to one of the small manor houses. You could choose which. It should be the most remote."

"I could not mention this to Humphrey of Gloucester."

"Indeed not."

"There is the Bishop of Winchester."

"He might suspect. He is very perceptive."

"There is, of course, the Duke of Bedford."

"By great good luck he is in the country now. Things are going badly in France and he will be here in consultation with the Council. Gloucester has helped to make England's position very grave indeed. I don't know whether Bedford would have time to see you. He could hardly refuse though, if you requested it. Moreover, he would be too preoccupied with affairs in France to worry much about your retirement from Court, I should imagine."

"I will try to see Bedford."

"That is the first thing. And in the meantime decide on the manor. Let it be small . . . remote from Court. We shall not want people continually calling."

"Oh, Owen, I feel so much better. I did not realize how frightened I was."

We clung together.

"We will come through this, my dearest," said Owen. "Put your trust in me . . . and in God."

The Secret Marriage

I had always admired John, Duke of Bedford. Henry had been very fond of him. His most reliable brother, he had called him; and although perhaps he had loved Clarence more, he had always known that the elder brother was rash and inclined to envy him, whereas Bedford was the essence of loyalty and had always borne in mind Henry's superior military skill, seeking to emulate him, certainly, but never giving way to envy.

He had aged considerably since I had last seen him. Keeping France in order was evidently a great strain. He was a brilliant administrator, stern, though just. My brother Charles, who was still called the Dauphin, was beginning to cause disruption in various parts of the country, and Bedford, labouring under the disadvantage of the waning friendship between himself and Burgundy, was hard pressed.

Nevertheless he came to see me. He was very gallant and at the same time kindly.

He asked me how I was faring and if I felt a little happier now.

I replied that I felt better than I had expected. He bowed his head, thinking that I referred to the loss of Henry.

"I find it difficult to adjust myself to Court life," I said.

"So many ceremonies," he murmured. "And you must attend them without my brother. It brings back many memories, I doubt not, and it does not allow you to forget our loss."

"How well you understand."

"It was a great tragedy . . . the greatest tragedy which could have befallen us all . . . and you, his Queen, suffered most."

There was another brief silence, then I said: "I trust, my lord, that you have been comforted."

"I am fortunate in my marriage."

Yes, I thought. To the sister of Burgundy. I had seen Anne once or twice but I could not remember what she looked like. Fortunate indeed he had been to marry Burgundy's sister. It made the straining link a little harder to break.

"Then I rejoice for you, my lord," I said. "And I must not encroach on your time. I wanted to ask your advice."

"I shall do my best to give it," he replied.

"I was telling you that I find Court life irksome. I want to live more quietly. There are too many memories . . ."

He nodded.

"I have been thinking that . . . if I could retire to the country for a while, live the life of a simple country lady . . ."

"Would that not give you more time for brooding . . . nursing your sorrows?"

"I think I could interest myself in country pursuits. I should have a few of my ladies with me . . . those who are my friends. If I could get away . . . for a time . . . I feel I could begin a new way of life."

"I see no reason why you should not. Henry would want you to find what comfort you could. His last words to me were of you."

"I know. He was good to me."

"Yes," said Bedford. "Why not make a break? Have you any place in mind?"

"There is the manor of Hadham."

"Hadham? That's in Hertfordshire, I believe. It is very quiet there, I am sure."

"It is quietness I seek."

"Do you not think that a convent might be more to your taste?"

"Oh no . . . no. I should brood all the time. All I want is to live a peaceful life . . . without constant reminders."

"Well then, I should say that Hadham is a good choice."

"Do you think that if I retired there . . . my wishes to be left in peace would be respected?"

"I would see that they were."

"My lord, you are so kind to me."

"As I told you, when Henry died he asked me to care for

you. He said you would be the most desolate creature on earth. I knew that that was so . . . and I gave him my word.''

I took his hand and kissed it; and he drew me to him and kissed me on the brow.

"I will do everything in my power now . . . and always . . . to follow his wishes. Go . . . go then to Hadham. I shall arrange that you shall live there free from disturbance.''

"I do not know how to thank you,'' I said fervently.

I felt joyous when he had departed. I had successfully cleared the first hurdle.

My next task was to prepare the household. Naturally I talked first to Guillemote.

When she was brushing my hair that night, I said: "Guillemote, we are going to Hadham.''

"Oh?'' she replied. Then after a pause: "Well, that is a pleasant spot. Small . . . and quiet. I should think that would suit us very well.''

"We are going to make it suit us. My Lord Bedford has been persuaded that I should be allowed to spend a little time in retirement.''

She stared at me in amazement. "You . . . persuaded him?''

"Yes . . . that I needed to be alone. He thought I meant to mourn for Henry.''

"But it is years since the King died.''

"The Duke still mourns him. He thinks it is natural that I should still do so.''

"He does not know that you have other ideas.''

"Guillemote, the situation was desperate.''

She looked at me in astonishment, and understanding began to dawn in her eyes.

"No,'' she murmured.

"Yes, Guillemote. I am going to have a child.''

"What will you do? How can you keep it?''

"I am going to, Guillemote . . . though as yet I do not know how.''

"Ah, Hadham,'' she said, her mind working quickly. "Yes . . . we might manage. A time in retirement. We shall make sure that we have our friends around us. But afterwards . . . a child! How can a child be explained? It will be . . . .''

I could not bear that she should use the word. I said: "No, Guillemote. It will not be. Owen and I are going to be married."

She drew a deep breath.

"When . . . is the child due? Where will it be born?"

"At Hadham, of course . . . and in about seven months."

She covered her face with her hands. "My lady, my lady. What are we coming to?"

"I do not know, Guillemote. All I know is that I am going to marry Owen, and this child will be my very own, this time. It does not belong to the state. It will be mine . . . mine and Owen's . . . and that is how it is going to remain."

"But you . . . the Queen!"

"The King is dead now, Guillemote. I am the Queen of this country only in name. I will not be used in these political games any more. I am myself. I am going to live my life as I want it. And that will be with my family . . . with Owen and my child."

She stared at me in amazement.

"I knew it had to come to this . . . sooner or later," she said. "When do we leave for Hadham?"

"At once," I told her.

Agnes and the Joannas were jubilant. Like Guillemote they had been anxious for a long time. After that incident in the hall when Owen had fallen into my lap, there had been a certain amount of gossip. It would therefore be a good idea to keep out of view for a while, they thought.

The fact that I was now to marry Owen and that our child was on the way thrilled them, and they were eager to have a share in the adventure.

Joanna Troutbeck said that we must pick the servants we should need with the utmost care. Only those who had proved their loyalty should be allowed to come.

"Better to be short of a few servants than have a traitor in our midst," she added.

How I loved them—those faithful friends of mine! They knew they were running a certain risk in conniving at our schemes, but they did not hesitate and threw themselves wholeheartedly into the project. Together we selected those who should accompany us; and it was not long before we were on our way to Hadham.

I was happy settling into the old manor house—in fact, I had never been so happy in my life.

We were eager that the marriage should be performed as quickly as possible, and I was deeply concerned for my confessor, Johan Boyers, who was the only one I could trust enough to ask to perform the ceremony.

We hesitated for some time before we could bring ourselves to put the proposition to him. It was a great deal to ask and we knew that he must be reluctant.

I spoke to him after confession.

"Dear Johan," I said, "I am in great difficulty. I am with child."

He stared at me in horror.

I went on: "I must marry the child's father, who is the man I love. I am asking you to help me . . . but if you feel you cannot . . . I will understand . . . though I cannot think whom else I could trust with this matter."

I saw his face whiten and there was a tightening of his lips.

"It is Owen Tudor," I went on. "We love each other, Johan. We must marry, for this child must be born in wedlock. I know of no one I could ask but you. Oh . . . I know the danger. The danger to you, to Owen and to myself . . . to us all. I do not command you, Johan. I throw myself on your mercy."

He said slowly: "This could be treason."

"I know. We intend to keep our marriage secret. I am no longer of importance. They have taken my son away from me, Johan. I want to beg of you, but I must not. It is for you to decide."

"If you do not marry," he said, "this child will be . . ."

I interrupted quickly. "I know. And I see that I am asking you too much. We must try to find someone who will help us."

"You could not ask a stranger. That would indeed be too dangerous."

"Yes . . . but I think we must risk it . . . for the sake of the child."

"Does Your Grace realize what you are doing?"

"I fully realize. Dear Confessor, you have always been a friend to me. I must ask you now to forget that I suggested this matter to you. It is dangerous. I am fully aware of that. But there is no law against marrying. I married once for state reasons. Now I would marry for love."

He was silent for a long time. Then he said he wanted to be alone. He wanted to pray.

I felt deeply depressed. Of course I understood. It was asking too much of anyone. If he married us and it were discovered that he was the one who had performed the ceremony, he would be blamed almost as certainly as Owen and I would.

The next day he asked if I would come to him.

I went, expecting a refusal.

"I have thought of this matter," he said. "I have prayed, and I think God has shown me my duty."

I said: "I understand, Johan. You must do as your conscience tells you."

"My lady, I have long cared for your spiritual welfare. I shall take this risk with you. I shall perform the ceremony."

"Oh, Johan!" I cried. "Oh thank you . . . thank you. But . . . are you sure?"

"Yes. For the child." His hand shook a little as he placed it on my shoulder. "And for you, my lady."

"I shall never forget what you have done for us, Johan," I said. "But I have been thinking. It is wrong for us to ask you to take such a risk. For Owen and for me . . . that is different. But for you . . ."

"My lady, you must marry and I must perforce perform the ceremony. We shall pray to God to protect us, for I do believe that in His eyes we are committing no sin. No. I am convinced of it. It would be a sin not to do this. What we propose to do is no sin against Heaven, though it could be called one against the State; and a sin against God is the only sin with which we need concern ourselves."

I was overcome with joy.

"We shall pray to God to preserve us, and if it be His will, that will be done."

And so came that never-to-be-forgotten day when Owen and I were married in the attic at Hadham which had been transformed into a chapel for the occasion.

Our witnesses were our trusted friends.

What we had done was highly dangerous, and it must never be discovered by our enemies. Everyone present knew that if it were, they would all be implicated. There was, therefore, a pressing need for us all to maintain the utmost secrecy.

As for myself, I was too happy to give much thought to the dangers as I settled down to await the birth of my child.

I was in a mood of deep serenity during those waiting months. My thoughts were all for the child, Owen and our future life together. At last I had found happiness, and everything that had gone before seemed worthwhile.

I could not think beyond those months—nor did I want to. I did not want to consider that I might be in a dangerous position—and Owen too, perhaps more than I. I did not even want to think of how we must act with the greatest caution and be ever on the alert. I only wanted to think of the coming child.

What preparations we made! Guillemote with Agnes and the Joannas would sit together sewing garments . . . talking of babies. Guillemote recounted incidents from my childhood. Ah, I thought, my child shall not suffer as I did. He—or she—will have a wonderful father . . . a mother who cares. Sometimes I thought of my poor father. I prayed that he was happy in Heaven as a good man should be. And my mother! What was she doing now? Communing with the English conquerors, I doubted not. And my poor brother? Was he going to struggle . . . hopelessly . . . to regain his kingdom?

My thoughts did not stay with them. I had happier matters on which to brood; and in my mood of serenity, I refused to consider the dangers and thought only of the blessings of childbirth.

And at last the day came. I knew what was involved, having given birth to Henry, so I was prepared. I knew something of the agonies but I also knew they passed and were quickly forgotten in the joy of holding one's child in one's arms.

They were all round me . . . my faithful servants. They had found a midwife who could be trusted, and in due course my child was born.

I could not contain my joy when I saw him. He was the perfect child . . . already I had detected a look of Owen, and when I pointed this out, they all smiled but they did not deny it.

I said to Guillemote: ''With my husband beside me and my baby in my arms, I am the happiest woman in England.''

We decided to call him Edmund and he was baptized at Hadham by Johan Boyers. Guillemote was, of course, his nurse, but nobody was going to stop me looking after this child as a mother should.

My little Edmund was mine; and I would not allow anyone to take him from me.

For some weeks we lived in complete bliss, the whole household refusing to believe that anything could disturb it.

Now and then we had news from outside our little world. Owen would ride into the village and talk to the villagers. They had been in awe of him at first because of his connection with the Queen's household but when they found he would talk to them as though he were one of them, they accepted him as such.

I had not been out for some time. I might have been seen at the time of my arrival at the house, but I had not dared risk anyone's seeing me in the later stages of pregnancy, so I always took my exercise in the walled gardens surrounding the house.

We had wondered how to explain the presence of a child. We decided that it should be thought that one of my ladies, married to one of the men of the household, had given birth. Then, if anyone glimpsed the baby, they would assume that he was their child.

Owen had said that we must think of all these details, for it was often some seemingly trivial matter which put one's enemies on the road to discovery.

One day there was disquieting news.

Gloucester had assumed the role of Protector of England now that Bedford was back in France. Therefore he had the power to induce Parliament to pass laws.

Owen was very disturbed. He said to me: "It would seem that he knows something because he has now put forward a statute which actually mentions your name."

"Tell me . . . quickly," I begged.

"He is threatening dire penalties on any who would dare marry the Queen Dowager—or any ladies who hold land from the Crown—without the consent of the King and his Council."

"What does it mean!"

"It means," said Owen grimly, "that we must not be discovered."

"But if he knows . . ."

"He cannot know that we are married, but he may know of our feelings for each other. There was that incident in the ballroom."

"Do you think that could have been the reason?"

"Very possibly. I know that there was talk about it."

"Owen . . . if they found out . . . what would they do to you?"

"They would have to capture me first."

"Let us take Edmund and get away from here. We'll go to Wales."

"My dear! Do you think we should be allowed to do that? No. To run away would confirm their suspicions."

"But what can we do?"

"We can stay here and be watchful. It is the only way, Katherine. But we must be for ever on the watch."

I knew that perfect peace was at an end.

For some weeks a cloud darkened our happiness. We waited for the blow to fall, for we were sure that Gloucester knew something of our relationship since he had caused such a law to be made.

But nothing happened. Each day went smoothly. I cared for my baby, sat at my needlework with my ladies, and Owen and I were together for most of the day. Sometimes we rode with a party into the neighbouring countryside, but we were always very careful.

Owen said that Gloucester would have other matters to occupy him which would be more important to him than our affairs. As Protector he had control of the King, although Warwick would have disputed that, for he had been commanded to take charge of Henry by his father and that was well known.

Moreover, it seemed that Gloucester was losing his popularity. The handsome, swashbuckling adventurer was looking a good deal less handsome, by all accounts. The profligate life he had led was leaving its marks. The people did not like his treatment of Jacqueline; they were aware of his relationship with Eleanor Cobham, and the women of London did not care that he should set a bad example to their husbands by discarding Jacqueline for the sake of one who, it was said, was a harlot.

He had failed to win Hainault, and one thing heroes cannot be forgiven is failure. Burgundy was now virtually in control of all the territories Gloucester had tried so hard to gain for himself, and Jacqueline had named him, Burgundy, her heir and co-regent of those territories. She had sworn never to marry without his consent, and had declared that she had never lawfully been married to Gloucester.

"You see," said Owen, "how very much the marriages of ladies in important positions mean to these ambitious men."

I did see and I trembled.

"But at least," I said, "this stops Gloucester from turning his attention to us. And people no longer think so tenderly of him. He is becoming a failure."

"Let us continue to hope that his thoughts will be fully occupied elsewhere," said Owen fervently.

"I don't trust him," I said. "I wish they would send him to France and Bedford would come back and govern this country."

"Bedford will not leave France, and Gloucester has already done enough to undermine the English position there. They would never send him to France as Regent."

"All I care is that he does not come worrying us."

"We will outwit him. All we have to do is to be careful."

"We are that . . . and especially so since we heard of this new statute. But I do not trust Gloucester."

"Nor I," said Owen.

The weeks passed and nothing happened. It occurred to us that, having promised dire punishment to any who dared marry me, Gloucester thought he had settled the matter, and turned his attention to other affairs which I imagined would be more important to him than I could be.

The months slipped by. Hadham was the perfect dwelling for us. The house was too small for entertaining. Its situation was in a backwater. People were forgetting the existence of the Queen Mother, and I refused to allow my happy life to be disturbed by fears of what dangers might be lurking round us. Even Owen thrust aside his misgivings. As he said to me: "Gloucester is pursuing his conflict with his arch-enemy, Beaufort. There is this matter of Beaufort's accepting a cardinal's hat from Rome, which gives him a real chance for a grievance."

"Well," I said, "everyone knows that a cardinal's first allegiance is to the Pope, and that puts his country in second place."

"Beaufort should think twice before accepting."

"It is certainly sometimes a millstone round the neck."

"Well, let us rejoice because it takes Gloucester's mind from us. Then there is his new wife, Eleanor Cobham. They say he uses a great deal of time and energy in her company.''

''What amazes me is that he is still allowed to retain his power.''

''I should have thought that, after all the havoc he has wrought, some attempts would be made to curb him.''

''He *is* the late King's brother.''

''But the Duke of Bedford is above him. After what he has done, I should have thought they would have seen that he could cause more trouble.''

''There is no doubt that things are not going well for the English in France, and it began with the uneasy relationship between England and her ally Burgundy.''

''Do you think Burgundy is necessary to the success of the English?''

''I think the quarrel between the houses of Orléans and Burgundy was England's biggest asset in the war.''

''And Gloucester's foolish attempt to get territory by marrying Jacqueline, which ended in failure for him, is destroying that asset.''

''Undoubtedly. It would never have happened if the King had lived.''

''Do you really think that Henry could have stopped Gloucester entering into an alliance with Jacqueline?''

''Indeed I do.''

''And you really think Gloucester would have obeyed him?''

''He would have obeyed Henry . . . if no one else.''

''Well, it is done and Burgundy is still an ally of Bedford, even though the bonds are weakening.''

''Well, of course, the two are friends and brothers-in-law. It was a wise move of Bedford's to marry Burgundy's sister . . . with Burgundy's consent.''

''It is a true love match, they say.''

''So much the better for them both.''

''Yes,'' I said. ''When one has the benefit of a happy marriage and learns the joy it can bring, one wants the same for everyone else.''

''That is because you have a generous nature, my love.''

''Oh, how glad I am that we were bold and brave. Just think, Owen. We might have turned our backs on all this happiness . . . just because we were afraid to take it.''

"My dearest," he said. "I hope you will never regret it."

I shook my head fervently. "No matter what awaits me in the future, I would not have missed the happiness I have with you for the whole world," I told him.

And so we continued in our blissful existence. It may have been that every day seemed more precious to us because somewhere, at the back of our minds, we knew it could not last.

How long should I be able to live secure with my family in this cocoon of secrecy?

There was strange news from France. Everyone in the house was talking about it. It was a miracle, some said. It was a wild rumour, said the more prosaic, put about by the French, who hoped to glean some advantage from it. They must indeed be alarmed to try such methods, said others.

Owen had discovered what it was all about.

"It's a peasant girl," he said. "She declares she hears voices which give her commands from Heaven. Apparently she is told by these voices that France will be strong again, and the English will be driven out of every part of the country."

"And the French believe this?"

"They were sceptical at first, naturally. An uneducated peasant girl from a place called Domrémy . . . working on her father's little bit of land . . . tending the sheep . . . such a girl to lead the armies of France! You would say the girl was mad . . . would you not?"

"And they do not?"

"It is strange. Apparently she has a way with her. She has accomplished all sorts of difficult tasks. Who would have thought a girl like that could have encountered anything but ridicule?"

"And what has she encountered?"

"She persuaded the Governor of Vaucouleurs to arrange for her to have an interview with the Dauphin."

"My brother saw her!"

"Yes. The story is that the men tried to poke fun at her. They took her to Chinon and into a room where the Dauphin was. They took her to one of his friends, telling her that he was the Dauphin and asking her to say what she had to say to him. But she *knew* they were deceiving her . . . and she went straight to the Dauphin and would speak to none but him."

I was trying to visualize my brother Charles. It was so long since I had seen him. To me he was still the little brother, the youngest among us . . . following us round with that bewildered look on his little face. I knew he had not wished to be Dauphin. Jean had not wanted that rôle either. The prospect of a crown had been thrust upon them. And what of Charles now? What was it like to be a Dauphin but no Dauphin . . . robbed of his crown which now belonged to my little Henry? What did he think of me . . . living in the enemy's camp? What did he think of my mother who had given her allegiance to the conqueror . . . passing over his crown to my little Henry . . . agreeing that it should be taken from her own son! Of course, that had made it better for her . . . to stand with the conqueror rather than the defeated; and when had she ever thought of her family? Her only concern had been for her own comfort.

It was difficult to imagine my brother Charles confronted by this strange young girl who came with messages from Heaven.

"And he received her?" I murmured. "This peasant girl!"

"It seems she overawed him as she had others."

"Can it be that she is indeed a messenger from Heaven?"

Owen said: "There is undoubtedly a strange quality about her. They say there is a certain radiance . . . a fearlessness . . . an indifference to ridicule. Her faith shines through her. She believes she has been selected from on high to be the saviour of France."

"The army will soon put an end to that."

I wanted to talk about the progress Edmund was making.

"We shall have to move from Hadham," I said. "For one thing the sweetening is becoming very necessary."

"We have been here so long. It is a pity. It is an ideal place."

"What think you of Hatfield? That would be possible."

In due course we decided to go to Hatfield.

Guillemote was very interested in the news which was coming from France. Naturally she had a great love for her native land. She had always been loyal to me, and during those days when I had had to adjust myself to a new country, her presence had helped me a great deal. Because I had been the wife of an English king, I had regarded myself as belonging to my husband's country; I understood that this was something Guillemote could never do.

She was very intrigued by what she heard of the woman they called "The Maid." I supposed the story of Joan of Arc was one which would arouse interest anywhere. A young peasant girl of no education to whom Heaven had sent voices commanding her to drive the invader from her tortured country!

It was a ridiculous fancy. Or so it seemed.

Guillemote had served me faithfully all my life but I think at this time patriotic fervour stirred within her and she dreamed of marching side by side with The Maid.

Her eyes glowed when she talked of her.

"There is an old prophecy," she said. "France would be ruined by a wicked woman and saved by a virgin maid."

The wicked woman, she implied, was my mother; and now here was The Maid.

Had there been such a prophecy? I wondered. Or were people telling themselves they had heard it at their mothers' knees?

I had never heard it. But then should I have done so during my days at the Hôtel de St. Paul and later in the sequestered atmosphere of Poissy? I was sure that many such prophecies were brought to light after the event which proved them to be true.

Little had been proved yet of this one, except that The Maid had seen my brother and had aroused in him a love of country to replace his hitherto languid acceptance of defeat.

And the people believed The Maid. Men were ready to fight beside her with new energy and purpose, because they were certain that God was their ally and that therefore they must prevail.

Then something happened to make all this seem unimportant to me. I was once more pregnant. I was filled with joy. Another child! And this time there would not be the same anxiety. I was surrounded by devoted friends. We had managed with Edmund, and we should know how to do so with a new child.

Owen was delighted and, although Guillemote pursed her lips and shook her head and wondered whether I was sufficiently recovered from the birth of Edmund, I could see that she, too, was overjoyed at the prospect of a new baby.

I suppose I should have been more interested in what was going on but my mind was wholly absorbed by thoughts of my coming child. So I did not ask myself what was happening at the siege of Orléans and if The Maid and her heavenly allies would succeed against the all-conquering English, but "Will the child be a girl or a boy?"

The journey from Hadham to Hatfield was a little trying. I rode some of the way because I did not want to arouse suspicions regarding my state of health, but Guillemote insisted that when I looked tired I should take to a litter.

I must say I was glad to see the walls of the palace before me and to pass under the gateway. I was exhausted by the journey, and Guillemote insisted on my getting to bed without delay.

My ladies were bustling around me to make sure that everything was in order.

There was an element of danger in moving to a new place. We had had everything arranged to our satisfaction in Hadham. Here there would be new servants, and servants talk.

I knew that I could trust Owen and my devoted friends to make sure that we were as safe as we possibly could be.

I needed to rest for several days after the journey.

"It has been too much for you," said Guillemote. "I am wondering whether it wouldn't have been better to have stayed at Hadham . . . sweetening or not."

"A foul place would have been no good for the baby," I reminded her. "And we had been there too long already."

"Nor was the journey any good for the baby," retorted Guillemote.

However, all seemed to be well, and after a rest I felt in good health.

Hatfield Place is a beautiful residence, grander than Hadham, and perhaps for that reason I had felt safer at the latter. We were nineteen miles north of London, which did not seem very far. I loved the long gallery and the chapel, which had some of the most attractive stained-glass windows I had ever seen. I liked to sit there and pray, with the light streaming through onto the dark oak floor. I would thank God for giving me the blessing of marriage to a good man, for my son Edmund and for the child I soon hoped to have. I was fortunate. And what I prayed for was to go on in my peaceful happy home, with my husband and children around me . . . free from danger.

My thoughts were completely absorbed by my family; so I listened half-heartedly to the news which filtered into the palace and was avidly seized on by the others.

Guillemote's stream of talk broke into my reverie.

"I believe it to be true," she said.

"What do you believe, Guillemote?" I asked.

"That The Maid has been sent by God."

"Oh, you are talking of that again, are you?"

"My lady . . . dear madam, *every*one is talking about it."

"Do they still think she is divine?"

"They do not think that she is divine . . . just that she is a messenger from God."

"Well, would that not make her divine?"

"She does not say that she is. She says she is a simple girl who hears voices commanding her to take up arms and lead the soldiers to victory."

I yawned slightly and stroked the little shift I was embroidering. "Orléans will fall to the French they say," went on Guillemote. "And if it does, that will be the turning point. It will be Paris next."

"Orléans fall!" I said.

"Yes . . . the siege. The English have been holding on. It is hoped that they are on the verge of surrender. Joan the Maid is there leading the men on urging them to break through the walls and rescue Orléans."

"How can she . . . a woman . . . ?"

"With the help of God," said Guillemote.

"Guillemote, you can't really believe . . ."

Guillemote looked at me steadily and said: "I do believe."

"The Duke of Bedford will never allow it."

"What hope has he? He is losing Burgundy's friendship. It only lingers on because Burgundy loves his sister Anne, who pleads with him not to desert her husband."

"This is gossip."

"Mayhap. But there is often truth in gossip. If Orléans should fall, men will flock to The Maid. It will prove that she has led her fellow countrymen to achieve what seemed impossible."

"You are bemused by this Maid."

"Madame . . . the whole of France is bemused by this Maid."

I could not take these tales seriously, but I soon learned that I should.

Orléans was taken and this was a resounding victory for the French.

I could not help thinking of my brother-in-law Bedford. He

must be disconsolate. It had been a sacred mission for him to carry out Henry's wishes and keep—and add to—the possessions in France. And now one of the key cities was lost. It was not only this loss but the effect the victory would have on the army which was losing its spirit as well as much of the land conquered by Henry.

Owen was dismayed by the news. He repeated his conviction that it could never have happened if Henry had been alive.

"I cannot imagine what this will mean," he said. "It is hard to believe that one victory like this can change the course of the war. But it seems this is not all. The Maid has aroused a new spirit in France. And when people are fighting for their own country, they seem to acquire a special strength."

"You cannot believe this story of The Maid's being sent by God?"

"There are many strange things that happen on earth which are beyond our understanding. This might be one of them. Moreover, we have to consider this victory, this new spirit which is arising in France. The Dauphin is now bestirring himself."

"My brother never wanted the crown."

"It seems that The Maid has inspired him to now."

Owen had discovered that messengers were constantly crossing the Channel. The Duke of Bedford was keeping the Council informed. Even I, absorbed as I was in the child I had and the one who was coming, could not be unaware that momentous events were taking place.

One day a messenger came to Hatfield.

I was alarmed. I had hoped that few had been aware of my change of residence, but the fact that this messenger came meant that the move was not unknown.

He was French and had been in the service of my father at one time; and I think it was for this reason that he had made the perilous journey to Hatfield to see me.

He wanted to give me the news in person, for he did not forget that, although I was the Queen of England, I was also a French princess.

I could see that he thought he had brought me good news.

I welcomed him, feeling greatly relieved that my pregnancy, as yet, was not apparent.

He told me that there was great rejoicing in France, and the news he brought was that my brother had been crowned in Rheims.

How could that be? I wondered. My little Henry was the acknowledged King of France. It had been part of the treaty of peace which had been signed between my parents and my husband who had graciously allowed my father to bear the title until his death, and my father was now dead. Henry would have been King had he lived, and then none would have dared raise a voice against that—but now he was dead and the crown had gone to his son Henry.

So how could my brother Charles be crowned King?

"The Maid came with him to the cathedral," said the messenger. "It was a goodly sight indeed. She carried her banner high. 'Jhesus Maria.' So bold it was that all could read it. Her face shone with glory, my lady. All knew that she was God's messenger."

"And my brother . . . the Dauphin . . . ."

"The Dauphin no longer, my lady, but King Charles VII of France."

I wanted to say: that cannot be. I could see Henry's face before me, shining with victory. If he had lived . . . oh, but if he had lived, everything would have been different. Owen would not now be my husband. Edmund would not have been born. I felt the child move within me as though to remind me of its presence.

No. If Henry had lived, it would have been a different story.

"Hope is springing up throughout France, my lady. It is hard to believe that this could have happened. It is a different country. The people have been given hope. And all through The Maid. But when you see her . . . my lady . . . that radiant goodness . . . it is not difficult to understand why."

I lowered my head, and the messenger seemed suddenly to realize that, although I had been a princess of France, that was no longer my country and he was talking of the defeat of the one to which I now belonged.

I wanted to ease his embarrassment. I said: "It was good of you to come to me with this news. I thank you. It must have been a very hazardous journey for you."

"I served your father. I knew of his love for you. I see now . . . ."

"No . . . no," I assured him. "It was good of you. I thank you. You must be refreshed. I wish you a safe journey back."

He left me . . . subdued.

The weeks were passing. My pregnancy was beginning to show itself. September was coming to an end, and the mornings were misty; the trees were taking on their autumnal tints. Before the year was out, my baby would be born.

I remembered the day well. Messengers came riding to the palace. They always caused me great disquiet. If my enemy Gloucester discovered that Owen and I had broken the law and married—even though the law was made after our marriage—I could not guess what our fate would be. They would perhaps not dare harm me, and as my brother now called himself the King of France, they would have to act with caution. It was Owen for whom I feared. They would call him a traitor. I trembled for Owen.

Guillemote came running to me, her face puckered in alarm.

"Can you not say I am unwell?"

She slowly shook her head. "They are from the Bishop."

"From Winchester?"

She nodded.

"He is a cardinal now," I said.

"I know. From the Cardinal then."

"What do they want?"

"Some message from him. Come . . . let me see. If you are seated, no one will know." She brought a rug and wrapped it over my knees and my waist.

"We will tell them you have a chill and are staying in," she said. "Mind you do not rise from the chair."

Someone was knocking on the door.

Guillemote went to open it. Two men stood there.

"We are from his Eminence the Cardinal. We have a message for the Queen."

"The Queen is suffering from a chill. She does not want to be disturbed," said Guillemote.

"It is merely to deliver a message, and we have instructions to speak to her and her only."

"Well then, do so," said Guillemote. "The Queen is here."

They came to me and knelt before me. I bade them rise and said in muffled voice that they should state their business as quickly as possible as I was feeling unwell.

''We are here to tell Your Grace that the Cardinal is on his way to you. He has something of great importance to impart to you and wishes to do so in person.''

Alarm seized me. I heard myself saying: ''Where . . . is the Cardinal?''

''He has already begun his journey, my lady. He should be with you in the early afternoon.''

I felt sick with fear. How noticeable was the change in my body? Would the Cardinal realize that I was pregnant?

I thanked the messengers and sent them to be refreshed before they began their return journey.

Guillemote came running in with the Joannas. They listened in dismay to what I told them.

''What are we going to do?'' I demanded.

''You could go to bed . . .'' suggested Guillemote.

I pondered that. It was a possibility, but illness had been feigned so often and the Cardinal, astute as he was, would be fully aware of that. It might arouse his suspicions, I said.

''I have it,'' said Joanna Courcy. ''All of us will wear the fullest skirts we can find. We will pad ourselves out with petticoats. We shall all look alike.''

''He will think we have a houseful of pregnant women,'' said Guillemote.

We all laughed but our laughter was a little hysterical.

''He will be full of his own thoughts,'' said Agnes. ''Perhaps he will not notice if we all look alike.''

''That's right,'' I said. ''He will see us dressed in a similar manner, as he will think, and it will not occur to him that one of us may be different. I think it is an excellent idea. We must get ready at once.''

We did so and I had to admit that it would have taken more than a cardinal, beset by his own ambitions, to be aware that my figure was any different from that of my ladies.

I sat in a chair covered by a rug. I should still keep up the myth of a chill.

The others ranged themselves round me. Joanna Belknap had a book on her lap as though reading aloud to us. The rest of us held our needlework. It was a peaceful scene—an indication of the life I lived in my chosen seclusion.

Guillemote had arranged that Edmund should be kept as far away as possible from my apartments.

And so the Cardinal found us.

He came to me and kissed my hand.

"You will forgive my remaining seated, Cardinal," I said. "I have a slight chill. They have been dosing me with their remedies, which has made me feel uncommonly lazy."

"Remain in a warm room," said the Cardinal. " 'Tis the best for a chill in the head."

"I believe that to be so. It is good of you to come and see me."

"A pleasure, Madam."

He looked at the ladies seated round me. I waved my hand, and they rose rather awkwardly in their padded garments. I watched the Cardinal closely. He showed no interest in their bulky skirts, I was relieved to see.

He had aged. The bitter feud with Gloucester had taken its toll of him. There were lines under his eyes, and his handsome face was slightly ravaged. It still retained its proud and haughty look which seemed to me to be reminding people that he was royal. Watching him, I had the conviction that Gloucester would never get the better of him.

"I trust Your Grace will soon recover from this indisposition which I rejoice to see is not great," he was saying.

"Thank you, my lord Cardinal. I am sure I shall soon be well."

"I would not have disturbed your peace," he went on, "but this is a matter of some urgency concerning the King."

I was alarmed. "He is ill?" I cried.

"The King is in the best of health."

My relief must have been obvious.

"Your Grace need have no fears on that score. The King is carefully watched over by several of us, and the Earl of Warwick gives good reports of his progress."

"I am glad to hear of it."

"If Your Grace came to Court, you would have more opportunities of seeing the King."

"I hear from him often. I pray that all will go well with him. What is this matter which so deeply concerns him?"

"Your Grace will no doubt be aware of the situation in France?"

"I know something of it."

"Bad news travels fast. This woman who has appeared on the scene . . ."

"You mean Joan The Maid."

"That is how she is known. She has created a certain amount of harm."

"A young girl can do that! I have heard that she *is* a young girl."

"She makes a great show of her virginity. Whether it is true or not, I have no idea. I rather doubt it . . . living with rough soldiers as she does."

"There is a great deal of talk about her. She seems to have achieved . . . miracles."

"The French have had some initial success, it is true."

"Which is attributed to her?"

"It would seem so. It is a form of hysteria."

"I have heard that it has resulted in the coronation of my brother. Is this true?"

"Yes, it is true. He calls himself the King of France now. But he is King in name only, of course."

"And the people of France . . . ?"

"Well, their mood has changed. They have, it is true, risen out of the lethargy which previously possessed them. They are telling themselves that God has sent The Maid to bring them victory."

"And this disturbs you?"

"It is nonsense, of course, but, as I have said, it has had a certain effect on the people."

"And she has recaptured Orléans."

"That is so . . . and there have been one or two other victories . . . minor, of course . . . but they have put heart into the French."

"And taken a little from the English?"

"These matters are very unfortunate. People are superstitious. They see omens everywhere. The French believe that God is fighting with them. He comes in the shape of a young maid. It is nonsense . . . but it has had its effect, since they have dared crown the Dauphin."

"Well, you say you do not regard it as important. You say it does not change the case."

"We do not like it. And this is the reason for my visit to you."

My heart started to beat wildly. I was wondering when he was ever coming to the point, but had feared to show my anxiety by pressing it.

"As soon as possible," he went on, "we shall take the King to France and have him crowned there. He is the true King. The throne was freely given by your father to the late King, your husband. It is a pity King Henry V did not have himself crowned at the time of his victory. Then there could have been no disputing who was the true King of France."

"He did not wish to deprive my father of his crown during his lifetime."

"Such gestures, while noble, often lead to confusion. However, we intend to right that as soon as possible. Our King Henry, young as he is, must go to France as soon as it is convenient to do so, that we may put the crown of France on his head. But as he has not yet been crowned King of England, we propose to do that at once, and it would be meet and fitting for his mother to be present on that occasion."

"You mean for the crowning here . . ."

"I mean for both. It will be advisable for you to go to the ceremony in Westminster, but necessary, I think, to that which follows in France."

I was filled with dismay. Go to France! Leave my babies? Leave Owen!

He went on: "The first ceremony will take place next month. I doubt not that you will need a little time to prepare."

Next month! I hoped I did not betray my consternation. Next month it would be impossible to hide my condition.

And to go to France . . .

I was on the point of crying out: I cannot. It is quite impossible. But I restrained myself. The last thing I must do was betray the true state of affairs to this astute man.

"I thought I should come in person," he went on, "to stress the importance of this. But of course you will realize that and how necessary it is for you to be present. The King is young. And at such a time he will wish to be with his mother."

I wanted to shout at him: yet you took him away from me. You gave him to Alice Butler and Joan Astley!

"And," went on the Cardinal, "your presence in France will be a great help. Especially now . . . when there is a sign of rebellion amongst the French. It will remind the people that the

King's mother is their late King's daughter. So I have come to ask you to come to Court within the next week or two.''

I could not go to London. That was certain. But what excuse could I give? I must have turned pale, for the Cardinal was a little concerned.

"I trust I have not tired you," he said.

"I . . . er . . . I must apologize for being in such a low state.''

"It was good of you to receive me.''

"Then goodbye, Cardinal. Thank you for your visit. They will send my women to me . . . immediately.''

He bowed himself out and no sooner was he gone than Guillemote and the others burst in.

"You look shocked," said Guillemote.

"So will you be . . . when you know what he came for.''

"Pray tell us and do not keep us in suspense," begged Agnes.

"They are going to crown Henry, and the Cardinal thinks I should be present at the ceremony.''

"When?" cried Guillemote.

"Next month.''

There was a shocked silence.

"You cannot go," said Joanna Troutbeck.

"That is certain," I agreed.

"It is simple," said Guillemote. "You will just be ill. What else can you do? It is well that you have set the stage. We will start right away. I shall get you to bed. Before the Cardinal leaves, it shall be known that you are less well than you were when he arrived, and your faithful servants, appalled by your condition—which has nothing to do with his visit, as they were aware you were more ill than you allowed it to be assumed— are getting you to your bed without delay.''

My son Henry was crowned at Westminster on the sixth day of November of that year 1429 in the presence of Parliament. His mother was not present. She was at that time somewhat unwieldy, keeping to her apartments and taking good care not to be seen by any but those whom she could trust—the birth of her child being expected in a matter of weeks.

Poor Henry! I was sad that I could not be with him. I wondered what he was feeling. At eight years old he was too young to have a crown placed on his head. He had always been a solemn child. I guessed he had become more so. He would need to be.

I wondered if he missed me. I felt a deep grudge against those who had taken him away from me. Was he thinking of me at this time? Did he *ever* think of me . . . or was I just part of that early childhood which must have become like a hazy dream to him.

I wanted to hear all I could about the ceremony.

Owen thought it was not only because they wished to take him to France and crown him King of that country that they had hastened his coronation in England; for when he was crowned, Gloucester would lose his post of Protector, and Owen imagined that it was the need to thrust Gloucester out of that important role which had been the deciding factor in this rather hasty coronation.

"Surely they will not expect my son to govern?" I said.

"No. But it is a way of getting rid of the present Protector. You are not the only one, my love, who sees him as a menace."

"I know the Cardinal does, for one."

"Others too, I'll swear."

We heard reports of that ceremony in Westminster Abbey. Warwick had led Henry in. He looked splendid, they said, in his rich coronation robes; and the people loved him for his youth. He was solemn and serious, looking rather sad and wise, as though he fully understood the significance of the ceremony and was already aware of the burdens of kingship which were being set on his young shoulders.

If I were not actually at Westminster, my thoughts were with him. I would write to him and tell him how sad I was that I could not be present at such a time. But that was not strictly true. I was carrying his little half-brother or -sister and that was a fact which made me rejoice.

But how I hated this web of deceit which I had been forced to weave about myself. I did not care so much that I must lie to Gloucester and the Cardinal; but I wished I did not have to do so to my son.

I had a letter from him which I treasured. In it he expressed his sorrow at my illness, and he was deeply distressed because I had not been present to see him crowned.

A splendid banquet had followed the ceremony in the Abbey, and during it a proclamation was made that in the New Year the King would be leaving for his French dominions.

During the weeks that followed, to the exclusion of all else, I was absorbed in preparations for my child's arrival. The same methods of secrecy which had been the order at the time of Edmund's birth were put into practice.

''We are getting accustomed to it,'' said Guillemote.

It appeared to be satisfactory for everything went smoothly. I often thought how lucky I was to have such loyal servants. I marvelled at this, for there was not one of them who did not know that what they were doing would be construed as a crime against the state and, if it were discovered, could result in imprisonment for them . . . perhaps even death.

The days were short now, and darkness was already creeping into the palace before four o'clock in the afternoon. The snow was falling heavily.

''That is good,'' said Joanna Troutbeck. ''It means we cannot have visitors catching us unawares.''

At last the time came. They were all around me and I felt safe with them.

My ordeal was not a long one. It was easier than it had been with Edmund; and when I heard the cry of my newly born child, I forgot the need for secrecy and all my fears in my joy.

''The child is a boy,'' Guillemote whispered to me. ''A bonny healthy boy. A brother for little Edmund.''

I saw Owen at my bedside, the child in his arms.

''Here he is,'' he said. ''Just look at him. He's perfect. Are you not proud of yourself to have produced such a child?''

''He is yours, too, Owen,'' I said.

And I felt: everything . . . just everything is worthwhile for this moment.

We decided to call him Jasper. ''Jasper of Hatfield,'' I said. ''Brother to Edmund.''

Edmund was brought to view his new brother. He looked with wonder at the small creature in the cradle.

''He is your brother,'' I said. ''You will always look after him, will you not?''

Edmund nodded gravely.

"You will always be good friends. You will always stand together. You will, Edmund, I know."

"Yes," said Edmund. And he repeated, "Brother Jasper."

He hunched his shoulders, smiling, as though it were a great joke that he now had a brother.

The Maid

Peace continued for a few weeks. Of course, we knew it could not last. We were prepared, for when the Cardinal had come to see me before Jasper's birth, he had told me of the imminent coronation in France. It was becoming more and more apparent that I should be expected to be there, in view of the fact that I was French and sister to the man who was now calling himself King of France. I was not sure what part I should be expected to play. Owen thought it would depend on the state of affairs which existed between England and France at the time. They would perhaps want me very much in evidence. On the other hand it could well be that they would want to keep me out of the public view.

"If this should be the case," I said to Owen, "why should they be so insistent that I must go?"

"They are taking no chances."

"Oh, Owen . . . *must* I go?"

"I do not see how it can be avoided. Your absence from the coronation at Westminster was acceptable. When the Cardinal visited you, you appeared to be unwell, so it was logical enough to assume that you were sickening for some illness. But if you plead illness again they will probably be sending doctors down to Hatfield to give a report on you. That could be very dangerous."

"I suppose so many people have used illnesses as excuses that it can easily become suspect."

"It is a good one if it can be substantiated."

"You really think I must go, don't you, Owen?"

"I am afraid, my love, that it would be highly dangerous not to do so."

"And you, Owen?"

"It might be that I could come as a member of your household. You will surely be expected to take some of your servants with you."

"If that were possible, I could bear it."

"We shall have to make it possible."

"We will. We will. Oh, but the children, Owen . . ."

"We cannot take them with us."

"No . . . alas. They must remain. But to be separated from them. How long, Owen?"

"It will surely be some months."

"I won't do it. I won't!"

"What excuse can you give?"

"That I am unfit to travel."

"It will not work twice."

"I will tell them the truth then. I will say, 'Leave me alone. Let me live my own life. I have my husband and my children . . . and my family. Rule this country as you will. Rule France too. But please do not try to rule me.' "

Owen took my hands and looked into my face.

"It is no use, Katherine, my love. Such talk will help us not at all. You will have to go or arouse suspicions. We cannot risk that. There must be no excuses this time. You must go as though it is a great pleasure to see your son crowned in your native land. It is the only way. It has to be done."

"I can't face it, Owen. Jasper has only just come to us. To leave him . . . to leave Edmund . . . for so long . . ."

"We have to do it. It's no use fighting against it. And when it is over, we shall return to this quiet, idyllic life. It will be all the more wonderful to us. You will see."

I wept silently.

"It is so hard to leave them . . . when they are so young."

He stroked my hair as he held me tightly in his arms. "Think. You will be closer to Henry."

"Henry is already lost to me. Do you think I shall ever be alone with him? I cannot see Henry now without seeing his crown. He is not so much my son as the King."

"Yet underneath his ceremonial robes and crown, he is only a child. Remember that. He may want to talk to you. He may need your help. It may be that he needs you more than Edmund and Jasper do. They will be left in good hands. You need have no fear for them. Katherine, we have to face this. We dare do nothing else.''

I knew he was right. I had to prepare myself for separation.

I tried to explain to Edmund that I was going away, that I hated to leave him, but this was a matter of duty. He was not quite sure what that was, and I was touched by the way in which he clung to my skirts as though to prevent my departure.

''Guillemote will be here with you. And Jasper will be here.''

That cheered him a little. He adored Guillemote, and I think that when she was around he felt safe.

It would be natural for me to take a small entourage with me. Owen was in this, and so was Joanna Courcy. The other two Joannas with Agnes were staying behind to help Guillemote with the children.

I prayed that I would soon be back but one could never be sure; and I doubted whether I should be received in France with the enthusiasm I had enjoyed when I rode with Henry at my side. The position had changed since then. I had not heard what was happening since the siege of Orléans, but I did know that there was a new spirit among the French and that the high hopes of the English had declined, with the result that there had been several French victories.

It was late February when Henry, after attending service in St. Paul's asking God's blessing on the proposed journey, made his way to Canterbury where he was to spend Easter.

I, with my little entourage, joined him there.

I was formally received by him, but I saw his eyes light up with pleasure as they rested on me, and I knew he was glad that I should be near.

I did have an opportunity of being alone with him, and it seemed then that he set aside his crown and stepped out of his ermine robes to be my little son.

''I have missed you,'' he said.

If only we could all be together! I was thinking of how I would introduce him to his half-brothers, Edmund and Jasper Tudor. If only that were possible! If only we could all be one happy family!

I laughed at myself. What an absurd flight of fancy. I wondered what Henry would say. They would have moulded him to their ways. I supposed Warwick was, after all, following his instructions. Kings could not be kept at their mothers' sides. They had to be brought up to ride, to shoot, to go into battle when the time arose. They were hurried through their boyhoods to make them quickly into men before they had had time to be young. They would say that was a woman's view.

"I have missed you so much, too," I said. "But I heard about your coronation."

"Oh yes, I am truly King now. The Earl of Warwick says that a king is not truly a king until he is crowned."

"Well, you are that now, my son. How like your father you are!"

"Am I?" he asked eagerly. "I have to be like him. They are always saying that. 'Your father would have done this.' 'Your father would have done that.' That is what they are always saying. If I do not please them, they say that my father would be ashamed."

"No, no," I said quickly. "He would have understood. He was a great soldier, but he was a good, kind man as well."

"I wish he had not died."

"A great many people wish that."

"If he were alive, I should not have to be King . . ."

I smiled at him sadly. "Your coronation must have been impressive."

"It was so long . . . and there were so many speeches . . . so many things to remember."

"But I heard you did your part well."

"Did they say so?"

"Yes . . . everybody did."

He looked pleased. "I thought the banquet would go on for ever, and they were all watching me . . ."

"Well, they would, you being the King."

"It is a strange feeling . . . to be a king."

"Yes, it must be."

"Why do you stay shut away in the country?"

"There is little I could do at Court."

"You would be near me."

"I would so rarely see you."

"I wish . . ."

"Tell me what you wish. You are the King. It should not be so difficult for you to achieve."

"What I wish no one could give me. I wish my father would come alive, and then I should not have to be the King."

My poor Henry, weighed down with honours which he did not want! His dearest wish was to be robbed of his crown!

I was glad that kingship had not given him grand ideas of his importance. Rather it seemed it had had the opposite effect.

We stayed in Canterbury over the Easter week and then made our way to Dover. On St. George's Day we were ready to cross to France. Cardinal Beaufort was a member of the party and he was in charge of the King's person. Ten thousand soldiers had joined us at Canterbury and they were ranged on the shore, ready to board the vessels when the order was given.

The sun was shining as we went on board, and very soon, with a fair wind behind us, we were sailing for Calais.

We were blessed with a smooth crossing, and about ten o'clock on a bright and sunny morning we landed.

The Cardinal insisted that we ride at once to the church of St. Nicholas, where High Mass was celebrated.

We stayed a short while in Calais and then the Cardinal said that we should make our way to Rouen where he hoped to find the Duke of Bedford waiting for us.

I gathered that we should remain at Rouen while arrangements were made for Henry's crowning at Rheims. It was an uncomfortable situation, as only recently my brother had been crowned and given the same title which was now to be bestowed on my son. I could sense, too, that there was a very different feeling among the soldiers from that which I had known when I came to meet that other Henry. Uneasiness had replaced triumph. I heard whispers of The Maid.

It was surprising to me that one woman—and a girl at that—could have so changed the outlook of people. In the towns and villages through which we passed we were regarded suspiciously. I knew that the soldiers were on the alert. This country was no longer meekly accepting the conquerors. In fact, the conquerors were on very uncertain ground. Could this all be due to one girl? She must have had divine help. Many believed that, and there was I being influenced in the same way as those superstitious people who thought that God had sent His help

through the person of a country girl, to drive the English out of
France.

I knew that the Cardinal was very uneasy.

I did not have much opportunity of speaking to him but now
and then he seemed to remember that I was the Queen and the
King's mother, and then there would be a little discourse between us.

He would not have spoken of his uneasiness if I had not
insisted on doing so.

I said to him: "Are you anticipating trouble, Cardinal?"

He raised those haughty brows and looked at me in surprise.

"It is clear that something has changed here," I insisted.

"In what way?"

"It would seem to me that the English are no longer regarded
as the triumphant conquerors."

"There have been a few setbacks, but nothing of any great
importance."

"So the fall of Orléans was of no importance?"

"It would have been better if it had not been allowed to happen."

"The crowning of Charles . . ."

"An empty ceremony. The Duke of Bedford is a great soldier
and a magnificent organizer. He has everything under control."

"I suppose it is hard to dispel a legend of this sort which has
risen up."

"You are referring to the woman who dresses up in men's
clothes?"

"I did mean the one whom they call The Maid."

"A momentary wonder. An exaggeration."

"It seems to have put heart into the French and taken something from the English."

"Whatever has been taken will be put back."

I was not sure how much importance he attached to Joan of
Arc, but I believed he was deceiving himself into thinking that
she could have no effect on the war.

I soon discovered that he was by no means unconcerned about
her, for as we marched through those villages, the change in the
mood of the people was decidedly noticeable—and it seemed
that a kind of despairing depression had fallen on our men.

Owen, who always rode in my party but never beside me, for
we had warned ourselves most severely about the dangers of

betraying our relationship and to be continually on the watch lest we betray it, made a discovery. He wanted to tell me, but as no opportunity presented itself, he gave the news to Joanna Courcy, asking her to tell me.

''They have captured The Maid,'' she said.

''The English?''

''No . . . not the English. The Burgundians, who were laying siege to Compiègne. Joan was on the march with three or four hundred men on her way to Crépy when she heard that John of Luxembourg, an ally of the Duke of Burgundy, had started to besiege the town. She went to the rescue of the besieged. Some people think there was treachery. There was a good deal of envy and some of those who should have been her staunchest supporters, being so jealous of her sought to trap her. Many of them got away in boats when the battle was going against them, and Joan with a few others assisted them in their retreat. There is a strong suspicion that her own soldiers may have betrayed her. In any case, the gates of the city were shut before she could get out. She is in the hands of John of Luxembourg and he has taken her to his castle of Beaulieu.''

''I suppose that is the same as being in the hands of the English?''

''Not quite. He will probably ask a ransom for her. He's Burgundy's man . . . and the relationship between Burgundy and the English is at the moment a little strained.''

''Poor girl. I wonder what will happen to her now.''

Joanna shook her head. ''It will be the end of her glory, I am sure.''

The Cardinal was clearly overjoyed, so I knew that his indifference to The Maid had been assumed.

I wondered what I should find when I joined my brother-in-law, Bedford, at Rouen.

Such was the state of affairs in France at this time that our journey to Rouen had to proceed with the utmost care. The fact that the King was one of our party meant that no risks must be taken. I thought of my little ones in England. They would be safe, Joanna was constantly assuring me. Guillemote would defend them with her life.

There were rumours about The Maid. She had escaped, said one. She had been recaptured, said another. Then . . . there had been no escape. She was still the prisoner of the Count of Luxembourg. She would be sold for a large sum of money, that was certain. And who would be ready to pay that large sum of money to get her into their hands? The English! And what would her fate be when she was their prisoner—she, who had been responsible for turning the tide of war against the English? However much they denigrated her, however much they pretended to ridicule her, they must realize the truth of this.

I must admit that my thoughts were mainly occupied with the desire to get back to my children. Moreover, I could not see a great deal of Owen. He had stressed to me the necessity to be careful. But at least there was the comfort of knowing that he was there.

So cautiously we processed on this slow and tedious journey, and although we had landed at Calais in April it was not until July that we arrived in Rouen.

Bedford was there, anxiously awaiting our arrival. He had changed a good deal. He looked careworn and much older. The events of the last year had naturally had their effect on him.

His great concern was for the King but he greeted me with the kindliness which he had always extended towards me. He was the sort of man who would never forget his brother's injunctions to look after me, and would carry out his promise to do so to the very best of his abilities. How differently I felt towards him than I did towards his brother Gloucester.

I was delighted to find that his wife was with him. Because of our relationship, Anne of Burgundy and I had seen each other now and then during our childhood, and we had always liked each other. It would have been difficult not to like Anne. She had grown very beautiful, with a beauty which comes from an inner goodness rather than from features.

I was able to talk to her more freely than to other members of the party—except, of course, Joanna Courcy.

She told me how anxious her husband was.

"The situation here," she said, "is worse than is generally admitted. It is incredible what this Maid has done. She has even aroused Charles from his lethargy sufficiently to get him to agree to a coronation."

"Poor Charles!" I said. "He never really wanted a crown."

"Nor did his brother Jean. How strange that so many fight to attain a crown and that those to whom it comes by inheritance would rather someone else had it.''

''Well, there are always many to fight for it. What a strange position we are in!''

''And you and I, Katherine, now owe our allegiance to a new country . . . and one which was the enemy of our native land. What a mess it all is! I think that, if there had never been this quarrel between Burgundy and Orléans or Armagnacs, everything would have been different.''

''But my husband was determined to take France.''

''And my husband is determined to follow his brother's wishes.''

''And we are caught up in it. Your case is different from mine, Anne. I was married to Henry as part of a treaty. You married his brother because you loved him.''

''Yes. I was one of the lucky ones. But you loved Henry. John says that Henry was above all other men. It was such a tragedy. John has never got over it. He worshipped his brother.''

''Henry was the sort of man people worshipped.''

She put her hand over mine and pressed it firmly.

I felt an urge to tell her. Do not be sorry for me, I wanted to say, for I have found a greater happiness than I ever had with Henry. If I could be left in peace with my family, there is nothing else I would ask.

I restrained myself. Anne was a good woman; she would be sympathetic, but her first allegiance would be to Bedford, and if she thought I had broken the law—which many might say I had—she would feel it her duty to tell her husband.

And sitting with Anne, I did realize fully that, however unimportant I had been made to feel, I yet remained the Queen, and it could be that the children I had by a second marriage might have some claim to the throne. Henry was the natural heir, of course, but Edmund and Jasper . . . oh no, the circumstances would have to be very extraordinary for anyone to think for a moment that they could be in line for the throne. But something of that kind must have been behind Gloucester's reasoning when he had forced that statute through Parliament. Perhaps there was something in his scheming beyond spite. No . . . no . . . the idea was too remote.

I said: ''Henry and your husband were such great friends. It was wonderful to see the brotherly love between them.''

"I felt they always wanted to protect each other . . . and themselves, of course. Their father's hold on the throne was not very secure, and that made them alert for danger. It drew them together as a family."

"The Duke of Gloucester does not appear to have the same family feeling."

"There are some who will always work for themselves and see everything as it affects them personally."

"And Gloucester is one of those."

There was a pause and at length she said: "He has caused John a great deal of anxiety. I have worried a great deal. My brother is very angry with Gloucester. It affects his relationship with my husband, for my brother is, I believe, the most powerful man in France."

"I know. There was the proposed duel."

"Which, fortunately, did not take place."

"I believe no one intended that it should."

"No. But the trouble is still there, and Gloucester has caused it. I could not bear to see the friendship between my husband and brother broken."

I nodded in agreement and she went on: "And now there is The Maid."

"She is in the hands of Luxembourg."

"Yes . . . and I believe he will sell her to the highest bidder."

"Poor girl!"

"She has wrought great havoc."

"To the English," I replied. "To the French she has brought hope."

Anne looked a little surprised. I could see that she regarded England as her country now. How lucky Bedford was! I felt a pang of envy. I understood completely their love for each other. Was I not blessed with similar devotion? But they did not have to hide their happiness behind a cloak of deception.

"I am so glad that I found you here," I said.

"I am with John whenever possible," she replied. "We hate to be separated."

"Have you any idea how long it will be before Henry is crowned?" I asked.

"John wants it to be soon. He always wanted it to take place in Rheims. It should. That will mean a great deal."

"Then why do we not go to Rheims? Why do we stay here in Rouen?"

"I will tell you why. Because there is so much disruption in the country. It is not safe to attempt the journey. The King must not be taken into danger."

"Is it so bad then? I thought . . ."

"The situation has changed considerably since The Maid took Orléans. There are pockets of resistance everywhere. John must be absolutely certain that the King could reach Rheims in safety before he attempts to take him there."

"How can a simple girl have done so much?"

"John says it is the legend she has created. Somehow she has made the people of France believe that she is being guided by God. John says it is not the girl herself. It is the myth surrounding her."

"But if there is a myth, she has created it."

"It is the people who have created the myth."

I could see that in her eyes all that John did and said was right. And I did not attempt to argue the point further.

As the weeks passed, I began to wish that I had made excuses not to come. I had not thought it would be so long. I had imagined that we would go straight to Rheims, the coronation would take place, and we should all return home. I had reckoned on a few months. How different it was! I certainly should have made excuses not to come.

But should I? When I thought of the consequences of discovery, I would be reduced to a state of terror. It was not for myself I worried, and I supposed they would not harm my little ones; it would be Owen they would seize. I saw that I must take every possible precaution against discovery. I must remember this and not grow too impatient at the delay.

It was brought home to me how precarious the situation was when Bedford and Anne left Rouen for a short hunting trip. I cannot think it was solely to hunt. Bedford would be investigating certain parts of the surrounding country, I supposed, testing its safety before allowing the King to move on. But it was no doubt wise to call this foray a hunt.

There was alarm when the members of the hunt came back without the Duke and Duchess. They were struck with horrified amazement to find that they had not returned.

The enemy were in the neighbourhood, they said. Could it possibly be that they had fallen into their hands?

While the awful contemplation of what this could mean gripped us all, Anne and Bedford came riding into the castle. Bedford was pale and tight-lipped. Obviously they had been in great danger.

I learned afterwards that they had become cut off from the party and had come very close to a company of French soldiers. By good fortune they had managed to keep hidden until the company passed, but it was only due to good luck that they had escaped capture.

It was an indication of the changed condition of the country and how close the enemy were to Rouen.

I was depressed. As Henry was with us and there could be such danger, there was no hope of our leaving Rouen just yet.

Anne told me about the adventure later. She had been very frightened.

"They were very close," she said. "We could hear their voices. We were lucky to be in a wood where the trees helped to hide us. Just suppose they had captured John! That would surely have been the end. There is no one who could take his place."

"You will have to be more careful in future."

"Oh, we shall be. John says we must take precautions before making the journey to Rheims. They will know the little King is with us. John thinks they would certainly make an attempt to capture him."

I was filled with alarm. "What do you think they would do to him?"

She was silent. I burst out: "He is only a child. What harm has he done? They would kill him . . . if they caught him."

"No. They would not dare. The most likely thing is that they would hold him to ransom. Be calm, Katherine. He will not be taken. He is safe here. John would never allow him to be taken. He has sworn a solemn oath to protect the King and serve him with all his strength."

"I know. Oh . . . but how I wish we could go home!"

"The crowning will take place and then you will go."

"But when . . . when?"

I might well ask.

* * *

The months were passing and still we lingered at Rouen. With the French so close, Bedford dared not venture out with the King.

Anne told me that he was abandoning all hope of getting to Rheims and that it might be necessary to crown Henry in Paris.

"Why not?" I said eagerly.

"Because Rheims is the place where the Kings of France are crowned and have been since the twelfth century, when Philip Augustus was crowned there. You know that, Katherine. And the French would not believe he could be truly King if he were not crowned at Rheims."

"Somehow I do not believe they will accept Henry as their true King wherever he is crowned."

"In time they will. John is certain of that."

But still the weeks passed and we remained at Rouen.

There was news of The Maid. The English had paid the ransom for her, and she was in their hands.

I guessed they would bring her to Rouen, which was a city more important to them than Paris because it was the capital of Normandy, which they had always considered part of England.

I was right. The Maid was close to us.

A hush seemed to have fallen over the castle. She was in everyone's thoughts. Those who had seen her said that there was a radiance about her and an innocence never seen before. To see her was to believe in her Voices, it was said. Now that she was a prisoner of the English—those who had suffered most through her—what would happen to her?

"Poor girl," said Joanna Courcy. "Sold to her enemies for 10,000 livres."

"How could Luxembourg have found it in his heart to sell her?"

"He was thinking of his pocket rather than his heart," said Joanna grimly.

"What will it be like for her in that prison?" I wondered.

"They may be in too much awe of divine judgement to harm her," suggested Joanna.

"I pray that will be so."

"But her judges will condemn her in the end. She has done too much harm to our cause."

"I wonder what she feels lying there."

"Your brother will save her surely."

"Why, yes," I cried. "Charles must save her. But do you think he can?"

"He will do all in his power. She has turned the tide for him. She has given him new hope, brought back his dignity . . . his crown, one might say."

"Yes, you are right. My brother will save her. But can he do so . . . if she is in English hands? Oh, to think the French sold her to the English for 10,000 livres!"

"The Burgundians," Joanna corrected me. "The French would never have sold one who was their best hope."

"How strange it is. Are not the Burgundians French? The Duke of Bedford will be rejoicing that there is still some friend-ship between him and the Duke of Burgundy. I wish I cold stop thinking of that poor Maid."

"People would say that we should rejoice because she is un-der lock and key."

"Oh, but she is so young . . . so innocent."

"An innocent girl who led an army to victory!"

"How I should love to see her . . . to talk to her . . . to discover for myself whether I could believe she truly heard those voices."

The Maid's name was on everyone's lips as Christmas came and we were still in Rouen.

I cannot say it was a happy Christmas. Few were in the mood for merriment. True, The Maid was no longer an inspiration to our enemies, and the fact that she lay at this time in her prison should have cheered us, but it did not. It was impossible to rid ourselves of the lurking belief that she was indeed inspired by Heaven and that the hand of God would be turned against us because we had made her a prisoner.

My thoughts were back in Hatfield with my children. Jasper was a year old. He would not remember me when I returned. Would Edmund? Oh, it was cruel to separate us. How much longer must we remain in France?

"Are we never to leave this place?" I demanded of Anne.

"Not until it is safe for the King to travel."

So the days passed.

I did have one or two opportunities of spending a little time with Henry.

He was deeply interested in The Maid.

"Do you really think that she hears voices from Heaven?" he asked me.

"I do not know," I answered.

"If it is true, we should not punish her."

"Perhaps we should let her go back to tend her father's sheep," I said.

"My lord uncle says that she would not do that. She would set herself at the head of the French army and lead them to more victories."

"Perhaps she would lead them to defeat."

"How could she, if God is with her?"

"Your uncle does not believe God is with her. He thinks she is a wicked woman . . . a bold woman who dresses like a man and lives with rough soldiers. Henry, tell me. Do you defend her . . . to your uncle?"

He turned to me, and I saw the bewildered look in his eyes. "I should mayhap," he said. "But I do not."

"Why should you?"

"Because it may be true."

"You really think that, do you not?"

"Sometimes . . . when I am alone . . . at night perhaps. And I pray to God and ask Him to guide me . . . to let me see the truth. But when I listen to my uncle and my lord Warwick and the Earl of Stafford, I think I am wicked to think that she who is our enemy may be working with God."

"Dear little King," I said, "they have put too heavy a burden on those young shoulders."

"They are putting her into the hands of the Bishop of Beauvais. I signed an order for him to set up a court and try her. My lady, could it be like trying God?"

"Only if you believe she is holy and has indeed been visited by the angels. Your uncle does not believe that."

"Oh no."

"So . . . you will not."

"My uncle says she is a witch, and if she is a witch, she deserves to die, does she not?"

"They will prove she is a witch if they want to, I'll swear."

"They do want to. Oh yes, they want to. But it must not be because they want to but because she is."

I soothed him, for I could see that he wanted comfort.

"We shall see," I said. "Whatever happens, you must not blame yourself. It is not your responsibility, you know."

"But . . . I have to sign the papers."

"That is only a symbol. You are not responsible for what the Regent does."

"But I am the King, dear mother."

"I wish . . ."

"Tell me what you wish."

I took his face in my hands and I was picturing him at Hatfield . . . in the nursery with his little brothers. Oh, if only that could be! If only I could wipe away that anxious look . . . if only I could make this bewildered little King into a carefree boy!

The year was moving on, and we were out of January—and still no sign of leaving Rouen.

I was growing restless. I sent for Owen.

He came cautiously but I flung myself into his arms. He held me firmly but I was aware of his tension. All the time he was wondering if we could possibly be watched.

"I am tired . . . tired of this, Owen," I cried. "I want to go home. I want to see my children. This is a nightmare which never ends."

"It must end soon," said Owen. "They will try The Maid. They will condemn her . . . and when she is dead, the French will say that as there was no miraculous rescue, The Maid deluded them. They will return to their old slothful ways, and the Duke of Bedford will be the feared and respected Lord of France once more."

"And what of my brother whom she has crowned King?"

"He will revert to his old ways. In fact, it seems he already has. It was expected that he would make some move to come to the aid of the girl who had done so much for him. But what did he do? Nothing."

I thought of Charles . . . indolent . . . self-indulgent. Oh Charles, I thought, have you no shame? Everyone expects you to make some effort to save this girl. But for her you would still be Charles . . . ironically called the Dauphin. You would never have done anything to bring yourself out of the rut into which you had fallen. But she did it for you. Are you going to ignore her now?

I feared that he would. Perhaps I knew too well that little boy who had been with me all those years ago in the Hôtel de St. Paul.

Winter had passed into spring, and we still waited. A feeling of doom had overtaken me. I should never escape.

I should have been bold. I should not have come here. I should have made excuses to stay at home.

It was already May. What were my children doing? Guillemote would keep my memory alive with Edmund. She would tell Jasper of his mother who loved him and longed to be with him. I could trust Guillemote. I thought of the spring in Hatfield. The trees would now have emerged from their winter nudity and be clothed in green leaves. How beautiful it would be in Hatfield, where my children were growing up without me!

Every few days there was news of The Maid. She had been passed over to the secular law. We knew what that meant.

The law would now pass on her that sentence which the Church feared to . . . just in case they were dealing with someone who had been guided by Heaven. How I despised them! How ashamed I was of my brother, who stood aside and made no attempt to help the girl who had done so much for him.

There was unrest everywhere and a tension in the air. People wondered what would happen when The Maid went to her death, for they had condemned her as a witch—and that meant death by fire.

Poor child! She was little more. Could they not show some mercy to one so young? Could they not send her back to her family . . . to the fields where she could once again tend her father's sheep?

But they feared her. Lurking in their minds would be the question: was she indeed the emissary of God? And if she were, what fate would befall those who harmed her?

I thought that right at the last moment someone would intervene to save her but, when the day came, no one attempted to do so.

It was 30 May. A hushed silence prevailed throughout the castle. The thoughts of everyone were with that young girl who had heard voices from Heaven and as a result had led an army and changed the course of the war.

How could a simple girl have done that without the help of Heaven?

I shall never forget that day.

People crowded into the streets to witness her martyrdom. We did hear details of it afterwards for those who had witnessed it were eager to talk—indeed, they could not stop talking of it.

Henry had asked that I come to him.

We sat holding hands. I was surprised that he, being so young, could be so deeply affected.

He said little. He just clung to my hand; and I knew he was thinking of The Maid.

There was a deep silence all about us. Instinctively we knew that it was over. And still we sat together . . . Henry and I.

His secretary, a man named Tressart, came into the room. He looked startled to see us there and was about to mutter an apology when Henry said: "Stay, Tressart."

There was a look of shock on Tressart's face and I guessed he had just returned from the square.

Henry said: "Tressart . . . you were there?"

"Yes, my lord."

"You saw . . . ?"

Tressart nodded; he was too moved for speech.

"Tell me, Tressart."

Tressart covered his face with his hands and still did not speak.

"Tell me, Tressart," repeated Henry.

"She . . . er . . . she died bravely, my lord. She asked for a cross that it might be held before her till the last. An Englishman in the crowd made a cross with two sticks and gave it to her."

"An Englishman," said Henry. "I am glad it was an Englishman."

"Cardinal Beaufort and even the Bishop of Beauvais wept when the faggots were lighted. Then someone fetched the cross from the church and held it before her eyes."

"God rest her soul," said Henry.

"And the Canon of Rouen cried out: 'Would my soul were where that woman's will now be!' "

"They should never have done it," said Henry.

Tressart stood very still, shaking his head. "We are lost," he said. "This day we have burned a saint."

It was later that day that Tressart came to me.

"The King is asking for you," he said. "He is distraught."

I found Henry in great distress. He immediately asked Tressart to leave us.

I went to him and took him in my arms. "Henry, what ails you?" I asked.

"My lady . . . mother . . . I cannot forget it. We have done this terrible thing, and it was in my name."

"You are thinking of Joan of Arc still."

"I cannot get her out of my head."

"It is a terrible tragedy, but these things happen now and then. It was no fault of yours. You have done nothing."

"It was done in my name."

"But that is another matter. You are too young to be blamed for what those about you do. They use your name, that is all, and you must obey them. It is they who are responsible."

"But I should have stopped it."

"There was nothing you could do."

"She was a saint, they say."

"She was the enemy . . . your enemy . . . the enemy of your country. She led an army against you. That is how you must see it, Henry."

"I cannot. I cannot. Mother, there is something I must tell you."

"Yes, my love."

"They took me to see her."

"In her prison?"

He nodded. "I did not speak to her. They made me look through an aperture in the wall. I saw her lying there. She was dressed like a man. Her hair was closely cropped. Yet she did not look like a man. Her lips moved. I think she was praying, because there was no one with her to whom she could be talking. I shall never forget her."

"You will, Henry," I said. "It is because it is so recent that you think this . . . and there has been so much talk about her, all this . . . hysteria, your uncle Bedford would call it."

"It is not that, dear mother. There was something about her . . . a shining radiance. And suddenly her lips stopped moving and she looked straight at me. She just looked . . . and looked . . . and I felt as though I were in the presence of holiness."

"My dear child, they should not have taken you."

"I wanted to go. I wanted to see her."

"Well, you did . . . and now it is over. Whatever was done cannot be changed now."

"But Tressart was right. I know he was right. We have killed a saint."

"Henry, you have to forget it. It is all part of war . . . and life. There will be other decisions . . . there will be many burdens. You are a king, remember, the son of a great father."

He covered his face with his hands.

"I do not want to be King. I do not want to have this on my conscience. I want to run away."

I held him tightly against me. I could feel the rising hysteria in him. I must calm him at all cost. He frightened me.

He held up his face to mine, bewildered and afraid, and there was a wildness in his eyes.

A terrible thought came into my mind: He looks like my father. I dismissed it at once. He had had a shock. He was only a boy . . . a serious-minded boy and already deeply religious. He took his duties seriously. The burning of that girl at the stake had had its effect on us all. And Henry, as titular Head of the State, felt himself to be responsible for it.

I rocked him in my arms as though he were a baby, and he clung to me. I was relieved that he wanted comfort and that I was the one from whom he sought it.

I talked to him. I told him how dearly I loved him and how sad I was that he had not been left in my care. But I was there if he wanted me. I was his mother. He must never forget that, and there was a bond between us which could never be broken.

I recalled incidents from his babyhood; how he had refused to leave Staines and had kicked and screamed to express his disapproval, and how they had said it was because he was so deeply religious that he would not travel on the Sabbath Day. I was pleased to see that he smiled faintly and that his features became more composed.

He sat for a long time close to me, and a serenity crept over his face so that he looked more like the boy I had always known.

I must try to shut out that terrifying image I had caught for a moment or so.

We were all over-wrought, I convinced myself. The burning to death of the saintly Joan of Arc had had an effect on us all.

* * *

How I wished we could leave Rouen! There were some who said it was a cursed city because in its square they had burned to death the saviour of France. The Goddams were damned, said the French. I had discovered that this was the name they had given to the English because so many of the soldiers in every other sentence used the words "God damn." The French had caught it. Hence the name.

The French might blame the English for sending Joan of Arc to the flames, but the English retorted that the French had done nothing to save her. And the French owed a great deal to her; the English owed nothing.

I wondered a great deal about my brother Charles. How would he feel when he contemplated the cruel death of the one who had lifted him out of his humiliation, who had made a king of him and had given his country hope?

Surely he felt as guilty as the English who had condemned this strange girl to the fiery death.

The summer was passing. I could scarcely bear to think of Hatfield, so great was my longing for it. But I did feel that Henry needed me with him, and it was some comfort to know that I had been at hand to help him, when my presence meant so much to him.

I had succeeded in soothing his fears and he was calm now. He really was a serious boy, not given to outbursts such as I had witnessed. Of course, he was over-wrought. They should never have taken him to see her. And how dramatic it must have been to peer through an aperture. What had she thought when she saw those young eyes staring at her?

I had never seen The Maid but I imagined she must have been impressive. Anyone who had the faith and courage to confront my brother and insist on his being crowned, any young girl who could inspire an army and lead it to victory, must have some divine quality. And Henry had been overcome by the experience of coming face to face with such a person. His reaction was natural enough. I had been unduly alarmed. I must not let myself think for a moment that he may have inherited his grandfather's madness.

It was not until the end of the year that the Duke of Bedford decided that it would be safe for the King to leave Rouen. Anne told me that he had now given up entirely the idea of taking Henry to Rheims.

There was not the same activity throughout the country since the death of Joan. There had been no startling victories for the French, but the English had not been conspicuously successful either. Joan of Arc had had an effect on both sides.

It would be Paris for the coronation, said Anne. There would be less fear of trouble there.

My one thought was that it would soon be over and we should return to England.

"December is not the best month for such celebrations," said Anne, "but I think it will have to be then. It is important to have it completed."

I agreed fervently, for only then could we go home. I was growing excited at the prospect. So was Owen, so much so that we had to restrain our elation which tended to make us careless. Even so there were delays.

It was nearly two years since I had seen my children. I tried to picture a two-year-old Jasper. Edmund would be nearly four. Owen and I would be strangers to them both.

It was 2 December before we entered Paris. Advent Sunday was a fitting date. There was no lack of welcome. The Duke must have Paris under control. The city had been decorated with gaily coloured bunting and, in spite of the somewhat chilly weather, the people crowded into the streets to cheer Henry as he rode in.

I suffered some qualms, for I was sure there must be many among the people who regarded my brother Charles as the true King and I was apprehensive for the safety of my son.

He acknowledged the cheers of the people with the quiet charm which won their hearts, and they were as susceptible to youth as any other people.

Cardinal Beaufort rode close to him. In due course he would perform the ceremony in Notre Dame.

Those days in Paris seem to me now like a hazy dream. This was the city of my youth and must necessarily arouse strange emotions within me. The old days came back to me so vividly . . . with memories of my brothers and sisters . . . so many of them now gone for ever. My poor tragic father was a sad memory; the Hôtel de St. Paul, the scene of my days of privation . . . I never wanted to set foot in it again.

My mother was in Paris. She wanted to see me. I hesitated. She had been part of the background of my youthful misery and privation—yet she was my mother.

She was living now, most unhappily, at the Hôtel de St. Paul. I wondered whether she repented of her evil ways, and I was filled with curiosity about her.

I was after all in Paris briefly, and our paths need never cross again. How could I leave the city without seeing her?

I took a small entourage with me—Joanna Courcy and a few others—and we were not recognized as we went through the streets. We chose the early afternoon when few people were about, and moreover it was a cold and miserable day.

As I went through the draughty hall, memories flooded back. I felt the chill creeping through the cracks and crevices and ill-fitting windows, and I thought of Marie kneeling by her bed, hands and feet blue with the cold. I thought of my father in his room, calling out for someone to come and shatter him because he was made of glass.

The past had come alive to haunt me.

And there was my mother.

How she had changed! She must have been in her sixties and the life she had led had left its mark on her. She was very fat but as voluptuous as ever. Her hair was curled in what must have been the latest fashion; her face was delicately tinted but nothing could hide the debauched appearance, the pouches under the eyes, the lines round the full, greedy lips. She was petulant now, dissatisfied, full of self-pity.

She called my name and held out her arms to me. She pressed me to her perfumed and overflowing bosom.

"My child . . . this is a happy day for me. Oh, what a happy day! My dear, dear daughter, the Queen of England. There are not many happy days for me now, daughter."

"You have no . . . friends now?"

"People are so fickle. I am old now . . . old and alone."

"In the old days you had so many friends."

She brushed the implication aside. "Your brother was never a good son to me."

"And you a good mother to him?"

She did not see the irony. She had not changed. Her own affairs had always been so important to her that she did not see beyond them.

"Children are so ungrateful," she said. "Charles is the tool of that woman."

"You mean his wife?"

"His wife! My dear child, you are ignorant of affairs here. His wife is a little fool. I mean his mother-in-law . . . Yolande of Aragon."

"Yes, I had heard that she influenced him . . . but for the good, people say. She is a strong and clever woman."

"Clever, I suppose, in seeking what is best for oneself. As for being strong—one does not have to be strong to govern Charles. What she has done is turn him against his own mother. And now he calls himself the King of France."

"There are some who would say he has a right to the title."

"It is our dear little Henry who is King of France now. How happy I shall be when the crown is where it should be—on his blessed head."

"*You* can talk like this! Charles is *your* son!"

"My son!" She snapped her fingers. "Is not Henry my grandson? Are you not . . . his dear mother . . . my precious daughter? Katherine, you were always my favourite child."

I did not know whether I hid the disgust I felt. Did she really deceive herself? Did she believe what she said? I could imagine her working out what stand she should take. In spite of the recent victories inspired by Joan of Arc, she still believed in the final victory of the English and therefore she would side with them against her own son.

I felt sickened.

She said: "How I should love to see him crowned!"

She would not be invited to the coronation, I supposed. I wondered what the people of Paris would say if she put in an appearance. I believed she was universally hated. But as I listened to her, I felt a certain pity. She had had so much. I thought of her coming to France at the age of fourteen, of my father's adoration of her. The chances she might have had to make a different life for herself . . . for him . . . and for us all. Was I wrong to blame the misfortunes of France on her? If I was, I was only doing what so many had before me.

"If I could but see my grandson before I die . . . ." She was looking at me appealingly.

I said: "That will be for the Duke of Bedford to decide. He and Cardinal Beaufort make all the arrangements for my son . . . not I."

She nodded.

"He is a beautiful boy, I know. I should be so proud . . ." She wiped her eyes.

I repeated: "It is not for me to make such decisions . . ."

And after a while I left. Having done my duty, I was greatly relieved that the task was over.

Henry did go to see her a few days before his coronation. I did not ask him what he thought of her. He did not know of her lurid past, I was sure, and I wondered if anyone would tell him. There was so much to occupy him. He was such a sensitive boy, and he had been crowned once in a country which had come to him as his rightful inheritance. That was very different from the ceremony when the crown had been taken in conquest. Being the boy he was, this would surely occur to him.

He was still recovering from the effects of the trial and death of Joan of Arc which had affected him so strongly, and I could not help feeling anxious as to whether he was ready, not only physically but mentally, to endure that which was being thrust upon him.

On the tenth of the month Cardinal Beaufort crowned him in Notre Dame. The ceremony was conducted with all the expected pomp, and it appeared that the Parisians, at least, accepted Henry as their King.

It was only afterwards that there were complaints because the English had not observed the custom of distributing largesse to the hangers-on, who had cheered and expressed their loyalty solely for the purpose of receiving this favour. In addition, there were no pardons for those prisoners whose families had been expecting to see them freed after they had offered such expressions of loyalty to the King. The old French customs had been flouted by the English, and there were loud protestations of anger.

I guessed that Bedford needed all the money he could find to keep his armies intact, and as for freeing prisoners who might become a menace, that would be sheer folly.

However, the French were displeased, and the mood of rejoicing which had been so evident during the first days after the coronation was becoming one of discontent.

Bedford acted promptly.

It was time the King returned to England, he said; and we made preparations to leave Paris for Rouen.

I felt a terrible sense of foreboding when we entered the city, and fears beset me that we should never escape from it. It was besmirched with the blood of the martyr Joan, and her spirit seemed to be still alive in the town. To drive past the square where she had been burned alive could not do anything but fill one with melancholy. While we were in Rouen, we should never be able to forget her.

Bedford's aim now was to get the King out of France as quickly as possible. The purpose had been accomplished, long drawn out though it had been; and Henry was now crowned King of France.

And so . . . before January was out, we arrived at Calais. I could scarcely wait to board that ship, and then came that moment when I was there on deck. There were tears in my eyes as I watched the approaching white cliffs of Dover.

A Visit from the King

How beautiful the countryside was! I saw with a deep pleasure the frost on the bare branches of the trees, the layer of ice on the pond, the pale wintry sunshine; I felt the cold tang in the air, making my skin glow. What a joy it was to be home!

Owen was beside me and I knew he was feeling exactly as I did. It was marvellous to share everything with him. We did not speak but each of us knew what was in the other's mind, for there was a wonderful communion between us.

I could not help thinking of my poor sad mother whose scheming adventures had brought her nothing of real value. *I* had my husband, my family . . . the happy, simple life we could share if only we could go on as we were now. If we could, I would ask nothing more of life.

We had sent a messenger to Hatfield to tell them of our imminent arrival.

And there it was at last. Hatfield, where we had known so much happiness, and would know more, I promised myself.

They were waiting to greet us. I looked for Guillemote but she and the children were not there. I was alarmed and disappointed. Then I was scolding myself. Of course she was not there. I had forgotten the need to keep up the pretence. Most of the household could be trusted, but we still had to remember the danger which could be lurking in the most unexpected places.

I embraced the Joannas and Agnes. Their looks soothed my anxieties. They were signalling me that all was well. They could not have looked so happy if it had not been so. And as soon as possible Owen and I would make our way to the nurseries.

What a happy moment that was! There was Guillemote, holding a child by each hand.

We stood for a second looking at them. I felt a pang of sadness because Edmund did not recognize me, but he looked at me with interest, so I guessed that Guillemote had told him that his mother was coming. The little one, the child I had left when he was a baby in arms, could not be expected to know me.

I ran to them and knelt before them. I put my arms around them and held them close to me. They studied my face intently. I looked up at Guillemote and there were tears in her eyes.

"They have been so excited because you were coming. Edmund will remember in time . . . Jasper, of course . . ."

Owen had picked up Jasper, and Edmund took my hand and smiled slowly. Was he remembering?

I felt a great sense of loss. I had missed so much of their babyhood.

But I was back. I was home. And all would be well.

Later Guillemote told me that life had gone very smoothly during my absence. They had lived in peace from day to day, constantly waiting for news, of which they had had very little.

There had been no visitors to the palace. Nor had they expected them.

And so we resumed our lives.

The children delighted us. They were two bright little boys, and very soon it might have been as though we had never been parted.

They were both devoted to Guillemote, who had cared for them so assiduously during my absence. I felt a little jealous of the affection they gave her. She knew this and told me that in time they would love me too.

"Already they are showing fondness for you," she assured me. "You should see their little eyes light up when I speak of you. And of course I talked to them of you all the time you were away."

We were so happy to be home. The springtime seemed more beautiful.

I became pregnant again. I was completely absorbed in my family, and I refused to think of anything outside my little cocoon.

But significant events were taking place in the world outside

Hatfield and that life I had created for myself. I should have noticed them, of course.

The English lost Chartres in the spring of that year. Owen said that luck seemed to be running out for Bedford. The French no longer had The Maid, and they should be feeling as guilty as the English for having killed her; but the tide had turned in their favour.

Bedford, whose purpose in life was to preserve his idolized brother's conquests, must be far from happy.

In the spring Henry opened Parliament. He was now nearly twelve years old and, it was said, mature for his years. He seemed to be grasping the duties of kingship and surprising people by his seriousness in carrying them out.

He was popular wherever he went. He presided over Parliament with a demeanour which won the admiration of Warwick, who set a high standard for his pupil.

Cardinal Beaufort's enemies were working assiduously against him. Owen said he had made a great mistake when he had accepted his cardinal's hat. Those who wanted to destroy him had brought charges against him, accusing him of giving his first allegiance to Rome. What did they expect of a cardinal?

I knew him for an ambitious man. The Beauforts were an ambitious family. Their very origins made that a certainty. I think Owen was right when he said that, if Beaufort's ambitions lay solely in this country, he would never have become a cardinal.

There were scenes in Parliament when his accusers attempted to brand him with treachery. The Cardinal defended himself with the skill one expected of him; and Henry listened intently. I was delighted and proud to hear that at the end of the debate he defended his great uncle and announced to Parliament that he was convinced of his loyalty.

They were all amazed at his judgement, which he gave in a lucid manner which was remarkable coming from a boy not yet twelve years old. So much so, that the case against the Cardinal was dismissed.

I wished I had been there to see his triumph.

It was an indication that Henry was growing up. Warwick was reputed to have said that the King had grown so much not only in stature but in wisdom as well, and was in full knowledge of his state.

It was an indication that Henry was no longer regarded as a child. He was stepping with dignity into the role of king.

I was so proud. I had cast aside my fears for his mental health. The fact that he had been so disturbed by The Maid's ill-treatment, imprisonment and finally death was evidence of his tender heart. I think something spiritual in her touched something similar in himself, for he was becoming more and more devout.

My great regret at that time was that I could not be with him. If only he could have shared our home and our domestic happiness, my joy would have been complete.

Summer had passed, and I was nearing the end of my pregnancy.

"We must not become careless," said Owen. "We must continually remember the necessity to preserve secrecy." Life had run smoothly. So much was happening in the world outside that we had attracted little attention; but that could change and we must be prepared.

My daughter Jacina was born in the same secrecy that had accompanied the birth of her brothers. We were delighted with her. We already had our two boys, and what Owen and I had wanted most was a daughter. We admitted this afterwards, although we had said nothing before, for we knew we should have been delighted with whichever came to us.

Our little girl was charming . . . healthy as her brothers . . . beautiful, bright . . . a wonderful addition to our family.

Guillemote was in her element. She loved all children but little babies had a special place in her heart.

I had not quite recovered from the birth of Jacina when I heard news which deeply saddened me. Owen had discovered this and he wondered whether to tell me before I was fully recovered, for he guessed that it would upset me. We were so close, Owen and I, like one person, and I was therefore very sensitive to his moods, and guessing that there was something on his mind, I demanded to know what was troubling him.

"I know you had a liking for her," he said. "She is young . . . it is a great blow. It will have its effect."

"Owen, tell me. Who is it?"

"It is the Duchess of Bedford."

"Anne!"

He nodded. "She is dead."

"But she was so young. Oh, poor John. He loved her so much."

"And as the sister of the Duke of Burgundy she was very important to him."

"I had not thought of that . . . only of the love between them. How did she die?"

"It was some illness which struck her down."

"But she was so young . . . younger than I!"

Owen put his arms round me and held me tightly. I knew he was thinking how precarious life was. We lived with danger. It could strike from any direction at any moment. Those who had been alive and well one day could be dead the next.

I said: "She was twenty-eight. I wonder . . . how is the Duke?"

"He is bowed down with sorrow, I hear. How strange it is that when ill-fortunes come they do not come singly."

"I wish that I could see him. I wish that I could tell him how sorry I am."

"It is unlikely that he will come to England now."

Later I heard that Anne had been buried with great pomp in the Church of the Celestins. She was deeply mourned by the Parisians who had called her "The Beautiful and The Good." The Burgundians were stricken with grief.

Owen said that this would most certainly loosen the already weakening links between Bedford and the Duke of Burgundy, for Anne had done so much to keep them intact.

Poor Bedford! I was sorry for him; but my delight in my new-born daughter was inclined to swamp all other feelings.

My sympathy for my brother-in-law was lessened considerably when in April of the following year he married again.

I was astonished and a little outraged on behalf of Anne.

"How could he?" I asked. "It is not six months since she died."

"Bedford is a ruler first, a husband second," said Owen. "Some men are like that."

Owen would not be. Nor would I. Love would come first with me. If I lost Owen, I should never marry again. I had loved Henry, I had thought; but now I had learned the difference between my feelings for him and those I had for Owen. Owen was the man for me, and I prayed fervently that we should never be parted.

There was a reason why Bedford had married so promptly. Owen was fully aware of the situation.

"The alliance with Burgundy is waning," he explained, "and Bedford needs to make a new one. The war in France is going badly. Bedford has tried to revive the old feeling of invincibility but The Maid has destroyed that. The only reason why the French are not victorious is because, without The Maid to urge him, Charles has sunk once more into his habitual lethargy . . . and his army with him."

Yet here and there still the spirit of The Maid lived on, and there were occasional French victories.

Owen said: "The house of Luxembourg is rich and powerful. An alliance with it might not make up for the loss of Burgundy, but it would be of some use. The Duke of Bedford is an anxious man and he cannot allow any opportunity to slip past."

"Another marriage of convenience then! And six months after the death of Anne, whom he professed to love so dearly!"

Owen smiled tenderly at me. "You must be kinder to him, my dearest," he said. "He is beleaguered at the moment. Burgundy is slipping away, and how much the English owed to the quarrel between the two most powerful houses in France everyone must know. The Duke is a man with a mission. His brother left him a sacred trust, and he is the kind of man who will sacrifice everything, including himself, in order to keep faith with his brother. Do not blame him."

"I do not, I suppose. I just cannot stop thinking of Anne."

Nor could I. I wondered if she could look down from Heaven and see the husband whom she had thought had loved her so devotedly, now the husband of Jacqueline, daughter of the Count of St. Pol of the house of Luxembourg . . . so important to Bedford now that he was in danger of losing the support of the house of Burgundy to which Anne had belonged and she who had been so instrumental in maintaining the weakening friendship between her husband and her brother, was now gone.

I could not help feeling a little cynical. How much, I wondered, had Bedford's love been for Anne, how much for Burgundy?

How different it was with Owen and me! We loved for love's sake only. And that was the only way to love.

I reminded myself that we must preserve secrecy at all costs. Our love was too precious to be harmed. We must never forget.

We must perforce endure this perpetual fear of discovery that we might never, by the smallest action, betray ourselves.

In June of that year Bedford returned to England with his new duchess.

There were no victory parades for him. The news of his marriage, as had been anticipated, had been coldly received by the Duke of Burgundy. The link was slackened still more. Bedford was missing that powerful ally. Affairs in France were in a sorry state. It seemed that neither side had a great enthusiasm for the war.

I wondered if I should have an opportunity of seeing the Duke and meeting his new wife. I could hardly offer condolences for the death of Anne now.

I was sure he was not a happy man.

It soon became clear that Gloucester was about to make trouble. When had he ever not been? And now it seemed he had a good opportunity. The brother towards whom he had always harboured some resentment, for the reason that he had been born his senior, if for nothing else, was no longer the conquering hero. He had come home in defeat rather than victory. Now was the time for Gloucester to move in against him.

He did it in typical Gloucester fashion. Rumour began to circulate throughout the country that Bedford had been careless. He had neglected his duty. He had spent too much time courting his new wife when his old one was scarcely cold. What sort of man was this who had taken on the sacred mantle of the great and noble King Henry V?

These rumours were clearly set in motion by none other than Bedford's brother.

Bedford made an announcement. He wanted all accusations against him to be made in the proper place, which was before the King and the Parliament.

Gloucester, of course, would not come forward and openly state his criticisms. He always liked to work in the dark. The result was that, when Bedford announced in Parliament that he wanted a clear statement of the attitude towards him, he received nothing but praise for his activities in France.

"It seems," said Owen, "that the little storm has blown over."

But Gloucester had no intention of abandoning his battle for self-aggrandisement. This quarrel with his brother kept him busy and was no doubt the reason why we were enjoying a period of comparative peace.

Gloucester was full of ideas, and the reason more mischief was not done was because he did not think them out clearly enough. He was impatient for action and so eager to promote himself, so furiously angry with the fate which had made him a younger son. He was determined—by fair means or foul—that that which would be due to him had he been born a little earlier, and because of his superior gifts, should be his.

Frustrated and restless, he could not see that he was making himself ridiculous. In a fit of rage and pique, he announced to the Council that he had plans for changing the fast-deteriorating situation in France. He would bring it back to what it had been in his brother's glorious reign.

He declared that Henry had often confided in him, discussed plans of action with him, consulted him and on several occasions asked his advice and followed it with the utmost success. He, therefore, felt he was in a position to take an army to France, and then they would begin to see results.

He had gone too far. It was known that on his deathbed Henry had asked Bedford to keep a curb on Gloucester's impulsiveness and not to allow him too much power. Gloucester's blustering conceit had served only to expose his weakness.

The Council most definitely refused to supply him with the arms and men he demanded; and Bedford announced that he himself would soon be returning to France.

I saw Bedford before he left. I had gone to Westminster for a week or so, which gave me an opportunity of seeing Henry. Owen and I had decided that this was advisable and that it would be a good idea if I appeared at Court now and then. We must always be on the alert, and Owen thought that, if I appeared occasionally, Gloucester was less likely to be suspicious of what I might be doing, hidden out of sight in the country.

Bedford looked old and careworn. I did not mention Anne. His new wife seemed very pleasant and fond of him. But I realized that he was an extremely anxious man. There was a certain desperation about him.

He was as courteous and friendly as he had ever been, and I wished that I could have told him how sorry I was for his misfortunes.

I returned to my family. We had moved back to Hadham now. It was quieter than Hatfield, and we were really fond of the place.

And I was once more pregnant.

During these periods, that happy indifference to all else but my family would descend upon me. I led the life of a simple country woman far away from the intrigues of Court life, and scarcely gave them a thought, except when some piece of gossip reached me.

Henry was growing up and since his coronation had assumed a new dignity. I supposed all the deference and homage he received must necessarily have an effect on him. He was serious enough to realize his great responsibilities, and he was of a nature not to permit himself to shirk them.

I did feel a twinge of uneasiness when I heard that Gloucester had instituted himself as a tutor to Henry. None disputed the fact that Gloucester was a very learned man. He was, in fact, one of the most complex characters I had ever encountered. A schemer, a voluptuary, reckless, impulsive, ambitious, and in complete contrast he was a scholar, a lover of literature, extremely widely read, an authority on the Latin poets and orators, well acquainted with Aristotle, Plato, Dante and Petrarch. When he talked to scholars of his own kind, a different man emerged, and it was difficult to reconcile him with the brash adventurer who seemed so completely lacking in judgement.

Henry himself had always been more interested in books than the warlike arts, and this made a bond between them, I supposed. However, I heard that Gloucester's tuition was very well received by the King and that the friendship between him and his uncle was growing because of this.

I was sure I was not the only one who was made uneasy by this disclosure.

I was heavy with child; in fact, I was expecting my confinement to begin very shortly, when a message came that Cardinal Beaufort and the Earl of Warwick were on their way to Hadham.

There was panic.

We had faced such a dilemma before, but then I had not been so far gone in pregnancy. Now it would be impossible to hide it. What could we do? Could we say I was ill? They would want to see me. If I were too ill to see them, that would mean that I

was very ill indeed and that doctors would most certainly be
sent.

There was only one thing to do. I must receive them. They
must be told I was ill. I hoped to be able to conceal my condition
and get rid of them as soon as possible.

"You must be in bed, of course," said Guillemote. "You
could be propped up with pillows . . . and we will tell them that
they must not exhaust you."

"What if they talk of sending doctors?"

"We will tell them that you have your own physician and that
all you need is rest."

It was a difficult ordeal. I was afraid my pains would start
before they arrived or, even worse, when they were here.

They sat by my bed—the Earl of Warwick and the Cardinal—
and they expressed great concern for my indisposition. I told
them that all I needed was rest. I had had these bouts before and
knew how to deal with them—which was true enough.

The reason they had come was that they were anxious about
the King, who was becoming more and more influenced by the
Duke of Gloucester.

"The King is serious for his years," said the Cardinal. "He
has made a good impression whenever he has appeared in Parliament. He listens gravely to the speeches and—amazing in one
so young—can add his contribution with remarkable intelligence. Had it not been for the Duke of Gloucester's prompting,
it would not have occurred to him that he wanted to govern . . .
alone."

"Govern alone! Surely not!"

"Surely not indeed, my lady," said Warwick. "The King
has always been a modest boy . . . aware of his youth and the
drawbacks it presents, but under the tutelage of the Duke, alas,
he has changed."

I felt the child move within me. Not yet, little one, I begged.
Wait just a while . . . not yet.

"It must be impressed upon him," said the Cardinal, "that
he is not yet of an age to govern, that he must pay attention to
all his advisers and not listen exclusively to one."

"That one being the Duke of Gloucester," I added.

"A man's knowledge of Latin literature does not give him
understanding of the skills of government nor the arts of war.

What we have to do is impress on the King that he is too young as yet to take his place as ruler.''

"I think he must understand that well."

"It is difficult for us, my lady, to tell him this . . . particularly when the Duke of Gloucester is telling him otherwise."

"Could not the Parliament explain to him?" I asked.

"They must indeed do so. But he *is* the King, and they are reluctant to tell him he is unprepared for this great task. He would listen to you. You are his mother, and you can talk to him . . . mother to son . . . not as subject to king."

"I see," I said.

"So we have come to lay the situation before you. We believe Your Grace could do much good by having a word with the King. He will listen to you . . . his mother."

"I will speak to him," I said.

"Thank you, my lady, and it would be well if there was as little delay as possible."

"I will see him as soon as I am well," I promised him.

"I doubt not that, if the King knew you were unwell, he would be happy to visit you here at Hadham."

"I would rather wait until I feel better. I assure you that, as soon as I am, I will visit him . . ."

I thought they would never go. The Cardinal must always stand on ceremony, and I supposed he thought it would be impolite to depart the moment he had secured what he had come for.

There was great relief as they rode away. Guillemote with the Joannas and Agnes stood at the window watching them.

Until they were out of sight we were ill at ease.

We had been fortunate again, for a few hours after they had gone my pains started.

Little Owen was born that day.

As soon as the child was safely delivered, we had to think of the difficult situation in which we had been placed. I could not leave my bed, yet if I did not, Henry might come to me. And Henry would not come alone. There would be at least a bodyguard with him—and some attendants . . . a few perhaps, in view of the fact that he was coming to a small place like Hadham.

Owen thought of all sorts of possibilities. Could I travel in a litter? What of the child? I could not leave him. And if Henry came to Hadham, what of Edmund, Jasper and Jacina? How could we keep them hidden?

We had managed successfully all these years to keep our marriage secret. That was because we had taken great care and had been surrounded by loyal friends and servants; but we had never faced a situation like this before. It had been comparatively simple to deceive the Cardinal and the Earl who came with four or five attendants and had not stayed for more than a few hours. But a visit from the King . . . that was quite another matter.

Guillemote was one of the most practical people I had ever known. She set about finding a wet-nurse in the village and when this was done the way was clear. She, Agnes and Joannas Troutbeck and Belknap would go to Hatfield with all the children, where they would stay until the King's visit was over.

I would keep to my bed; and as soon as the King had departed, they would return.

The more we considered it, the more it seemed the only possible solution.

Owen would remain at Hadham with Joanna Courcy and the other members of the household.

Henry would be with a hunting party, and we had word that he would call to see me as he had heard that I was unwell. It was a relief that they would not be expecting to stay at Hadham, for the house was too small to accommodate a party of any size. Owen's great fear was that some members of the party might wander into the nearby village and perhaps pick up a little gossip. That seemed hardly likely, I said, for we had always been so careful to keep the secrets of our household inviolate.

The wet-nurse was a healthy young country girl who had been delivered of a male child at the same time as Owen had been born; she had enough milk in her ample breasts to feed two babies.

I felt a terrible sense of foreboding as I lay in bed listening to the sound of their departure. To Edmund, Jasper and Jacina it was an adventure, and they had their beloved Guillemote with them, so they were happy.

Owen came and sat by my bed. He took my hand and felt the pulse at my wrist. "Your heart is pounding," he said.

"Owen," I said, "I am afraid."

"It will be all right. The children will be safe with Guillemote."

"But to have to send them away . . . secretly. Sometimes I am very much afraid . . . as now."

"We always knew there would be difficulties, Katherine."

I nodded.

"And yet we did it. Was it worth it?"

"Completely. But how I long for a peaceful life . . . an ordinary life . . . the sort of life which comes so naturally to others."

"All have their difficulties, my love. And we must face ours. And whatever happens, we must remember this: it was all worthwhile."

"It seems wrong that we should have to pretend that that which means everything in the world to us does not exist."

"As long as we know it exists, it does not matter."

"These years . . . they have been wonderful, have they not, Owen?"

"Aye, and will go on being wonderful. Do not talk as though they are in the past. Here we are . . . our children growing up around us. We shall grow old together, Katherine . . . happy until the end. It is rarely that two people are blessed with the happiness you and I have known."

"It is true. I must remember that."

"There is nothing to fear. Henry is coming. Henry would never harm you. All you have to do is talk to him. You have always enjoyed those times you have had together. You have often complained that they are so rare. Well, now he is coming to see you. The children are well away. Soon they will be back, and it will be as it was before."

I lay back on my pillows. I did not want him to leave me, but even in our household we had to be watchful of ourselves all the time. He kissed me tenderly and left me.

I lay back, awaiting the arrival of my son.

It was mid afternoon when he arrived. The children would be at Hatfield by this time, I assured myself. Owen was right. There was nothing to fear. Henry might only be a boy, but he was the King, and wherever he went there must be a certain amount of pomp.

I could imagine them all, lined up below to receive him. Then I heard the trumpets announcing his arrival.

I should have been down there to greet him.

He came into my bedroom. There were two of his courtiers with him. Guards, I supposed. He would be used to
having them with him.

My heart gave a little bound of pleasure at the sight of him.
He was not yet fourteen but he looked a little older. He was still
a boy though.

With a regal gesture he dismissed his guards.

He came swiftly to the bed. "You are sick?" he said anxiously.

"I am recovering," I told him.

He took my hands and kissed them.

"I am so happy to be with my lady mother," he said.

"And always I find great joy in your presence."

He smiled. "Dear mother, tell me of your illness."

"It is nothing. I grow better every day. In a week I shall be
up and about as usual. It is just that . . . at the moment . . . I
am a little weak."

"What illness was this?"

I lifted my shoulders.

"Could not the doctors discover? I should have sent my physician."

"Oh no . . . no. It was soon over. Do not let us talk of my
ailments. How have you been?"

"I am well. But when they said you were unwell and wanted
to see me, I was greatly distressed."

"Did you think you would find me on my deathbed?"

A look of anxiety came into his eyes. Poor little King! He
was so young after all. How cruel it was to thrust such a burden
on those frail shoulders. I wished that I could tell him everything
. . . introduce him to his half-brothers and -sister . . . say to
him, "Leave all that pomp of kingship and come and live with
us . . . with your stepfather and half-brothers and -sister. We
will teach you what it is to be truly happy apart from the fears
that your secret life be discovered and attempts will be made to
destroy it."

"How relieved I am that I did not," he said.

"Oh Henry," I told him. "I often think how happy I should
have been if we could have been together always. But that is not
the way of life, is it? It is only the humbly born who can have
the pleasure of their children's company. I often wonder why

people envy us. But you are wondering why I am talking thus. Oh, it is good of you to come and see me.''

"I would come often if that were possible.''

"I know it, and it gives me the greatest pleasure. You will never forget that I am your mother, will you? And that, I believe, gives me special privileges to speak to the King.''

"Dear lady mother, the privilege is mine.''

"Ah, you make pretty speeches. Is that what you learn from your uncle Gloucester?''

He smiled and I went on: "You enjoy your sessions with him, do you?''

"No one understands literature as he does. His talk is most beguiling.''

"I remember that you always had a feeling for literature rather than riding, hawking, archery and the use of arms.''

"It is far more interesting, dear lady.''

"And the Earl of Warwick, does he think so?''

He gave a rueful laugh. "I think the Earl believes the study of literature to be a waste of time. He would not know Dante from Aristotle.''

"He is nevertheless a good and worthy tutor.''

"I expect that is true.''

"But you, of course, enjoy more what you discuss with the Duke of Gloucester.''

"But naturally. We talk of matters of absorbing interest. I am tired of warlike activities. They tire me as the great writers and thinkers never do.''

"And the Cardinal?''

"He is of the same mind as the Earl of Warwick. My uncle Gloucester thinks I give them too much liberty.''

"They have been good tutors for you, as you admit.''

"My uncle is of the opinion that I should no longer suffer their restraints.''

"Henry, you are not very old, you know.''

"I shall be fourteen years old in December.''

"It is too young to take on the burdens of kingship.''

"My uncle would help me.''

"Gloucester!" I could not hide my dismay.

"Yes. He says that Warwick cannot think of me as anything but a child . . . and the Cardinal is the same. They want to hold me back. My uncle says that I have shown signs of maturity and firmness. Do you know, dear mother, I spoke to them in Parliament when the Cardinal and my uncle Gloucester were disputing together . . . and I was able to solve their differences. My uncle says that I have enough wisdom to rule without the Cardinal always at my elbow . . . and if I were in any difficulties, he would always be there to help me.''

"Gloucester!" I repeated in derision.

"He is very clever, dear mother. He charms people. He is very merry. He makes them laugh. They all love him."

"Not all," I said. "The Cardinal and the Earl of Warwick evidently do not. And I believe there may be many others who feel as they do.''

"But I am the King."

"Yes, you are the King, but this is a great country. It has to be governed with care. There can so easily be trouble . . . and kings can lose their crowns. Experience is needed to rule a country, Henry, and you are too young to have had any."

"Yes, but you see, I can learn from my uncle. He would be there to help me."

"Help you to destroy yourself. Henry, I am your mother. My great care is for you. I want you to be happy. I want you to be a great, good king like your father."

"That is what I aim to be."

"Then you must not assume responsibility until you are ready to carry it. The demands of kingship are great. A boy of fourteen, however clever, would be unable to meet them."

"But I should not be alone."

"You are too young to see that your uncle is working for himself . . . not for you. He is an ambitious man. He seeks to rule this country through you."

"Oh no, my uncle Gloucester is not like that. He wants me to be King."

"No, Henry. You cannot rule yet. You must listen to your Parliament and your Council. You cannot break away from the Cardinal and the Earl of Warwick. They will guide you. They will help you. And you must listen to the wishes of Parliament. The worst possible thing for a king is to be in opposition to the will of his Parliament and the people. When you are older, you will understand that. In the meantime, put out of your mind those notions. You are a boy yet. In time you will be a great king, but only if you listen to the wise men about you and do not let yourself be taken in by flattery.''

He was looking at me in amazement.

''Henry,'' I went on, ''whatever you may think, know this: here is a mother who seeks nothing for herself and whose only concern is for your future greatness and above all your happiness. You do know that, do you not?''

''I do,'' he said fervently.

''Well then, take heed of what I say. You want to take over the rule of this country. You cannot, Henry. It is a man's task, and even then he must be a very clever man. You have done well so far, beyond what could be expected of one your age. That is true, and wise as you have shown yourself to be, we shall see that you are even wiser. You are going to put yourself into the hands of . . . not one who wants to rule through you . . . but those men like the Earl of Warwick and the Cardinal and the members of your Council who have proved their wisdom and their desire to serve their country well.''

He listened intently. I was proud of him. He really wanted to be a good king, worthy of his father. He was not seeking self-importance—in fact, he rather shunned it. He wanted to be a king with his uncle Gloucester beside him, because they shared a taste for literature and he liked to be with him.

''Henry,'' I went on, ''it may be that the Parliament will point out to you that you are as yet too young to take over the government. I do not want this to be too much of a shock to you if it comes. I want to prepare you. You must fall in with their wishes . . . whatever advice you get to the contrary. To do anything else would be dangerous for you. It might even result in civil war.''

''War!'' he cried. ''I hate war. How I hated going to France. I did not want to be King of France.''

I said: ''You do well to hate war. It is something which brings no good to either side . . . winner or loser . . . and then how long does the winner remain the winner?''

He nodded in agreement.

''Henry, I am forgiven for talking thus?''

He looked at me questioningly.

''I have spoken to you very frankly,'' I continued, ''but it is out of my love for you. You know that, do you not?''

''Indeed I do.''

"So . . . all is well between us?"

He took my hands and kissed them. "How could it be otherwise?" he said.

"And you will . . . ?" I began.

"I see that I am too young to govern," he replied.

"You will grow up, Henry, soon . . . too soon perhaps."

"Dear mother," he said. "Why do you stay here in the country? I should like you to be at Court."

"This life suits me, Henry."

"But we should see each other often."

"We should."

"Then we shall."

I smiled at him ruefully. How could we? I wondered what he would say if he knew of my new family, which was his too? Surely he would love his little half-brothers and -sister. If only I could explain to him!

I said: "I feel sure the Parliament will point out to you that you are too young to assume kingship. You will now be prepared, Henry, and I know you will accept their decision graciously."

"I understand, dear mother," he said. "Yes, I must indeed wait . . . until I am older."

I took his hand and held it fast. "I would I could keep you here with me. I wish you could share my life . . ."

"You must get well quickly and come to Court. I will send my physician to attend you. He is very good."

"I do not need him. I am much better. To see you and to know that you are not too important to listen to me gives me great pleasure."

I was proud of him. He was clever enough to realize his own shortcomings, and surely that is a sign of greatness in a man?

He will be as great a king as his father was, I told myself, though I prayed not a warlike one. Let him be a king who gave his attention to learning . . . to the building up of culture in the land. Surely that would make him a king of true greatness?

Death in France

As soon as Henry left, Owen came to me and I told him what had taken place.

"So he listened to you and is taking your advice. He will be a good and great king, I believe."

"Gloucester must have flattered him considerably to make him feel that he is quite capable of taking on the burdens of state. I am surprised that he was taken in. But, of course, Gloucester stressed that he would always be there to help."

"Which of course was the main purpose."

"Gloucester terrifies me," I said.

"We have managed so far," replied Owen. "And we shall continue to do so. And having succeeded in this rather delicate matter, we shall have had practice in case a similar occasion should arise again. You see, it all worked out very smoothly. Guillemote managed the matter of the baby very well."

"How lucky I am to have had her all these years."

"She is as one of us."

I agreed with that.

"Now," went on Owen, "we will send a messenger over to Hatfield and let Guillemote know that she may bring the children back."

I was awaiting the arrival of the party which would bring the children to me. It was mid afternoon. I lay in bed drowsing. Very soon I should be up, and everything, I hoped, would return to normal. I was congratulating myself on the resourceful manner in which we had dealt with the difficulties of Henry's visit and, after all our fears, how smoothly everything had gone, when I heard the sound of horses' hoofs.

They had come home. It would be wonderful to see them. Guillemote would bring them up to me immediately because she would know of my impatience to see them.

I sat by the bed waiting for the sound of children's feet . . . waiting for the door to be opened, for them to dash into my arms.

I could picture the beaming face of Guillemote looking benignly on.

The door was opened suddenly. It was Joanna Courcy. She was white and trembling.

"Joanna . . ." I began.

She was thrust aside and standing there, glaring at me with undoubted malevolence in his whole demeanour, was the Duke of Gloucester.

"My lord . . ." I stammered.

Joanna was trying to keep him out of the room. "The Queen has been ill. She is recovering . . ."

He looked at her coldly and said: "You may go."

Joanna glanced at me. I nodded for her to obey him. I was glad that I could hide my trembling hands under the bedclothes.

I heard myself saying, and I was surprised by the steadiness of my voice: "I do not understand why you come bursting thus into my bedchamber."

"Because I would speak with you, Madam," he retorted.

"Of what?" I asked.

His face was scarlet. I could see he was trying to control his temper, which I knew, from repute, could be violent. I wondered briefly whether he had come to kill me. I thought quickly: no, not even he would dare do that. His methods would be more subtle.

"I have come to ask why you should malign me to the King."

I knew at once to what he was referring. Had Henry told him? If he had it would be because Gloucester had forced it out of him. Or perhaps his spies knew that the Cardinal and Warwick had visited me, asking for my help. He would have his spies in many places.

I have often found it useful to feign ignorance of the language, which is plausible enough when it is not one's native tongue.

So, to give myself a few moments to recover a little, I pretended not to understand.

"Please . . ." I said. "You mean . . . I cannot understand . . ."

Showing a certain petulant exasperation, he said slowly: "The King has been here. He has talked to you."

"Yes . . . he visited me . . . recently. I see so little of him. That is sad for me . . ."

"And you have spoken to him against me."

"But no, my lord. I have spoken against no one. My son tells me that you are so conversant with the Latin poets . . . and what pleasure it gives him to learn of them."

"I know you have told him not to listen to me . . . not to take my advice."

"To listen to you? But no. I have told my son . . . because he asked me . . . that he is a boy yet. He will govern his kingdom one day . . . but not yet."

"The King is my nephew."

"Oh yes . . . and he is my son."

"I vowed to my brother to care for him . . . to give him what he lacks through his father's tragic death."

"I know my husband commanded the good Earl of Warwick to teach him the use of arms . . . and what he should know . . . how to lead his armies as a king must when the need arises. My husband's dear brother, the Duke of Bedford, and Cardinal Beaufort have cared for my son. He is not yet fourteen. A boy of his age cannot take on the government of his country. That is what he is and that is what I tell him. No . . . no . . . I say. It cannot be just yet."

"But the King is unusually endowed. He has the spirit of a ruler. He has special gifts. He has inherited these from his father."

"His father told me once that he was wild and reckless in his youth. It was only when he was a king that he changed his ways . . . and that was because he was of an age to understand what kingship meant."

"The King is very serious. He is more interested in learning than the use of arms. He will be a great king."

"Yes . . . in time. That is what I tell him. But he must wait for that time. Until he is of age he must rely on his advisers."

"He would have the best advisers, my lady. He understood this. But since he has talked to you, he has lost his confidence."

"The King has the wisdom to come to the conclusions he came to."

"I trust, my lady, you will not consider it discourteous of me if I suggest that living shut away in the country, you cannot have a grasp of matters of state. May I add, Madam, that you have allowed yourself to become the tool of that arch-villain the Cardinal and that fool Warwick."

"No, my lord, that is not so. I have come to my own conclusions in the matter. They are my own and not those of others."

"It may be that you would be wise to keep out of matters of which, by the very nature of the life you lead, you know nothing."

"And you, sir, I wonder if you would leave me in peace to recover from my illness."

He stood regarding me somewhat insolently. He looked round the room.

"Did you hear me?" I asked.

"Perfectly well, my lady. I am just about to depart, but there is one thing which has set me wondering."

I waited in trepidation, for there was evil in his countenance. The heat of passion had passed and it was replaced by something cold, deadly and evil.

"I was wondering what you . . . such a beautiful lady . . . find to amuse you in the country?"

"I enjoy country life, my lord."

"Here! With a few ladies-in-waiting? And men-at-arms, of course. I would say that that Welshman has quite a presence. Would you, my lady?"

He was looking at me maliciously. I thought in terror: he knows something.

I felt my colour deepening and I was beginning to tremble.

"Did not he distinguish himself at Agincourt?"

"The King thought highly of him," I said. "He was in his household . . . and he continues to be in mine."

"That must be a very desirable situation. Though this is hardly the place for a soldier. Why is he not in France with my brother Bedford?"

"I have no idea," I said. "Some soldiers tire of perpetual war."

"I'll swear he has a liking for country life. Please, sister, do try to be a little kinder to your poor brother-in-law. It is a great sadness to me to know that you are not friendly towards me and suspect me of . . . I know not what."

"This matter has nothing to do with my friendship towards you, my lord. My son asked me for my opinion and I gave it to him because I felt that it was the right one."

He bowed to me. "You must come to Court," he said. "You and I must get to understand each other."

He was at the door. I sank back onto my pillows, and as I heard his clattering footsteps going down the stairs, I could not stop myself trembling.

Joanna Courcy came in.

"I could not stop him," she said. "I wanted to get up to warn you."

"I know. There was no help for it."

"Why did he come here? Does he suspect anything?"

"I know why he came here. And I think he suspects."

"Oh God have mercy on us! What next?"

"Where is Owen?" I asked.

"He is in the gardens, I think."

"Does he know Gloucester was here?"

"I do not know."

"He must keep out of the way. I do not want him to be seen. Gloucester talked of him . . . in a certain way."

We heard the sounds of departure below, and Joanna went to the window. "He is leaving with his men," she said.

"Thank God he has gone."

"I will go and get something to steady you."

"No . . . no . . . stay. I wish Owen were here. I must talk to him. The way Gloucester spoke . . . I fear he knows . . ."

We were silent, and almost immediately there were sounds of arrival. I heard Edmund's voice.

Guillemote was coming back with the children.

They were home again. My heart was leaping uncomfortably. And Gloucester was just going.

Could it be possible that they had met as Gloucester was leaving the house?

Guillemote brought the children to me. Edmund and Jasper scampered across the room, Jacina toddling after them. They threw themselves into my arms. I held them so tightly that they protested and wriggled free. I was trying to stifle the terrible fear in my heart. I gazed over their heads at Guillemote. She was standing still, holding the baby, and I knew by the expression on her face that she had met Gloucester.

The children were all talking at once, telling me about their journey . . . how Edmund had ridden with Jack on his horse, and Jasper with Dick. Jacina had been in the litter with Guillemote and the two babies—Daisy's, who was the wet-nurse, and little Owen. I feigned an interest but all the time was wondering what had happened.

They had gone to the big house, Edmund told me. They had all slept together . . . except the babies. They had played in the gardens.

I knew that Guillemote was longing to talk to me, but by tacit agreement nothing was said until the children had gone to the nursery.

Owen was with me. He had been in the gardens, had seen Gloucester's arrival and had thought it wise to keep out of sight. Then he had seen his departure after the brief visit and had been about to come to me when Guillemote had arrived with the children.

"I was horrified," he said. "It seemed certain that they had met."

Guillemote explained to us.

"We were turning into the palace when he came riding along with his small company. I was in the litter with little Owen and Jacina and the wet-nurse and her child. Edmund and Jasper were riding with two of the men. I recognized the Duke at once and I was very shaken. We could not turn back. We were too close for that and he had already seen us. We had to pass each other."

"What did he do?"

"He drew to one side of the road . . . signing for his men to do the same. They stopped. He lifted his hat and bowed his head. He seemed to be staring at us all. I was not sure whether he knew who I was. He would probably know some of the ladies. I thought it hardly likely that he would have noticed me from the past when he may have seen me once or twice. He looked at the children and . . . we passed on. The way he was looking at us sent shivers down my spine."

"Is that all?" I asked.

She nodded.

I looked at Owen. It was enough, we both knew.

We were certain that Gloucester would take revenge. The only thing we were unsure of was when; but we believed it was only a matter of waiting.

He had always had the notion that, in view of my position, I must be watched. He had been determined that I should not marry again. I had been wife to the King, and he probably thought that any children I might have could imagine they had pretensions to the throne. It was hardly likely, of course, but a man such as Gloucester would be alert for possibilities.

My son was King; it was likely that he would marry and have undisputed heirs to the throne. But strange things happened in the royal line. And at the moment between Gloucester and what he coveted there was Henry and after Henry, Bedford. And Bedford had no heirs. I believed Gloucester had not worried a great deal about my activities in the past—but certainly enough to try to prevent my marrying again. Yet I had been a mild irritation until now. The King was growing up, and it might be that my influence over him might increase. And now I had openly offended Gloucester. He believed I had turned my son from falling in with his wishes. Gloucester was a man who did not like to be flouted. He would regard what I had done as an insult—and insults must be avenged.

I guessed, therefore, that sooner or later he would strike. And I am sure the blow would have come more quickly but for a dramatic turn of events.

The French were heartily tired of the war. I supposed the English were, too. No one was winning. If Henry had lived, people were saying, the conquest would have been completed by now. France and England would be one country under the domination of the English. But what was the case now? True, the King of England had been crowned King of France. Who was to say which was the King? What was the point of paying taxes just to continue a war which was coming to no satisfactory end? It was different before the coming of The Maid. Truly, she had changed everything, and although she had not brought complete victory to the French, she had made the English position very difficult to hold . . . and it was becoming more so.

At this time there was a meeting in Arras which must be

causing a great deal of anxiety to the Duke of Bedford. I thought of him as I had last seen him, his face casreworn and a desperate sadness in his eyes . . . in fact, a certain hopelessness.

The meeting in Arras was an attempt to bring an end to the war and to unite the royal house of France with that of Burgundy. If this succeeded, it would be a fatal blow to English hopes in France.

Looking back over the events of the past years, I could see what an effect that quarrel had had on our history. The Duke of Burgundy and my brother Charles were both Frenchmen—moreover close kinsmen—and the quarrel of the Orléans-Armagnac faction with Burgundy had been the downfall of France. It was not until a simple peasant girl had restored that country's faith in itself that the misery of failure and defeat began to lift.

It was quite clear that Philip of Burgundy and my brother Charles must become allies so that France could grow proud and strong again.

It was tragic that the two leading houses in France should be fighting against each other when an enemy was attacking the country. There must be an end to this talk of revenge. The welfare of France must come before petty family quarrels. Frenchmen must not make war on each other.

The English refused to give up their claim to the crown of France, and Bedford left Arras and went to Rouen. I could imagine his thoughts as he entered the town. This was the place where they had burned The Maid, but she was indestructible. They may have destroyed her body, but her spirit lived on.

I remembered Tressart's words: "We are lost. We have burned a saint."

It might well be that he was right.

And there in Rouen, the city of bitter memories, Bedford would be waiting the outcome of the meeting of Arras. His relationship with Burgundy had suffered even further since the death of Anne. It was she who had helped keep it alive. Bedford had respected Burgundy, and Burgundy had respected him. They had been brothers-in-law. And then Bedford had married again and so soon after Anne's death. True, there was an advantage in the match but it had surprised me . . . and no doubt others. Moreover, the marriage had naturally displeased Burgundy and could only be expected to widen the rift between them. Perhaps

Bedford realized during those days in Rouen that his marriage had been a mistake, for it was still of the utmost importance to England to keep on friendly terms with Burgundy—far more important than any advantage which could be obtained elsewhere.

I had always admired Bedford. He was undoubtedly the best and most honourable of Henry's brothers. He had been a good friend to me and a good guardian to my son.

When I heard that he had died in Rouen, I was overcome with grief and a sense of foreboding.

The first thought that occurred to me was: the Duke of Gloucester is next in line to the throne.

We had waited in trepidation for some reaction to his discovery. I was sure he had heard rumours about my relationship with Owen, for, careful as we were, some little indication must have leaked out. There was that occasion at the dance when he had fallen into my lap. That had happened a long time ago, but at the time I was sure it had been talked of. Sometimes such things are greatly exaggerated and a minor incident is turned into one of significance.

After he had forced the statute through Parliament about my remarrying, Gloucester had done nothing. That might well have been because he had matters of more significance to occupy him. But now that I had presumed to advise the King, I had brought myself to his notice, and I was sure he would have taken some action if it had not been for his brother's unexpected death which had taken him a step closer to the throne; and he would have thought for nothing else at this time.

Later I heard accounts of how the Duke of Bedford had died. He was a sick and disappointed man, obsessed by the fear that he had failed in the mission his brother had left to him. He had gone wrong somewhere, he was convinced. He should never have allowed them to burn The Maid at the stake. It was said that that—and much else—was on his mind when he died.

He had been disturbed by the effect The Maid was having on the war, and he had felt at the time that she must die. But then he began to wonder whether he had offended Heaven and whether, even from a practical standpoint, it would have been better to have let her live.

I was sorry for him. He had been a good man, kindly if stern.

He had always tried to do what he considered right, and what more can a man do?

He lacked Henry's genius, but who did not? Events were too much for him. It was tragic that such a good man should die disappointed.

His death was the final break with Burgundy. It was timely, too. It really seemed as though God's hand was against the English, for it happened just at the time of the Treaty of Arras and must have decided Burgundy.

There was no Englishman whom Burgundy trusted as he had trusted Bedford. So he had made his decision. Frenchman would not fight Frenchman again.

We heard of the rejoicing throughout France. People were dancing in the streets. Burgundians shook the hands of the Orléans-Armagnacs. They drank together. They vowed never to fight each other again. The only cause for which they would fight would be that of France.

The Duke of Burgundy had signed the Treaty of Arras.

"Long live Charles the King!" shouted the people. "Long live the Duke of Burgundy!"

I believed that England's hopes in France were doomed from that day.

But my main thought was: Gloucester is now next in line to the throne. If Henry were not there, he would be King.

Paris was about to be taken back by the French. The English were leaving; and in the midst of this turmoil, my mother died.

I cannot believe that she was sorry to go. Her life must have changed drastically. She was old and fat and full of gout, and to a woman who had used her beauty and set such store by it, using it to satisfy her ambitions, old age must have been hard to bear.

I wondered what she felt on her deathbed when she was about to leave the world which had meant so much to her. She must have known that the English were preparing to leave Paris and that her son's triumphant army would soon be in possession of the capital. And what did she think Charles would say to her? She had scarcely been a friend to him, and certainly not a good mother.

He had been at one time beset by doubts as to his legitimacy. It was Joan of Arc who had convinced him that he was the King. His mother had sided with his enemies . . . against him. She had been responsible for so much misery that had befallen his country; and his mother-in-law, Yolande of Aragon, had shown him what a mother could be.

He would hate his own mother. Would he show any mercy to her now?

That was something we should never know, for she died before the English left.

They showed a certain respect for the dead. They had her body laid in a coffin which was placed in a barge and carried down the river to the Abbey of St. Dénis, where she could be buried among the kings and queens of France.

So there were two deaths in one short month.

"Gloucester will have other matters with which to concern himself now," repeated Owen.

From the peace of Hadham, Owen and I kept an eye on what was going on.

The death of Bedford, we assured each other, had made such a change in Gloucester's prospects that he had almost certainly turned his attention from us. We began to settle into our peaceful life once more.

Looking back now, I feel that we seized those days with great eagerness because we felt we had to live each one to the full, being fearful of what disaster could come upon us at any moment.

The quarrels between the Cardinal and Gloucester persisted. Now that Burgundy and the King of France were allies, the English cause in France seemed hopeless, and the Cardinal wanted to explore plans for bringing about peace.

Gloucester was of a different opinion. He declared that there had been mismanagement. All we needed was a return to the methods of his brother, and we should be successful again. He was the man, he tried to assure the country. But although he was cheered in the streets, for his great asset was his charm and a certain bonhomie which he could produce at a moment's notice, no one really thought he could attain the victories which had come to Henry.

Owen said: "We should be thankful that he is so occupied. It is certain that, in the midst of all this, he can give no thought to our little matter."

The Cardinal thought that Henry should make a marriage

with the eldest daughter of my brother Charles. He got so far as putting the suggestion before the French. To my relief, they treated it with an indifference which infuriated the English. I could not help thinking of my father, whose madness many believed had come to him through his mother. That was what had made me fearful that it might have been passed on to Henry. But I had consoled myself that it was only when he had been disturbed by The Maid that I fancied I had seen signs of instability. But everyone had been affected by The Maid. And what of Charles? He had always been rather odd . . . and his daughter . . . what of her? They were only faintly uneasy thoughts which came to me, but I was glad when the match was put aside.

Then Gloucester went to France, and we settled down to peace. And during that period of peace I became pregnant again.

Once more I settled into that state of contented serenity. I often wondered afterwards how I could have shut my eyes to all that was happening about us; but I did. When I look back, I can see that some of the happiest times of my life were when I was expecting a child, because then I seemed able to forget all fear of what trouble might be brewing for Owen and me.

We heard items of news. The English were doing badly. They were somewhat demoralized by the loss of Paris. Calais had been assailed, and that was one of the reasons why Gloucester had left England to rush to its defense. To the English, Calais was the most important port. It was the gateway to France.

Gloucester suffered a blow to his vanity because Edmund Beaufort, nephew of the Cardinal, saved Calais before he arrived. I could imagine his chagrin. It would make him feel even more venomous towards the Cardinal.

I laughed about it with Owen, but my main thoughts were with the coming child.

Then Gloucester came back to England.

Bermondsey Abbey

It was a hot summer's day. We were in the gardens.

Owen was toddling now; the two elder boys were running about, playing some mysterious game, and as usual Jacina was trying to share in it and they were somewhat reluctant to allow her to.

I was early enough in my pregnancy not to feel unwieldly and I sat back enjoying the fresh air and the contentment of having my family about me.

Suddenly the silence was broken by the sound of horses' hoofs. I started up. Owen had risen. Guillemote came running towards us. She gathered the children together and was murmuring that she had something to show them and they must come with her at once.

Owen and I exchanged glances. We were always prepared for unexpected arrivals. We had planned for such an event many times. He turned and went towards the stables. Guillemote was hurrying the children into the house, and I followed.

I was surprised. Important visitors usually notified us of their imminent arrival. This, therefore, could not be anyone of standing; however, we must be prepared.

I stood at the window watching. The Joannas and Agnes had come to stand beside me.

We saw about twenty guards below. They swarmed across the gardens. One of them had taken hold of a stable lad and was obviously questioning him.

My heart leaped in terror. The boy pointed to the stables. That was where Owen had gone. Two of the men had taken their

279

stand by the door of the house, one on either side. The others were making for the stables.

Then I saw a sight which terrified me. The men came out of the stables, and Owen was with them. He glanced up at the house.

I could no longer restrain myself. I ran down the stairs and out through the door. The two guards standing there were startled. They stepped forward.

"I am the Queen," I cried. "Stand aside."

They let me pass. I suppose they knew I could not get far, and in any case, the rest of them were straight ahead with Owen.

I went to them. "What is this?" I cried. "What are you doing in my house . . . in my gardens? Do you know who I am?"

The men bowed. "We have orders to arrest this man," said their leader.

"Whose orders? How dare you! He belongs to my household."

"He is the Welshman, Owen Tudor. He does not deny it."

"Why should he deny it? Release him at once and go. Go, I say! You will hear more of this."

"Begging your pardon, my lady, we have been sent here to arrest this man, and that we must do."

"Go away . . . go away. On what grounds? How dare you!"

"On the grounds of treason, my lady. Treason against the laws of the land."

"Owen!" I cried and ran to him.

The agony in his face was terrible to see. He was shaking his head, warning me. I could see his fear for me in his face; and I thought I should die of anguish.

"Where are you taking him?" I asked.

"To London, my lady. Those are our orders."

"Why? Why?"

"Orders, my lady. We are sorry but it is our duty and we must obey."

He moved towards me but they held him back, and for a few moments we stood there, just looking at each other.

I saw his lips move: "Katherine . . . my love . . . always my love . . ."

"I will not allow . . ." I began.

He smiled at me tenderly, resignedly. "I will be back," he murmured.

"They have nothing . . . nothing . . . of which they can accuse you."

"No . . . no," he soothed. "It is a mistake."

But we both knew that it was not. Gloucester was back in England. This was his doing.

So often we had thought of something like this happening; we should have been prepared for it. We were in a way, but perhaps we had always deluded ourselves that it would never come. But we could not have imagined misery such as this.

I was almost fainting. I was aware of Guillemote and Agnes. They were holding my arms. I could only cry out: "No! No!"

And it seemed as though from a long way off I heard the sound of horses' hoofs as they rode away, taking Owen with them.

I do not know how I lived through the days which followed. At every sound I would start up, telling myself that Owen had come back, trying to delude myself that I had been living in a nightmare of horror conjured up by my imagination. We had feared it; we had planned for it; and because of that I had thought it had really happened.

I could not eat; I could not sleep.

"You will be ill," scolded Guillemote. But she was the same. I knew how her thoughts ran, for they were similar to mine. Where was Owen? What was happening to him now?

We worried about the children. What could we tell them? Edmund and Jasper were too old not to know that something was wrong. Jacina knew too. They watched us with frightened eyes.

I could think of nothing but Owen . . . gone . . . taken by those wicked men. Should I ever see him again? I dared not think of that possibility. I could not bear to consider what my life would be without him. I was numb with misery.

I must do something. I must go to London. I must find him.

There was my son, Henry the King. He would help me. Bedford was dead. He was one who might have understood. How could I plead with Gloucester? I pictured him as I had last seen him. He had been so angry with me. Even then he must have been planning his revenge.

I must see Henry.

"Guillemote," I said. "I am going to see my son. I am going to beg him to send Owen back to me."

"How could you see him?"

"I will go to London . . . to Westminster . . . wherever he is. I will go to Court. I will explain."

"You could not travel in your state. My dear, dear lady, think of the child you carry. You must not distress yourself so."

"Oh, Guillemote, why do you talk thus? They have taken Owen. How can I help being distressed? I *must* see Henry."

"You cannot travel."

"I will write to him. I will ask him how they dare arrest Owen as though he had committed some crime. What has he done?"

"My lady, he has married you."

"Why should he not? We love each other, do we not? What harm do we do?"

"It was against the law."

"Gloucester's law! In any case, we were married before that became law."

"I know. I know. Write to the King. He loves you well. It may be that he will come to your aid."

"He will. Of course he will. He is my own dear son."

I could not gather my thoughts. My hands shook so that I found it difficult to hold a pen.

"Henry," I wrote. "You must help me. They have taken Owen away. You must order them to send him back. You must save your mother, for surely I will die if Owen does not come back to me . . ."

That would not do. I must write clearly. I must explain. "I did my duty for my country and for your country, Henry. I married the conqueror of France. I bore his child, you, my dear one, and now it is only just that I should know some happiness. Please Henry, if you ever had any affection for me, help me now. You can. You are the King. You must remember that. You can command these wicked men to undo the evil they have done to me . . ."

There were sounds of arrival below. I dashed to the window but I could see nothing.

Guillemote was running into the room.

"Guillemote, Guillemote, what is it?" I cried. "Owen has come back. Oh, tell me Owen has come back."

"There are men to see you, my lady."

"And Owen?"

She shook her head. "They are saying they must see you at once."

"Oh Guillemote, what now? What now?"

"I know not, my lady."

"Where are the children?"

She nodded her head upwards.

"What is it, Guillemote? What do they want?"

"They will tell you, my lady."

I followed her down the stairs. They were standing there. Guards . . . like those who had taken Owen away.

"My lady . . ." they began and hesitated.

"What have you to say to me?" I asked dully.

"My lady, we have come to take you on the King's orders to the Abbey of Bermondsey."

"To Bermondsey? But . . . why . . . why should I go to Bermondsey?"

"You will be cared for there by the abbess, my lady. It is the King's orders."

"My son's orders? I do not believe it."

He unrolled a scroll of parchment and showed me Henry's signature.

"I do not understand . . ." I began.

"The King's orders are that you should be taken to the Abbey of Bermondsey and put into the care of the lady abbess there. We must leave within an hour."

I said: "The children . . ."

"We have orders for them, my lady. They are to be put into the care of the Lady Katherine de la Pole, the Abbess of Barking."

"But Barking is not Bermondsey!" I said foolishly. "I am to go to Bermondsey."

"That is so, my lady. And we have to leave very soon."

"I will not," I said.

They looked at me sadly. "Our orders are to take you, my lady."

I felt helpless, for they were implying that if I did not go willingly they would take me by force.

"Where is Owen Tudor?" I asked.

They looked at me blankly.

"The children should be made ready to leave," said one of the guards. "You too, my lady."

Guillemote was standing behind me. I turned. We just looked at each other. I had lost Owen. I was going to lose the children . . . and Guillemote, the Joannas, Agnes . . . and all those who had served me well . . . everything I cared for would be lost to me.

This was cruel. This was unbearable. How could anyone do this wicked thing!

It was no use pleading with these men. They were only obeying orders.

Guillemote took my arm, and together we went up the stairs.

So they took me to Bermondsey. I was numbed by bitter misery. I did not say goodbye to the children. I feared to frighten them. I cannot forget the memory of Guillemote's white face, her eyes wide with pain as they dwelt on me. There was a sense of desolation about the entire household. Everyone now knew that the disaster which for so long we had feared had come upon us.

I cannot remember very much of the journey. The abbess received me with deference. Her prisoner I might be, but I was still the Queen. My room was simple—bare walls except for a crucifix. I hardly noticed. Two nuns came in and helped me to bed. I lay in those unfamiliar surroundings, staring before me, seeing Owen walking across the grass between the guards . . . Guillemote hustling the children away.

They tried to make me eat but I could not.

The hours passed. Night came. I did not sleep. I just lay there in that austere bed wanting to die.

The abbess was a kindly woman. She was concerned about me and tried to make me talk.

"You must find peace," she said.

"There is no peace for me," I replied.

"God will help you."

I was impatient. "All I want is my husband and my children."

She was indeed a good woman. I saw compassion in her face.

"Would you not pray with me?" she asked.

I turned my face to the wall.

"I want to help you," she said.

"Then give me back my husband and children. That is all I

want. The right to live as the humblest woman is allowed to . . .
the right to be with my family.''

She left me in despair.

Another day. Another night.

''You must rouse yourself,'' said the abbess. ''You will lose
your reason if you continue thus.''

Lose my reason! Her words had sent me back to the Hôtel de
St. Paul. I was hearing that wild voice calling for help. I was
seeing my son bemused by the sight of The Maid. The abbess
had reminded me of the shadow which hung over my family.

Be calm, I said to myself. Think of other things.

But I could think only of Owen and the children around us
. . . a bright sunny day . . . and such happiness suddenly shattered by the sound of horses' hoofs coming towards the house.

I was alone. The abbess had left me in despair.

I started to think back over the years of my childhood, to my
first meeting with Henry, to my life with him . . . the birth of
my son. They were not unhappy days. But it was only when I
knew Owen that I discovered what true happiness was. Few
people find it as Owen and I had. What a tragedy that we should
have had to hold it so carefully until it was finally snatched
from us.

The words of the abbess kept coming back to me. ''You will
lose your reason.'' There were times when I was not sure whether
I was in the past or the present. Sometimes in the night I would
think I was in the Hôtel de St. Paul, lying close to Michelle for
warmth while Marie prayed at the bedside. I thought: I must be
calm.

The idea came to me that the only way in which I could live
through the days was by writing it all down. Perhaps I should
discover where I might have acted differently. Could this have
been avoided? Was there a way in which Owen and I could have
been together and there was no cruel parting? Was it just possible?

It was true that I felt better. The abbess was pleased that I
had this occupation. She could see that it helped me.

Writing materials were supplied to me, and through the days
I wrote. I became fascinated by the project, I think largely because for hours at a time I could lose myself in the past and shut
out the desolate present.

The summer had gone. I had no knowledge of what was

happening to my family. I was sleeping a little better now . . .
I did not dread the long nights as I had, for, having written of
the past and in a manner lived it again, I felt a certain exhaustion
at the end of the day which I welcomed.

I would sometimes dream that I was happy again, that Edmund, Jasper or little Jacina was telling me what they had done
that day, that little Owen was talking to me, in his quaint baby
way. I cherished those dreams, for they brought a fleeting happiness into my dreary existence.

It must be nearly Christmas time. I was trying not to think of
last Christmas. I had covered so much paper with my writing.
I was getting near the end. It was almost unbearable now because I was writing about my life with Owen and the children,
and all kinds of little incidents came to my mind . . . too trivial
to record but precious to me.

One early morning I awoke in agony.

I had allowed my grief to overwhelm me. I had not thought
of the life I carried within me.

My baby. Would they allow me to keep the child? They must.
They could not part a mother from her newly born child. The
abbess was no monster. If I could have my child with me, perhaps I could find some solace.

But there was some time yet.

It was two months before my child was due.

They were at my bedside. I had been oblivious of all else but
pain. I had even forgotten the loss of my husband and my children. There had been nothing but agony.

"My child . . ." I murmured.

I saw my dear confessor, Johan Boyers, and I thought: I am
dreaming. But it was not so.

"My lady . . ." he said.

"Johan!"

"I came when they sent for me."

"Johan . . . where is Owen? . . . Where are the children?"

He shook his head. "You must rest."

"My baby . . ."

He lowered his eyes. "The birth was premature . . ." he said
gently.

I murmured: "I see. Not content with ruining my life, they
have killed my baby also."

He said: "The child still clings to life but I think I should baptize her without delay. What name shall she be given?"

I don't know why I chose Margaret. It just came into my mind.

"Margaret," he repeated. "She shall be Margaret."

"Johan?"

"Yes?"

"You will not go away."

"I will come back to you later," he said.

I lay there, exhausted. So I was to be denied even the blessing of my new-born child.

Johan Boyers brought great comfort to me during the days which followed.

He said: "They sent for me when you were so ill."

"I must have been near death or they would not have done so."

"You were very ill . . . but you will recover."

"Shall I, Johan?"

"The shock of everything . . . it brought on the birth . . . too soon . . ."

"And I lost my child . . ."

We were silent for a few moments. Then I said: "You were there, Johan . . . what happened?"

"I can tell you that the children are well."

"With strangers?"

"The abbess is a good woman. She will do all she can for them."

"They will want me. They will miss Owen. They will need Guillemote."

"Guillemote is trying to get to them. The abbess is a compassionate woman. Guillemote hopes that she will be able to get into the abbey . . . to look after the children as she has always done."

"Oh, God bless her!"

"And Owen . . ."

He was silent for a moment and I prompted him: "Please tell me. Tell me the truth."

"He is in Newgate."

"The jail?"

He nodded.

"On what charge?"

"Treason . . . in marrying against the law."

"It was before the law was made."

"That will certainly help."

"Johan, you have done me so much good."

"Would you like to confess?"

"What should I confess, Johan? I have sinned in these last months. I have railed against God for taking from me all that I cared for."

"Let us pray together."

"There is one thing, Johan. My first husband, the King, I did sin against him. He asked me to make sure that our son was not born at Windsor. Yet I allowed him to be born there."

"Why did you do this?"

"I cannot say. It was some compulsion. I could have left Windsor before it was too late . . . but I did not. I stayed on. I cannot understand it now. Was it the prompting of the Devil?"

He shook his head. "God meant the King to be born at Windsor. That is why it happened."

"Yes," I said. "Let us pray together."

It was wonderful to have him with me. He was part of the old days.

He did not go from the abbey until I was able to leave my bed.

Christmas had passed and January was coming in, with wintry weather.

I thought of the great fires we had had at Hatfield and Hadham, of Owen telling the children stories. They loved to hear of the Welsh mountains and the days of his ancestors.

I felt the tears falling down my cheeks.

I was very weak. I could not walk about my little room without feeling exhausted.

The abbess was alarmed. She said she must get the physician to see me.

I think people sometimes have a premonition that the end is near. I did, and it had a calming effect upon me. I knew this austere cell would not be my home for much longer. I knew now that I would never see Owen and my children again; and, oddly enough, I experienced a strange feeling of reconciliation because I could feel this world slipping away from me.

When this year of 1437 came in, I believed I should never see the end of it; and I knew that was not a fancy; it was a revelation.

I wondered that Henry had not come to see me. He would have done so, I was sure, but he was very much under the influence of his uncle Gloucester now. Gloucester was the heir presumptive to the throne. I trusted Henry would be well looked after. He would have come to me, I knew, if it had rested with him. He had always loved me, even though we had been so little together.

They must have been worried about my health, for Johan Boyers was sent for again.

His coming was a great joy to me—not only because he was a familiar face from my happy past but because he had good news for me.

He waited until we were alone, then he said: ''Owen is free.''

''Free!''

''He has escaped from Newgate.''

''Oh . . . they will catch him.''

''He will not be caught. He will be too clever for them. He eluded the guards and got right away. He is in Wales, I believe. He got a message through to me for you.''

''Oh, Johan . . . is this true?''

''He says . . . he will be with you . . . as soon as it is possible. He said, 'Tell the Queen that we shall be together again. It will be my greatest aim that this shall be so.' ''

I was silent. I was unaware that I was weeping until I tasted the salt tears on my lips.

I shall never see Owen again. When he comes it will be too late.

Everyone around me knows it. They are very kind and gentle.

I was so shocked when I came to them. I became so weak . . . too weak to recover from the premature birth of my little girl.

So . . . I am dying. I still have the strength to hold my pen. My spirits have lightened a little. I no longer have to look ahead to long years without Owen and the children. I shall be reunited with them one day. I know it.

Today is New Year's Day.

I had a gift which gave me great pleasure because it was from my son. So Henry had not forgotten me. He would have come to my aid if he could, I always knew. And this was his way of saying so. He had sent me a gold tablet on which was a crucifix set with pearls and sapphires.

My poor Henry! He is only fifteen years old. The tablet tells me that he would have helped me . . . if he could.

I prayed then . . . deeply and sincerely . . . for him, my son. May his life be easy. May the burden of the crown sit lightly on his head.

I am too tired to write more. It cannot be long now. I pray for Owen's safety and for the happiness of my children and all those who have loved and served me well during my life, which is soon to end.

Bibliography

Aubrey, William Hickman Smith, *National and Domestic History of England*

Batiffol, Louis, translated by Elsie Finnimore Buckley, *National History of France*

Castries, Duc de, *Lives of the Kings and Queens of France*

Church, Rev. A.J., *Henry the Fifth*

Earle, Peter, *Life and Times of Henry V*

Fabre, Lucien, translated by Gerald Hopkins, *Joan of Arc*

Goodwin, T., *History of the Reign of Henry the Fifth*

Green, John Richard, *History of England*

Guizot, M., translated by Robert Black, *History of France*

Hudson, William Henry, *France*

Hume, David, *History of England*

Lang, Andrew, *The Maid of France*

Lindsay, Philip, *King Henry the Fifth*

Mowat, R.B., *Kings and Queens of England*

Oman, Charles, *Political History of England*

Stenton, D.M., *English Society in the Middle Ages*

Stephen, Sir Leslie, and Lee, Sir Sidney, *Dictionary of National Biography*

Strickland, Agnes, *Lives of the Queens of England*

Timbs, John, and Gunn, Alexander, *Abbeys, Castles and Ancient Halls of England and Wales*

Vickers, K.H., *Humphrey, Duke of Gloucester*

Wade, John, *British History*

ABOUT THE AUTHOR

Jean Plaidy is Victoria Holt. Under the Plaidy pseudonym she has written over forty-five historical novels for Fawcett Books, including the Georgian Saga, the Plantagenet Saga, and the Queens of England series. Ms. Plaidy resides in England.

JEAN PLAIDY

THE QUEEN OF HISTORICAL ROMANCE PRESENTS THE QUEENS OF ENGLAND